LURKERS

LURKERS

—

SANDI TAN

SOHO

Published by Soho Press, Inc.
227 W 17th Street
New York, NY 10011

Library of Congress Cataloging-in-Publication Data
Tan, Sandi, author.
Title: Lurkers / Sandi Tan.

ISBN 978-1-64129-255-9
eISBN 978-1-64129-256-6

I. Title

PS3620.A6836 L87 2021 813'.6—dc23 2020028033

Interior dog illustrations: © Vi-An Nguyen

Interior design by Janine Agro, Soho Press, Inc.

Printed in the United States of America

10 9 8 7 6 5 4 3 2 1

So violent and motley was life, that it bore the mixed smell of blood and roses. The men of that time always oscillate between the fear of hell and the most naïve joy, between cruelty and tenderness, between harsh asceticism and insane attachment to the delights of the world, between hatred and goodness, always running to the extremes.

Johan Huizinga
The Waning of the Middle Ages

I.

GIRL IN THE WINDOW

–

May 2006

to

July 2006

– 1 –

HOT DAMN

The only time Rosemary remembered seeing her father happy was when he was playing *Vice City*. Instead of jacking cars, shooting hookers and tussling with cops, he strolled along Ocean Beach, its simulated Miami beachfront, minding his own business. From the boardwalk, he would gaze out at the undulating orange waves. For hours.

If he got in the way of a stray bullet or became the unlucky victim of a mugging, he picked himself up and started over. When he was released from the hospital, he'd walk, and walk, and walk, until he got back to the water. At no time would he steal a car or hijack a bike to speed up his journey—that, he knew, was the surest way to attract attention.

Sometimes, for a change of pace, he headed to the bridge leading to Starfish Island. This was the most isolated spot that he knew of in Vice City. And he would stand on its pedestrian ramp, staring out at the bay where the water was blue, not orange, and the lapping of waves could be heard.

If anyone walked in on his game, he'd turn around and say, "Boring, right?" He'd say this grimly, like a scientist pushing technology to its limit in order to collect important data. Not that this was any different from the way he pursued everything else; the man was terminally embarrassed to show pleasure.

"Maybe all he wanted was to be someplace else," Rosemary said to her younger sister, a week after his funeral. "Maybe he should have just taken a vacation."

"Don't be obtuse," said Mira, looking up from her homework. "He hated traveling. He hated, like, airport security asking him perfectly normal questions. He even hated being on the freeway, away from the *two* gas stations he ever used. Can you just imagine him, like, on a Greyhound bus, with all those winos and child molesters?"

"Remember how he played *Vice City*, though?"

"Yeah, so?"

"Maybe he just wanted to be someone else. You know?"

"Blond dude in a Hawaiian shirt?"

"Maybe he did."

"Maybe, maybe, maybe . . ."

THE GIRLS FELT a certain nostalgia for how simple life had been just a month before, when their father was alive. There was a time for everything then. They were home from school at 3:40, ramen boiled at 3:45, homework was pulled out at 4:00 and at 4:02, the Mystery Boom Box started blasting its infernal melodies.

Like clockwork each day, Christina Aguilera's voice bounced off their house, their garage, the brick floor of their patio, as well as the walls, garages, and patios of the five other houses with yards that backed onto theirs.

The sisters could never figure out where the boom box was; echoes made pinpointing impossible. But it had to be one of the houses visible to them from their den, or that their den was visible to. The music always began just as the girls laid out their books, as if some diabolical imp with birding binoculars had been watching and waiting by his stereo.

"I freakin' hate that album!" Mira got up and slammed the windows shut. "Someone should go out and just shoot whoever's doing this to us!"

"I vote for Dad," said Rosemary. They both giggled.

Their father, Mr. Park, was sixty years old and a man of the old school. He hailed from the South Korean port city of Pusan, where even his degree in electrical engineering could not guarantee him work. Apparently, there had been a glut of engineering grads in his province and many of his classmates wound up working in fisheries or as stevedores. After fifteen years as a security officer at the port, he emigrated to America and found work at a second cousin's tofu restaurant in LA's Koreatown, becoming its oldest busboy at forty-two. It was in that lively, compact enclave that he met and married the girls' mother, Joon, a woman then half his age and the only daughter of an embittered pastor. When Joon's father died a year later, dutiful Mr. Park, whose conversion to Christianity was as new as his marriage, left the restaurant and took over his father-in-law's ministry.

He believed in hard work, family and, incrementally, the values of the Korean evangelical church. After the '92 riots destroyed much of Koreatown, he and his young wife took their two-year-old, Rosemary, and retreated to Santa Claus Lane in Alta Vista, a family-centered community crouching in the benevolent shadow of the San Gabriel Mountains, twelve miles north of LA.

Santa Claus Lane was idyllic compared to Koreatown. It was about a third of a mile long, lined on both sides with mature deodar pines and protected at both ends by stop signs. A sign that said DIP stood at its middle, right outside the Parks' house. Had

Mr. Park's English been more proficient he might have taken it as a slight—he was always touchy—but linguistic prowess and malice being absent, everybody lived peaceably.

He remained nervous around black people but decided that settling down in what their realtor called a "mixed neighborhood" would be the best way to assimilate Rosemary—and her soon-to-be-born sister Miracle—into the American way of life. Besides, before buying their careworn bungalow, he'd counted the number of churches within its two-mile radius and come up with thirty-four. Black people of faith didn't scare him, not even the singing kind.

In the years immediately following the riots, Mr. Park withstood stares and taunts from all kinds of people while doing simple chores around town. Once, a black woman threw a carton of sour milk at him while he was filling up at the gas station. But he rarely feared real trouble. His faith in God grew stronger by the day, and with his savings he started his own ministry, All-Friends Worship, the local chapter of a vast Korean evangelical network whose flagship was a literal cruise ship docked in Gyeonggi Bay.

All-Friends Worship was a blue clapboard Victorian with an improvised, concrete slab extension. It looked as if a semi had backed into a strip mall, dropped off some old granny's house, then vamoosed. Not that aesthetics mattered to his flock. There were small pockets of Koreans, refugees from the riots, scattered around the San Gabriel foothills, and for many of them, Mr. Park's church was the one place they could meet others of their own kind and speak uninhibitedly in their own language. For the women of this type, All-Friends became a home away from home. They came to church to compare their children's test scores and exchange crockpot recipes; they discussed gaming the discount racks at Macy's and how to find the one sales rep who would speak Korean if her supervisor wasn't around. One enterprising woman even started a Texan line-dancing club, whose sessions boldly collided with Bible Study Thursday.

Because of these women, Sundays at All-Friends had the chatter level of a fish market back in Mr. Park's home city of Pusan. When it didn't bring him nostalgia, it brought him the shivers. Because of these women, Mr. Park decided against letting his daughters learn Korean. Korean inspired a henhouse insularity in women that he didn't want his daughters to have. Whereas with men, Korean was a stabilizing force—it was blood, gave them identity. It was not something they clung to out of desperation because they feared all else.

Not learning Korean was fine by the girls. Rosemary detested the Korean language on aural grounds. When Korean rolled off the tongues of Westerners who came to the language late in life, it took on a strange baroque musicality, like drunken Italian. But when native Koreans like her parents spoke it, it sounded guttural, coarse, accusatory. It skewed combative whether one was asking someone on a date or threatening them with a cleaver.

Sometimes Rosemary didn't know what bugged her more—having to hear Korean spoken all Sunday, or the fact that her father's church had a name with bad syntax. All-Friends Worship. First, there was the weird hyphen; then the ambiguous logic: Was it an exhortation for all friends to worship or a worship belonging to all friends, in which case an apostrophe was missing?

At school, the kids who took an Asian language were mainly adopted Chinese girls. They studied Mandarin only to please the parents who'd rescued them from the fleapit orphanages of Fujian—and they always looked miserable about it. If she'd had a say in her own ethnicity, Rosemary would have opted to be a Latina, not of the stumpy Central American variety but the whippet, Gap assistant kind; she wanted to be the type who could bleach her black hair chestnut and still have it look natural. Like a less trashy Christina Aguilera, with quadruple-pierced ears and a Grumpy Bear hoodie from Hot Topic. In other words, just Latina enough. And oh yes, a nose stud.

Rosemary didn't mind the Mystery Boom Box as much as Mira did. Sure it was loud, and whoever was playing it had to be either deaf or out of their mind. But at least there was a reliable schedule to the madness. It began at 4:02 every day and ended at eight. Two rounds of Aguilera's *Stripped*, followed by a couple hours of KROQ. It might have made it harder to concentrate on calculus, but she did enjoy watching the reactions it provoked in her otherwise sedate, otherwise non-communicative parents.

It became dinner conversation.

"Kee Hyun, the music. We must stop music," her mother would say. "For the girls."

Her father would grunt and chew on a pickle. "Maybe they stop soon."

"Stop soon?" Her mother would take her father's bowl before he was done eating. "Music has been here three weeks. Girls hard for study, Kee Hyun."

"Maybe I go tomorrow." Her father would grab his bowl back.

"You always say tomorrow. Yesterday you say tomorrow. Last week you say tomorrow."

"Maybe I go tomorrow this time."

"You always say maybe. Maybe, maybe, maybe!"

"*Hot damn!* I go tomorrow." It would be the only time the girls ever heard their father swear.

One evening, Mr. Park went looking for the boom box. He had considered wearing his minister's uniform but decided against it lest it appear he was using the Lord's authority to settle petty scores. He walked back and forth past ten different houses before he found what he hoped was the correct one. It was hard to tell because of the rush-hour traffic whizzing past on Lake Ave.

Under the roar of the cars, he practiced over and over his opening words, "Excuse me, Sir, Madam, I am your neighbor," improvising a series of friendly gestures and a facial expression approximating a smile. During a lull in the traffic, he took a deep breath and entered the property. It was a Craftsman bungalow, just like his, but desperately in need of two new coats of paint. Under his breath, he practiced, "Excuse, Sir, Madam, please, I am your neighbor," as Christina Aguilera's singing vibrated through his skull, threatening to mix up his words.

He walked up the driveway quietly and peered into the back-yard. Shivers. Propped up on a couple of apple crates, speakers aimed at the back fence, was the Mystery Boom Box. Booming. The rest of the yard was a patchwork of junk—dented aluminum siding, rusted barrels, rotting fruit from a dying grapefruit tree. Yet on the back of the old Mustang resting on cinder blocks was a gleaming Jesus fish, a reassuring sign that he would find common ground. He jogged to the front of the house.

Before he got to the porch, a fat woman in a red housecoat pushed open the screen door and bellowed: "What ya want?"

"Excuse me, Madam, please, I am your neighbor," he began. He gave her a little wave.

"Git outta my yard!" The woman's orange hair was slick from the shower and her thick glasses made her eyes emphatically huge.

"Please, your music, Madam. I live over there." He waved vaguely toward a bunch of houses, not wanting her to know where he lived. An overweight teenage girl in shorts joined the woman at the door. She had her mother's freckles and square jowls.

"Music too loud for ya?" the girl said, in the same jeering tone her mother used.

Mr. Park nodded and started to back away. He felt that he had registered his point, and gave them a quick wave goodbye. As he walked briskly off their property, he heard one say something to the other. The mother started cackling—the throatiest, most lurid laughter he'd ever heard coming out of a woman.

Approaching home, he half expected his daughters to sprint out and give him a hero's welcome, the kind of lapping affection they'd routinely showered him with when they were younger. Instead, it was his wife who came out the front door—scowling.

"What's matter? You don't find house?"

"I found house," he said, his pride wounded. "Of course, I found house!"

"Then why still music?"

Mr. Park glared at his wife and walked into the house. There, he saw the girls doing their homework, with the den windows still tightly sealed. His heart sank. He plodded to his bedroom and shut the door.

Mr. Park said very little that weekend. The girls took it as a sign that his mood was improving when on Sunday afternoon, he agreed to their usual game of post-church badminton, even with the boom box going full blast.

As a student in Korea, Mr. Park had been a badminton champ who stunned opponents with his ruthless, lightning-fast smashes. But in America, with his daughters, he played American badminton—soft strokes, big loops, lots of laughter, lots of pointless running. He always took on both the girls at once, and deliberately let them win most of the time just so he didn't have to watch them sulk.

The girls noticed something different about his game that

evening—the old Park Kee Hyun of South Pusan Technical University was reemerging, stroke by stroke. Soon, he was slamming the shuttlecock across the net at such velocity that at one point, it grazed Rosemary's arm and left a crimson line. And he wasn't letting the girls win, either. Mira called the game off when she realized they never got past two or three volleys. Their father grabbed a few loud gulps of iced barley tea and retired to the house with his head held high.

With their Dad out, the girls played a leisurely round—swooping parabolas, giggles punctuated with cries of "Oops!" and "D'oh!" They must have lost track of time because the boom box had stopped and it was dark by the time they were done. They ran back into the house, reeking of perspiration and bug spray.

Their father was still in the shower, which was very unusual. They could hear the water running. After knocking on the door five times and getting no answer, Rosemary asked their mother to get the master key.

Mrs. Park banged on the door herself before sliding the key into the lock. Finally, with jittery hands, she pushed the bathroom door open.

Mr. Park, head minister at All-Friends Worship and father of two, sat lifeless in a sea of murky red, his knees tucked under his chin. A box cutter with a yellow plastic handle sat neatly in the soap dish, its blade retracted so no one else could hurt themselves. He faced the door with his eyes closed, and under the endless cascade of the shower, he looked like he was still crying.

PEOPLE WERE UNEXPECTEDLY generous to the family in the week following Mr. Park's funeral. Even Kate Ireland, the solitary, vaguely Asiatic brunette across the street came over with a bag of decaf beans from Starbucks and a Hallmark look of sorrow. Kate's mother would have done a lot more, but coming from Kate, the Parks knew this was plenty. In the early days, when Mr. and Mrs. Park were still new to the area, Kate never even waved hello.

In all their years as neighbors, the Park girls hadn't had any contact with her, always telling each other that she was the kind of person they would hate to grow up into—mousy, friendless, repressed. Kate's mother, on the other hand, had been an exuberant, retired white lady right out of the Lifetime channel, bringing by star-shaped cookies around Christmas; sadly, she had moved away. The girls liked Kate's German shepherd all right, when it was still alive and would wag its tail from behind the window. But why have a dog if all you did was lock it indoors like a cat?

Mrs. Park insisted she was responsible for Kate's new neighborliness. A few days after the German shepherd's death, Kate had gone into some kind of trance while watering her geraniums. She hadn't noticed as water gushed down the sidewalk. It was Mrs. Park who ran over, turned the hose off, sat the woman down on her own front step and let her sob for ten minutes. It was then that Mrs. Park finally learned the dead dog's name: Bluto.

"Death bring living people together," Mrs. Park said to her girls. "Even though dog dying not as bad as people dying."

Somebody sent the grieving family a book called *When Bad Things Happen to Good People*. They couldn't figure who it was until they scrutinized the packing slip in the Amazon box and found a greeting from Mira's cello teacher: "I'm Sorry."

Church volunteers returned all the personal effects from Mr. Park's office, and Mrs. Park told them that neither she nor her girls would show their faces at All-Friends again. Going back there would only remind her of her husband's lack of peace with

God even as he pretended to serve Him. How could she look any one of the parishioners in the eye? Her husband had betrayed all of them by simply giving up.

There was one saving grace. His body was not interred at All-Friends, which didn't have the right building codes, but in the mausoleum beneath the biggest Korean church in Orange County, fifty miles away. This meant she had an excuse not to visit as often as a widow should.

As the period of mourning faded away, Mrs. Park's concerns sharpened. How would they buy groceries? She couldn't drive. How would they make the money to buy groceries? She had nothing but a high school diploma, from a provincial school near the North Korean border. The Koreans she knew in America had never heard of her district, let alone her high school's excellent cheerleading program.

For the first few weeks, she walked to the nearest mini-mart where she picked up milk, bread, ramen and peanut butter. It was three-quarters of a mile away, not a difficult walk on a cool spring day, but it would be far less pleasant in the fast-approaching summer. Once a week, her husband's Koreatown relatives would bring her tofu and surplus produce such as cabbage, lettuce and spring onions, and she tried to make these last. But she knew this arrangement couldn't go on forever. These distant cousins weren't generous people—they were acting out of duty, and duty, unlike charity, had a limited hold on the American mind. She learned to take the bus to a supermarket three miles away. But the interminable wait at the bus stop, often with suspicious-looking types, made her fear carpal tunnel from gripping her purse so tight.

Once, she waited twenty minutes with a frail, white-haired black woman in a security guard's uniform who tried to put her at ease with friendly conversation. But she was nervous about her poor English and didn't say anything back. Later, she regretted her unfriendliness and thought about how melancholy the woman had made her feel—a woman that age shouldn't have had to work, let alone wait for the bus home after a twelve-hour shift watching a vacant lot. That said, the old woman had a job, which put her in a better position than Mrs. Park herself. All she had was a 2003 Camry with a full tank of gas sitting in her driveway, not going anywhere at all.

Her husband had left behind the modest bank account of a decent, naïve minister. His poor financial planning was, she knew, partly her own fault. Five years before, she hadn't let him spend $500 to take part in a regional church seminar on money management. As it turned out, all the younger, more ambitious Korean ministers in LA and Orange Counties attended and, according to the church circulars, gleaned inspiration about fund-raising and business development, while Mr. Park lagged farther behind.

The mortgage payment was $1,200 a month, and they had seventeen years to go. If they lived very frugally, with both girls maintaining good enough grades to remain in their schools' scholarship programs, Mrs. Park reckoned that they could survive for two years on her husband's savings. But that would mean absolutely no meals out, no movies, no overnight excursions to Ojai with the Girl Scouts.

Mr. Park's cousin, whose tofu restaurant had become so successful that they opened three branches outside Koreatown, dutifully offered Mrs. Park a job waiting tables at his Alhambra outpost. He rescinded the offer as soon as she accepted, saying her English might not be good enough for his clientele—young American-born Koreans.

Mrs. Park talked to her girls about planting their own

vegetables—eggplants, tomatoes, maybe even bok choy. Rosemary kept her dismay to herself and said she would take Driver's Ed as soon as the course was offered at school. Mira, the truth-teller, spelled it out to their mother: "This is America. You have to drive. And you have to have a job. Or else you might as well forget it."

Her words bruised Mrs. Park. There was no way around it, she had to find a solution. For the first time in over a decade, she prayed.

ROSEMARY WAS EATING a bowl of ramen and watching the news in the den. Not long after her father's death, she began following a story she'd found personally appealing: a fifteen-year-old schoolgirl from New Jersey had gone missing. Five weeks later, the saga was still unfolding.

The story gripped her because this was the first time in her memory that the news media had ever picked up on a missing-teenager story where the girl wasn't blond and blue-eyed. This time, she was a silky Eurasian Rosemary's own age, a scholastic all-rounder who was in the Girl Scouts as well as her school's math decathlon team. She went to a chichi girls' school. Her father was a therapist and her mother was a professor at one of those picture-perfect Seven Sisters colleges that Rosemary dreamed of attending.

She felt a surge of abstract pride whenever pictures of the missing girl flashed on the screen. She liked the fact that there was rarely any mention of the girl's ethnicity, except on the Fox News network where she was continually misdescribed as "Japanese teenager Brittany Ann Yamasato."

The Yamasato family was holding a "live" news conference just then. While the girl's father wept in the background, the mother, a tall brunette who resembled the actress Sigourney Weaver, announced gravely that FBI agents had finally broken into her daughter's computer and found that she'd been communicating via AOL Instant Messenger with a sophomore from a West Coast university. From the salvaged message fragments, the authorities had reason to believe that Brittany had run away with this boy, after a series of coffee shop rendezvous. As if on cue, the mother broke down, pleading for any leads surrounding the young man who went by the name Paul. Sobbing, she confessed that she and her husband had "*no* idea" that their daughter had been "*so* unhappy." When the news conference ended, CNN brought on a dour panel of educators to pontificate dryly on Alienation in the Honor Roll League.

Mrs. Park walked into the den and clicked off the TV.

"Ma!"

Then she walked over to the windows and shut them, muffling the rock music pounding from the Mystery Boom Box.

"Ma! What're you doing? I finished my homework!"

Mrs. Park sat herself down on the sofa, and stared at her calloused hands.

"Baby, today I clean closet, I find something was your Dad's."

"Was it money? . . . A gun?"

"It is paper . . ." Mrs. Park looked up at Rosemary, smiling, but her eyes brimmed with tears. "He write many story! But was secret. He never tell me! I not know!"

"Really? Dad was a writer? Since when?"

"I not know."

"Can I see them? Where are they?"

"They still in closet."

"Well, did you read them? Are they any good?"

"I not know."

"What do you mean? Didn't you read them?"

"No. They in English."

MRS. PARK PLACED the stack of stories on Rosemary's desk. They were hand-written on letterhead from All-Friends Worship and numbered in total about sixty pages. She ordered a Domino's pizza (Hawaiian, busting the week's budget) and made hot cocoa in preparation for the girls' reading.

There was a lightness in Mrs. Park's step but the girls had a sick feeling about the stories when they spotted titles like "The Dancing Banana Woman" and "Child Toucher."

"We make book to sell, yes?" Mrs. Park backed out of Rosemary's room, nodding and bowing like an innkeeper in an old samurai flick. Once the door was closed, the girls looked at each other and made faces.

They divided the stories into roughly two equal piles and started reading, quickly trading the pages they'd finished. Their father's handwriting was neat and square, and he rarely made any corrections.

The story "Cheater Man" began: *The lawyer Harvey Finkelstein was down to his last pack of cigarettes when he remembered his dear old father. It had been over a year since he had paid the old boy a visit. Perhaps Father would be dying soon and he would will the entire lot of his remaining wealth to me, thought Harvey. As he approached his father's mansion, he was surprised and delighted to see the undertaker's van parked in front of the house . . .*

The Harvey Finkelstein character was forever saying things like, "Another day, another dollar!" and always seemed to have a pastrami sandwich or bagel stuffed into his pocket. As the story went on, Harvey got mixed up with heroin smugglers who lived in peach-colored condos facing the water. Mr. Park's gangster underworld sounded like something dreamed up by a child after Adderall and *Vice City*. At the end of ten pages, all the characters perished in a terrorist attack on Miami Beach.

"Wow," said Rosemary, passing the pages to her sister. "You certainly can't accuse him of being formulaic."

"Wait till you read this one," Mira said. "It's almost avant-garde." She handed over the story "Child Toucher."

Rosemary's eyes widened. She read, "'In fact, he scoffed at people who were occasionally hauled into court for acts of peepism . . .' *Peepism?*" She cast the story aside and squealed. And Mira squealed, too, for good measure.

The girls could have stopped here but there was something morbidly enticing about reading such bizarrely bad writing—by somebody so close to them, and so dead.

"The Dancing Banana Woman" the girls saved for last because of its title. It had to be savored. They read this one out loud together: *Venus Washington loves to dance cha-cha. Never mind that she is not terribly good at it and woe betide the man or woman who is silly enough to tell her the truth. She is cushioned by false praise from her dancehall partners, and the adoration of her husband Leroy, who brings a new dimension to the word "wimp" . . .*

The girls groaned, but read on all the same. There were questionable spots of fluidity: *The wrinkles on her thighs which used to dissipate after an afternoon at the spa now seemed reluctant to desert her* and *Leroy moved at a pace thought not possible for someone as corpulent as he.* They pointed out sentences like these to each other with mounting suspicion that he might have plagiarized them. Rosemary, in particular, found it hard to picture her white-haired father sitting at his desk, writing the final line of the story: *As he lived, so he died, in the most fitting manner and in the most appropriate place—in a brothel.*

"This feels like the first one he wrote," said Rosemary. "It's got a beginning, middle and end. Like, structure. Before he felt confident enough to break free and, like"—her fingers crooked into scare quotes—"*experiment*."

"Isn't it weird that Dad wrote all this stuff and yet he wouldn't let us read Harry Potter because it's got wizards?"

"He was always a hypocrite."

As they gathered up the pages, they wondered why the story was called "The Dancing Banana Woman." Bananas did not figure in the least, except perhaps as a crude sexual metaphor. Then Rosemary's cheeks burned with mortal embarrassment. It hit her—Venus Washington was African American.

"We have to burn these," she whispered. "We can't *ever* let anyone see them."

They stared at the papers on Rosemary's pink coverlet, chilled with the awareness that these were their father's most personal items of legacy.

"If this was how he saw the world, no wonder he was so unhappy," Rosemary said.

"Hot damn!" Mira exclaimed.

"Hot damn," Rosemary echoed.

ROSEMARY WATCHED HER mother sink deeper into the sofa.

"I'm sorry, Ma. But they're, like, slightly disappointing."

"Don't backpedal, Stinky," Mira cut in. She plopped herself down on the sofa and grabbed her mother's arm. "Ma, the truth is they're truly, deeply bad. He really shouldn't have bothered. I mean, *honestly*, man."

Mrs. Park gripped the pile of stories to her chest, not saying a word.

Mira sighed dramatically. "Look, if you can't, like, face up to reality, then I don't know what else to say to you!" She stomped to her room and slammed the door. A second later, her head popped out to glower at her sister. "Rosie, tell her! She obviously doesn't believe me. Don't be a freakin' two-face, alright?" The door banged shut again.

Mrs. Park was staring at a stain on the carpet three feet away. Rosemary reached for her mother's arm but her mother pulled away. "Ma . . ."

Mrs. Park got up and headed to the front door with the stories. She kicked off her "inside" slippers and shoved her sullen feet into her "outside" slippers (which were the same exact slippers except not stained and frayed).

"Where are you going, Ma?"

"You only child, you not know anything!"

"Ma, we can't let—"

But the door slammed shut.

– 2 –

THE CRAFTSMAN

Raymond van der Holt pondered the catalog. Would a seven-candle chandelier bring the front room into balance? The twelve-candle model that came with the house was excessive. He'd been thinking of downsizing for months and the Restoration Hardware sale had come to the rescue. Then again, if he could just wait it out, there was the discount weekend in December . . .

This was how Raymond had been spending the past five or six years. Pondering catalogs, being selective about what he wanted, and being even more selective about what he actually bought. He couldn't spend as giddily as he used to—the royalties and movie options would dry up, and he'd be left with only his 1924 Craftsman house and the beautiful, pedigree-free objects within it. (He never antiqued—germs!)

At fifty-five, he kept himself smooth-skinned with a panoply of Kiehl's ointments. He retained a full head of hair, which was a source of pride because his father had gone bald at thirty-nine, and he combed this silver nest before answering the door, no matter who rang, mailman or Jehovah's Witness. He was not vain, per se; he just had an old-fashioned sense of decorum, and he liked what he liked: grownupness. During times of distress, he perked himself up by channeling Cary Grant gliding down the stairs with a highball. There was an original Batchelder-tile fireplace in his living room, muted and mellow with rabbits and pinecones. Gazing at it also calmed him, but Cary Grant had better dimples.

Many years ago, as a Midwestern man of twenty-seven, he'd churned out a grisly trio of novels, the Deathwatch cycle. Within two years, all three had become international bestsellers. By the time he was thirty, he'd been anointed a savant on both sides of the Atlantic, not to mention Japan, where his most ardent (and terrifying) fans lived.

His subjects were grave robbers, necromancers, zombies and—his favorite—vampires. Part of his success lay in his resistance to the term "horror" and his refusal to play the schlock-meister; he preferred that reviewers and fans alike refer to his works as "blood epics." He found it gratifying, for example, when the *New York Times* described his books as "chilling chronicles of necromania," tying him more to Lovecraft and Poe than to Stephen King. Although his characters were fantastical, he steeped his tales in truthful emotions—real wants and real fears, the other components of his winning formula. His zombie stories were allegories of xenophobia and race hate, and his vampire saga contained his own anxieties about aging. He never had mummies leaping out of the wardrobe just to say boo.

After a successful run of ten books, Raymond decided he had nothing more to say. It became tiresome to keep up with shifting expectations. Worse, he found himself too frequently invited to soirees with other practitioners of the genre. It wasn't the competition he dreaded, it was the homework. Having to thumb through multivolume sagas so there'd be something to discuss—writers of this type were notoriously solipsistic and couldn't handle conversation outside of their own invented realms. Anyway, their stories were never as vigorous and heartfelt as his, and there were few things more unbearable than an insincere werewolf epic.

Then, there were the fans. The disturbing ones, who sent him dead animals and decomposed body parts, lived in Japan, and he found them easy enough to ignore. But his target audience, the people for whom he started writing his books in the first place, were nowhere to be found.

In his naïveté, he'd hoped that his writing would draw in legions of tousle-haired, doe-eyed teenagers he could lure into his bed, ruby-lipped androgynes who wore Mom's pantyhose late at night while listening to jazz or Terry Riley's *In C*. Boys with faces like angels, and minds like devils. But instead, Raymond found—to his genuine horror—that the great majority of his readers were suburban housewives. These denim-wrapped females formed book clubs and organized role-playing weekends around his books; they invited him to inaugurate picnics and autograph raffle tickets. They squealed freely at his book signings, and too frequently, the chubby ones came dressed as sirens from his zombie cycle. He shuddered thinking about the way they bumbled around, jibberingly exchanging homemade business cards and Wiccan greetings. Whenever he read at a Barnes & Noble in the suburbs, he smelled the strip mall tacos on their breath.

Male children didn't read books anymore. It broke his heart to see in the news how children now went on the Internet to broker friendships with strange, older men. He believed in Headloin Love, massive acts of spontaneity propelled by a lightness in the head *and* a fire in the groin. Being in the moment, being in the flesh. How he missed the boys who'd cover his face in kisses when he brought them ice cream and silk dresses. Modern boys wanted cold, hard cash—or gift cards from Blockbuster or Best Buy. He recoiled at their bluntness, their unabashed declarations that "I'm in it for this, I'm not really a fag." The boys he loved best from the old days never had the time for grotesque words; they kept their heads down and their knees bent.

Dismayed, he channeled his energies into his house. Moving west from New York in the mid-nineties, Raymond had been in search of his own castle. But with new Hollywood money eating up most of old Los Angeles housing, he never managed to find a compound that was comfortable enough, stylish enough, yet affordable enough. Finally, his realtor sold him on the Craftsman aesthetic, a harmonious beam-exposing, grain-deifying style that was popularized at the turn of the twentieth century by a Wisconsin builder named Gustav Stickley. Classic Craftsman houses were chockablock in Alta Vista, a foothill area as yet undiscovered by the media throng; Raymond was instantly seduced by their shaded porches, shingled roofs and aw-shucks charm. He bought one on Santa Claus Lane, in cash.

Even though his own research told him that Stickley's prototypes were one-story, one-bathroom models of economy, his realtor insisted that his sprawling, two-story purchase was the only authentic Craftsman on the street. The others, she said, were copycat kit houses from the Sears, Roebuck catalog, pretty but nonetheless nailed together like log cabins.

His was a beautiful house whatever the vintage, and he liked having a space he had to live up to. It was rustic yet regal, hanging back from the street like a diffident suitor. He hoped against hope that a slight boy with bee-stung lips and opalescent eyes, drawn to the amber glow of his mica-shade lamps, would someday prance up his porch, asking to borrow a cup of confectioner's sugar.

That was the kind of visitor he waited for, not the bedraggled

Korean neighbor who was currently waddling toward his door, Lord knows why.

He watched her from his picture window, hoping she'd change her mind and turn back. She was teary-eyed, clutching a bundle of paper. Probably some kind of a petition. Oh, shoo! When she stepped onto his porch with the dull, flat-footed *thupp*s familiar from Jehovah's Witness church marms, he sighed, got up, and combed his hair in the mirror.

"Hello, dear," he said, at the door. "And what can I do for you?"

She refused to look him in the eye, possibly still raw from their encounter two years prior when he refused to retrieve her girls' shuttlecocks from his roof.

"Hello," said the Korean woman. "My husband, he say you writer. Yes?"

"Yes," said Raymond. He counted seven plastic barrettes in her hair.

"You write book. Yes?"

"Yes. I wrote a few books."

"Can you help me?"

"What, dear, would you like me to do?"

She paused and organized her thoughts. Then, casting aside fears about her lack of grammar or diction, she shoved the bundle of papers into his hands.

"Please. This my husband book. He write this. Please read. Finish read, please, you tell me if good or if bad . . . okay?"

Raymond glanced at the papers, smiling wryly at the letterhead: All-Friends Worship. The word *Viagra* on one of the pages leapt out at him. Hah.

"When do you need these back, dear?"

She flinched, stunned that he'd taken so little convincing. A smile of relief burst across her lips: "When you finish."

She nodded her thanks and backed off his porch, bowing painfully low.

"I see you later," she said. "Okay?"

"Okay." He watched her scurry back toward her house, then remembered something. "Oh, wait, Mrs. Kim!"

She stopped and turned. "My name is Mrs. Park."

"Mrs. Park . . . I've been meaning to ask you. You know that music that comes on at four o'clock every day? Does that"—he paused to find the least aggressive words—"bother you? It's not from your house, is it?"

She seemed genuinely startled that someone would have thought that. "No, no!"

"I thought not," he smiled, waving her goodbye. "I didn't think it was . . . demographically probable."

MRS. PARK PULLED out bunches of chives and green onions she'd been saving all week. She dropped them into batter and fried savory Korean pancakes, their oily aroma filling the entire house. The girls circled her in the kitchen, miming gestures to each other, trying to decode her. She hadn't said a word all evening, not since she returned from the creepy old neighbor's house. Thirty pancakes, stacked high on a platter. Glaring at the girls, she turned off the stove and plucked off her apron.

"No touch!" she cautioned. "Pancake no for you!"

She ran into her bedroom and carefully put on a white cotton dress and white pumps. In the bathroom, she combed her hair, fiddled with a tortoiseshell barrette and applied red to her lips.

Mira blocked her in the hallway. "Ma, what's going on? Are you trying to seduce that guy? Trust me, it's not gonna work."

Mrs. Park said nothing. She brushed past her daughter and dipped into the kitchen to collect the pancakes. Before exiting the front door, she looked right through Mira and called out to her firstborn.

"Rosemary, what's meaning 'democratically proper-ba'?"

"What's *what*?"

"Democratically proper-ba."

"I have no freakin' idea."

"Is good thing, no?"

"Possibly. Depending on the context."

"Okay, okay. You wait, I come back."

RAYMOND VAN DER Holt was enjoying the view of the mountains through his picture window when the Korean hausfrau invaded the frame, again. She was dressed entirely in white this time. What now? He got up, combed his hair again and answered the door.

"Oh, Mrs. Park, I haven't started on the stories yet. I know, I know. Bad boy." He slapped his own wrist.

"Is okay." She pushed a platter of soggy grey discs with green stripes into his hands. "I make the pancake for you. You doing work, you eat the food, okay?"

"Yes, ma'am."

She peered over his shoulder and into his house. "Very nice, your lamp."

"Right, so it is."

She stood there for a moment, as if she wanted to be invited in. "Pancake is no MSG. All veggie-table. I not know if you eat the meat."

"Thank you, Mrs. Park, in fact I do eat the meat." He took a step back into his house. Hint-hint for bye-bye. "It's very kind of you."

"Oh!" she suddenly exclaimed. "I forget soy sauce! I come back."

"No, no! Please don't! I have soy sauce. I'm sure it'll suffice."
He looked down and saw the scaly, unpainted nails peering out
her open-toe pumps. "Good night now, Mrs. Park."

"Gooda night."

THE LAST WOMAN to step into Raymond's house had been
his secretary, Adele Hollister. He preferred the term assistant, she
preferred secretary—in any case, she was a thick-wristed little
woman from Mississippi who put three kids through community college with her rigorous transcriptions. She was the one
person who could decode his hieroglyphs. In her five years with
Raymond, he'd only caught one typo in her work—"maldorous"
instead of "malodorous."

Raymond himself wrote longhand, using black Pilot roller-
ball pens on cream-colored loose-leaf Maruman paper from
Japan. Adele came in twice a week to transfer his words into a
chunky IBM laptop that lived for the most part in the supplies
closet. It depressed Raymond to look at that machine—drab,
serious, redolent of rote work.

When he first hired Adele, he warned her firmly that she
might occasionally encounter rude words and macabre sexual
situations. But from the start she was unflappable. She came in
at nine in the morning and tapped away till three. She didn't care
what words he used or didn't use. When she was done, she baked
cookies and made a pot of mint tea, leaving the house enveloped
in an aromatic dream of mother and maid.

Raymond liked her so much he kept her on even after his
oeuvre had waned. A year after his announced retirement, a big
publisher gave him a generous advance to write a memoir of his
youth, *The Lost Boy*. But what was the use of memoirs? He felt
that "nonfiction" was a genre cherished beyond what it deserved

by NPR-addled Americans. Because was "nonfiction" even *that*? Didn't the scrim of memory render fugitive every supposed truth? He'd much rather write up an inspired adaptation of his youth, where he roamed Manhattan in a vampire's cape, than recount tawdry evenings waiting by a mossy glory hole. Who'd want facts? After a year's deliberation, he returned the money— and on a tighter operating budget, he let Adele go.

These days, he couldn't even reenter the marketplace if he wanted to. Bookstores crippled him. A few years ago they were bad enough, filled with tomes by authors who took macho pride in the plainness of their prose, writing about burnt coffee and trailer parks and midday highs. But now, now was worse. Historical thrillers set in olde Europe, doleful as doorstops and stuffed to the gills with encyclopedia vomit; slim compendia by "modern humorists" who chronicled painfully ordinary situations and parlayed their modest gifts into radio programs, TV appearances and campus tours; and the absolute pits—catty *romans à clef* about life in New York's upper crust written by venal young things in stiletto heels.

He longed for the days of clichés he only partly despised— women's stories where empty tumblers of Dubonnet and old 78s, played over and over, stood in for romantic agony, or war stories where likable heroes got wounded and actually died. He'd rather starve than compete with the hacks of today, thank you very much.

HOLDING THE STORIES by the dead Korean, Raymond walked out to his backyard the following morning. He'd reheated the chive pancakes in his oven and the first of them now crunched warmly in his mouth. Not bad, not bad at all.

He pulled over a wrought-iron chair from the patio and put it under his oak tree. Facing him, across his privet hedge, was the Parks' yard. Through a bare patch in the hedge, he glimpsed his bête noire, their abandoned blue sofa. Its cushions bore a thousand slashes, inflicted by some insomniac cat, and moldy foam rubber was pushing out of its wounds. An eyesore matched in noxiousness only by the mysterious blasts of slut-rock.

Raymond turned his chair so he wouldn't have to see that thing. He reminded himself to talk Mrs. Park into getting rid of it in exchange for reading the stories.

The stories. He sighed. Oh, the stories. He started at the top of the pile. "The Dancing Banana Woman." Oh, God. The naïve, unschooled prose. The knee-jerk misogyny, the oblivious racism. The odd turns of phrase and lines lifted wholesale from some shabby paperback or other. And then he'd read all the stories, eaten all the pancakes, and was in need of a compensatory Scotch.

THAT EVENING, MRS. Park returned. Raymond had washed and dried her pink melamine platter, and it sat on the demi-lune console by his door waiting for her.

"Thank you for the pancakes. They were scrumptious."

He handed back the set of stories, which he seemed to have ironed flat for her. He'd also secured them with a black binder clip.

"And thank you so much for sharing your husband's stories."

"Oh! You finish!" She hugged the sheets. "Maybe you can help for selling?"

Raymond chuckled instinctively, then caught himself. The woman was dead serious.

"Would you like to step inside? I only have mint tea to offer you, but maybe we could have a quick little chat."

MRS. PARK SAT lightly on the red leather chesterfield. The dents her heels made in Raymond's thick Chinese rug made her feel like a barbarian, yet he wouldn't let her take them off. She sipped at the mint tea, wiping away traces of lipstick on the bone china with the piece of tissue she'd kept in her bra. She observed how he held his teacup with his pinky aloft and she did the same.

His house was at least twice as large as hers. Even the paint on the walls looked expensive. Built-in bookcases were everywhere. Many of the books had matching spines containing the words *Raymond van der Holt*.

"What type of books you write?" she asked.

"Oh, I don't know . . . One could say they're all love stories, essentially."

"Oh! Romance!"

"Well . . ."

"What is your name?"

"Raymond van der Holt. There—you can see my name emblazoned on all the books in this room. Awfully narcissistic, I suppose you're thinking, but I spare myself the embarrassment by never having people over." He glanced at her. No reaction. "I may even have Japanese editions of my novels upstairs. But I don't suppose they'll be of any use to you."

She pointed at the framed picture of a young man on his grand piano. "Your son?"

"No, I'm afraid that's Marlon Brando." When she drew a blank, he explained, "In his earlier, funnier days."

"You play piano?"

"Alas, you shame me again, Mrs. Park. I don't. That's set decoration. Like the books. And the photo."

"Is nice piano."

Raymond cleared his throat. "About your husband's stories, Mrs. Park . . ."

She put her teacup down and held herself up.

"They no good, right?" She had an I'm-tough-I-can-take-it grimace.

"They were very entertaining. You should be proud of your husband."

"But . . . they no good, right?"

"People toil for years before they produce anything, and believe me, even experienced midlist authors don't often find people who want to publish them. Writers in America now go away to school for four years and come back with just one short story and forty thousand dollars of debt. Your husband wrote five, what, six stories?"

"Tell me they bad. Tell me." Tears were welling in her eyes again.

"Good and bad are very subjective terms. And as you probably already know, like everything else out there, the publishing world's run by idiots."

She nodded and rose to leave. He handed her the melamine platter by the door.

"Maybe my husband stories too dark?"

Now Raymond had to smile: "They're not dark, dear. They're just poorly lit."

She headed to her house without looking back.

"Be brave, Mrs. Park," he called after her.

Minutes later, he kicked himself for forgetting to ask her about that blue couch.

LATE THAT NIGHT, way past his bedtime, Raymond was swirling his third glass of Muscadet and reading Johan Huizinga's

The Waning of the Middle Ages while Josephine Baker sang "Blue Skies" on his faux Victrola. When he lifted his head to yawn, he was startled by a mop of black hair in the lower edge of his picture window. From its movements, he could tell that it was no hirsute Pekingese but something more intelligent—someone was watching him with eyes hidden behind that curtain of hair. It surveyed the living room, scanning it from one end to the other.

He stood up and waved his arms wildly. *I can see ya, ya little cunt.*

No reaction.

Then the curtain of hair rose with a sickening grandeur. A black tulip blossoming. Raymond shuddered. His spy stood lankily in the picture window, framed like a Goya of a girl completely in the nude, her skin pale against the dark velvet night. The hair remained over her face like a lustrous ebony mask. Her pubis, meanwhile, was tauntingly exposed—a bristly chimney sweep's brush.

"Stop that! Come on, stop that right now!"

Arms akimbo, he gave her his most authoritarian stare. Peter Lorre, then Charlton Heston.

The girl took several steps back. Then, with no regard for her personal safety, she slammed her entire body hard against the glass. *Thwack!*

"Hey! Hey, I mean it!" He stopped himself from stepping outside lest it was a trap set by the unhinged Mrs. Park. He'd hate to be caught berating a naked girl, especially if the cops were already on their way.

Instead, he waved his finger at her from indoors like a chiding schoolmaster.

"Fuck off! Just go away, will ya?"

The girl peeled herself off the window. She took three slow

steps back and again smashed herself against the glass. *Thwack!* And yet again—*thwack!*

Raymond froze. This was antique leaded glass, impossible to replace, and the fiend didn't seem likely to give up until it broke. Who was this? What did they want?

At her fourth *thwack!* Raymond thought he heard a crack in the glass or in its frame. That was it. A man had the right to protect his property. He gulped down the rest of the Muscadet and stormed to the door.

"You're asking for it, sweetie!"

She must have had quick feet because when he opened the door, there was nobody on the porch. A cold draft rushed past him and into the house. There was nothing out there but the night. The chirping crickets gave nothing away.

He walked to the window and surveyed the damage from the outside.

There were two smudges in the center of the pane, shaped exactly like greasy nipples.

THE GIRL IN THE WINDOW

Summer was murder on the lawns of Alta Vista. The San Gabriel Mountains held the July air down in a valley chokehold and the parched grass went from green to white to gray to brown in a single breath.

The people of Santa Claus Lane took the heat personally. They either kept longer hours at air-conditioned offices or hid in their homes until night made it safe to breathe again. As the sun went down, the rattle and hiss of lawn sprinklers covered up the whines of rash-covered infants and the whimpers of sunbaked pets. There were no evening soirees organized around cold drinks to commiserate—everybody withdrew. But had someone created opportunities to mingle and snipe, all the neighbors would have agreed that the only home on Santa Claus Lane that seemed exempt from the inferno was the Big Brown House.

Raymond van der Holt's house loomed larger, was set back deeper and painted darker than the others. Like many fancy homes in folksy neighborhoods, it tried to camouflage itself with common shrubs and trees. The effect of all that greenery was that Raymond's house resembled some opulent forest hideaway in the Pacific Northwest, cool and aloof even when pounded by the hottest heat. Not true, of course, and Raymond had the electricity bills to prove it. When the heat subsided one evening, he emerged from his air-conditioned refuge and activated the sprinklers. The boom box–playing maniac had been uncharacteristically silent. He could only hope she was dead from sunstroke.

He slipped on rubber clogs and unleashed a hose on the thirsty patches the sprinklers missed. The sound of flowing water relaxed him. The sky was darkening, and there was a loamy fragrance from where the moisture loosened the soil. Earthworms were probably farting without a care. If it weren't for the mosquitoes, Raymond would be sipping Bandol in the shade of his oak, making believe he was in an abnormally prosaic aerie in the south of France.

A cool breeze kissed his arm, as if a fugitive blast of igloo air had slipped out the back door and found its way out to him. He looked up at the house, dark and still. The back door and windows were shut. Maybe a cold front was moving in. One could dream.

He tugged the hose to the far end of the yard and drenched the base of his oak. Watching the water unleashed the ancient urge—as it often did. He undid the crotch of his pants, and looked around. With only the Parks' ravaged blue couch as a potential witness, he peed freely.

A myopic hawk flew overhead, grazing the treetop and sending leaves cascading. Then a flock of smaller birds, all cawing madly in pursuit.

"For fuck's sake!" Raymond zipped up his pants.

Could these actually be the elusive, possibly fictional, feral green parrots of Alta Vista the realtor had yapped so excitedly about? In the evening light, these birds looked more charcoal than chartreuse. Raymond turned off the hose, painstakingly coiling it around the tap so it wouldn't flatten the grass in the shape of a comatose snake.

Out of the corner of his eye, he caught something through his study windows. He rushed closer, trying to recall if he'd locked the front door.

"Who's there?" he bellowed, more a statement than a question. Looking around the yard for a possible weapon, he freed a rusty, cobwebbed tomato stake.

Glancing back at the window, he saw the pale orb again. This time, a human form, made gaunt and vague by bug screens and privacy tinting. Then the specter seemed to register that it'd been spotted, and retreated in a flash.

Raymond ran to the back door wielding the rusty stake. It was locked, from the inside. He kicked at the door in a rage, then power-walked to the front of the house.

"I'm going to kill you!"

The front door was wide open. The sprinklers on the lawn soaked the legs of his pants as he passed.

Through the doorway, his home looked like one black hole. He gripped the stake and neared the threshold. Then he removed his wet, grass-stained clogs and left them on the porch. He entered the house, closing the front door behind him.

Once inside, he darted from light switch to light switch, flicking on every one he could find. The lights did nothing. All he had were dim, wimpy accent lamps with their stupid copper shades—mood, not security lighting. Worthless, effete set dressing. He cursed himself.

He sluiced through the hallway, past the oxblood dining room, toward his study in the back. He peeked around every dark doorway before taking the next step, the way he'd seen detectives enter strange rooms in movies.

"Don't even *think* you can escape now."

Behind him, the front door of the house slammed shut.

Hadn't he already closed it? He turned, ran briskly to the front of the house, and opened the door.

The sprinklers were on full blast. In the half-light, he saw watery prints of bare feet on the dry stone pathway. He followed the footprints as they led off his property, to the center of the street, where they . . . vanished.

It appeared that the intruder had made a beeline for Kate Ireland's house across the street. He thought of ringing Kate's doorbell to warn her, then decided against it. He didn't want to sound like a crazy old coot, showing up at her door, sweat rings under his arms. Not that she seemed completely sound herself. He'd run into her several times at the liquor store, hunching along the whisky aisle with her many bottles, as if anyone in a liquor store would judge. No, as long as the housebreaker was gone, he wouldn't bother. It didn't look like anything was missing. Of course, the next time they showed up, he'd teach the punk a lesson with his knives—plural.

The phone was ringing when Raymond got to his porch and set down the stake.

"I can't talk now, Dad," Raymond said to the master of impeccable timing.

"Why not?"

"I'm really tired. I'll call you Sunday."

"I just wanted to hear your voice," the old man said.

"You wanted to hear my voice?"

"Yes, son. I just wanted to hear your voice."

"Remember that DVD I sent you of the movie they made out of my book *Black Grave*?"

"*Black Grape*, did you say?"

"Black. *Grave.*" His dad had never read any of his books, citing moral objections.

"Oh, yes."

"If you put on the DVD, and anyone working at Dartmoor would be able to do that for you, you can hear my voice on the commentary track."

"I'm not so sure. They aren't so bright, the girls who work here."

"What're you talking about? Students from Yale intern there." Raymond sighed. "Look, I really have to go now. Somebody just broke into my house."

"Good Lord! Are they still there? Have you called the police?"

"I can't, can I, Dad? Not when you're keeping me on the phone with you."

"Raymond, why are you being so mean?"

"Oh, for heaven's sake! What do you want from me?"

"I'm your father."

"Yes, and as my father, I'd expect you to have the maturity and decency to realize that I, your son, am a fully grown, fully realized adult and that I have my own life. And with that, my own problems that I need to solve." Raymond took another deep breath. "I have to call the police now."

"Please call sometime, won't you?" That plaintive voice again. It was the kind of thing that led to patricide. "You won't forget, will you?"

"I'll call you, I'll call you. Goodbye, Dad."

It seemed unimaginable that this old scarecrow could have ever been a meat packer, a taciturn man's man who spent his days alone in an icy locker hanging carcasses. Now, one minute left to himself and he was nervous as a cat.

Whenever Raymond suggested he make friends with the other residents, he'd say he didn't feel at ease with the retired surgeons and accountants, implying that Raymond had thrown him into an elite facility as an act of perversity. He'd never sat in a real leather recliner until he moved there, or even tasted a martini—and all that was just fine; it was the looks he thought he got from the ones who marched down the halls in golf clothes as if they owned the place.

Raymond's mother, on the other hand, would have thoroughly enjoyed Dartmoor. She would have Jazzercised with the other whitehairs every morning and played bridge every night, with nary a thought as to anyone's background, not least of all her own. She would have loved the party buses into Manhattan to see *Les Miz*.

It was probably the biggest regret of Raymond's life that he hadn't placed them both in Dartmoor while she was still alive. His mother died an undignified death in their ramshackle Wichita duplex, choking on a piece of meatloaf during *Jeopardy*. His Dad had been in the other room, sleeping off a Blue Nun bender.

Raymond opened his front door. The sprinklers had stopped. The intruder's footprints had evaporated, leaving absolutely no trace. What would be the point of calling the cops now?

He went back inside, locking himself in for the night. With a thimble of Lagavulin in his hand, he sauntered to his study to locate the damage, if any. He found himself humming, then singing a fortifying tune that his mother had sung to him as a boy:

> *Shine little glow-worm, glimmer, glimmer*
> *Shine little glow-worm, glimmer, glimmer*
> *Lead us lest too far we wander*
> *Love's sweet voice is calling yonder . . .*

He flicked on the light. His mahogany writing desk was

untouched. Even the half-eaten bag of low-fat chips lay exactly where he had left it, next to his reading glasses, on top of the book on the Middle Ages he'd been perusing.

He moved to where the intruder might have been when they appeared in the window. It was a sliver of space between the desk and the pane—and the desk was too heavy to be moved. Nobody could fit in there. He peered under the desk to where his or her feet might have been—there he saw dark, red-black droplets of blood. He jumped in terror.

His teak floor!

He dashed to the kitchen for a sponge and wood-cleaning soap, his head pounding. It was only after he'd finished scrubbing and rinsing the blood off the floor that he realized he'd wiped away all evidence of the intrusion.

Bah! He took a Xanax, then a Klonopin, and chased them down with whisky for good luck.

THE CAMRY SAT on the driveway under the blazing sun.

"You have to get in there!" Mira screamed at her mother.

"Trust me, Ma, it's not going to explode." Rosemary spoke calmly. Someone had to be the voice of reason.

Mrs. Park stared at the car, the key ring in her hand. She squeezed the button—*cheep-cheep!*—and unlocked the doors.

"Get in there, Mother!" Mira opened the driver's door and pushed her mother to it. "Now!"

"Wait, wait . . ." Mrs. Park gripped the edge of the door, panting. ". . . Slowly!"

"Take your time, Ma," Rosemary said.

"*Take her time?* It's been, like, three months." Mira rolled her eyes at her painfully diplomatic sister. "Tell her. Tell. Her."

Mrs. Park looked to her older daughter for kinder words.

"Ma, we . . . bought a book," Rosemary said. "On driving."

"We're going to study it ourselves," Mira cut in, "since you're incapable of it."

Tears welled up in Mrs. Park's eyes. The girls couldn't tell if she was moved or insulted. When her brow furrowed, they had their answer. She slammed the car door shut and hit the button on the key ring, locking it. *Cheep!* Avoiding their eyes, she stalked back into the house.

"You see? We shouldn't have told her," Rosemary said, pulling a spiderweb off the car's wiper. She wound it around her finger like a loom.

"How else will we get through to her? She's not Amish, you know."

"I know, but she's, like, super bueno mucho upset now."

"I can't tell you how sick I am of eating that ramen she buys from the am/pm. I'm anticipating bone loss from the MSG."

They turned to the house as the screen door opened. Mrs. Park popped out.

"I make a plan." She met their eyes. "We go back to Korea."

THE MYSTERY BOOM Box had not boomed in more than two weeks. The last time the girls heard it was the Fourth of July, when it blasted patriotic songs by country-singer types.

Mira thought, *If only Dad had waited another few weeks. If only I hadn't used the music as an excuse for not doing my homework. If only Ma hadn't pushed Dad to the brink with her incessant sea-hag nattering.* It wasn't even that she liked her father much, but she liked the idea of moving to Korea even less. There, she imagined, all the men wore fake Air Jordans, burped kimchi and spent their spare time beating up their wives.

She and Rosie were in a race against time. After giving away all of their Dad's belongings to the Salvation Army, their mother had begun packing their things into old cardboard boxes. She'd already thrown ten years' worth of *National Geographic* into the recycle bin and said she'd deal with the crockery the following week.

Nights, Mrs. Park made phone calls to friends and relatives in Korea, always beginning friendly and ending desperate, her eyes rimmed with red and her arms entangled in telephone wire.

"Do you even know anyone there anymore?" Mira would ask her. "You left twenty years ago. That's, like, a *really* long time ago!"

Mrs. Park wouldn't answer; she'd keep her eyes tilted away from the questions, defiant. Mira was only a child, and a spoiled, mean-spirited one—what did she know about obligation? The girl's histrionics always ended the same way anyhow, with her screaming "I hate you!" and storming out of the kitchen, then returning two minutes later in tears, pleading, "Please, Ma, please don't make us go!"

Mira found a way to distract her mother. After dinner, she read to her from *When Bad Things Happen to Good People*. Though it was a hideous task having to explain each line to her mother in language she could understand, it prevented Mrs. Park from disappearing to make those calls to Korea and it kept her from noticing that Rosemary was outside, trying to figure out the Camry's controls with *Driving for Idiots* in her lap.

Mira read aloud from a chapter entitled "Why Do the Righteous Suffer?" She couldn't wait to get to the chapter called "Sometimes There Is No Reason" just to watch her mother lose her mind.

"*The misfortunes of good people are not only a problem to the people who suffer and their families . . .*"

Her mother interrupted her, tapping at the words on the back cover.

"What is this say?" Mrs. Park asked.

Mira flipped the book over.

"For anyone who has ever been hurt by life . . . It means that this book was written for people who feel cheated and eff-ed over by their circumstances. Like you."

Her mother nodded.

"You also, yes?" she said, hopefully.

"This book was written by a rabbi. I'm probably not 'hurt by life' in the way that he's talking about."

"You not feel missing your Dad?"

"I guess . . ." Mira gazed at the hairy mole on her mother's neck. "But this is not about me. It's about you."

Mrs. Park looked wounded.

"You pray to Jesus?"

"Ma, that's too many questions. Can we just continue reading this thing?"

Mrs. Park pushed the book away and tried to get her daughter to look at her.

"You asset Jesus Christ as Lord and Savior?"

"Ma . . ."

Mrs. Park grabbed Mira's wrists and forced her palms together in prayer.

"You asset Jesus as Lord and Savior. Yes?"

"Stop it. You're creeping me out." Mira snatched her hands away and stood up. "Can I ask you something, Ma? Do you feel persecuted?"

Mrs. Park stared back blankly.

"When we were studying the legacy of slavery, a boy in my class asked a really interesting question. He said, 'Why aren't there great Asian American chroniclers of suffering?' He meant that the Jews have their Holocaust museums, and African Americans have Frederick Douglass and Hurricane Katrina, but Asians don't really have anyone. Like, George Takei's kind of upbeat. And I got to thinking maybe *you* could be our spokesperson, Ma. Because you're so gifted at grievance."

Mrs. Park covered her mouth with her hand. "You say garbage, Mira!" She buried her face in her hands, and began sobbing.

Mira was startled by the power of her words. She was only funning.

Rosemary crept into the house just then, *Driving for Idiots* tucked under her shirt.

"Ma? What's wrong?" Rosemary glowered at her sister. "What did you do? What did you say to her?"

"Nothing." Mira backed away from the couch. "I asked her a rhetorical question and she misunderstood me. You know how it is."

Rosemary followed Mira into her room, plunging her nails into Mira's arm.

"Ow! Quit that! You're hurting me!"

"What did you say to her?"

"I asked if she felt persecuted. I know it sounds totally cruel out of context but . . ."

Rosemary closed the door behind Mira.

"Listen to me," she hissed. "We're in a really, really delicate situation here. I'm not sure you realize how serious this is. That woman, a.k.a. our mother, wants to take us to Korea, where we will both suffer grievously and, like, never meet our fullest potential. Now, can you get that into your thick skull?"

"I have that inside my head every second of every day!" Mira wriggled to get out of her sister's iron grip. Rosemary released her, and Mira fell against the bed. "I'm going to get bruises from this, I swear. People at school will think I have an uncle who rapes me. And I'll say I do."

"Can you be serious for one minute? I know you're going stir crazy here but we have to keep Ma calm or she might actually go through with this."

"I'll probably just kill myself." Mira grinned, her braces gleaming. "Seriously."

"Don't talk like that. The last thing we need is another irrational freak-out in this house. Right now, from what I can tell, it looks like she's having no luck getting someone to, I don't know, take us in."

"Why am I not surprised? That woman has no people skills whatsoever. Couldn't we put ourselves up for adoption? Couldn't some rich gay couple in New York adopt us? Couldn't we say we're poor girl babies from China?"

"Miracle Park, you don't even know what real poverty is."

"Yeah, like you're Miss Rwanda Baglady."

Rosemary pulled the driving book out of her shirt and threw it at her sister.

"Your turn."

"Any luck tonight?"

"I figured out high beams, low beams. Which means we can make a getaway, in the dead of night."

ROSEMARY RODE THE bus to school twice a week for summer drama. The kids unfortunate enough not to be attending camp or loitering around piazzas in Italy sometimes signed up for the class, just to have something to do apart from PlayStation, or porn.

But Rosemary was actually serious about the class. There was nothing to keep her at home—the Brittany Ann Yamasato saga had run its course. Two months before, sightings of her were reported as far north as Vancouver, where she'd been seen riding in a wood-paneled van with an older man, and as far south as Corpus Christi, Texas, where witnesses said they saw her stick her tongue through a glazed donut. But those leads tapered off. A cuter, younger kid—a missing Boy Scout from Utah—was now the hot item; all the cameras were trained on his blindingly blond family as they prayed.

The drama class's main draw was Mr. Zehring, a boyish man who could have been twenty-six—or forty. His light-brown hair bounced on his head like a toupee whenever he made jazz hands, which was often. And he did so derisively, which was odd for a theater guy. He always seemed at a slight remove from the room, a bit soliloquyishly meta. She thought he looked like a handsome JFK, though his patter was less presidential, more motivational speaker. He made the kids call him Mr. Z, for short, and some actually called him by his first name, Bryce.

At first, the class wasn't something that Rosemary was dying to do—theater kids and their transatlantic affectations gave her the creeps—but the guidance counselor had suggested she take up an extracurricular activity that wasn't purely academic so her college application would look less stereotypically Asian. She started Mr. Z's class and enjoyed his approach so much that she didn't feel insulted when he funneled her into a supplementary class with three other students of East Asian descent who had trouble, in his words, "releasing their face." Until they learned to be expressive with their bodies, he said, they would be of no value in a regular drama class.

He said that as someone who was raised as a Lutheran in the upper Midwest, he had some of the same problems—his face was "all closed up" and his feelings were "compacted." He'd been programmed not to show emotion because his father believed that emotion in boys was evidence of weakness.

"It was like my entire face was cast in concrete, and the real me was roiling underneath." He ran his splayed fingers down his face. "I knew that what I was on the inside and what I was on the outside were two very different things. Separate entities, even. And that's not even counting *what I thought I was* versus *what I wanted to be* versus *what I really was*. You follow?"

The kids nodded placidly. He went on:

"But people couldn't *see* my true self. People couldn't look past my carapace. And it was incredibly, incredibly frustrating for me, as I'm sure it is for you. They thought I was this dull, well-behaved boy with nothing remarkable to say about anything—if they thought of me at all."

Mr. Z said he had to "reprogram" his face, doing funny expressions in the mirror every morning and night, massaging his forehead and the areas around the eyes to relax the muscles. There were tongue and mouth-stretching exercises, too. *A cheap and chippy chopper on a big black clock . . .*

"Think of yourself as a tree. If you let your fears and inhibitions fall away, only then can you start conquering them, picking up each negative feeling like a rotting piece of fruit and mashing it up in your hands." He was a great mime. Rosemary could almost smell the sourness from the imaginary peach that was macerating between his palms.

She did all his facial exercises in the bathroom for a half hour every morning. They chased away her terror of being in her dad's death chamber—the grout around the tub was stained tea-brown. After two weeks, Mr. Z told her she had succeeded in smiling with her eyes and gave her two thumbs up.

In the final session before the four East Asians were allowed back into the drama class, he screened the movie *Dead Ringers*. He asked them to watch how the lead actor—"a Pinteresque British mummy"—released his face during the course of the film.

The movie, directed by David Cronenberg, whom Mr. Z singled out as "the sickest director in the world," told the story of identical twin brothers, played by Jeremy Irons. Rosemary recognized him as the voice of Scar in *The Lion King*. The brothers were both gynecologists, and in love with same weird French Canadian lady. But because they had a twisted relationship, one of them dominant and the other submissive, the rivalry for the lady evolved into a deeper psychic battle. There were nude love scenes too bizarre for the kids to find sexy—and none of them were into watching the middle-aged fuck.

Rosemary found the movie spooky and touching but couldn't quite articulate why, and so kept those thoughts to herself. In contrast, Alicia Hwang paraded her enthusiasm, repeating everything Mr. Z said.

"You're so right—it *is* about the split in each of us. The ego and the id!" Alicia Hwang was the kind of Asian suck-up that would make most Asian suck-ups vomit.

After class, Mr. Z pulled his Nissan Maxima up to Rosemary at the bus stop. "Hop in." He said he had to run an errand anyway. His car smelled like toothpaste—or mouthwash. When they turned onto Santa Claus Lane, he slowed his car down. She felt herself get goosebumps, waiting for him to just say something.

"Did you know that this area used to be a giant graveyard for the Pascualite Indians? The only thing that grew here was poppies. Then, in the 1890s, a man named Luther Burbank brought these deodars over from the Himalayas and planted them here." He pointed up at the beardy pine trees lining the street. "He was a brave guy."

"For planting trees?"

"Well, for one, he told people he was a freethinker, but he was really an atheist. And you know how they went for nonbelievers in those days . . ."

He pulled the car over to the side of the road, and she felt her stomach tighten.

"He published a pamphlet called *Why I Am an Infidel* in which he wrote, 'Science, unlike theology, never leads to insanity.' Pretty bold stuff, huh?"

"I guess," she said.

"Ironically, deodar means 'tree of God.'"

"Huh. That's funny."

He looked out the window.

"Are you a believer, Rose?" The way he said it made her hair stand on end. He cooed it, like he was asking if she loved him.

"My dad was a pastor."

"No kidding? Was? Has he retired?"

"In a way. He killed himself."

"Oh. I'm so sorry, Rose." He winced with his eyes but his mouth was still smiling.

"No, it's okay." She wanted both for him to drop her home so the awkwardness would end and for the ride to keep going. "How come you know so much about . . . trees?"

"I absorb all kinds of information. My wife calls me a sponge— an animal and not a mineral, by the way, nor a tree."

Rosemary waited a moment then said: "You're married?"

"You assumed I was gay, didn't you?" He inhaled dramatically and raised an eyebrow. "Because I teach drama. And care somewhat about my appearance."

"No, it's not that. It's . . . you don't wear a ring."

"How right you are. I don't wear a ring. I'm allergic. My skin's very sensitive. Um. So . . . where exactly do you live?"

She turned red—she'd never said. She waved her hand five or six houses down. Mr. Z pulled into the center of the road and started driving. He stopped outside Raymond van der Holt's house.

"Whoa, nice crib, girlfriend!"

"No, mine's that little gray thing next door to it."

Rosemary gathered her things together slowly and opened the car door. She unbuckled her seat belt last.

"Rose," he said. She turned. "If you ever need anything or just someone to talk to, call me. Let me give you my cell number."

The term "cell number" always made her think of prison. Her heart leapt nonetheless. He brushed her bare thigh when he opened the glove compartment and reached for a red plastic pen. Then he scrawled his number on the back of an old gas station receipt and unthinkingly handed both pen and paper to her. She took both, pocketing the pen before he could notice.

"Thanks."

"I'll see you at class on Monday. If not sooner." He waved as she got out of the car. What did he mean, if not sooner?

Suddenly, he exclaimed, "Did you see that?"

"See what?"

"In the window of that big old house."

"Where?"

"It's gone now. I thought I saw a naked girl in there looking right at us."

Rosemary turned to the van der Holt house. Was he putting her on? "It's unlikely . . . I'm quite positive the guy who lives there doesn't like girls."

"Hmm. Then I must've imagined it. That's what I get for watching *Dead Ringers* with you."

II.

GIRL ON THE PLANE

–

December 1975

to

April 2006

HOMECOMING

Mary-Sue Ireland's path to Santa Claus Lane began at her father's funeral in 1975, in a land that felt completely alien to her, the kind of place she'd never dream of visiting, let alone dying in. She would sooner find common ground with a Hindu mendicant on the streets of Calcutta than with any of the well-fed citizens of this dreaded town.

She had rarely given Des Moines, Iowa, a moment's thought (except to curse it) since her jailbreak at age eighteen. Since then, she'd visited her father at his retirement home maybe four times, which was four times more than she'd wanted to. Even with the cloud of Alzheimer's, Bob Ireland always managed to pull himself together for enough time each year to send her an airline ticket from San Francisco. His checks kept Mary-Sue coming back, and she was too proud to make any bones about it. He'd been a distant father to her, spiritually absent even when physically present, and if this was his way of making up for it, she'd take every penny.

Of course, he'd gotten on just fine with her little brother, Bobby—in those days there were no two Ioway men baseball couldn't bond. Mary-Sue knew she was too old to let such inequities eat at her. She was thirty-three. When Daddy was her age, he'd already built a splendid career and had been for five years the head of a Midwestern rubber company that dealt in condom technology. What had she done?

Driving up ice-slicked Locust Street, Mary-Sue saw the blistering gold dome of the state capitol in the distance. That was the big-city beacon of Daddy's youth, his beefy adolescence squandered in a farm town named Anita where the big excitement every night was waiting for the Rusty Razor barbershop sign to light up. Des Moines was far from a metropolis in his day and even less of one now. Its streets had become exemplars of wounded glory, gray with once-grand office buildings that collected more echoes and shadows with each passing winter. It was a ghost town in progress.

She'd gotten a call about her father's death from some kind of relative who still lived in Des Moines and worked part-time at the hospice where he'd spent his last days fighting liver disease.

"Everything's been arranged, dear," said the cousin-lady, with her overly soothing switchboard voice. "All you need to do now is show up."

Mary-Sue remembered screaming into the receiver: "Where do you get off talking to me like this? I'm his fucking daughter!" The rest of it, from the packing of black clothes to the flight from San Francisco to Des Moines, was a complete blur. She had vague recollections, however, of lighting up a joint at the Denver airport and stubbing it out when some silver-haired cowpoke stared at her.

Cruising along the streets of Des Moines, pointedly avoiding her old neighborhood, she peered into the other cars and surprised herself thinking that, apart from the overeaters and the high-waisted geezers with the Dust Bowl faces, Iowans were, by and large, a good-looking people. Donna Reed had been an Iowan originally. John Wayne, Jean Seberg. The people at the airport were all easygoing, wholesome types. A far cry from the hollow-eyed crazies she often encountered roving the streets of San Francisco, vibrating with such intensity they scared even her. She'd always thought that her father was good-looking in his prime, just enough off-handsome he might have been plopped into movies as the leading man's valet. She had inherited her father's brown curls and big, watchful eyes; now if she'd simply stop smoking so many damn cigarettes and put some of her old chub back, she'd probably pass for a wholesome Iowan herself.

Out in West Des Moines, her happy thoughts about iconic Iowans faded. A panhandler stood by the intersection, wearing a raggedy Santa suit. The red had bled into the white and his buckle dangled loose off the belt. The Yosemite Sam beard was the man's own, chest-length and snow-dusted—he could have been a rogue member of the Manson Family. Bony fingers held up a cardboard sign: WILL WORK 4 BUS TICKET. Mary-Sue entertained the idea of paying him to attend the funeral in her place, and this made her laugh so hard she narrowly missed a flatbed full of hogs. The driver gave her the finger. She rolled down her window, called him a country-ass pigfucker, sped away, and felt *good*.

The funeral was very tasteful. Nameless former colleagues from Cedar Falls had driven through a small blizzard to be there. Nameless relatives from the Iowa countryside showed up in ill-fitting borrowed suits. One of the Cedar Falls sophisticates remarked on how classy it was for the funeral home to have hidden its hearses from the visitors' lot.

What Mary-Sue had been told was correct—she didn't have to do anything but show up. The entire program had been planned without her. The moment she arrived at the door, she was escorted by Mr. Evans, the funeral director, to the front-row pew and handed a box of Kleenex. The aunt or whatever who'd spoken to her on the phone smiled at her smugly from the far end of the chapel but never once came over; she planted herself by the row of wreaths, greeting well-wishers and fiddling with the hundred gold bangles she wore on her arm like Slinkies. Mary-Sue was grateful she'd smoked a joint in the parking lot or she'd be running at her with a clenched fist.

On the stage, atop a table with a burgundy silk runner, sat a jade-colored urn. She hadn't even known that her father wished to be cremated. Everybody at the funeral, it seemed, knew her father better and loved him more than she did. She was a stranger.

When the service began, a fifty-ish pastor with a comb-over came to the lectern. He had the face of someone who'd fallen asleep at the sewing machine and woken up with his features stitched together funny. Then the aged organist with shaky Parkinson's hands played a couple of songs from *The Music Man*, which Mary-Sue felt were wholly inappropriate. Some people cried during this time—perhaps they knew these songs had meant something to her father.

Nobody stopped to talk to her after the service. They were all too busy. A couple of old biddies nodded sympathetically at her before hurrying over to the pie and cookie cart, where the snickerdoodles tasted like sawdust (and she was stoned). When did Iowans stop knowing how to bake? She'd had better at a macrobiotic cantina in the Haight where the cook was often too baked himself to tell sugar from salt. She exchanged nods with a teenage boy who'd been dragged there by his infirm grandmother, car keys jangling impatiently in his hands. Everybody was occupied. She'd make a clean getaway.

She was halfway across the lot to her red rental Mustang when somebody came running after her, shoes shushing in the snow, asking her to wait. It was Mr. Evans, the slow-talking funeral director. He wanted to know if she'd be taking the ashes.

The ashes. She hadn't even given them a second's thought.

"No!" she said, then repeated in a calmer voice, "no, but thanks."

"I didn't think so." The funeral director pursed his lips and started back to the home, snowflakes melting on his bald pate as they landed.

Mary-Sue watched him walk away with mincing steps, shaking his head ever so slightly. Now it was her turn to run after him. She followed him back to the entrance of the building.

"What *the fuck* did you mean by that?"

"I beg your pardon, Miss Ireland?"

"What did you mean 'I didn't think so'? You don't even *know* me, you parasite! You feed off the misfortunes of others and you think you're entitled to judge me?"

"I'm sorry if I've upset you in some way, Miss Ireland. I really didn't mean any disrespect at all."

"God! You passive-aggressive motherfucker!"

"Well, I really should be going back in to see how the others are doing. Please take care of yourself, Miss Ireland. You obviously need to get some rest."

He leaned forward to give her a hug. She returned with what her gut told her to do—she clocked him hard on the face with her handbag. Its large metal clasp hit him square in the left eye and an inch-long cut under his brow began to bleed. He staggered back a couple steps, stunned. Before either of them grasped what had happened, Mary-Sue struck him again. This time, he fell back onto a snow-covered bush, sending clumps of white into the air. There was more blood on his face now, and the snow he touched instantly turned scarlet.

"Please, Miss Ireland . . ."

"Stop saying my name, you condescending asshole! You don't even *know* me!"

She lunged for him but did not strike him this time. He fell to the ground in anticipation all the same. He tried repeatedly to stand himself back up but his patent-leather shoes kept slipping on the ice. Mary-Sue laughed. Each time he fell, he became more and more disheveled.

"Help . . . !" His voice was hoarse. "Somebody help me!"

"Look at you, Mr. Evans. Look at you now."

She walked briskly to her car, got in and vroomed away.

MARY-SUE GATHERED UP all the little bottles from the minibar. She lined them up like a firing squad in front of the TV and drank them one by one. She was in a suite that had been booked for her at the Hotel Fort Des Moines, another old landmark that had become as shabby as the rest of the Midwest. Anyone who had any sense at all moved out to try their luck in California or New York; the ones who stayed either had no imagination or no choice. Her father she once imagined had both, but he'd chosen to remain in his home state out of some spiritually ruinous notion of loyalty.

She made a toast to the capitol building, shimmering against the black winter's sky. She toasted the uneven tan on the wallpaper. She toasted the decades of toe cheese in the thick-pile wall-to-wall. She toasted the butt sweat in the leather club chair, the tumbler that probably once held some old industrialist's dentures. The whole hotel was a dying white man. Iowa. Fucking Iowa, man.

When she was done toasting, she shut off the lights and crawled into bed.

MARY-SUE SPENT HER teen years in Des Moines plotting her escape, reading *New Yorker* listings in the public library and studying the subway map that her father brought home from a business trip. Cosmopolitan Manhattan, she believed, was where her destiny lay, and she vowed that once high school was over, she'd hop on the quickest train there and never look back. When the time came, she did just that.

Life wasn't exactly what she expected. The real East Coast people, like her roommates at Barnard from whom she first learned that *bourgeois* was a bad word, were WASP natives with beach houses, and they formed an impenetrable tribe that would never let her in long enough to belong. On weekends, she'd be their special guest star, the Midwestern charity case who was offered a peek at their peculiar rituals involving boat shoes, gingham napkins and thank-you notes, but she'd read enough Wharton to know that she would be a fool to try to parrot their ways. She learned the meaning of "shabby genteel" when she made her first Boston friends. They sleepwalked through life with passed-down manners borne of creaky Nantucket estates long since carved up, fought over, and lost. The Iowan in Mary-Sue felt that their frayed aristocratic style was vastly overprized, especially when it showed itself in their inability to locate the post office or, more pointedly, to pay for their share of a meal. The smart Jews were the ones she most longed to run with, but even the ones she bedded made her the brunt of quips about rednecks and anti-Semites. Most of these New York smart alecks had never been out of the five boroughs, let alone west of the Mississippi, yet they talked as if they knew *every*place and *every*thing—a quality she once admired but quickly found repellent. She also had another disadvantage—she couldn't stand jazz.

With school not providing the social nourishment she craved, she dropped out in her junior year and bounced up and down the Eastern seaboard, trying to find a perch to call home. After a few years, she headed west. Her third month working at a desolate used book store in Grass Valley, she met Chad, a prairie-voiced drifter from Omaha who caught her eye when he spent two hours picking his way through a copy of the *I Ching*. He seemed soothingly familiar to her—loose-limbed swagger, corn-fed grin; she wanted to scoop him home right away and make him pot roast or read his palms. But he had ideas of his own. He and his friends were starting up a commune on the coast north of San Francisco and needed one more person to make the rent. He told her, somewhat sheepishly, that the other six were also exiles from the Midwest. She jumped at it.

In their shared, wood-frame house over the eucalyptus-scented cliffs of Gualala, two hours north of the Golden Gate bridge, the group lived an idyllic existence. The women made and sold kites and wind chimes to passing motorists and the men rented themselves out as Sherpas to hikers who wanted to explore the nearby hills. Mary-Sue and a girl who'd grown up on a farm in Wisconsin made cheese using milk from the goats they raised; one of the boys brewed organic tofu in the feed barn. They grew their own food, made their own clothes. At night, they often discussed books but not to the exclusion of any slow readers, so the standbys were *The Great Gatsby, Catcher in the Rye*, *The Wizard of Oz*. Mary-Sue donated her collections of Rimbaud and Céline to enrich the communal stash but as far as she could tell, nobody cracked a single tome, not even out of curiosity.

Every month or two, the residents got punch-drunk and gave

each other haircuts. Every week or two, they traded partners. Mary-Sue shared her bed with Chad for about three weeks, off and on. When a former cattleman from Colorado moved in, she went with him as soon as she saw his big hands.

Bobby came out to visit the summer their parents were separating. Their mother had been strident in her demands, and Daddy began retreating into dark afternoons of bourbon and Bullwinkle cartoons. He wanted to tag along whenever Bobby went tooling around for skirt and that was more than the boy could take.

"Daddy's losing it. I'm blowin' this pop stand." That was how he'd put it on the phone. Within twenty-four hours, Bobby was strolling through Mary-Sue's front door in Gualala, licking his lips when he glimpsed the ocean through the kitchen window.

Though Bobby was Mary-Sue's baby brother, she never felt she needed to protect him. He'd leapt out of the womb with a natural knack for taking care of himself. It might have been his lopsided smile. You could have dropped six-year-old Bobby in a Harlem sandbox or the dining hall of an English boarding school and he'd be telling jokes and shaking hands. Unlike Mary-Sue, he always belonged.

Bobby stayed in the group house for three weeks, and nobody complained. He regaled the men with news of Iowa inter-city politics—regurgitated from Daddy's mutterings—which for some reason they found fascinating. The women he charmed by playing the new boy with the greedy, greedy penis. He slept with the farm girl from Wisconsin until her Hare Krishna boyfriend put an end to it. After that, Bobby bicycled into town for fresh bait, some of them housewives more than twice his age.

Every day Bobby was there was further torment for Mary-Sue. She resented his intrusion into the private universe she'd found for herself, the way he appropriated everything of hers as his. Even worse, she knew he was primarily there so he could make a grand entrance when he returned home as the prodigal son. Her family was never huge on biblical thinking but everyone everywhere went *awww* for that one.

Finally the last straw. Mary-Sue was enjoying a couple hours of afternoon delight with her Colorado cowboy, Steve. Because locks went against house rules, Bobby walked into her bedroom while Steve was going down on her, right as she was about to come. Instead of leaving, Bobby stood and watched. Mary-Sue's thighs were hiked up over Steve's shoulders, her head and torso falling off the side of the bed like a trapeze in flight. She shrieked, plucked whatever books she could off the floor, and hurled them at Bobby until he finally cackled and walked away, leaving the door wide open.

"Nice jugs, sis," he said. She made him pack his bags before the hour was up.

After Bobby went home, Mary-Sue's housemates spoke so fondly of him that she realized she'd been living with a bunch of halfwits. The peach had lost its bloom. Mary-Sue split Gualala and joined a colony of modern ascetics up the coast in cold, wet Humboldt County, one hundred miles south of the Oregon border. These colonists lived in single huts in the redwoods with the barest necessities: electricity tapped from a nearby power line that went out without warning and a grimy communal cold-water shower. It was as far from a suburban split-level as she'd ever encountered; everything about it made even the group house in Gualala seem plastic and phony. *Bourgeois.*

The colony didn't care what you believed in as long as you believed in something and kept yourself clean, kind, solitary and silent. There were a handful of Buddhist, Hindu and Roman

Catholic hermits but the rest of them didn't have names for their beliefs yet—they were still too new, still too original.

And in that atmosphere, she strove to be good. She stopped smoking, stopped drinking, kept celibate, ate only whole grains, seeds and vegetables, and scrubbed herself in the shower till her skin was raw. Sadness, she felt, was a by-product of baggage—material wealth, family, lovers, all of which were physical reminders of the past and instigators of unnecessary regret and desire. The simpler she kept her existence, she felt, the easier it would be to chase away unhappiness. It helped that the colony permitted neither televisions nor radios, and only the elders kept luxuries such as fridges and space-heaters. Life was uncomfortable, medieval even, but it had meaning because everything, from brushing her teeth to boiling water, posed a challenge. She stopped taking things for granted, especially tampons. She rose at five and went to bed at midnight. The nights without electricity, she sat by lumpy tapers and just listened—owls, crickets, the rustling of leaves in the wind.

Gradually, the sadness went away, overtaken by the cold, the damp, fleas and general anxieties about her health. When she cried her endless tears, it was from sheer exhaustion. And exhaustion heightened all amazement. The mute beauty of a sunset, the elaborate fretwork on an acorn, the clear taste of stream water, all of it was more pronounced than ever before. If this was mystical ecstasy then she had found it, through cuts, bruises, scabs, blisters and painful wood splinters too tiny to be extracted by candlelight.

Three years into Humboldt County, there came a letter from her father. It was, inevitably, about Bobby. After the shooting of war protesters on campus, Bobby had decided to drop out of Kent State and enlist in the army. He wanted to go to Vietnam and "kick some ass." Daddy was beside himself. Even though he considered himself an old-fashioned patriot, he didn't want his only son going over to fight a war on a side that wasn't winning. He asked for Mary-Sue to call home collect and help talk her brother out of it. To speed her up, he'd enclosed a check for $500.

Mary-Sue was reluctant to break her calm of the past three years and let the world back into her life, with its Pandora's box of chaos, anger and grief. She needed her father's money but she'd learned from experience that anything to do with Bobby was poison. Once she picked up the phone, the orderly life she'd made for herself would be no more. She could not do it. She could not sacrifice her peace.

But she acted honorably. Because she didn't call home, she never cashed the check.

From the jungle, Bobby wrote her—not their father—a series of long letters, full of braggadocio and operatic violence. Science fiction, as she thought of them, stories from another planet. It was as if he was trying to incite some kind of sisterly reprimand from her, but she refused to take the bait. She never once wrote back.

The morning her father's accountant told her that Bobby was killed, she vomited right there in the phone booth. Her only pair of sandals was now permanently wrecked.

Not long after, she received word from the colony's elders that her behavior was interfering with "the equilibrium" of the others. She wasn't surprised. One evening, feeling paranoid, she'd thrown a sandbag at a Buddhist monk named Nguyen. But because the community did not believe in the brutality of expulsion, they requested that she leave voluntarily. Quietly, she packed up her things.

She drifted from town to town in the Northwest like a ghost, stopping wherever she saw signs for organic produce. Daddy never contacted her to discuss Bobby. She knew it was on her to call him, and she wasn't about to do it. No fuckin' way.

THE DAY AFTER her father's funeral, Mary-Sue woke up from her alcohol-induced coma, jumpy and discombobulated. She pulled the drapes open. It had snowed heavily while she slept and the city appeared to be covered in icing sugar. The capitol looked beneficent with its white papal beanie. *I absolve you, Mary-Sue Ireland.*

She drove to the funeral home and charged right into the chapel. An easel with an old woman's portrait named the honoree as Mary Susanna Lombardi. Mary-Sue took a seat in the back while the organist with Parkinson's played a hymn that seemed well-known to everyone but her. Only about seven guests were in attendance. Mary Susanna Lombardi's body lay serenely in a steel coffin that looked to Mary-Sue like the hood of a Rolls Royce. The coffin trade—what a racket. She glanced around for Mr. Evans, the funeral director. It turned out he was standing at the far end of the stage, his eyes fixed on her. There was a flesh-colored Band-Aid over his brow. He nodded at her slowly and began his approach.

"Hello, Mary-Sue. Would you like to sign the guest book, too?"

Mr. Evans led her to his office in the rear of the home, and gestured for her to sit in one of two overstuffed armchairs.

"Honestly, I was hoping I'd see you back here." He closed the door and retreated behind his desk. There was a smugness to his smile. "You know, I didn't file a police report. I thought we'd settle this mano a mano."

He was baiting her. She held her fist down. "I came to get my father's ashes."

"Oh?" Mr. Evans feigned surprise. He leaned his swivel chair back. "Your aunt said she'd come and collect them this afternoon. Should I call and tell her not to?"

"Yes. Do that."

"All right, I will do that. It shouldn't be a problem. You had the right of first refusal after all. All children do." His fingertips leaned into one another, forming a pyramid. Then darting forth, he withdrew a single-sheet pamphlet from his drawer and slid it across the desk to her—"On Anger." The author was one Gregory H. Evans. "In case you're wondering—yes, I wrote this myself. I write most of the guides we produce. Many people have told me that this one was especially helpful. I know you're a woman of strong opinion and I will be curious to hear your feedback."

"You want me to read this now?"

"No, no, take it with you. You can always tell me later. Grief lasts." He studied her reaction and, when she expressed no ire, gave her a wink. Still nothing. "Now, let me go and fetch your beloved father."

He brushed by her shoulder deliberately as he took his mincing steps out of the office. While he was gone, she studied the plaques and framed photographs on his walls. He was evidently a good friend to old women. There were multiple certificates in the mortuary sciences, a state of Iowa registration for the practice, and a Master of Fine Arts in Fiction Writing from Iowa City. On his desk, a plastic organizer overflowed with paper clips, rubber bands and Bic ballpoint pens with their caps gnawed into odd shapes. Scrawled on a Precious Moments memo pad in bubble letters were the words *order formaldehyde!*

Mr. Evans returned to the room with the jade-colored urn.

"Your aunt made a fine choice—this is genuine jadeite, from

our Exquisite Treasures line. We listed the urn alone at eighteen thousand dollars."

"It was my father's money anyway."

"I don't doubt that. He was quite handy with the pocketbook. Or so I was told."

Mary-Sue took the urn and got up to leave.

"Hang on, I'll need you to sign this." He put a stack of carbon copies in front of her and offered her one of his pens. "It proves that you collected the ashes and that they didn't just vanish into thin air. Though that has been known to happen from time to time."

She signed the documents without reading.

"Very trusting."

"Very impatient."

"And please don't forget my pamphlet." He folded the "On Anger" tract and placed it in her hand, grazing her skin meaningfully. "Let me know your thoughts. I know you can be brutally honest, but I'm a big boy. Really, I am."

He walked her to the door. "When I phone your aunt, is there anything else you'd like for me to tell her?"

Yeah, tell her to eat shit and die, she thought. "Tell her, thank you."

"Very good. I shall do that very thing."

As soon as she'd driven a block from the funeral home, she crushed Mr. Evans's pamphlet into a ball and flung it out the window as far as she could. She hoped it would land in the mobile home park called Club Paradise.

"Sayonara, sucker!"

It landed in the middle of the street.

WHEN SHE GOT back to San Francisco, Mary-Sue found a stack of mail waiting at her door. There was a condolence card from her landlord, Mr. Antonio, a letter from her father's accountant, and a bulging envelope from FCVN, Friends of the Children of Viet Nam. It was the last piece of mail that she tore open first, and with greatest optimism.

– 5 –

KATE IRELAND

Mary-Sue grabbed the pale blue dress with the smocking across the chest. Size three. For ages two to three. She pulled out a size four and compared the two side by side. Size four was only a little bigger, longer mainly, but this could make all the difference.

Kate, as she'd already named the daughter she hadn't yet met, was three years old and due to arrive the following day. Mary-Sue had no idea what she looked like, whether she would be small for her age, like the Third World orphans she'd seen on TV, or sized more like her Kmart counterparts. She took both dresses, and a large stuffed panda to remind Kate of her Oriental heritage.

The trial-and-error nature of family life terrified Mary-Sue. Her Des Moines clan had enjoyed every chance of success. In a more scientific universe, they might have been a control group— handsome Daddy, pretty Mom, teenage daughter and cute little Junior, tucked away in a sprawling ranch house next to a blue-grass fairway. Yet the Ireland family experiment had failed—in strengthening community, in fostering stability, in producing happiness. When she was young, she assumed that blood bound everything, but as she got older, she came to realize that blood bound *nothing*. Family was a coincidence of birth—it was no more than spilled soda. She figured she could do no worse on her own, creating a nuclear-nuclear unit with its variables lowered from four members to two, and the odds for failure reduced by half.

She stopped at the market on the way home to pick up things a hungry child might enjoy—milk, apple juice, vanilla ice cream, chocolate-chip cookies, Cheerios, frosted cornflakes, Grape-Nuts and pretzels. She added a carton of soy milk, just in case Kate turned out to be lactose intolerant. Later that evening, she went to collect the Mickey Mouse–shaped cake she'd ordered from her neighborhood bakery, panting as she bustled up Telegraph Hill to her apartment with it. Such a large cake might have been excessive for one little girl, but the next day also happened to be her own thirty-fifth birthday, and such a doubly auspicious occasion called for as much sugar as they pleased.

Myrna LaBoeuf, her counselor from Friends of the Children of Viet Nam, called at dinnertime to run through the next evening's program at the San Francisco airport. President Ford had just given the mission a name, "Operation Babylift," and the FCVN social workers who'd been toiling for months were relieved to have their mission legitimized at last, even if the name he chose sounded like a playground contraption.

"We just heard from the embassy in Saigon and they said the kids are all gathered at the airport over there, all hundred and fifty of them." Myrna sounded chipper.

"Did they say anything about my little one?"

"We didn't get specific news about any one child. But I'm sure she's doing just fine. Listen, we've just been informed that the president will be at the airport tomorrow to receive the babies and—whether we like him or not—we're thrilled about this because it means we're finally getting the respect we deserve. The downside is security will be tight. So make sure you get there early and find us. And don't forget your papers."

"Does this mean I'll have to get all dolled up?" Mary-Sue asked.

"Oh, wear anything but black pajamas!" Myrna chuckled. "Personally, I think simple and elegant is best. There'll be a ton of photographers."

"I'd rather not be photographed with our so-called president, if that's possible."

"Oh, come on, hon. Tomorrow's not just gonna change your life, it's gonna change history! What's a little smile? You're doing a good thing. You should be very proud of yourself."

"Pride has nothing to do with it. I just want my first encounter with *my daughter* to be private. Not some fucking baby-kissing photo op."

A pause at the other end of the line.

"Well, listen, Mary-Sue, I have to go now. Plenty of calls to make tonight. We'll see you at the airport tomorrow, alrighty?"

Mary-Sue pulled out her squarest-looking outfit, the sedate black dress she'd worn to her father's funeral, resenting that she was being coerced into wearing mourning clothes to greet her new daughter. She had originally planned to wear her favorite sweatshirt and blue jeans to the airport, but goddamn the president of the United States. She stood outside her second bedroom, which had been painted pink and turned into Kate's room, trying to picture what her life would be like in twenty-four hours. No more lonely nights. Saturdays and Sundays staring out into nothingness—those were luxuries she could afford to miss. Trips to the toy store, the park, the dentist, errands that would give her no choice but to get herself organized. A little voice calling her "Mommy" might finally force her to give a shit.

Sometime close to dawn, the phone rang. She damn near jumped out of her skin. Cursing like a trucker, she picked up the receiver and croaked: "Yeah?"

It was Myrna LaBoeuf, weeping:

"There was a crash."

Mary-Sue sat up. She gazed at her clock. It was 5:07. Her blood froze.

"What? When?"

"About . . . six hours ago."

"*Six* hours ago? Why the hell didn't you call me then?"

"We only just heard ourselves . . . The army . . . it's classified, hon . . . The plane crashed right after takeoff, nobody knows what happened . . . Some are saying it mighta been sabotage . . ."

Mary-Sue took a deep breath.

"Were there survivors?"

"Yes . . . but . . ."

"Did my Katie make it?"

"I don't know, hon. I really don't know anything at this point . . . They said . . . They said there are tiny little bodies . . ." her voice broke, "strewn all over the Mekong Delta . . . Oh God, Mary-Sue, I am so sorry . . . I am so sorry . . ."

THE C-5A GALAXY was the largest cargo plane of its day but it was still just a cargo plane, which meant that it came with no seats and none of the safety provisions found on a basic passenger jet. Moreover, many of the babies were so small that seats were of no use to them anyhow—they were placed in boxes with only faith and fate holding them down. The nurses and attendants were outnumbered. Soon after takeoff from Saigon, one of the Galaxy's doors popped open, and the pressure inside the cabin plummeted. Witnesses said they saw infants and babies being sucked out of the plane like rag dolls. The pilots managed to turn the plane back toward Saigon but it missed the runway, crashing into rice paddies near the Mekong River and breaking into four parts. Mary-Sue never saw the worst pictures, nor did any American without top-level clearance—almost all the photos were destroyed by the US Army. The ones released showed only the survivors.

Mary-Sue waited anxiously by the phone. She never left the apartment, chipping away at the Mickey Mouse cake bite by bite. She listened a little to a military expert on the radio gassing on about how the plane was built by Lockheed, and how that model had a history of malfunction. Some help this was now. She didn't dare turn on the TV in case she saw footage of the crash. Though she had no idea what her Katie looked like, she was convinced that if she even glimpsed her face—or mangled body—she'd recognize her in an instant and lose her mind.

Days later, Myrna called with news. Three-year-old Kate was among those who survived, and she was—miraculously—unscathed. A young South Vietnamese nurse had held on to her as the plane plunged into the rice fields. When their part of the plane caught on fire, she covered Kate with a blanket and shielded her from the flames. Kate had been one of the lucky ones. The army reported its final tally—155 out of the 328 on board were killed, 98 of them infants and babies.

"So when do I get to see her?"

"They've put the kids on rotation. The flights that were scheduled to leave will still do so but they'll be putting survivors on those planes whenever they can find space for them."

"What the hell's that supposed to mean?"

"It means, Mary-Sue, be patient."

The Operation Babylift flights continued as Saigon fell. Then on one of the final airlifts out of the city, Kate was brought to San Francisco without fanfare. The South Vietnamese nurse, who suffered 20 percent burns from the crash, was on the same plane. The skin on her face was gone, as was most of her nose; she was to go through reconstructive surgery at the UCSF Medical Center, thanks to contributions from the American people. In the weeks following the crash, she'd grown desperately attached to the little girl whose life she had saved, and at the San Francisco airport, refused to let Kate go, calling her "bé cưng." Darling baby. Mary-Sue watched as nurses injected the woman with sedative and snatched Kate away as soon as her arms let go.

Kate was small and nondescript, but somehow eerily complete—her arms and legs worked, she could see, hear, respond. She had silky dark-brown hair that was a clue to one non-Asian parent, probably a GI. Although she wasn't immediately adorable, something about her was very familiar. When the FCVN woman put her in front of Mary-Sue, her piercing brown eyes registered everything—and her silence was damning.

Mary-Sue was terrified of her. She held the big stuffed panda bear between them like a shield. Little Kate, after some hesitation, walked to the bear and hugged it and hugged it and hugged it. Not once afterwards did she look back at the disfigured nurse who saved her life, now slumped in her wheelchair.

Mary-Sue spent the next few years keeping Kate all to herself, teaching her how to eat, dress, potty, spell, and rub her little button nose against hers in the Eskimo fashion. Under Mary-Sue's tutelage, Kate developed quickly into an American child, with no memory of the orphanage in the coastal village of Quy Nhon where she'd spent her first years. Or of the crash. The only time Mary-Sue received a prickly visitation from Kate's past was when, at age five, she started crying uncontrollably as soon as she heard Bing Crosby singing "White Christmas." Later, reading a Friends of the Children of Viet Nam newsletter, Mary-Sue learned that the song had been used by the US Armed Forces in Vietnam as a signal. Whenever it had come on the radio, Crosby's warbling was accompanied by the live orchestral boom of choppers and the satanic timpani of guns and bombs.

WHEN KATE TURNED seven, Mary-Sue found work as an executive assistant at a human resources company in Southern California, and they moved. She wanted her Katie to assimilate into the real America, and San Francisco, that artificial oasis of tolerance, permissiveness and multiculturalism, was too much of a bubble for that. Not that she'd ever consider moving them back to the comatose heartland of her youth.

Mary-Sue found the homey old Craftsman houses of Alta Vista inviting—and different enough from Des Moines that she didn't experience debilitating pangs of déjà vu. Compared to the Bay Area, a modest sum bought you a decent house with a yard in this part of the state, so she took out some of Daddy's endowment and set down new roots. She became a suburbanite homeowner, like the rest of the people on Santa Claus Lane. The majority of her neighbors were Anglo working families who'd been there at least two generations, very square in their way but also very comforting. There was also a smattering of black folks who seemed like remnants from a different era—stragglers from the Great Migration too downtrodden to pick up their things and run north after their kin. Mary-Sue wished they would say hi but they mostly kept to themselves.

Putting down roots felt good, and right. When the holidays came round, Mary-Sue and Kate signed off on Christmas cards as "The Girls of Santa Claus Lane."

The backyard became their haven. Together, mother and daughter harvested oranges off their own tree and ran about, year-round, on bare feet. A family of pet hamsters had their last rites read to them in rapid succession under their shady oak. Weekends, Mary-Sue took Kate for pancakes at the Good Ol' Times cafe; for culture, they went to nearby Pasadena and took videos out of the public library. And if that wasn't good enough, there were parks and all kinds of fun that cost no money at all.

Kate, meanwhile, had trouble at school. Teachers found her quiet and, well, spooky. Especially the way she refused to look people in the eye. She lacked the earnestness and messiness they were accustomed to. When they saw her in the hallways, they nodded at her, as one would to a colleague one passed on the street.

Struck hard on the head by a medicine ball during PE, Kate didn't cry—she simply got up and went on. Her mental sums were flawless, and when she was awarded a prize for math, she didn't express either pride or pleasure. She came across as unflappable, but not in a happy way—to everyone aside from Mary-Sue, she seemed incapable of feeling. She found satisfaction in homework while her classmates planned slumber parties and discussed unicorns. Her best friend, by default, was an asthmatic French Canadian boy named Paul Corot with whom she shared an aversion to other children.

Mary-Sue worried about her little girl. Where was all this drive coming from? It certainly wasn't from her. She never pushed Kate to do anything, never volunteered incentives if she made a certain grade or threatened her with time-outs. The only unconventional thing about her child-rearing was that she spoke to Kate as if she were a full-grown person, a wholly cognizant roommate. Whether they were discussing the food pyramid or women's lib, there was never any baby talk.

One day in the fourth grade, Kate's teacher Mrs. Hansen took her away from the classroom while the other kids were coloring rainbows, and led her to the principal's office. There, Mrs. Hansen, the principal and another fourth-grade teacher convened in whispers, while Kate sat like a thief awaiting judgment. After ten excruciating minutes, the adults ended their caucus. Before they could speak, Kate said, in her still, little voice: "I'll be good."

The principal smiled wryly. "The problem isn't that you're no good, Katharine," she said. "The problem is that you're *too* good. You belong elsewhere."

"We're all so proud of how you've overcome the difficulties of your history," Mrs. Hansen said, kindly. She squeezed Kate's tight little shoulder. "Don't you see? You're another one of those Vietnamese overachievers."

Another one of those . . . Kate's eyes welled up with rage, and for a moment, she thought the principal looked afraid. She held in her anger as the principal showed her brochures of campuses with lush green lawns and even one with an old campanile. These places all had names ending in "Academy" or "Institute" that made them sound like reform schools or asylums. And expensive ones at that. These witches, ganging up on her. She wanted to bolt.

"I'm *not* one of those . . ."

"Kate, your teachers mean well," the principal said. "But they have reached their limit. They just don't know what to do with you. We'll have to call your mother in to have a little chat."

This was blackmail, Kate knew. And she was too powerless to counter it. "No, no, please don't." She scrunched up her face like she'd seen other children do before their tears arrived. "I don't want my mother to worry. Please, give me a chance. I'll change."

She kept her promise. To prevent herself from being shunted around like some Dickensian urchin—she'd been reading *Oliver Twist*, which was way more engaging than those vapid Ramona books—she deliberately and unhappily botched an IQ test. That was just the start. She laid down speed bumps in her brain; instead of reading the thesaurus during lunch, she steered her thoughts toward scratch 'n' sniff stickers and Strawberry Shortcake play-sets. She started stating half thoughts instead of waiting for full ones to form, aping the unfocused speech patterns of her peers. Slowness was painful at first. Then it brought new pleasures. She made friends trading stickers and sharing poetry dedicated to Han Solo. She diligently avoided Paul and his magnetic chess set. "He's a mouth breather," her new friends had hissed.

Her mother worried anew. One day Kate was reading *Moby Dick* and the next she was tuning in to *Who's the Boss* and asking for candy bracelets. She'd wanted Kate to reap the full benefits of American freedom and become a true individual. Instead, quite overnight, Kate had turned into liberty's lazy spawn, the conformist. The girl had been such a delight to raise—a pal, really—but after puberty, it was as if she'd been replaced by a stranger in pink blush and bubblegum lip gloss. Everything was either "Ew!" or "Gross!" Mary-Sue didn't know how to articulate her disappointment to Kate without sounding cruel—and they used to be able to discuss everything, everything.

Finally, Mary-Sue blackmailed her into joining the chess club ("or no Walkman for you!"). That move turned out to be a winner. Because of chess, Kate again spent more time hanging out with Paul, who Mary-Sue deemed a positive influence.

Paul had greasy hair, wore Izod shirts in pastel hues and was an impassioned member of Greenpeace—an eccentric package that Mary-Sue, much more than Kate, found enchanting. A quiet boy, he lived in a room above his parents' garage on nearby Mount Curve. Like Mary-Sue, Paul's folks were displaced cosmopolitans, but unlike her, they were fuddy-duddy foreigners, completely oblivious to youth culture. Paul's pink Izod shirts were his mother's idea; his Quebecois father wore cravats to dinner! From time to time, Mary-Sue would leave anonymous parcels outside the boy's door containing albums by bands like The Doors, The Who and Joy Division, and videotapes of movies like *A Clockwork Orange* and Pink Floyd's *The Wall*, hoping that once he developed a taste for them, it might find its way back to Kate.

Both her daughter and Paul had blossomed from strange little grim-faced children into demure and altogether good-looking teenagers whose beauty was evident to all but themselves. Kate had grown lanky, and at fourteen, was taller than Mary-Sue, with long, lustrous almost-black hair that turned brown in the summer. She had fleshy rose lips, unlike Mary-Sue's increasingly thin and pale "fish lips," and high cheekbones that made her elusive smiles radiant. There was something in Kate's look—the set of the mouth, especially—that made Mary-Sue think of her brother, Bobby, though she didn't dare let herself entertain the possibility that he might have been her father. Paul conquered his asthma with conscientious lap-swimming and emerged a muscular jock, physically if not psychologically. He had dark, wavy hair that he grew to collar-length—out of indifference, not vanity—like some Romantic poet. Mary-Sue found herself fantasizing about Kate and Paul becoming lovers, sharing the kind of sexy, intense partnership she'd never had with anyone. She didn't have a clue whether they harbored any erotic feeling for each other—Kate never told her anything anymore—and the pair of them seemed blithely virginal, like the stranded innocents played by Brooke Shields and Chris Atkins in *The Blue Lagoon*.

One day, Mary-Sue succumbed to temptation and left a copy of a tantric sex manual at Paul's door. It had a whole chapter on female ejaculation that had stumped even her. Whether these secret dispatches worked or not, she never knew for sure. Her beloved Katie spoke to her less and less as the days went by, locked into teenage solipsism and an acculturated inability to talk to "parental units." Again, Kate was never bitchy about it, but polite and impenetrable as a lodger, which actually hurt more.

On Kate's sixteenth birthday, Mary-Sue gave her one hundred dollars to spend on whatever she wanted. She enclosed the cash in a birthday card and left it on Kate's pillow. Inspired by the Indian takeout she'd had for lunch, she wrote this on the card:

> *Dear Ranjit,*
> *I know that life is hard but as my late lamented father*
> *Poori used to say,*
> *The fun is in finding a clean river to shit in.*
> *May you find your river, my darling!*
> *Happy 46th! Chooti Hooti Hay!*
> *With love and kisses from your sad old maiden aunt,*
> > *Chitrajeet*

To her pleasant surprise, Kate returned with a note, written on rough, recycled paper. She left it on the fridge door for her mother to find, under a Hamburglar magnet:

> *Dear Gurmit,*
> *I hope this finds you well. Thank you for the generous*
> *bag of rice. I heard you have sprained your back in an*

unfortunate mango-picking accident, and I hope that your injuries are healing quickly. I have been enjoying the rose water and aromatic lime chutney that I almost sent to you for your speedy recovery.

I know that as childhood buddies we have been through many ups and many downs. We have both won and lost many a game of cricket. Sometimes my lassi is sweeter than yours, but your achar is still the best even if I will never admit this to your face.

Someday, after the next monsoon, we will talk about bigger things. We will build a tidbits shop to rival that of Mr. Ali and his wife, Mrs. Ali. They are nobodies. They are brigands. They sell moldy popadams. We will do better than that.

Until then, let us dream of banana trees and hammocks. One day we will both have bungalows in the shade. They will be pink and they will be wide. Monkeys will run from us. But listen to me, Babu, you must never forget your secret powers. Do not forget, in your haste to become a world champion mango-picker, to use your special powers. Only one or two people in the whole of our beautiful province are able to mimic the cry of horses as well as you. You are the Neigh King.

When you neigh, I will come. I swear it on your turban.

> *Take care of the little pooris, and of yourself,*
> *Your Test Match partner,*
> *Apu*

Meanwhile, Kate went on being a teenager of few words, eating dinner in front of the TV, slinking sullenly into her room, giving no indication that she'd actually composed that note. It was an infuriating charade. Mary-Sue folded the letter carefully and put it in the steel safe where she kept all her important documents. Then she left another little note on Kate's pillow, crossing her fingers and toes that this new level of communication could be sustained:

> *My dearest Sunil,*
> *Your note was duly noted and highly appreciated.*
> *Perhaps we could continue our discourse over lassi and*
> *tidbits at a restaurant, and speak of our plans for the*
> *future? It will be my greatest privilege to host this*
> *dinner.*
>
> > > *Your humble confidante,*
> > > *Jalil of Jalalabad*

A reply appeared on the fridge the next morning:

> *Vishnu,*
> *Don't push it.*
>
> > > *Your very distant cousin,*
> > > *Kali*

And that was that.

When it came time for college, the girl insisted on Pomona, a respectable liberal arts college thirty minutes from home, in the middle of the suburban nowhere. She had good enough grades for Berkeley and elsewhere, but she chose this poky school because they'd offered her a full scholarship. It wasn't as if they couldn't afford to pay their own way—the inheritance from Daddy had been set aside for this. Mary-Sue was distraught:

Had her frugality given Kate the false impression that they were poor? Paul had applied to colleges in New York, to get as far as he could from his parents. If Kate had done something similar, it might have broken Mary-Sue's heart, but kids were supposed to break their parents' hearts. Kate couldn't justify her choice. All she would say was that she liked "the look" of Pomona. Nothing could dissuade her. In her stubbornness, she was Mary-Sue's daughter after all.

For all her forthrightness, Mary-Sue found it harder and harder to express herself to Kate as she watched their interests diverge. Kate, on the other hand, felt that her mother's loneliness was unbearable—all the more because Mary-Sue never complained or engaged in any kind of guilt-tripping. Going to college close to home meant that she could always come and keep her aging mother company. Mary-Sue was getting old—in ten years, she would be sixty. Kate knew that Mary-Sue liked her job fine, but how satisfying could it be for a well-read, opinionated woman to spend her days reordering Sharpies and rubber bands and keeping track of who was in or out of some lawyer's office? She never dated, or did so only on the sly, and as far as Kate could tell, she didn't have any relatives or close friends.

Kate could never forget watching Mary-Sue put on her bra in the morning the way a TV cop might strap a holster across his torso—a daily ritual against unsettling dangers. Mary-Sue's body was not like the ones Kate had seen on TV. She wasn't at all fat, but she had bumps, folds, cellulite (which Kate initially took for surgical stitches, and found terrifying), stains caused by vaccinations and bug bites. It was clear early on that she was indifferent to her body, even ashamed. They never went swimming, for instance.

Even as a child, Kate knew that it was loneliness, rather

than compassion, that had led Mary-Sue to adopt a child from a war-torn country. She envied the unquestioning birthright of natural-born heirs like her friends at school, asking and getting from their parents without having to psychoanalyze every move beforehand. Not that she yearned for anything extravagant—but even the simplest request for lunch money always came tainted with guilt. She wasn't *actually* Mary-Sue's daughter, no matter what Mary-Sue thought; she was a just lodger renting space in Mary-Sue's heart. And until she was strong enough to fend for herself, she would try to consume the minimum, to deplete Mary-Sue's resources as little as possible.

It made it no easier on her that Mary-Sue did things like buying two kinds of toilet paper: she put the good, soft kind in Kate's bathroom and the rough, cheapo kind in her own. Kate had objected tearfully as soon as she discovered the racket but her mother refused to stop. Mary-Sue's way was not to be messed with. She continually refused to spend any money on herself, cutting her own hair and wearing old shoes till their soles wore thin, then covering the holes up with duct tape. She insisted on going around in a broken pair of reading glasses held together at the center with a Band-Aid. In the evenings, while Kate watched TV, she sat under the bare bulb of the kitchen reading library books like *War and Peace* and drinking a foul-smelling tea called Fallopian Friend. The only nice thing she owned was a silver-plated picture frame holding a photo of her brother, Bobby, that she kept by her bed, but even this was in no way fancy.

When Kate was eleven, the year she hit puberty, the flashbacks started. In her perfect upstairs bedroom on Santa Claus Lane, across the hall from where her mother slept, the visions descended upon her every night she had her period. They were no less horrific for their repetition: a peaceful sort of floating, then baffling pandemonium, flying torsos, a loud bang. Suddenly she was sinking chest-deep in a warm, viscous mix of blood and mud. A woman with a charred face was trying to pull her down. As the waters rose, her eyes grew used to the dark, and she'd see the single worst image—the headless body of a little girl see-sawing, half in, half out of an airplane window.

That little girl, Kate always felt, was her. Or at least, some form of her that had died alongside the others that fateful morning.

She never told Mary-Sue about these nightmares. A woman who'd martyr herself over toilet paper would certainly flip out at the least hint of psychological misery. Nor did she tell the school counselor. She felt like enough of a misfit at school—and besides, any confession she made might go straight back to Mary-Sue.

She resolved to cure herself of these visitations, taking pointers from dusty manuals on Zen meditation and lucid dreaming that she quietly pulled off Mary-Sue's nightstand. Inspired by Luke Skywalker's Jedi training, she willed herself to detach her emotions from unhappy memories. Like the Buddhists, she didn't try to eradicate unwanted thoughts, she simply pulled herself out of the fracas and became an observer—the visions became scenes out of a movie or a book. Soon, the nightmares lost their power. But unlike a Zen master whose discipline made life richer, her methods sapped from her a certain immediacy with the world. Emotions came to her secondhand, filtered. Where other people just *felt* things, she lived life as if it were beamed to her on tape delay.

In high school, these shortcomings went unnoticed as her best friend, too, in his own way, shunned intimacy. Paul had come to be known as Bluto, after Popeye's nemesis, because he had unusually large biceps for a skinny kid whose most vigorous form of exercise, as far as people knew, was moving the castle across the board until it struck the queen. Together Kate and Bluto wrote comic Brechtian one-acts starring characters from *The Facts of Life* and made fake agitprop collages out of discarded issues of *Time*—a favorite featured Bill Cosby choking Idi Amin with one of his hideous wool sweaters. Their moods meshed perfectly— they cooked up their own kind of cool and feasted on irony. Being teenagers became the perfect alibi for their extreme disaffection, and high school with Bluto by her side was bliss. "You're my soul mate, man," he even told her one day, a prelude to clammy, platonic hand-holding. Yet when it came time to pick colleges, he chose New York without a second thought.

Miserable at Pomona, Kate took a shitty job at a pizzeria to pay for her living expenses; asking Mary-Sue for help would have made her feel worse. Sometime during her junior year, pressured by professors tenured in identity politics and eager herself to seek some kind of closure, she picked up the phone.

"I'm thinking of going to Vietnam," she told Mary-Sue.

"Why on earth would you want to do something like that, for your first trip out of the country? Why not London or Paris?"

"I met some other kids who were . . . placed, like me. And, well, we're thinking of going back."

"Back?"

"To visit. I feel like I really need to do this."

"Who are these other kids?"

"I told you, Mom. They're orphans, like me."

"You're not an orphan, Katie."

"You know what I mean."

"Where did you meet these people? Did they try to recruit you?"

"It's not like a cult. Someone put up a flyer at school and I saw it."

"It doesn't follow that you have to respond. That's peer pressure."

"It's not. I'm not. Nothing's set in stone."

"Those tours, I've read about them. They're like caravans of grief. I would go so far as to call them traveling circuses of guilt. They'll exploit you. They'll use your testimony to recruit more followers, just you wait."

"I still feel I need to do this."

A pause.

"Well, if you really feel so strongly about it, I'll give you the money . . ."

"I'll pay you back. Promise."

"Oh, don't worry about that. But, honey, I just don't think you should go there with those types of people."

"Who? The orphans?"

"They're not orphans any more than you are, Katie. But yes, those people."

"You prefer that I travel alone?"

"I'm sure you could find some friends who wouldn't mind taking the trip with you. That way, you might go and do something fun, instead of spending the whole time visiting orphanages and feeling lousy. Maybe you could go to Thailand and, I don't know, do some snorkeling."

"What's the name of that orphanage again? The one I was in?"

"I don't know, baby. That's ancient history."

"You must have it somewhere."

"I threw all that stuff away. Your life began the day I picked you up at the airport. You know that, don't you?"

KATE TOOK THE trip to Vietnam the summer of 1993 with three friends from her Southeast Asian Studies class, none of them orphans of the war or even Asian. A professor with embassy ties helped them with entry visas and names of local contacts should they get into any kind of trouble—washed-up, ex-CIA Kurtzes, Kate reckoned.

Up in the plane, Kate saw the curvy brown snake that was the Mekong River eating its way through the verdant patchwork of rice fields. Her head throbbed and she felt nauseated, furious that she'd chosen to return to this place. What good could come of it? She forced herself not to vomit when they touched down (bump, two, three) at Tan Son Nhat airport, in what used to be Saigon but had since been renamed Ho Chi Minh City. Even that, a mouthful. When they stepped into the blazing, cloudless day, the humidity coated her skin in a way that made her edgy. It wasn't déjà vu exactly—she felt no nostalgia or sadness, just a vague feeling of impotence and outrage. The airport was decrepit. The air seemed insolent, a silent bystander through decades of violence and poverty, deliberately doing nothing while everything fell apart. Yolanda, who'd sat next to her during the entire flight reading *The Executioner's Song*, noticed her grim expression and held her hand in solidarity. One of the boys, Jules, draped his arm around her protectively and she brushed it off, but with thanks.

They spent the week at a backpacker's inn, living like equatorial flâneurs. They woke up late, ate insanely cheap croissants, drank milky *café* and rented bicycles to ride around the tree-lined boulevards—the French, unlike the Americans, had left some nice things behind. The bicycles came in handy for eluding the street beggars who chased them around, trying to sell them old wartime currency. Contrary to what the guidebooks said, Wrigley's gum wasn't enough to send them away. Kate saw young women with missing limbs plying the streets for spare change—this could easily have been her if it hadn't been for Operation Babylift. The thought spooked her to the core.

Crossing busy intersections on foot without the aid of traffic lights was for Kate and her friends a harrowing rite of passage. After the convulsions of hysterical laughter subsided, they were ready for anything. Two of them followed a tout outside the crumbling Hotel Continental, made famous by writers like Graham Greene, to a blind alley where an opium den flourished. The boy, Dan, got a massive headache after his five-dollar smoke while Yolanda, his girlfriend, felt only a light buzz. Then they all hired cyclos and had the riders pedal them around the city, crossing perilously into the paths of other cyclos, bikes, mopeds, buses, even trains—all the while screaming and lifting their arms in the air like they were on a theme-park ride.

They bought conical rice-planter hats from street vendors and wore them around town, bumping their wide rims into the throng at the Ben Thanh market. This was the central market housed in a French colonial building that Jules said reminded him of run-down train stations in Prague and Budapest. There Kate saw an Amerasian around her age wearing an *ao dai*—the Vietnamese national dress—on her haunches, skinning frogs under a running faucet; this, too, could have been her if she hadn't been airlifted to America. When the girl looked up and met her eyes, Kate felt nauseated. They could have been sisters. Not just metaphorically.

In a fit of romanticism, Jules traded in his perfectly good Teva sandals for a pair of rubber flip-flops that fell apart the moment he stepped out of the market. He went back to the stall but the vendor would only return his Tevas for "ten dollah." An altercation was averted when Kate produced the money and grabbed the sandals, handing them back to Jules. They ate a ton of twenty-cent chocolate éclairs at the next stall to forget about the whole thing.

On the fourth sultry day, Jules and Kate split away from the others and headed for French-style *glacés* at the celebrated Fanny ice-cream stand in the center of town. The ice cream was nothing special by North American standards, and it liquefied as soon as they stepped out of the shade. As they walked back to their hostel, licking their cones, a scrawny, barefoot boy in a faded Bart Simpson T-shirt leapt out from behind a tree across the street and sped toward them like a brown torpedo, crying: "Gra-gree! Kwai-Meri-Can! Gra-gree!"

"Fuck! Three o'clock!" Kate said, without turning. "Wanna make a run for it?"

Jules, surfer blond and California friendly, turned instinctively to look.

"No! Don't make eye contact with him!" whispered Kate.

But it was too late; the boy knew that he'd hooked Jules, and started trailing him, tugging at the back of his T-shirt, yelling, "Gra-gree! Gra-gree!"

Jules looked at Kate and shrugged. He offered two sticks of gum to the little boy. Up close, they saw that his Bart Simpson shirt was a crappy knock-off with the eyes drawn too far apart. The boy took the gum but continued to walk close to them, his voice getting more cracked and demanding.

"Gra-gree! Kwai-Meri-Can!" He plucked at the pale hairs on Jules's arm.

"Oww!" But it made him giggle all the same. "That hurt, little man!"

The boy grinned at the laughter he provoked. He tried it again.

"What's he want, you think?" Jules looked at Kate.

"How should I know? I don't speak Vietnamese. Just watch your pockets."

"Gra-gree . . ." the boy pleaded pathetically and pulled out of his shorts a thick pamphlet in clear plastic. He showed it to them but gripped it tight with his rough, chapped hands as if Jules or Kate might try to run off with the valuable document. They looked at it. It was a murky photocopy of Graham Greene's *The Quiet American*, two paperback pages smeared across each sheet, the whole thing stapled together crudely.

"Oh, I see now . . . Kwai Meri-Can . . ." Kate tugged at Jules's arm. "Let's go. Come on. *Now.*"

The kid grabbed Jules's other arm, glaring at Kate. "Five dollah!"

"You gotta be kidding!" Kate said to the boy. She tugged at Jules to leave, walking on ahead of him.

"Five's way too much, dude," Jules said helplessly. "No five."

"Jules! Don't even talk to him . . . Come on!"

"What about one dollar?" Jules asked the kid. He pulled out a crisp dollar bill and dangled it in front of the kid. The kid lunged for it. Jules let him.

"Three dollah!" the kid said while pocketing the buck.

"Jules, you idiot! I can't believe you're entertaining him!"
Kate ran back.

"Keep your stupid book," she told the kid. "He already gave you a dollar . . . Now, please, get lost!" Kate pushed the boy away from Jules, but his feet held the ground. He grabbed ahold of Jules's arm like a barnacle.

Together Jules and Kate tried to pluck the boy's fingers off Jules's arm one by one. When they succeeded in freeing his arm, the boy wrapped his legs around Jules's knee. Then the skinny tentacles came back with a vengeance, locking themselves in the crook of Jules's arm.

"This is fuckin' ridiculous!" Jules laughed, almost enjoying it. "Help!"

They looked around to see if people were staring at them but the locals were minding their own business. Perhaps in Saigon, this was bookselling.

"Maybe you should try to walk home like this," said Kate. "It's all your fault, you know. Just watch your wallet." She turned to the little Vietnamese boy, "Hey, can't you tell you're not wanted? He already gave you a dollar! Why do you keep bothering us? Why do you have to be such a fucking little creep?"

She charged ahead and made it to the steps of the Notre Dame cathedral, which resembled an Etch A Sketch version of the Parisian original. The little boy suddenly released himself from Jules and sprinted after her, shrieking: "You Vietnam whore?"

His words hit her in the gut. "What did you say to me?" She faced the boy squarely. He reached barely higher than her waist but could have been anything from six to thirty years old.

"You Vietnam whore?" the boy repeated, defiant.

Before she could stop herself, she'd slapped the boy's face. He appeared to be a veteran of hard knocks and didn't even flinch.

"Kate! What are you doing?" Jules ran to her, glancing around nervously. "We could be arrested for this! He probably doesn't even know what he's saying!"

The boy snickered. "Whore!"

Kate shoved the kid and kicked him hard in the shins. He buckled to the ground, by the cathedral steps. As Jules ran over, she kicked him again.

"*Kate!*"

"I'm American, okay, you little piece of shit!" she screamed at the kid. "Fuck you to hell, you fucking rat!"

Jules held her back while she struggled. The boy curled up into a protective ball like an aardvark. His vertebrae showed through his T-shirt, a notched serpent.

As Jules led Kate away, the little boy picked himself up and brushed the street dust off his legs.

"Don't look back," Jules told Kate. "Keep your eyes on the road ahead."

She tried—for a minute. Then she turned around and saw the little boy sticking out his tongue at her. He lowered his shorts and mimed taking a dump, even squeezing out a real fart.

"Vietnam whore!" he yelled, wriggling his bare ass.

She broke free of Jules's arms and tore after the boy. He zooted across the street, dodging speeding bikes, squealing, gleeful, impossible to catch. When he got to the other side of the street, he yelled back at Kate till his demonic voice cracked: "VIETNAM WHORE!"

"I'll kill you, motherfucker! I swear I will!" she screamed. People stared now. Jules wrapped his long arms around her, and she realized she was shaking. He held her so close to his chest that she smelled the Old Spice under his arms. He put his lips against her hair and shushed her.

"Let it pass. Let it pass."

The rest of the trip was a blur. She remembered the others teaming up against her, saying she was wrong to attack the Vietnamese boy. Gullible guilty liberals, always on the side of the supposedly oppressed! Yet they'll brag about haggling down old ladies trying to sell them Tintin T-shirts for two dollars. After a series of quarrels, they left her alone in the hostel so she could sleep every day till noon. She remembered going over to the coffee bar next door where she ate croissants, drank coffee and listened to mid-eighties pop on the jukebox, ten years out of date. Wham!, Sheena Easton, Pet Shop Boys, Chaka Khan—Chaka

Khan, for hours on end. She remembered crawling back into bed as the afternoon monsoon rains fell. One of those afternoons she bumped into Jules, who had returned to switch shirts after a sweaty excursion to the Cu Chi tunnels where the Vietcong once hid. They had comforting sex in the shower—she came, he didn't—before he once again brought up the incident with that little rat.

"Maybe you overreacted a little?"

Her mother had been right. She should have gone to London or Paris.

She tried to forget about Vietnam after that and stopped seeing those "friends" of hers. She took on a second job and within two months, paid her mother back for the trip and never talked about it.

Vietnam, however, refused to release her. The flashbacks returned, every bit as vivid and ferocious as they'd been when she was eleven. And as then, they tormented her whenever she was menstruating, keeping her awake all night, rendering her worthless the following day. She tried her mental exercises but this time they did nothing. She got a prescription for Xanax at the psychological health center but the drugs made her dopey during class. Besides, she liked having an edge.

The only thing that seemed to be able to quell those nightmares was driving home from Pomona in the dead of night and crawling into Mary-Sue's bed. The one place in the entire world where she had always felt completely safe was at her mother's side; how better to steal an extended closeness with her than while she slept? Kate would fall into dreamless sleep next to the snoring, oblivious Mary-Sue and the steady, reassuring clips made by the plastic alarm clock on her nightstand. At first light, she slipped out of bed and took off for school without waking Mary-Sue.

Until graduation, this would be the only way she could get any rest on those nights of the flashbacks.

MARY-SUE NOTICED EVERYTHING, of course. She'd wake up in the middle of the night to pee and there they were—the warm body in her bed, the car in the driveway, the tampons in the trash. She didn't say anything because she knew Kate would be on the defensive about it. If she woke in the morning before Kate did, she lay completely still and kept her eyes closed until Kate rose and tiptoed out of the room. Sometimes this tactic made her late for work but she didn't care. She had to resist the temptation to leave packs of cookies on the breakfast table for Kate to take on her way out. That would break the charade; kindness went against the rules of this game.

As soon as Kate graduated, she moved back home, and Mary-Sue didn't try to stop her. She didn't want her to feel unwelcome. Far from being a freeloader, Kate got a job and bought all the groceries and paid all the bills. But Mary-Sue was perplexed when her grown daughter began again to creep into her bed on stormy nights. Perhaps Katie was a late bloomer, too. After all, she'd been in her mid-thirties herself before she did the one right thing in her life: import Kate. Nevertheless, Mary-Sue hoped it would be a matter of months before her daughter got up on her own two feet and moved away. She longed for the sweet sorrow of missing her.

THE MID-1990s WERE an interesting time on Santa Claus Lane. Nervous Alta Vista families fearing the aftershocks of the LA riots moved out to new exurbs built around shopping malls beyond the county line. New people moved in—Latinos, Armenians and Koreatown transplants who wanted nothing to do with the free-floating anger that had permeated many parts of the city. Mary-Sue suddenly became one of the longest-standing residents of the neighborhood, a grande dame. She realized how easy it was to gain currency as an old hand in California; she'd been in her house 15 years but it might as well have been 150. The new people came to her for advice on everything from how to take care of camellias to where to get their cat spayed. With her salt-and-pepper hair and accentless speech, she must have seemed to them positively patrician, and this amused her no end. Kate, however, had no interest in these strangers who kept coming to their door with stupid questions, least of all the Korean pastor who once stared at her funny because she hadn't worn a bra.

Mary-Sue felt an instant empathy for Mr. Park, the Korean pastor, and his young family. They seemed completely overwhelmed from the moment they moved in across the street. Soda bottles, toilet rolls and tins of baby formula would fall out of their overstuffed shopping bags and tumble down the driveway. Rosebushes would go unwatered and burn. The lawn would remain unmowed until Vector Control monitors came by to warn them that their tall grasses were harboring mosquito larvae.

Once, Mary-Sue entered their home while helping them with some shopping and saw that the inside of their house was mostly bare. The Parks had sunk all their money into acquiring the property; there was none left for furniture, not even a crib for the second little girl that the pretty young wife was about to have.

"We really have to help them," Mary-Sue told Kate.

With Kate's help, Mary-Sue placed her blue pull-out couch on a set of wheels and rolled it across the street to the Park's. No one would mourn its absence from their den but in the Korean family's house, maybe it'd make an extra bed.

Mr. Park received the kind gesture with a lot of nodding and a minimum of words. He was too proud to accept their charity, and too proud at the same time to say no. Little would Mary-Sue have guessed that as soon as she left his door, the blue sofa would be moved from Mr. Park's living room to the edge of his overgrown, disheveled backyard.

BY 2000, IT was clear to Mary-Sue that Kate had no intention of ever leaving home. She knew the limited allure of Alta Vista—most young people would be raring to flee. Not her Kate. Like only Mary-Sue could, she blamed herself. Kate's dysfunction was the direct result, she felt, of lousy parenting. Rather than expel her beloved daughter, Mary-Sue decided to withdraw more of her father's money and, in a word, flee. Even weighing her snobbery, she settled on South Florida.

The widow of an eccentric fern collector sold Mary-Sue their estate in Homestead, just outside Miami, well below its market worth; evidently, the old woman was eager to move on. The house was built on the highest point in South Florida—a grand elevation of three feet. One couldn't see the street from it, let alone the coast, but that was fine by Mary-Sue. The antebellum-style villa, complete with ornamental shutters, came cocooned in five wooded acres, hidden like a militiaman's lair deep in the agricultural heartland of Dade County. She could be a hermit all over again if she so chose, pursue any life philosophy she damn well pleased. She felt the same giddy freedom she experienced when she first arrived in California in the '60s, before Katie, before Santa Claus Lane, before she managed to botch up her one attempt in her entire life to become a normal human being.

South Florida was filled with old people—Jews, in many cases—and they read. That meant that Mary-Sue could, for culture, dip into nearby Coral Gables for its bookstores. On top of that, the local campus of the Miami-Dade community college held interesting lectures from time to time, ranging in topic from the sexual imagery in pre-Columbian pottery to the reproductive lives of microscopic plants, and through those occasions, she met new people, some of them bearable enough to be considered friends. For food, she had mango, orange, key lime, loquat and guava trees in her yard, and the Publix markets sold cheap avocados and everything else she could possibly need, aside from the company of her Katie. But distance was good for them—they both needed to grow up, independently. Yes, she reminded herself, even she, a woman in her sixties.

Kate came out to visit twice a year, speeding in from the Miami airport until she reached the big, Spanish moss-draped cypress that concealed Mary-Sue's driveway. Why her mother chose to live in a place like this confounded her.

On balmy evenings, they sat in the covered porch swatting mosquitoes and listening to monkey calls. Raccoons left poop valentines on the doorstep every night. At no time did they ever talk about unhappy things. Instead, they ate fruit from Mary-Sue's trees, drove down to the Keys and, on Kate's most recent visit, popped over to peek at the giant sinkhole that had appeared in the yard of Mary-Sue's neighbor, Larry, a short, ruddy man who did some kind of building-contractor work.

"The Lord won't never let us forget the whole of Florida's one big swamp." Larry hawked a loogie past his potbelly and into the void. Simple man, Kate thought.

No longer roommates who took each other for granted, mother and daughter opened up more. They discussed terrorism in big cities, picked hurricane shutters out of a catalog, debated the morality of local restaurants that served turtle fresh from the Everglades. It surprised Kate that Mary-Sue had evolved over the years into a perfectly plausible Southerner. She belonged in Florida. She wore sandals to restaurants whether appropriate or not, stacked unwanted items in the yard, and developed a sweet tooth for any kind of nut roasted in brown sugar. As each visit drew to a close, it always became clear that all Mary-Sue wanted was to assure Kate that she was doing fine on her own, and that her self-transformation was complete. Kate envied—and slightly resented—Mary-Sue's confidence and adaptability. Most of all, she missed her bustling energy around the house. The German shepherd she'd rescued from the pound was a very poor substitute. She knew it was unreasonable to hope that a pet could replace her mother; still, she never expected to be stuck with such a timid, sickly lump of a dog.

At the end of her last visit to Homestead, after their usual unsappy, pat-on-the-arm goodbyes, Kate felt sorrier than usual when she had to leave—a huge part of her wanted to move into her mother's tropical paradise and forget all about Alta Vista. As Kate backed down the driveway in her rental Saturn, feeling the queasy separation anxiety she always felt, Mary-Sue ran over and rapped on her window: "Oh, I almost forgot! You wouldn't guess who I ran into at the Borders on Dixie. I wouldn't have recognized him if he hadn't called out to me first."

"Who was it?"

"Oh, I better not say." Mary-Sue was coy as a schoolgirl. "He asked me to keep it a secret. I think he's going to surprise you in California one of these days."

– 6 –

DOUBLE-DIP

Kate and Bluto hadn't spoken in years. Centuries, it seemed like. Then out of the blue, he'd breezed into town and given her a call that spring morning, asking if she had time for a "sundae on Sunday." This was the kind of shtick that passed for wit when they were kids, Bluto having also been, as he liked to say, a cunning linguist. The arrival of the call that particular Friday seemed inevitable to Kate somehow. She was at an impasse, having gone nowhere professionally or romantically, and she'd been waiting for some kind of spiritual release, some fast-moving freight train out of nowhere to ram her out of limbo. She left her sick dog by a bowl of water, and drove out to her local Classic Shakes.

When Kate arrived, it took a while before she spotted him in a Naugahyde booth with a girl—Eurasian, she instantly knew—who looked about fourteen. The child was wearing a pink T-shirt with "Kiss Me I'm Irish" in green glitter. That, and jeans that frayed midthigh. Cutoffs, Kate supposed they were still called. She never wore those anymore. They were sitting at the far end of the diner though the place was practically empty. The girl's dark, shoulder-length hair was wet and glossy from the shower or the pool.

Kate felt it was low of Bluto to spring his daughter on her like this, having said nothing about her—or his marital status—on the phone. She studied them as she made her approach, passing the chrome soda fountain, the glass dome with its leaning tower of pink donuts. If this kid was fourteen, that would have made Bluto her father at eighteen—the first year of college. That might explain, even excuse, his radio silence. Perhaps there was a wife sitting at home or working two jobs in New York. Or maybe he was now divorced, or widowered . . . was that even a word?

Bluto stood up and gave her a hug that felt both intimate and by-the-book. They'd never even hugged before, she realized, such gawky teenagers were they. His torso felt ribby against her, but his arms were bulky, like he lived half his life in a gym. She tried to recall if he'd always been built like this, a plastic action figure. As they disengaged, his cheek grazed hers. It felt rough. Grown up. She saw the creases on the sides of his eyes when he smiled. Crow's feet. He looked weathered, and that made him manlier, sexier. How unfair.

She sat down and ordered a decaf. Bluto and his daughter were sharing a plate of fries, which the girl dipped in both ketchup and mayonnaise. Kate froze. She didn't know anybody else who did that apart from herself.

"See that?" said Bluto, proudly pointing out his girl's ritual. It seemed likely that he'd trained her. "Uncanny, wouldn't you say? Plus, your hair, your eyes."

They ordered burgers, and then Bluto really got to talking. He spoke of all the years they'd been out of touch, of graduating and falling flat on his face, of the three long years he spent "couch-surfing" in Brooklyn, of making a poor living as a landscaper, of car trouble on the Tappan Zee, of antiquing in historic Rhine-beck with rich widows, of falling serially for essentially the same, interchangeable person—the unappeasable blonde who didn't care for books or music. He threw around a lot of New York place names, but there was no mention of the girl's mother. Maybe she was some kind of Thai hooker he was embarrassed about.

The girl kept her eyes fixed on Kate, as if studying the way she bit into her cheeseburger and how she chewed. Kate was careful to deny the girl the pleasure of seeing her double-dip her fries. Every time Kate tried to include her in the conversation, the girl's eyes flitted down to her food or to Bluto, and her fingers rushed to fiddle with the monogrammed gold necklace around her neck.

Finally Bluto brought her into the conversation. He said her name was Brittany, like the province in France, not the singer. She was fifteen. He said that until he met her, he'd wasted too much time deceiving himself into thinking he'd be happy with a woman when all along what he'd wanted was a girl. He leaned across the table to Kate and whispered—"fire of my loins, a relentless cum machine"—about Brittany, the surly child who, until ten seconds prior, Kate had assumed was his daughter.

Kate stared at Brittany, who was twirling her hair as if nothing unusual had been said, her nonchalant affect gaining a new level of noxiousness. "This is a joke, right?"

Bluto laughed, and swatted the air with his hand. He had met the girl on the Internet, where he'd posed as a college freshman named Paul. At their first rendezvous, he said, she hadn't been shocked to find a thirty-two-year-old man waiting for her at the Starbucks; she told him she just *knew* he'd be "middle-aged." He took her on a plane and brought her out West to celebrate their one-month anniversary.

"Her parents think she's on a camping trip with the Girl Scouts." He smiled. "I know, I know, it's not exactly legal, but I thought my secret would be safe with you."

Kate felt like slugging him and fleeing the place, but she didn't want to make a scene. She played with her lettuce, while her insides grew queasy. When it came time for dessert, all three ordered hot fudge sundaes, but when they arrived, Kate couldn't touch hers. Bluto gave the girl his maraschino cherry, which sent her into nauseating spasms of gratitude. It was the only time Kate would see her mad, crooked grin.

"What do you want to be when you grow up?" Kate asked the girl.

The girl shrugged, knowing that her devil-may-care attitude was the privilege of youth. "Movie director?"

Kate snorted. She couldn't help it. Bluto warned her with a look to Be Nice. "It was Brittany here who wanted to see you, you know. Honestly, I was just going to take her straight to Disneyland. I wasn't even going to call."

Kate got her purse and stood up. "You know what, Bluto? You're sick. Fuck you."

"Well, it was very lovely to meet you," the girl said.

Bluto draped a protective arm over the girl and stroked her porcelain chin. It was two against one.

"I suppose it's my fault. I talk about you way too much," he said. "I kept telling her she reminded me of you. And so she got excited by the idea—"

"Not excited, curious," the girl corrected him.

"Either way, she wanted to see the genuine article. So here we are."

Kate pulled out money for her share of the food and slapped it down. "I don't know why I even bothered to come." She was beginning to shake. "I mean, my dog is dying at home!"

"What kind of dog is it?" the girl asked, just as Kate was walking off.

Kate turned and growled: "He's a German shepherd."

The girl clapped her hands. In derision, Kate thought.

"What?" she snapped.

"I've got a German shepherd, too," the girl said. "What's your dog's name?"

"Bluto."

THE NEXT DAY, Bluto phoned Kate and asked how her dog was. She should have hung up on him that second, but she'd just returned from the vet, where the other Bluto had been put to sleep. She agreed to meet him for a drink, provided the girl didn't tag along. She picked a cheesy sports bar in Old Town, a place she was certain they wouldn't run into anyone she knew.

She found him nursing his second beer, slouched at the counter so his shoulders formed angel wings inside his shirt.

"I thought you'd be flattered," he said, "that I picked someone so nakedly based on you. A virtual carbon copy."

"Obviously, all Eurasians look alike to you."

"Very funny." He gave her arm a little pinch. "If we'd fucked back then, we might have a kid her age today."

"Hah!"

He laughed. "Now you sound exactly like your mother. *Hah!*" He took her hand and fed her a jalapeno popper. "Ah, old times . . ." He sighed dramatically. "How's Santa Claus Lane? Still suffocating?"

"Pretty much," Kate said, quietly. She freed her hand from his.

"And yet you never left."

She was silent.

He tried again: "We were given legs, you know, so we can move around."

"Why exactly did you come back here?"

"I turn thirty-three soon. They say thirty-three's a pivotal age.

I've realized that over the years, I've never been able to recapture the kind of . . ." Just like that, his eyes turned to water. "You travel four thousand miles to seek perfection when all along it's sitting right here . . ." He leaned toward her, and his words fell to a whisper. "I've emerged from my years in the wilderness. Now I need to cleanse myself of the darkness and reclaim the innocence of my youth."

She grabbed her keys. "Fuck you. Maybe you should've joined an ashram or the Peace Corps, not stolen somebody's daughter."

His eyes flared, but cooled off in seconds. "Maybe. But I guarantee—the daughter's more fun." He gestured for more beer, one for him and one for her. "After our first meeting, Brittany and I went back to my car and fucked our brains out. There was no hesitation, no awkwardness whatsoever. She was clearly . . . educated." He gave her a tender smile. "I did to her everything that I should have done to you, when we were fifteen, sixteen, seventeen, eighteen. Heck, twelve. All those opportunities we had, you and I, and we just blew it. Did you have *any* idea how hard you got me?" Another look. "Anyway, Brittany and me, we went on and on till all the windows steamed up and my dashboard smelled like her pussy."

His knee brushed against Kate's thigh—and she felt herself shudder. She got up and walked away without looking at him.

A minute later, she returned. "Since you're here . . . Could you do me a favor?"

"SAME AS IT ever was," Bluto said, when they pulled into Kate's driveway on Santa Claus Lane. "The light. The paint. Every blade of grass. The same."

"Except my Mom's moved to Florida."

"I know."

Kate looked at him but decided to let it go. As they got out of the car, she saw Mr. Park, the slab-faced Korean pastor, watering his lawn across the street. It was something he did about once a month with remarkable half-heartedness. He looked at her and Bluto expressionlessly, but was obviously passing some judgment inside his warped head. She pointedly didn't wave—there was no point in acting friendly.

There was the spot at the back of her yard, under a shady oak tree, earmarked as her dog's final resting place. She watched as Bluto worked silently with the shovel, making a hole in the ground and excavating old hamster bones. His big arms glistened with perspiration. Then, just as wordlessly, he set the shovel down and lifted the dead German shepherd up from the turf. Without waiting for a final word from her, he dropped the lifeless body into the void and began methodically covering it with dirt. Kate's heart thought it heard the dog whimper, but her head knew it to be untrue. When the ground became level again, she got choked up.

"Thanks." She handed him a towel. "Thanks for coming here and doing this."

She showed him to the shower. He shrugged off his clothes and didn't shut the door. She watched, noting how the rest of his body looked compared to his arms. He also had an outsize, TV anchor's head, matched by an outsize dormant penis. When he finished showering, she toweled him dry and found him ready for sex. He found her, with a quick thrust of his fingers, to be the same.

"You have to use a condom. I don't want that girl's cooties."

Surprisingly, he came prepared.

Kate plucked off her clothes while they kissed. Before she could replace her oily smelling pillowcases, he'd grabbed her from behind and plunged himself into her, stopping her in her tracks. Carefully, they moved themselves down to the mattress as one. He opened her up with each stroke. Then he placed her on her back and fucked her steadily, grabbing her breasts and staring into her eyes. She tried to give herself over to the moment but her mind kept racing: Was this what he did with Brittany? The same moves? Would he go back and report it so they could desecrate this moment by reenacting it?

"Where are you?" Bluto sounded impatient. He jerked her down to the carpet with him and pinned her under his thighs until she surrendered with moans. Then very roughly and very suddenly, he rolled her onto her front and took her, his chin digging hard into the back of her shoulder. She screamed. His intensity threw everything into focus: she'd waited half her life for this. They were together at last, whole at last—at least until he pulled out, ripped off the condom, and came.

They showered together afterwards, sneaking in another round while soaping each other. He rubbed her clit while biting her neck, and she stunned herself with her continued ability to climax—intensely—while standing. She reciprocated, pleasuring him orally as his fingers found traction on the tiles.

They smoked a joint together in the nude, not exchanging a word. Whoa, it was stronger stuff than they used to know. By nine that night, they were both dressed but had done it so dancingly, so leisurely-ly, they seemed teleported into her car with no memory of how they got there, and were now backing down the driveway like a make-believe married couple. Would this be their life if they'd gotten romantic decades ago? Would they have had kids? Nah, no kids. No kids. They'd prefer continuous fucking. The condom, what a wonderful invention.

As she drove, high, fighting the giggles, she imagined she was chauffeuring him to the late shift, brown-bag supper in his brief-case, change for the pop machine in his pocket. Nah, nah, nah, to read the ten o'clock news at KCAL. Nah, nah, nah, to his high-paying job measuring earthquakes at Caltech. It felt true, for one, two, three minutes. They were time travelers. They'd dipped backward and bent the clock, broke it maybe. How could they possibly be thirty? That was *old*. They smelled of the same soap, the same shampoo. They were passing through the same streets they knew. Come on. Really. They were fifteen, playing house. That thing with the other girl, whatshername—that wasn't real. This thing, *this* was real. They were destined, him coming back just when she most needed a big bump in her life. Like that guy in *Terminator*. What was his name? What was his name? Oh . . . *Kyle Reese!* she shrieked. *What?* he said. It's like she'd con-jured him up with some kind of voodoo. Wait, had she though? Honestly she couldn't even remember. So what if she had? He was looking so damn cute she had to lean over to french him.

He tasted like soap. Floral, but bitter. Huh. She turned back to the road. Huh. There was something not right with her pas-senger. He seemed replaced, like an artificial breast grafted from a thigh. The effects of time travel, she supposed. It changed you from minute to minute. She peered in the rearview mirror: oh whew, she was still fifteen . . . ish.

When she pulled into the Slumber Inn lot, Bluto was fast asleep, his fingers draped over her knee. She woke him by blowing air across his lashes.

Outside room 105, he lifted a hand to wave goodbye but it appeared to take a great deal of effort. His arms, those heavy arms, were slack. His face, on the other hand, was waking up, and growing gently confused.

AT THREE IN the morning, Kate was awakened by the phone. She expected to find Bluto in his doggy bed when she opened her eyes, but seeing it empty, she remembered with a jolt that he was dead—and buried. Never again would he sit on the bathroom floor and gaze up at her blankly while she shaved her legs.

It was the other Bluto on the line. Crying. In her sleepy haze, she thought he'd picked up on her sadness about the dog. It dawned on her that he was talking about something else.

"You gottahelpme, Kate . . ." His words grew increasingly incoherent. "Don't leavemeherealone, please . . ."

She told him to be calm. She grabbed her keys and, still in her flannel jammies, drove back to the Slumber Inn. This better not be a prank or a trap.

Outside room 105, she tapped on the door quietly, just as he'd instructed. After some rattling of locks, the door opened and she saw Bluto, his face funereal. She felt a queasy chill when she heard him quietly close the door behind her.

"I was asleep when it happened." He gestured at the bed. King size, she noted. There was a humanoid lump beneath the floral bedcovers. "She's gone."

"What do you mean, gone?" Kate backed away. With one swift motion, he yanked off the covers. Girlish clothing scrunched together there, molded into a human form. Kate spotted the "Kiss Me I'm Irish" T-shirt from their first meeting, as well as the jean shorts. There was a lot of skimpy underwear—price tags were still on most of them.

"She's gone," Bluto repeated, more bleakly than before. "We went to sleep. And when I got up to pee—she just wasn't here."

A pink gym bag sat unzipped, emptied out, on the carpet. Glossy flip-flops lay splayed nearby. Her monogrammed gold necklace was draped around a lampshade.

"Is there a pool here? Maybe she went swimming."

"No, there's no pool here." The life had gone out of his eyes. "She just vanished. I don't know what to do. I mean, she's got no clothes."

Kate moved around the room, peering under the bed, opening closet doors and ripping aside the shower curtain. Could this be their idea of a prank? Was she hiding somewhere, videotaping this and giggling? She grabbed the empty pill bottle on Bluto's side of the bed. Sleeping pills, prescribed for him by a Dr. Yamasato.

"What did you do, Bluto?"

"Nothing!" He raised his hands, like a perp proving he wasn't armed.

Kate made for the door, "All right. I've had enough."

"No! Please, don't go . . . You have to help me find her."

When she turned back, he was crumpled on the floor, holding his knees to his chest, despondent.

She moved a stack of dirty underwear and sat him down in the room's lone chair. Motels like this made no bones about their purpose: if you were traveling, you checked in to sleep; if you were local, you checked in to fuck. You certainly didn't check in to sit around with an old friend.

"When I came back from your house, she made a big stink about being left here all by herself. She was jealous, clearly . . ."

"Did anyone see her when you checked in?"

"No, I always made sure she stayed inside the car with her head down low. And she knew about stranger-danger. If anyone talked to her, she'd give them a fake name. Like Kate."

"Kate?"

"It's a common name."

"Does she have friends or family out here? People she could've run off to?"

"I was her only friend. If she was a well-adjusted girl she'd never be with me, let's just put it that way."

Kate surveyed the room and returned to the clothes on the bed. The queasy feeling returned. Why had Brittany left all of her stuff?

"Why don't you go and take a shower while I think of something."

Bluto nodded obediently and rose from the chair, wobbly on his feet. Lumbering forward like a zombie, he gave her a final pleading look before disappearing into the black hole of the bathroom. "You *have* to help me, Kate . . ."

When she heard the shower running steadily, she let herself out of room 105 and raced to her car, heart pounding. Her hands were icicles and she panicked that her engine wouldn't start, the way it would have stalled at precisely this point in a movie. But the car did start and she backed out of the lot with her headlights off. She kept her head low until she reached a major street, and then hit the gas with a vengeance.

As she sped home, she felt the unflappable eyes of the missing girl on her. She looked up at the rearview mirror—they were her own eyes, of course. Bluto hadn't lied. She and Brittany looked almost exactly alike. Separated by a lifetime, and now, by the inscrutable night.

She made a left onto Santa Claus Lane.

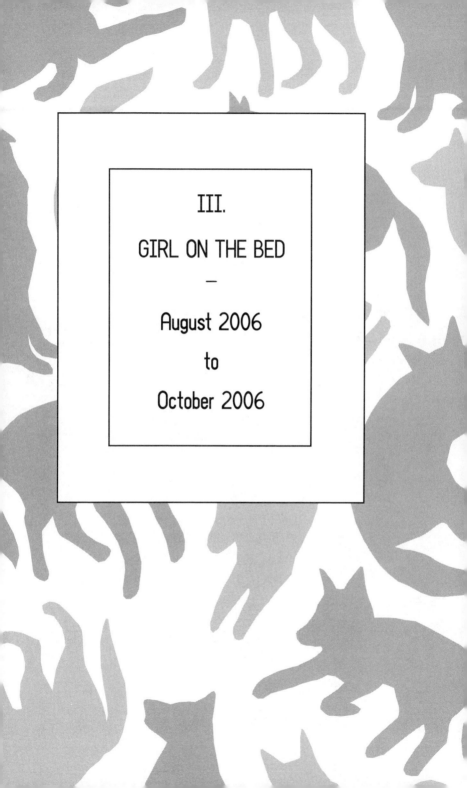

III.

GIRL ON THE BED

–

August 2006

to

October 2006

MAGICAL THINKING

Mr. Z pulled down the projection screen. Rosemary noticed he behaved very differently with this class, maybe because there were now twenty-two of them and not just four. He was less intimate, more formal, as if some of these kids had parents he needed to impress. In other words, he acted exactly like a schoolteacher.

"I want to show you two of my favorite paintings in the world. They're both created by an underrated nineteenth-century Frenchman named Hippolyte Delaroche, known to his friends simply as Paul. Paul Delaroche was a Romantic, with a capital *R*."

He clicked on the first slide. Two little girls with page-boy haircuts perched on the edge of a creepy-looking four-poster bed. One looked off to the side with vivid dread on her face, and she had an illuminated manuscript in her hand. The other girl leaned on her companion for support, staring back at the viewer with a nauseated expression. Near them was a lapdog peering into the void beyond the bed.

"Can anyone tell me what this is?" Mr. Z asked. Blank stares. He answered his own question: "The Princes in the Tower."

Oh, thought Rosemary, so they're *boys*.

"This was painted by Delaroche in 1830 and it now hangs in the Louvre museum in Paris." He turned back to the image. "Can anyone guess what's going on here? Come on, people. This is not an art history class. I want your emotional response, not your intellectual response. Remember, heart, not head."

"Are they . . . lovers?" a boy named Arik asked. Nervous giggles.

"Are you saying that because they're sitting on an unmade bed?"

Arik shrugged.

"Good guess, though, because something unholy is definitely going on here. One of these boys is Edward V, aged twelve, and the other one's his nine-year-old brother, Richard, the Duke of York. They're in the Tower of London because why? Anyone?"

"Somebody put them there." Smart-ass laughter.

"That's right, Charles. Someone did put them there. And that someone was their uncle, Richard III. Edward was made king of England when he was twelve and his wicked uncle didn't think a kid deserved that title. So he decided to get rid of him. By the way, you may know Richard III as the hunchbacked king from Shakespeare."

Murmurs of recognition. Alicia Hwang raised her hand:

"He was played by Ian McKellen in that movie."

"Yes, Alicia. Very good." Mr. Z turned back to the screen. "Look at this. The tension in the frame. At any moment now, some muscly henchman is going to come up those stairs, burst through the door and haul them away to have their heads chopped off."

With his laser pointer, Mr. Z brought attention to the boys' faces: "Deep anxiety here in little Richard. Resignation in Edward—in fact, he looks like he's falling asleep. The different ways we deal with trauma." He pointed at the lapdog. "And of course, here you have the silly pup who gazes directly into the darkness, with no conception of fear. Just look at the tension in the scene. The *drama*."

"How do you know which boy's which?" someone asked.

"I assume that Edward is the resigned-looking one wearing the rings and stockings of royalty. As the older child, he had to know that resistance was futile." Mr. Z paused, pursing his lips. "In the end, nobody ever knew what really happened to the boys. If they were killed, their murders were never recorded. And if they were freed . . . Well, there was no way their uncle would have let them live."

A hush. Mr. Z clicked on the next slide.

"On to something jollier . . ."

It was a painting of five people—three women and two men—wearing costumes from the Middle Ages. The woman in the center had on a dress in blazing white. She knelt, blindfolded. Her left hand was outstretched, looking for support. A balding man in a fur cloak guided her toward the wooden block where her head was to rest. On the extreme right, a sinister guy in red tights leaned on the handle of a humongous ax. There was straw on the ground, ready to soak up blood.

"Whoa," someone said.

"Anyone?" Mr. Z crossed his arms, smiling at the room.

"Joan of Arc?" Alicia Hwang ventured.

"Good try, Alicia. In fact this is a piece called *The Execution of Lady Jane Grey*, painted by Paul Delaroche in 1833. Another scene set in the Tower of London. The original hangs in the National Gallery in London and it's huge—I've seen it—eight feet high and ten feet wide. When you're standing in front of it, these figures are life-size. You feel like at any second, they'll start moving and they'll chop off her head." Mr. Z looked at the picture in awe, adding softly: "It's . . . electrifying."

Rosemary tried to imagine the original painting. Even as a slide projection it achieved the effect of palpable dread.

"Lady Jane Grey was deposed as the Protestant queen of England after just nine days in 1553, when she was fifteen years old. Again, she was done in by a jealous relative, in this case, her sister-in-law, Mary. Mary gave Jane the option of converting to Catholicism before they executed her, but Jane politely said no thanks. So much for blood ties . . ."

To Rosemary's mortification, Mr. Z directed his laser pointer to her chest. The red spot bounced around her left breast like a neon flea.

"How old are you, Rosemary?"

"Fifteen," she mumbled.

"Then you can probably imagine what the poor girl must have been going through." He gave her one of his smiles that also looked like a wince.

"Who are those two ladies lurking behind her?" someone asked.

"Her loyal maids-in-waiting. Again, look at the different ways of dealing with trauma. Jane is completely calm while her two maids are in hysterical agony. One of them has her eyes closed and the other has her back turned to the action. In fact, look . . ." Mr. Z moved his pointer across all five characters on the screen. "Not one of them is looking back at us at all. You can't even see their eyes. That's part of the horror of the scene. It is so intimate, so hermetically sealed-off. As a result, we feel as if we're witnessing true, unmitigated emotion."

He shut off the slide projector. "All right. Enough art." He clasped his hands together. "Time for some trust exercises."

MR. Z OFFERED Rosemary a ride home again, saying he had another errand to run near her house. This time, he took a different, longer route to Santa Claus Lane. They passed the Whole Foods and the Baklava Factory, even the four discount mattress stores on the other side of the freeway. She pretended she didn't notice.

"Lot of churches around here," said Mr. Z, like that was funny or strange. Rosemary had no idea how to respond to that.

After several minutes of silence, she said: "Those paintings you showed us, they were really cool."

"I hope I didn't embarrass you, calling on you in class."

"No, it was fine. You just caught me by surprise."

He gave her a smile so full-bodied it instantly made her feel small and insincere. He looked so kind.

"I wanted to know how you'd be about performing in front of people. You see, I'm thinking of casting you in a play."

Again, she didn't know how to respond. Would it be ungrateful to decline the role of the non-speaking maid or the tree? She'd told herself no more shrubbery.

"I want you as the lead."

"No way." He *had* to be kidding her.

"Yes, way!"

"What play is it?"

"A mystery play. I wrote it myself. We'll stage it around Christmas."

"A mystery play—like a Nativity play?"

"No, no," he took a breath. "Mystery as in intrigue and surprise."

"Oh. And you wrote it?"

"I thought it was probably high time I pulled it out of my drawer and dusted it off. I didn't think I could do it until I found my leading lady, i.e. you."

She hadn't actually heard anyone say the letters *i.e.* before and suppressed her conditioned impulse to snicker. If only Mira were here.

"So what do I play?" She was almost afraid of his answer. A cat? A tree?

"The femme fatale."

"What."

Mr. Z turned his car onto the side street that would turn into Santa Claus Lane. "And just in case you thought I was kidding, we begin rehearsals next week."

ROSEMARY KEPT THE red plastic pen she'd stolen from Mr. Z in her underwear drawer. It was a fragile thing of beauty that felt snug in her hand. The clicker released and retracted the nib crisply. And except for the faint USA imprinted on the metal clip and the local 626 area code of the phone number on its body, the pen could have been an artifact from Italy. BUCA DI BEPPO, UNA FAMIGLIA was printed on it in white.

Its black ink was frail and flowed unsteadily, so she used it sparingly, for crucial notation only, like marking on her calendar the rehearsal dates given to her by Mr. Z. The sessions hadn't yet begun, and all she knew about the play was that it was a two-hander where she'd be acting opposite a cute boy named Arik Kistorian, and that the performance was tentatively set for Christmas Day.

Helicopters buzzed over the Park house as the girls ate their ramen dinner and watched *Extra*—Hollywood ingénues had called each other vaginal epithets again, someone was gaining weight, someone else was losing weight. The police choppers had been circling their area ever since a slew of break-ins was reported at the start of the summer. They zipped around for ten to fifteen minutes at dusk every couple of days, looking for men in hooded sweatshirts roaming the neighborhood.

"*What* did they just say about Lindsay Lohan's crotch?"

"Didn't hear it! That dumb chopper!"

"Crank it up, man!"

"You have the remote. You do it!"

They turned up the TV and immediately their mother started yelling from the kitchen: "Don't make so much noisy! Mama have headache!"

Their mother was wrapping up ceramic dinnerware in old newspaper and stuffing it into boxes. The girls never offered to help, hoping that as Mrs. Park grew more and more exhausted, she'd come to the conclusion that her Korea plan was doomed to fail.

The girls turned off the TV and bussed their bowls to the kitchen sink. Seeing their mother packing up nice-looking plates that had never made it to their dinner table, they rolled their eyes at each other.

"When did we get these?" asked Mira. "I've never seen them before."

"Wedding present," Mrs. Park answered, her widow's peak drenched in sweat. "Many years old."

"How come we never used them? They're so chic."

"They too good," Mrs. Park said, matter-of-factly.

"Too good?" Mira picked up one of the plates and turned it over. "This is, like, IKEA."

Rosemary pinched her sister's arm hard. She knew Mira was just trying to pick another fight with their mother.

"Ma, Rosie's hurting me!"

Mrs. Park was wise enough not to respond. She continued packing.

The girls slumped listlessly back to the den where the ceiling fan rattled, and sprawled out on the cool tile floor.

"Do you think we'll make it to Christmas, staying here?" Rosemary said.

Mira kept quiet.

"Hey, I'm talking to you."

"I am be-ing hyp-no-tized by the ro-ta-ting blades . . ." Mira stared at the fan, then flaunted her crossed eyes. "Frankly, I don't think we're ever going to leave this gulag."

"What do you mean? In a couple of hours, she'll be on the phone calling people in Korea again. At some point, someone's going to say yes!"

"I can't let myself consider it. I'll go insane—and then die. In that order." Mira turned to her side and hugged her knees. Then she released a resounding fart.

Rosemary threw a pillow at her. "I really, really despise you!"

Mira cackled. Then just as suddenly, she grew grave. "Can I tell you something? It concerns both of our fates."

"What? *What?*"

"I read somewhere that girls between the ages of thirteen and sixteen are especially prone to paranormal visitations. Especially poltergeists."

Rosemary kicked her sister, and stood up.

"It's true!" Mira insisted. "It's to do with hormones, girls our age! We have too much estrogen."

"I'm not even going to dignify that with a response." Rosemary stormed off.

"I've been thinking about this. We could harness our rage, together! We could summon up a spirit. We could even summon up Dad, and he'll help us against—"

Rosemary slammed her bedroom door.

"Who make a big noise?" Mrs. Park came shuffling in from the kitchen.

Mira closed her eyes, crossed her chest with her arms and became an exquisite corpse.

ROSEMARY PULLED OUT the slip of paper with Mr. Z's phone number. Would it be too weird to call him? Technically it wasn't late at all—a little past seven-thirty, but it was well past school hours and it was dark out.

Although she'd been instructed to conserve her minutes, she used her cell so there'd be no risk her mother might pick up the extension and hear her with some man.

Her fingers were ice-cold as she punched in Mr. Z's number. She actually didn't need the paper—she'd already memorized the digits like a mystic PIN—but his handwriting was talismanic. He crossed his sevens. She sat by her open window, as far from her door as possible in case Mira was eavesdropping. Ringtones. Once, twice, three times. She prepared to hang up before his voicemail clicked on.

Then she heard his voice, "Hello, Rose," on the other end. She tingled all over when she realized he'd seen her name on his caller ID.

"I hope I'm not bothering you." Her voice was small and tight.

"You'll never bother me, Rose," he said. "You don't have to worry about that."

RAYMOND'S AGENT, LENA Ozova, was in town from New York. Five years had passed since he'd sat with the scrawny Pole, and he was curious to see if her facelift had held up. They went to Musso's in Hollywood where they split a bottle of Albariño and shared a chef's salad which she picked at as if eating an extra leaf might send her to Canyon Ranch. He had the calf's liver. She was careworn and brittle—her vertebrae had not been kind—but her face looked youthful.

"I can get you into an anthology," she said, in her Slavic lilt that men of all persuasions supposedly found irresistible back in the seventies.

"Who with?"

"What does it matter who with? You need to get yourself back into circulation, my dear. Look at Stephen King—he wrote *Carrie* in 1974 and there he is, still plowing away at it, top drawer, bottom drawer, all the drawers."

"So Steve's actually going to be in this thing?"

"No . . ." said Lena, carefully. "It's a new crowd. Fresh blood. That's why we think it'll be good to have you in the mix. You get to be the *éminence grise*, baby."

"You promised we wouldn't be discussing the book business."

"But we are not—it's a magazine anthology."

"Magazine?" Raymond lost his appetite. "Yeesh."

"All right, *journal*. Do you want to spend the next hour talking semantics? There'll be slots for you—two, three times a year. Mid to high word-rate, so don't sulk. Guaranteed slots, so you won't need to suffer the humiliation of submission." She watched the muscles above his jowls tighten. "Raymond, I worry about you. You behave as if you're some mummified corpse. It's a colossal waste. All I'm trying to do is *wake you up*."

"I've been percolating, that's all." Raymond called for the check.

Lena raised a kohl-painted eyebrow. "That's not the best way to make coffee. Nespresso will tell you that. So what's brewing?"

"I've been toying for some time with the idea for a book, sort of. It'll draw parallels between modern American life and the

Middle Ages in Europe. You know, the atmosphere of fanaticism, witch-hunting, the belief in the supernatural, and so on . . ."

"Fascinating." Lena squeezed his hand, which meant shut up. "But in the meantime, why don't you cook up a couple of short stories? You used to be able to whip those up in no time. You used to understand fear so well." She watched him squirm, and savored it. She grinned like the Cheshire cat: "Just think of your father."

LENA WAS RIGHT. His old man was the real horror. If he hadn't had to pay for his old man's expenses, he would have put in a pool years ago. He would have turned his garage into a gym-and-sauna combo. He would have done all that plus maybe bought a house in Cabo or the Palm Desert. Paying for his dad to live at Dartmoor was like sending two kids to Harvard for the rest of their lives. Twenty-four-hour call buttons, low-sodium cordon bleu dinners and Jazzercise with Nobel laureates.

He switched his computer on, a thimble of Glenfiddich nearby to steady his nerves. It'd been a while since he had googled anything other than "Raymond van der Holt" and he was now about to research this "new blood" Lena mentioned. His future peers, she'd said, with an insouciance that was hard to read. Was he to be flattered? Amused? Intimidated?

His indignation led him deeper and deeper into the web. What he thought would take just ten minutes, tops, kept him hooked at the terminal, clicking, clicking, clicking. These novices were mostly in their twenties. Many of their biographies listed illustrious college careers, famous mentors and bogus-sounding prizes (the Charles Bukowski Spirit Award; Bread Loaf African American Writer of the Year).

"Graduates of the Namedroppers Academy," Raymond muttered, and poured himself more Scotch.

The majority of them had their own websites, replete with links to online retailers selling their work, printable excerpts and signable guestbooks. The page belonging to one female poet he could barely tell from a sex worker's ad, there were so many affidavits of support under her sultry, leggy portrait. But—and this was the thing that really bugged him and kept him up looking for counterexamples—all of their writing samples had snap. In some cases, he detected the palimpsest of tricks he too had utilized: sneaky changes of POV, extended flashbacks, unannounced tone shifts; nevertheless he worried their work surpassed his in verve, content and enterprise. No doubt these young scriveners had an unfair advantage. If he'd grown up with the entire Internet at his fingertips, by now he'd have won a PEN award, an Edgar, probably even a Tony for the Broadway musical of his werewolf cycle. He wouldn't be like them, guest players in an *anthology*.

AT UNION LIQUORS, the only liquor store in the area not set up like it was anticipating a holdup, Kate no longer dawdled by the paper cartons of Merlot. Nor did she stop to admire the cellophane bundles of honey-roasted cashews the way she used to.

The first time she saw Raymond at the store, a couple of years ago, she observed him quietly from a distance, then as soon as he left, bought exactly what he bought because he looked so damned knowledgeable plucking whisky off the shelf, not even pausing to read the guff on the labels. Since then, she'd wasted no time, heading straight from the door to the whisky section and grabbing whatever was on special that day, two or three bottles at a go. The maker made no difference, as long as it was *whisky*—the Scots spelled it without the *e*. This guaranteed that it was made with Scottish spring water and not some kind of industrial bog runoff from a place like Kentucky; or so Raymond had said to her once at the store.

"Pour this into a crystal tumbler, two fingers deep, and give it a tender swirl," he purred. "Highland peat is hard to beat."

Ordinarily she hated the bossy free advice of strangers, but she'd seen the way he talked to the storekeeper and realized that this was the way he acted with everyone. His condescension was avuncular. She began looking forward to running into him in the whisky aisle. This happened every month or two, always on a Sunday. He would be dressed like a dandy on his way to the races: silk pocket square, straw fedora, but there was usually something amiss—unbuttoned fly, flip-flops, bags of sweating frozen pizzas waiting in the car.

"Absolutely no ice. To release its flavor, add a touch of water. Just a touch. But whatever you do, never, *never* American tap water, unless the taste of chlorine appeals to you." "Blends are junior high; you want college, at the very least." "A blood tub is a very small cask some distilleries use to speed up maturity. It's faster because there's more contact with the wood. But I prefer my whisky to fester in its own time."

Around their fifth or sixth encounter, they introduced themselves to each other. No plans for any whisky meetups were made—they knew their kind of drinking was best done alone.

She found it soothing as she drank in the solitude of her living room that Raymond was doing the same in his house across the street. She often watched him from one of her upstairs rooms. Framed brilliantly in his picture window, he was like a silent movie that replayed itself over and over every night. He sat in his favorite armchair with a crystal tumbler of something, holding animated conversations with people she never saw, conducting symphonies she never heard. Once in a while he would get careless and stagger around the house with his robe wide open, forgetting that a window *worked both ways*. It was delicious how she never ran into him at the supermarket or the bank or the drugstore—it was only ever Union Liquors.

It was also at their liquor store that he asked her, a few weeks ago, "When are you due?"

Mortified that he'd noticed her recent weight gain, she accepted his misguided joshing with a chortle.

"No, seriously, my dear," he said, "you shouldn't be drinking like this if you're having a baby."

KATE DROPPED TWO slices of bread down the toaster and twisted the lid off the strawberry jam. While she waited, famished, she gulped down her third glass of milk.

The greeting card sat on the kitchen counter. Her mother had a habit of sending her goofy cards—Hanukkah cards for Valentine's Day, get-well-soon cards for her birthday and Kwanzaa cards for no other reason than pure silliness—but never before had the greeting matched up so fully with the actual occasion. The card opened to reveal a very pregnant mama squirrel. Shit.

She hadn't told Mary-Sue about her pregnancy; yet it seemed as if her mother, with her uncanny sixth sense, had simply known. *Congratulations!* chirped a chorus line of squirrels. They'd had no contact in over a month, and the card was probably just a friendly reminder for her to call. Mary-Sue had always been nothing less than kind and generous—a nun with a checkbook. She'd never known the *real* Kate—violent, haunted, ruled by chaos and disappointment. A *Vietnam whore*.

She could kill Bluto. Him and his busted condom. He hadn't called her since that night, which was just as well since she didn't want anything more to do with him. Their encounter might as well have been a hallucination born of a lonely spring night.

Yet certain facts remained irrefutable—that girl Brittany had made the news, still missing. And the incubus was no dream. It grew daily in size and temperament; it had very specific demands and exacted very specific punishments if those demands weren't met. At four months, it had become harder for Kate to deny or disguise her state. She sometimes still harbored dark thoughts about getting rid of it.

On the bright side, she knew that Mary-Sue would welcome the baby with a benevolence that Kate didn't herself possess. Mary-Sue would detach the reality of the baby from the reality of its provenance and overwhelm it with a love that would render history inconsequential. Nothing would matter beyond the fact that it was flesh and blood, and yelping for supervision . . . Not that this made it any easier to pick up the phone.

The August heat was hard on her body. She'd already thrown up that morning, running from her bed to the toilet, hand over mouth, at seven. Now, the merciless sun was beating down on the house, unearthing old stinks. A sick dog with halitosis. A poorly covered grave. Dead babies floating down a muddy river.

She rushed again to the bathroom.

KATE KNEW HER own history of terrible impulses only too well. Only a few years ago, she had been a grade-school teacher in south Los Angeles, with its appalling teacher-student ratio. She taught math, reading and writing at an elementary school where not once did she meet an Edward James Olmos who prescribed calculus for self-respect.

Kate got goosebumps the first time she heard "motherfucker" coming from the mouth of a seven-year-old girl, but that was dignified compared to the other things the kids called one another. The baggy-pants look began for boys in the first grade. The girls wore gaudy spandex and had sopping infections from DIY pierced ears. Spot checks uncovered cigarettes, bullets, condoms, even a handgun in her third-grade class—her most prized student, Keneesha, kept a hunting knife in her lunch sack. Protection from what or whom, it was never clear. The child didn't want to say, and the school shrink gave up.

There was a boy named Marco in her class, a six-year-old Filipino Mexican, slight even for six. He did his homework on time, never called her any names and stayed out of trouble. His mother sold fake Louis Vuitton purses at a swap meet downtown, his father had worked construction until a falling scaffold took off his arm. Like many of the kids at the school, he spoke mainly Spanish at home; his English came dented by the barrio, and he tried hard to shake its imprint. Then things got strange. Often when Kate would be writing on the blackboard, this kid would fix his eyes on her. She would feel him watching her every move, staring at her breasts, her hips. It wasn't a crush, that much she knew. The boy was six. She could tell that he didn't like her, didn't trust her and was sussing her out for some other possibly criminal opportunity. In looks and manner, he reminded her of somebody from the past but she couldn't quite place who.

One day as she was driving out of the school parking lot, she saw him waiting for the bus. His eyes met hers, but instead of flinching or smiling a hello, he kept on staring. It was like a contest. She had to look away. When she stopped for kids at the crosswalk, Marco materialized, his palms pressed flat against her window.

"What are you, Miss Ireland?" he asked. "Who are you?"

She hit the gas. The nerve of the little prick.

The next day at school, Marco accosted her in the hallway. Again, he stared at her in his searching way.

"Miss Ireland?" A rosary dangled from his hand. "Did you come to save me?"

She gestured for him to walk ahead of her.

"My mother received a message from God," he kept on, looking back at her as he walked. "She said there is an angel at my school. She said the angel will save me." At the stairwell, he turned back to look at her again as he held on to the handrail and carefully descended the steps.

"Well, kid, that's a nice story," she said.

Suddenly, she watched him close his eyes and swoon, his legs giving way under him. He plummeted without resistance down the stairs, head and shoulders first, landing at the bottom of the staircase in a passive, twisted heap. He was still clutching the rosary. Students and teachers rushed over. Some of the kids made catcalls and laughed. Kate raced down the steps to where Marco was, calling for the school nurse. The kid's mouth poured blood, and one of his arms made a right angle in the wrong place. He murmured when they tried to move him but otherwise made no complaint.

Kate was called to the principal's office. In a fit of keenly felt déjà vu, before gentle, gray-haired Principal Simmons could even question her about the incident, she bolted from the room, yelling "I'm done!"

She then gave private English lessons to foreigners, immigrants who wanted to improve their language skills in order to land better jobs or post comments on the Internet without getting heckled by creeps. Her sideline was accent augmentation, targeting those who wanted to pass as native speakers for professional or romantic reasons.

To improve their conversational skills, she asked her students to talk about their lives, and their confessions produced some of the strangest and sweetest stories of new American striving. There were three Thai sisters who wanted to expand their massage-parlor business into the gated suburbs, a Russian mail-order wife sent to learn English by her dying televangelist husband, a Peruvian car dealer who'd been in the US for twenty years and wanted to branch into Hummers.

Mr. Park, the Korean pastor across the street, had been her single dullest student. Unlike her mother, she'd never warmed to him, but he asked to hire her and the terms had been more than fair. Her tasks were simple: drive to his church twice a week and teach his staff rudimentary English, then stay on to converse with him for a couple of hours more. He swore her to secrecy, saying he didn't want anyone to find out about his lessons. She inferred that by "anyone," he meant his wife and daughters. His chauvinism—sexual, cultural, generational—was there in the way he sat, with his legs apart, one peasant foot perched on the seat like a pasha. It was there in the way he coughed, his open mouth exposing his tonsils for all to see. It was there in the leisurely way he scratched his balls, then slyly ran his fingers across his nose.

The funny thing was he actually spoke the language better than he let on; it was just his accent that was a bit hard to penetrate. He said his daughters laughed at him whenever he tried to converse with them. Inhibited—although he didn't put it that way—he retreated into pidgin and monosyllables. By default, Kate became the only person he could talk to, and he seemed to really enjoy her company. He told her about his past as a badminton champion in South Korea, and how he missed the charred beef aroma of street carts selling *galbi* late into the night.

Several times he tried to hug her after class, praising her for being "such a good listener."

But she really wasn't. When he confessed that he had ambitions of becoming a writer in English, Kate encouraged him to put his stories down on paper so she wouldn't have to hear him stutter on pitifully about them. He got to work immediately, writing hard every day. The next week, she was surprised by the quantity of his output—sixty pages—having expected only a tedious haiku or two. The quality of the work was another matter altogether. But these were language lessons, not fiction workshops. She concentrated on fixing his English and made no comment about his chosen subjects—lechers, philanderers, the full gamut of completely revolting men. Obediently, he wrote his stories out several times over, his grammar and handwriting improving with each successive draft. She was considerate about them, using value-free terms like "different" and "unexpected."

When he finally assembled his stack of six short stories, as polished as he could make them, he invited Kate for coffee at Starbucks. To celebrate, he said. There she found him trying to read the ads at the back of the *LA Weekly*, his mouth open like a carp. She was mortified when the barista took them to be a couple.

As they sat down, Mr. Park thanked her for her continued encouragement and asked if she could help place his stories in reputable newspapers or journals. His primary interest was to impress his "very clever" daughters, both of whom adored *The Simpsons* and *South Park*, and possessed, according to him, "the very sarcastic type of humor." Eventually, he'd want to go on to write novels or television sagas, with his clever daughters' help, perhaps. Epics involving a whole cross-section of society, "like Charles Dickens and *Simpsons*, all together." He would tell the stories of everybody, rich and poor, Korean and black, Latino and Jewish, and he'd make their lives intersect in refreshing ways. He clasped his hands together: "Old world plus new world!"

He waited eagerly for Kate's response, the soy foam canopy on his latte growing cold and quietly sagging.

Kate's face was red. She tried to find something nice to say.

"Mr. Park, I really . . . I'm not sure I know what to tell you."

"Yes? You see it?" He tapped the table for emphasis. "I pay you extra if you find publisher for me. Our secret. Two hundred dollars."

His offer wasn't just idiotic, it was incredibly insulting. Kate pushed out a smile and said, neutrally, "I don't think you should be thinking about ditching your day job yet."

"No!" Mr. Park guffawed, hearing only what he wanted to hear. "No, I don't quit until I make bestseller! I have responsibility of my family. I am not old maid like you."

Confident in his talent, he sat himself erect, pulled his knees apart and cleared his throat noisily. A few people turned to stare, but he remained oblivious. He hacked a lump of phlegm into his napkin and left it crushed up on the table, perilously close to Kate's coffee. She pursed her lips.

"How should I put this?" she finally said, pulling her cup away. "Your stories aren't good enough for publication anywhere. I mean, quite honestly, they're garbage."

"But you said . . ."

"I know what I said. And I'm sorry for misleading you. I just didn't want to hurt your feelings." She looked at him. There was soy foam on the side of his mouth—or what she hoped was soy foam. "Mr. Park, your clever daughters would be horrified. Some of the attitudes expressed in your stories, Americans will find downright . . . disgusting." She hadn't meant to use *that* word, but she was inspired by his loogie.

Mr. Park nodded too quickly. He took in her words as he drank his latte in large gulps. Once he was done, he swept his hand briskly across the tabletop to clear it of crumbs and stood up. He thanked her for her time and, avoiding her eyes, left.

The whole way home, he thought about his next badminton match with his daughters and how he wouldn't let them win again. He didn't do them any favors deceiving them into thinking they were better than they actually were. God help him if they ended up man-haters like that Miss Ireland. And to think he once found her dangerously attractive. He knew she'd never warmed to him—Western women seldom did, her mother had been a rare exception—but he thought he would gradually win her over, story by story, draft by draft, check by check.

His wife had been right all along; he should have let the girls study Korean. What was Spanish going to do for them? It was bad enough they already thought in English. He sensed trouble farther down the road. Already they questioned him and disrespected him at every turn—this would mutate into hate and shame. Oh, the way they looked at him sometimes. As if he were the stupidest person in the world, put on this earth by God just to annoy and embarrass them. Clever as they were, his girls were raised wrong and there was no one to blame now but himself.

IN MR. Z'S car, a kind of off-key, weird old song played.

Trumpet and piano. Then someone singing off-tempo defiantly about "sudden cheese" and "strange foot." And blood.

Rosemary felt Mr. Z watching her from the corner of his eye.

"Like it?" he asked.

"Um . . . yeah."

"It's called 'Strange Fruit.' Know it?"

She shrugged.

"Billie Holiday."

"Oh, yeah! I've heard of him."

"Her."

Oh, hah. It was *southern breeze*, not sudden cheese . . . And it's *strange fruit* hanging, not strange foot . . . Duh.

"It's probably one of the most powerful songs of the twentieth century, and one of my personal favorites." He looked at her. "I might use it in our play. What do you think?"

"It's a cool song."

"I'll burn you a CD of it if you like."

She nodded: of freaking course, *I like*.

He stopped the car on a quiet, sloping street called Mount Curve. Rosemary and her sister often pedaled up it on their bikes, panting like dogs, then spun around and sped down without braking.

The day was overcast. Used cotton balls sequestered the shy blue sky.

"Think it's going to rain?" He pulled up the handbrake.

"It's been grey and muggy like this for days. Nice and moody. I like it."

He cleared his throat. "So, I think workshop today went great."

Funny he should have mentioned that. She was dying to ask him what the session had been all about. There was still no script and no one was part of the workshop other than the so-called male lead Arik and herself. Mr. Z spent the whole time talking about French movies and making the two of them hold hands. They were supposed to work at seeming like "a convincing couple," which she at first misheard as "a conceiving couple." She hobbled around the rehearsal room like a pregnant lady until Mr. Z asked her why she was walking so strangely.

"What do you think of Arik?" Mr. Z asked.

"He's okay." Tall, wavy brown hair, shadow 'stache, dimply like an Armenian-American Josh Hartnett. She wondered what it'd be like to lie in his fuzzy arms.

"Just okay? I know for a fact he thinks you're foxy."

Rosemary made a face. *Foxy?* What a word.

"What's the matter?" he asked. "Don't believe me?"

"Not really, no."

"I'm telling you he's really into you. It was electrifying just watching the two of you together." He looked at her. "There's nothing wrong with being foxy, you know."

She squirmed again and looked down at her hands.

"Well, I guess he *is* kind of conventionally cute."

"Finally! An opinion." He squeezed her arm. "Brava."

She smiled, turning away so he wouldn't see her blush. Her cheeks prickled. She gazed out at a short tree brimming with bright orange apricots in somebody's front yard, set against a storybook cottage painted in robin's-egg blue. She and Mira had been watching these apricots ripen in slow motion for weeks. She loved this house, always had—it stood out on a street of faux adobe-style boxes painted in various shades of taupe. Three fat crows were working on the fruit that had fallen onto the freshly mown grass. She imagined that anytime now Snow White or Grumpy or Doc would come charging out of the little house with a broom to shoo the birds away.

"What do you think of this cute little house?"

"It's, like, my favorite. Whoever lives there's probably really happy. And well-adjusted. When I was little, I used to fantasize about living there." She saw his smile and instantly felt like a moron for sharing such unguarded enthusiasm.

"Like apricots?" He called them A-pricots, like a country boy.

"Um, I guess they're okay."

"Then why don't you run out there and go grab us a couple?"

"That would totally be stealing."

"If they're on the ground, it's only looting. It's not as if any of them'll survive those crows. Better us than them, right?"

She noticed she'd been sitting on her hands and extracted them from under her thighs. They were clammy things. She looked at the house. There wasn't a car in the wisteria-wrapped carport, nor even a bike.

"Wait. Is this a dare?"

"I don't care for apricots either way. I was really just thinking of you." He shifted his eyes to the tree and then back at her. "Go for it."

She placed her fingers on the door latch. He was about to say something else when she sprang the door open and bolted across the green lawn. One crow squawked a warning to the others, and all three flapped away from the tree, apricots jammed into their beaks. The fruit was all hers now. Stretching out the front of her T-shirt like an apron, she filled it with the fuzzy little things, avoiding the mushy ones that leaked juice, yet they still stained her shirt. She turned to Mr. Z in his car and stuck out her tongue in victory. He gave her a thumbs-up, which pleased her more than she could fathom.

The next thing happened in a flash. A hairless man with beady eyes and a snarling snout leapt out of the bushes at her. All she saw were teeth. Incisors like knife blades. She sprinted, releasing fruit as she ran. When she looked back from the safety of Mr. Z's car, she saw it.

A white bull terrier on a chain, its short legs pacing the perimeter. It couldn't have gotten her, but it sure got close. She laughed hysterically. Her hands were shaking.

"Are you all right, baby?" Mr. Z caressed the back of her neck. It felt so good.

"That freaking mutt came out of nowhere!" Her fear was turning to outrage. "I lost everything!"

"Not everything." Mr. Z reached over and picked up the one apricot that had rolled down the seat, between her thighs. He brought it to her lips. When she caught her breath, she took a bite. Juice ran down his fingers. "How is it?"

"Not worth risking life and limb for."

Mr. Z took a bite of the fruit himself, then sucked at the rivulet of juice in the dell between his thumb and index finger. He smacked his lips.

"Oh, I think you're being a little hard on the poor thing."

He passed the fruit back to her and wiped his mouth on a Kleenex. With sticky fingers, he pulled down the handbrake and started steering the car with the ball of his hand. She saw now that her shirt was covered in juice splotches, evidence of her crime.

"By the way, for your future reference, that was my house," he said, grinning. "Anytime you feel like apricots, feel free to plunder. That's Constance. I promise you, she wouldn't hurt a fly."

– 8 –

TURF

"Let's take a look at the master bedroom."

The guy walked up the stairs of Raymond's house.

"So what kind of business are you in?"

"I wrote books," said Raymond. "Silly books, that people seemed to like."

"Nice work if you can get it," the guy said, and Raymond detected no sneer in there. Refreshing. The guy glanced at his clipboard. "Raymond van der Holt?"

"Yes, humbly so."

"Never heard of you. No offense."

"None taken."

The guy walked ahead of Raymond, pausing in the hallway outside the bedroom.

"May I?" Before Raymond could answer, the freckled, forty-ish guy was in his bedchamber, pulling aside the bisque-colored Thai silk drapery and poking around the casement windows. He continued counting under his breath, "Thirty-three, thirty-four . . . thirty-five," and made a note of his new tally.

"Would I really need to wire these upstairs windows?"

Raymond asked. "Those little magnetic boxes you stick on them are just so hideous."

"It's beauty or safety, take your pick," the man said. "Our boxes are highly sensitive. The alarm goes off half a second after the magnet on the window loses contact with the magnet on the frame. That's a half second faster than our leading competitor."

"I choose beauty." Raymond trailed after the guy, smoothing out his drapes.

The guy gave him an estimate for the downstairs doors and windows, and said he would include a motion detector in the entry hallway "for free." Raymond thanked him and asked to schedule an installation ASAP. They shook hands coolly, and parted.

Ever since Raymond bought his house, he'd been exposed to the world of Guys—the lawn guy, the tree guy, the drywall guy, electricians, plumbers, these very interchangeable manly men who knew how to fix things and work things, and therefore kept people who couldn't fix and work things themselves at their mercy. The Guys he employed were straightforward, hardworking, life-loving men who played with Tonka trucks as little boys and grew up knowing they wanted to tear things down, blow things up. They were the ones who caused bottlenecks on the interstate when they vegged out at the wheel, gazing at construction zones; Raymond imagined that most of them emerged from the womb operating forklifts. They made huge investments in the American dream by breeding and buying, and constituted a formidable market force that sucked up a gazillion bucks' worth of gas, porn, NASCAR tickets and freedom fries. Even their toddlers were champs—running marathons on Home Depot wall-to-wall. One could never fault these Guys for thinking that someone like Raymond, with his funny accent and Persian rugs, was phony or marginal, or a serial killer. Every TV show they watched trained them to think so. The USA was theirs and they knew it. Raymond was merely visiting until his visa expired.

As long as they did their job and charged honest rates, Raymond couldn't give a rat's ass what any of these subliterate lunkheads thought of him. He didn't even need them to like him. No, as long as his house was comfortable, and safe, he didn't care if they took their sons to the shooting range instead of the ballet. Let them get ass cancer on deep-fried pizza.

With his home security system installed, Raymond came and went with greater peace of mind. He began to enjoy locking himself in at night. It was poetry: *Armed to Stay, No Delay*. Beep-beep! The decals the security guys stuck on his windows became protective talismans, and the yard sign poking out of the flower bed was his secular crucifix.

One Saturday afternoon, he drove home from the Starbucks in a funk after reading a *New York Times* op-ed that declared American fiction dead, at least according to dwindling sales figures. The vile pundit claimed that ever since 9/11, Americans had been opting for nonfiction because they felt they needed to re-engage with the world and learn "real facts," and that literary magazines had been cutting back on fiction pages or axing them altogether to make way for CEO profiles and reportage. Well, screw them all, Raymond thought, these selfsame people would have sent Faulkner packing off to punctuation school. Even the Guys who worked on his house sought comfort in the Bible—they were not the enemies of fiction.

The true enemies of fiction were the ponderous autodidacts who tyrannized him at readings with lists of factual errors found in his books, plainspoken guardians of regional arcana out to prove him out of touch with local lore and politics. Oh, and the literal-minded boneheads who showed up just to call him an old racist and wish him dead. These were the dreamless zombies of American life he wouldn't mind seeing exterminated en masse. He was grateful he was out of the writing game—good fucking luck to those MFA-wielding kids Lena Ozova told him about. Let them cater to the capricious whims of the statistics-mad, the politically correct and the metaphor-challenged who made up the shrinking anemone once known as the American book-buying public. Good fucking luck to them.

Parking his Jaguar, he noticed pink rhododendron petals scattered across his lawn. They made a trail from the driveway to the front door. The sign from the security company had been plucked out of the flower bed and thrown facedown on the grass like aluminum roadkill. A police chopper was circling the afternoon sky. Something was definitely up down here.

He rushed into his house, power-walking to the control pad, and saw that he'd forgotten to arm the system before leaving. Fuck! He reached behind the front door for his baseball bat and moved through the house, taking practice swings, thirsting for a hit.

The downstairs was clear. Upstairs, he found no one either. Nothing.

Then the phone rang. He let it ring five, six times before succumbing to its tyranny.

"Hell-o, Dad."

Silence. The old man on another guilt trip.

"I said I would call you Sunday."

Still nothing.

"If you're not going to say anything, I'll hang up . . . I have better things to do in this life than wait for you to speak up. Are you there, old man?" He waited. "Hello-o?" The line clicked and was dead.

Rat bastard. Replacing the baseball bat, Raymond felt a queasy twinge of guilt. Perhaps he'd been too harsh. The old coot was never one to thrive under the hard talk of ultimatums. He was probably now balled up in his recliner, weeping into his shirtsleeves. Raymond caved in and called Dartmoor.

"Hello," his father answered phlegmatically.

"Dad, it's me again." Raymond put on his most contrite voice.

"Son, can I call you back later? The game's on." The TV could be heard in the background blasting some kind of live sporting event.

"No, no, don't call back. I just wanted to say . . . Well, I'm sorry for yelling at you just now."

"What?"

"When you called me."

"Why on earth would I be calling you in the middle of my game?"

"Because you have been known to act against reason."

"Did you phone me up to pick a fight?"

"No!" Raymond shook his head, cursing himself. "Forget this conversation ever happened."

"What?"

"Yes, exactly. What."

Raymond walked to the bathroom, perplexed. As he lifted the toilet seat, he noticed that he was standing in a puddle of clear liquid about two feet wide. It wasn't water from any leak—he looked up for telltale mold on the ceiling. He crumpled down on his haunches and dipped his fingers into the puddle. It was gooey, thicker than water but lighter than paste, and had a consistency close to that of Woolite.

"Goddammit." He recognized the substance. "Oh, for heaven's sake!"

He paced the living room, trying to think what he should tell the police if he called in a report. *Hey officer, there's Astroglide on my floor . . .*

Minutes later, it hit him. That was no Astroglide! How could he have forgotten? Ectoplasm. He'd written about it so much in the past. *Oh, you know, officer—it's that primordial ooze created out of moisture and dust by, well, ghosts?* Ah, but ectoplasm sounded even worse than Astroglide.

Raymond had dealt with otherworldly beings so much on the page that it never once occurred to him he might have to deal with them in life. He neither believed nor disbelieved in them. They were literary props to be exploited, as philosophy-free as piano wire or ice picks. Unless he wanted to encourage a high-maintenance relationship with this entity, he'd have to treat it like a nuisance to be evicted, like a smelly possum in the basement. The worst they could do was irritate the hell out of you with their now-you-see-me, now-you-don't routine. The main question was, why now? Why, after years of his writing stories about them, had one finally decided to make contact? What did it want?

He smiled. He was flattered by the attention.

No sooner had he finished mopping up the damp spot than the phone rang again. He felt a shiver. He let it ring a few times more. He picked it up without saying a word, and was met with the same sickly silence on the other end. Seconds later, "Raymond?"

He sighed. "Hello, Dad."

"Game over."

"What?"

"The Jayhawks won. I can talk now."

"Unfortunately, now's a bad time."

"Why is it a bad time?"

"I'm afraid I don't have an answer for that, Dad."

MR. Z TOLD Rosemary and Arik that the two of them were henceforth exempt from attending class with all the others. They could show up just for the play rehearsals—what he now called Workshop—and have that count toward a credit. They were that special. Mr. Z immersed them in European literature, showed them movies. They read the lyric poems of Rainer Maria Rilke and the medieval love letters of Abelard and Heloise, and watched films from the French New Wave like *Breathless* and *Jules et Jim*, which Mr. Z praised for their fresh, passionate naturalism. Afterward, they engaged in trust exercises that would look to any outsider like creative riffs on Twister. Workshop became to Rosemary and Arik a gateway to an earlier, more romantic world.

Mr. Z said he demanded raw honesty in his "company"—the grandiose term he used when referring to his two star pupils. His company had to be one where trust was *the* key operating principle. Nothing that happened within the Safe Room—their windowless black box studio—was to be shared with the outside world, and nothing that happened within would ever be considered weird, dumb or taboo. He said trust was so crucial in the creation of drama that it was why the Sundance Institute held its workshops for writers and directors in the isolated mountains of Utah. If the outside world was ever allowed to intrude, the magic of their Arden would be lost.

"Safety, and in particular, the safety of emotional freedom, is a very fragile thing," he said.

In this hothouse atmosphere, Rosemary found herself enjoying the company of Arik, who, beneath his rugged good looks, turned out to be a shy, oddly sensitive boy who swallowed his words. He worried excessively about his low, manly voice, yet neglected to shave off the downy Fu Manchu patches bracketing the sides of his mouth. He and Rosemary found a shared connection in the fact that they both had fatherless homes—Arik's dad had "gone out for smokes" years before. His housewife mother, who couldn't prove that she started college in Yerevan and graduated in Beirut because her papers were lost, worked as a seamstress at a dry cleaner's. They liked to say his father was dead but sightings of him continued to surface, making dignity hard; he'd be spotted buying baklava in Glendale or driving an airport taxi on the 405. Arik had an eight-year-old brother whom he both adored and abhorred; both of them were bound by embarrassment and pity for their mother, a hirsute bowling ball of a woman who pickled her own root vegetables and spoke with an impenetrable accent. Their living room, he said, was crowded with other people's suits and gowns that his mother brought home to alter while she watched Lebanese soap operas and wept.

In one of the final sessions of the summer, Mr. Z kicked Workshop up a notch. He wanted Arik and Rosemary to talk about their most private desires. Nothing would be too profane, he stressed. They must learn to channel their insecurities into narrative art.

As usual, they sat cross-legged on the floor, in a small circle facing one another. Circles represented openness and community, Mr. Z liked to say. But with just three people, the shape they formed was in fact a triangle.

Mr. Z gave Arik's shoulder an encouraging tap. "We don't judge here. We share. Now, tell us what you *want*, tell us what you *need* . . . and remember that wants and needs are two separate things."

Arik cleared his throat self-consciously and tilted his head from side to side to loosen his neck.

"I was having another one of my feuds with my mother . . ." He paused, looking sheepish.

"Feuds are fun," nodded Mr. Z. "We are nothing without conflict. Go on."

"As much as she disses my dad, I can't help but miss him," Arik mumbled. "I can't get over how somebody who seemed so normal and so there, could just disappear like that, like some kind of a ghost . . . But then I realized it's not my dad that I'm missing but, you know, like, a *conceptual* dad?" Arik found his groove and began to let go, stretching his long legs out and letting his voice rise with his emotions. "I realized that the thing I've been wanting and needing all my life is somebody who could tell me which bands were cool in the eighties and what books to read and how to dress . . . all that stuff. My dad, when he was still around, never even played catch with me, he didn't know shit about American sports . . . I *want*, I guess, a cultural dad. And I *need*, I guess, a positive male role model, someone to impose their tastes on me so I can rebel against them. Right now I have nothing to rebel against . . . My mom is fine with everything I do because she doesn't know *anything*."

When he was done, he looked at Mr. Z for approval, his Adam's apple bouncing up and down as he swallowed and waited. Mr. Z blinked slowly, then shook his head with a wry smile.

"Come on, you can't be serious," he said, not unfriendly. "*Those* are your wants and needs?"

Arik looked genuinely wounded. "Are they not good enough?"

"In this day and age, when you can get anything your heart desires, *anything*, and all you want is dear ol' Daddy?" Mr. Z laughed. "Come on, Sweet Prince. Dig deeper."

In a quiet voice, Arik said: "I thought you said there'd be no judgment in the Safe Room."

"Well," Mr. Z scratched his chin, "I'm speechless. I truly am." An unnatural pause. "What about you, Rose? What do you desire?"

Rosemary gazed downward demurely. "I think I'll take the Fifth on that."

Mr. Z looked at his two acolytes, with their lowered heads, and sighed.

"All right. I feel like I owe you both an apology. I wrongly assumed that we were more comfortable with ourselves than we are. I wrongly thought we'd get to the Truth."

"But I *was* saying the truth," Arik objected, still wounded.

Mr. Z refused to meet his eye. "Now that we've reached a certain understanding, I'd like to inform you that next week we're going to start you two kissing. That's right, each other." He caught the kids exchanging a look. "Look, we can't have star-crossed lovers in our play who, when they finally get together, only want to hold hands and listen to Coldplay. Come on, people! When real soul mates hook up, you can't tear them apart. That's how I want you two to be."

Arik reached for Rosemary's hand to show Mr. Z he'd be a good sport about it and make up for disappointing him. She didn't resist and let his clammy paw lie atop hers. A shiver of pleasure shot through her as he gently squeezed her hand, lightly running his thumb across her palm.

"That's a good start," Mr. Z nodded approvingly. "Free your mind and the rest will follow. Before you know it you'll be rimming her."

"Excuse me?" Arik dropped Rosemary's hand.

"Oh, nothing. Just a mismanaged joke. My bad judgment. I apologize." Mr. Z pointed at their hands. "Continue. Continue."

As they locked up the Safe Room and prepared to leave, Mr. Z nursed a secret smile the entire time. His jangling keys echoed as he walked the kids through the empty Arts building.

"Do you guys know the meaning of the term *terroir*?" he asked.

"You mean, like, terror?" Arik said, as if it were a trick question.

"No, terroir. It's French. It means territory or terrain, and it pertains to grapes that go into making wine. The idea is that grapes grown in one type of soil, in one location, receiving a certain amount of rain and sun, taste different than grapes of the same species that are grown in different soil, in a different location, and exposed to a different climate. It's why Cabernets from Napa taste different from Cabs from Chile, or why Rieslings from Oregon are different from Rieslings from Alsace."

Arik and Rosemary were straining to follow.

"In fact, vintners have noticed that a grape grown in one part of a vineyard could be more or less tannic than the same grape grown just two yards away."

He saw the kids exchange glances.

"You two are not oenophiles, are you?" asked Mr. Z. The two shook their heads meekly. "Ah, it's so easy to forget you're only children. But here's how terroir is relevant to you—I find myself just fascinated by the fact that you two are such prime examples of terroir as applied to human beings."

"We're like grapes?" asked Rosemary.

"Don't be obtuse. What I mean is that you are who you are because of *where* you are. For example, all things like money and genes being equal, the Rosemary Park born and bred in Seoul would taste different than the Rosemary Park we know and love who's born and bred in LA County. Similarly, the Arik Kistorian from Yerevan would be entirely different from the Arik Kistorian we know."

"Isn't that just nature versus nurture?" Arik said.

"Well, it's a bit more than that. I don't think culture is everything. Terroir also covers natural influences like sunshine and air quality. For instance, you two are gorgeous. You both have that wonderful California tan, that slouchy unformed charm—I mean it lovingly! If you two were doing manual labor in some other part of the world or had to enlist in a children's army, you wouldn't have the posture you have, your hands wouldn't be as soft as they are. In other words, you exhibit all the privileges of your terroir."

As their mentor walked ahead of them, Rosemary and Arik exchanged another uncertain look. They'd never seen Mr. Z like this, rambling on, making weird slips. But neither of them wanted to be the one to say it. And Rosemary needed to pee.

When Rosemary emerged from the building, Mr. Z was leaning against his car.

"Need a ride?" he asked. She paused, uncertain.

"*Want* a ride?" he asked. She nodded.

She watched Arik get on his bike and leave the school gates before she climbed into Mr. Z's car. He handed her a rewritable disk in a paper sleeve.

"Here's the CD I promised you. Sorry I took so long." Song titles were listed in hasty Sharpie writing that looked like chicken scratches. Somehow she'd imagined something more special, like a CD in a plastic jewel case, personalized with his doodles in three or four colors. The songs didn't remotely fill up the seventy minutes the CD could hold—there were just a couple of songs by Billie Holiday, including "Strange Fruit," and a couple of tracks by a guy called Van Morrison she'd only vaguely heard of.

"Thanks." She shoved the CD into her satchel and slumped

back, wanting him to notice her displeasure. She watched the familiar streets fly by her window.

"What do you think of Arik now?" he asked her after a while.

"I like him."

"Are you excited about kissing him?"

"Kind of."

"I thought you might be."

They sped uphill toward Santa Claus Lane. When they got to her block, he parked the car on the side of the street and undid his seat belt. He leaned across to her suddenly, and her natural mechanisms pulled her back against the window.

"No, no, don't be afraid. Don't be afraid. I just want to ask you. Was that your secret desire? To kiss him?"

"I don't know." Her voice rattled.

"Remember, now that I've unlocked your face, I can tell your every thought . . ."

She swallowed. His face was only inches from her.

"And for the record, that was a bogus story he told about wanting a dad. Which is why I gave him grief for it. I know what he really wants. He told me—it's you."

Darting forth, he pressed his lips against hers, systematically kissing her upper lip, then her lower lip. She tasted the cool mint breath strip she'd seen him place on his tongue like a communion wafer. His lips were shockingly soft. She tilted her neck back instinctively, and felt herself pinned to the seat.

"Part your lips. Just a little." He nudged his warm tongue inside her mouth, and she gasped, stunned by the urgency of his intrusion. She tried to get her own tongue out of the way but it kept rushing back to meet his. He cupped both sides of her jaw with his hands and kissed her deeper, producing the kind of sucking noises she'd heard in movies. The way he held her face, she felt she was levitating. This kissing thing . . . it almost didn't matter who was kissing her, she could do this kissing thing forever.

Slowly, one of his hands reached down her neck toward the opening of her T-shirt. And she wanted it, she wanted him to put his mouth where his hand was. And to rub his hand between her legs.

Then, he withdrew. The sudden retraction was more violent than a slap.

"Oh, I'm so sorry, Rose . . . I got carried away."

"No, don't apologize. It felt really nice." Her lips were still on fire.

"You could say I was In The Moment." He gave her a bashful schoolboy's smile, which made him seem twenty years younger. Cute. He's actually cute. He drew her hand to his crotch, and she turned her eyes away instantly. She didn't *want* to see it, yet she didn't move her hand—she *needed* to know. Her fingers felt him inside his pants, stretching the fabric taut like a dog in a snake's belly.

"Think of Arik tonight."

He started up the car and neither of them said another word.

– 9 –

ICE CREAM SOCIAL

Rosemary watched the truck pull up in front of the house.

"Get up, the man's here!" she hissed at Mira, who was flat on the sofa, gazing up at the fan like a vegetable. "I have stuff to do for school, or I would do this myself."

"I'm too hot to move," Mira moaned. "I'm completely stuck to the leather. If I move, it'll tear my skin off in one piece, I swear."

"Get up, freak, he's at our door now."

"You know that if I do this, I'm, like, aiding and abetting in our forced removal to Korea, right? Besides, I'm on my period. Cut me some slack."

The doorbell sang its tinny, electronic *Godfather* theme. As Mrs. Park's slippered feet shuffled through the house, she glared at her daughters in the living room, neither of whom had budged an inch. Rosemary pointed at Mira: "She said she'd do it."

"Thanks for nothin', sister."

Mrs. Park pulled her hair back into a severe ponytail and opened the door with the neutral, apprehensive smile she reserved for workmen and delivery people.

"Good morning, you must be Mrs. Park." The PestBusters rep was a laconic middle-aged guy in a denim shirt and faded jeans.

He had a ponytail too, longer than Mrs. Park's. "My name's Dave Keller. We spoke on the phone about the termite inspection."

"Yes. Please come in." Mrs. Park waved him in. She stared at Mira to come to her side. "My daughter, Mira. You tell everything to her."

Mira harrumphed to the doorway and shook Dave Keller's hand.

"Should I take off my shoes?"

"Nah, it's OK." Mira looked at her mother, who nodded.

"Thanks. You wouldn't have liked the smell of my socks." He followed Mira into the house. Mrs. Park shuffled along after them. "When was your last inspection?"

"Never," said Mira. "The house is crawling with all kinds of creatures."

"Nice."

Rosemary went to the stereo and set "Strange Fruit" on repeat. She turned the music up to cover the sounds of Mira leading the termite man around and Mrs. Park padding like a dog after them in her terrycloth slippers. Then she lay down on the sofa and closed her eyes. Oh, what she'd give for an iPod.

The termite guy disappeared up the black hole leading into the attic. When they failed to hear his footsteps overhead for a couple of minutes, Mrs. Park tapped Mira on the shoulder and pointed up there. She mimed drinking.

"Be patient, Ma. Let him do his job."

Mrs. Park tapped on her shoulder harder, insistent. Mira scowled at her mother, and took a couple of steps up the creaky ladder.

"Excuse me, sir? Are you all right up there? My mother doesn't want you hurting yourself on her property because she's paranoid about getting sued."

The termite man's head popped out of the hole, and both women gasped.

"Drywood termites," he said, drolly. "Looks like they've been set up here forever. They're way down at the eaves."

"Termites?" Mrs. Park covered her mouth, nausea rising.

"I can point 'em out with my flashlight if you want to climb up here."

"No, no," Mrs. Park said.

Mira interpreted: "We'll take your word for it."

"You ladies are real trusting." The termite man climbed slowly out of the hole, grunting as he lowered himself down the ladder. "You're lucky you're dealing with me. I've been in this business twenty years. There's all these fly-by-night guys out there now who'll tell ya you need to fumigate the whole place when all they've found's a fly."

Mrs. Park tapped Mira on the shoulder again, and again mimed drinking.

"Now, is she calling me a drunk?" the termite man asked. "Just kidding. I'm fine for water."

He put on a jumpsuit and over the next hour or so, poked inside the basement, inspected the garage, and scraped and tugged at the unloved toolshed in the yard. Besides termites, wasps and the endless stacks of old newspapers in the basement—"Tell your mom she really needs to move them, it's an inferno waiting to happen down there!"—he found five rodent carcasses in the crawl space under the front porch, likely the forgotten treasures of some absentminded mutt.

After everything, they stood on the porch for the debriefing. The termite man's jumpsuit had him looking like a break-dancer who'd just moonwalked through a sandstorm. He marked up a floor plan he'd drawn on the spot, labeling the areas where he'd found undesirables. There were ten spots, including an entire wall of the garage that was home to a colony of subterranean termites.

"I have to recommend you let us tent the house and the garage."

"What do you mean, tent?" Mira spoke for her mother, who looked confused.

"We'll cover the house up like a circus tent and pump it full of Vikane, which is a colorless, odorless poison that only trusted companies like ours are authorized to use. It'll blast to hell every lil' sucker living in this structure."

"So you can't just go in there and scoop them out?"

"Well, no. Termites live deep underground. You got to think of them as Al Qaeda sleeper cells, know what I mean? They're just sitting there quietly, then one day you wake up and find your whole house collapsed on top of you." He folded his arms gravely. "What you want to do is introduce poison into the bowels of the house, using those tunnels that they've dug. You can kill as many termites as you want but it ain't over till you get down to the queen. And I know the analogy's a little corny but you have to think of the queen as the Osama bin Laden of termites."

"Somehow I could tell that was coming."

The man handed his clipboard over to Mrs. Park. The figure he put down was something even she could read: $4,600.

"Oh! Very expensive!" Mrs. Park shook her head in disbelief.

"Well, if you're planning to sell, I don't see what choice you've got. The buyer will bring in their own termite guy, and once they see what you've got here, the deal's going to fall through. I see it happen all the time. I assure you, not a happy thing."

Mrs. Park moved her lips while she did the silent math in her head, gravitating to her own corner.

"I know what we do may look invisible to you but it's all about vigilance," the termite man whispered to Mira. "Success to us means nothing happens." He paced the porch, caressing and knocking on the support beams. Mira shadowed him.

"Good, solid wood." He shook his head. "Houses built these days look like they came out of a box from IKEA. A little shake and down they go."

Mrs. Park returned, smiling graciously.

"We think about this. We call you later, okay?" She gripped Mira's shoulder, pulling her away from the man.

"Fine by me. But the longer we wait, the greater the damage." He winked at Mira, cueing her to talk sense into her mother. "Is it okay if I wash my hands?"

Mrs. Park led him back into the kitchen. They passed Rosemary sprawled on the sofa, listening to the loop of "Strange Fruit." While the man washed his hands, Mrs. Park fluttered back to the living room and slapped Rosemary's bare thigh.

"Rosie!" she hissed. Rosemary opened her eyes and saw her mother gesticulating: her shorts! They had ridden up her thigh and part of her butt was exposed.

The termite man came back through the living room with clean hands.

"That's a great song," he said to Rosemary.

"Yeah, it's really poetic."

"A little creepy don't you find, though?"

"How do you mean?" She tugged at the hems of her shorts.

"Black bodies hanging from the trees? Are you hearing the same song I am?"

"Well, yeah . . . It's a song about strange fruit . . ."

The termite man smiled for the first time.

"It's about lynching, honey."

MIRA DARTED OUT the door after her sister. Rosemary was already on her bike.

"Where are you going?" Mira called. "Wait for me, I want to come."

The evenings were getting shorter again, even if the days were still hot and stubborn with summer. Sprinklers seemed to be running on every yard on the block except theirs.

Mira cajoled her bike out of the garage and pedaled after Rosemary.

"What's your hurry, Stinko?"

"You're the one who wanted to come! I didn't invite you."

They biked uphill fast. Rosemary was making for Mount Curve.

"Slow down, jerk!" Mira called after her.

"Just go home!"

"Don't you want to know what the termite man had to say?"

"I don't give a fuck what he had to say!"

Rosemary stopped outside the blue cottage with the apricot tree, Mr. Z's house. Mira slowed down and stopped as well, panting. She got off her bike and turned it so it faced downhill, in the ritualistic way they'd done for years.

"Wanna race?" Mira asked. No answer from Rosemary, who was busy gazing at the cottage from where they stood. There was a new-looking silver Ford Taurus in the carport; Mr. Z's Nissan wasn't there. The apricots were all gone, and the white dog was dozing, half-concealed by shrubbery.

"Hell-o?" Mira flapped her arms wildly. "Why are you staring at that house?"

The curtains in the blue cottage were partially open and they could see that the house was bathed in the warm glow of lamp-light. The aroma of home cooking—roast chicken?—was in the air, full of warm, garlicky goodness. Somebody turned the chandelier on in what must have been the dining room. Rosemary caught a glimpse of her—a svelte Indian lady in a silk floral blouse, perhaps in her mid-thirties. She was carrying a small vase of roses, and they looked fresh; she leaned forward to put them down on the dining table. Rosemary couldn't see if she wore a ring but had to assume that this woman was Mrs. Z. She hadn't expected Mr. Z's wife to be anything but a generic white girl who'd loaf around in an old college sweatshirt and elastic-waist pants as soon as she got home from work, yet here she was—Mrs. Z. Elegant, exotic, gorgeous. Her hips got to meet his, night after night after night. This was the woman he chose.

Mira tinkled the bell on her bike several times.

"Shut up! What are you doing?" Rosemary shot daggers at her.

"I've been talking at you for, like, five minutes . . . You're scaring me. Why are you acting like some Peeping Tom?"

"I think it's a really cool house." Rosemary sounded a little wistful.

"We've been by here like a million times, and you never even noticed it before."

"Yes, I have."

"No, you so haven't. So . . . do you want to race or not?"

"Not."

"God, then why did you even come here?"

Rosemary got back on her bike dully.

"Where are you going now?" asked Mira. "I want to tell you my termite plan."

"Stop tailing me!" Rosemary rode downhill for a block, then swiftly swerved left and sped along one of the tree-lined cross streets that would take her east, toward the Armenian neighborhood.

Mira felt intensely alone. She looked at the blue cottage. Her sister was right—it *was* cool. It was perfect. She wanted to live there. The dinner smells made her stomach rumble. Buttery mashed potatoes. Roast chicken. Love and protein.

A silver Mercedes slowed down as it approached Mira and her bike, flashing its headlights at her in friendly warning. It turned into the driveway and parked snugly behind the Ford Taurus, as if the driveway had been constructed to accommodate those two cars exactly.

The back doors popped open and two little mocha-skinned girls, about seven years old, maybe twins, climbed out of the car. At the same time, the front door of the house opened, and the Indian woman in the silk blouse stepped out. The girls squealed "Mommy!" and ran into her arms. The white bull terrier woke up to bark a hearty welcome. Finally, the driver of the Mercedes emerged. He was a silver-bearded Sikh who looked like a surgeon or a psychiatrist, a specialist in any case who was senior enough to wear his turban to work. He locked the doors of his vehicle with a beep before strolling into the house. The pretty mother of the girls greeted him with a peck on the cheek.

Just before the front door of the house closed, Mira saw the man turn his head and throw her a suspicious glare. He had every right to do it. She was a total stranger standing on his sidewalk, staking out his family under the darkening sky. The curtains on all their windows pulled shut, one by one by one.

ROSEMARY SLOWED DOWN when she hit the block where she supposed Arik lived. She didn't know his exact address, except that he had mentioned two walking-distance landmarks: Sam's Dry Cleaning, where his mother worked, and Dominic's, the pizzeria where he often grabbed a slice.

The houses on his street were small, modest, Spanish-style bungalows painted in innocuous shades. In the twilight, she couldn't make out if a house was orange or pink—he'd said his was a ghastly salmon. Everything blurred into one big gray area. She walked her bike past the houses, narrowing down what might have been Arik's to about four or five, based on details he'd mentioned—disheveled camellia bush, dried-up lawn, his mother's garish taste in curtains. Then it got too dark to see anything, and invisible dogs started growling and barking wherever she walked.

She got back on her bike and cycled home.

ROSEMARY AND MIRA hid in their rooms while the Korean realtor lady visited again. She'd been over for tea twice in the past week, talking like a foghorn, flashing her crimson nails. She wore short skirts and really high heels, and because of her flat, angular build, she looked to the girls like a man in drag. Her business card had become a fixture on their fridge, pinned under a Hello Kitty magnet: QUELLIE SOO, LICENSED REALTOR, TIP TOP ESTATES (EAST DIVISION).

She worked Mrs. Park hard, impressing her by throwing into her Korean some awkwardly formal English: *I tell you, isn't that something? To see it is to believe it, believe you me.* The girls had never seen their mother join so agreeably into conversation, and for hours at a time. Together the realtor and Mrs. Park nibbled all afternoon on kimchi, chestnuts and seaweed crackers, gulping down liters of tea brewed from expired corn. Sometimes, the lady brought over snacks made from red bean paste and Mrs. Park would whoop with joy. Today, she made Mrs. Park clap like a circus seal when she showed up with a Styrofoam box of gummy dill dumplings.

Mira barged into Rosemary's room. "Everything about her is so fake," she said. "What if Ma's being had?"

"Whatever, I don't care." Rosemary turned back to her library book on Pre-Raphaelite painters. Her sister snatched it from her.

"John Everett Millais. Is he famous?" Mira flipped through the book, seeing pages upon pages of auburn-haired maidens dancing in forests, kissing knights, floating still on top of lakes. "He's got three names. Just like a serial killer."

"Give it back. It's for Workshop."

"Are you studying to be, like, a waitress at Medieval Times?"

"No."

"Please, Rosie, tell me you're not going to start wearing those puffy Ren fair dresses like all the chubby Goths at school."

"Shut up."

"Please don't become a chubby Goth, Rosie."

"Go away."

"I haven't told you about my termite plan yet." Mira bounced on the bed. "House-buyers hate termites, right? And termites *love* stinky, damp places. So I was thinking if we flooded the basement and attic with our pee, we'll start, like, a super infestation, then Ma won't be able to sell the house. And, though we'll have an incredibly stinky house, we won't have to go. End of story." She beamed.

"Of all the stupid things you've ever said, *that* is the *stupidest* I've ever heard."

Mira sat catatonic, disbelieving, for a minute. Then she bolted.

Meanwhile, in the living room, Quellie Soo was explaining the concept of "staging." In order to have a successful open house, Mrs. Park needed to "stage" the event, to give the buyer the impression that they'd stumbled onto a happy place inhabited by happy people. For that to work, Mrs. Park couldn't have their furniture and effects packed up or shipped away just yet—the house had to look lived in, as if its owners had simply stepped out for a pint of milk for the cat. Vacation photos in gold frames, Quellie said, were key to a smooth sale. New curtains and paint, too. Mrs. Park had to consider making these upgrades because too many flaws were visible; there was no way they could show the house in its current state.

When she saw Mrs. Park sinking into another one of her cushion-clutching internal monologues, Quellie formulated an economical alternative to reel her back: sell the house at Christmas, when the trees on Santa Claus Lane would be all lit up. The spirit of goodwill might make buyers overlook its flaws. As she left, she implored Mrs. Park again to get the house fumigated. She knew it was the $4,600 fee that was holding her back.

"Sell the car, my dear," Quellie said in English, and left for her next appointment.

AT DAWN, MIRA popped out of bed and crept barefoot out of her bedroom holding a plastic yogurt cup filled with her own piss. She flicked on the light to the basement and, wearing her mother's slippers because her own were too precious, ran down the steps into the musty underground, trying not to giggle.

The air was freezing down there. It was a real dump, all germs and cobwebs. The termite guy had been right—it *was* a firetrap, filled with Korean newspapers from the Neolithic Age. And cans of paint with their lids sealed with rust. And old flashlight batteries. And—could this actually be?—that decrepit Big Bird doll encrusted with her baby puke. Unbelievable!

Mira doused the crawl space just under the wooden floorboards of the kitchen with the piss, careful not to get any on her clothes or skin. When she was done, she pulled down her pants and squeezed out more pee on a stack of vintage newspapers. She looked at them for a second.

Shit! The one on top showed the Twin Towers under attack— she could have auctioned it off on eBay. Oh well, too late now! She doused the burning towers with more pee, and cackled.

The door to the basement slammed shut. She stifled her instinct to scream. Very carefully, she crept up the steps, turned the doorknob, and peered out.

"Rosie?" she whispered. "That you?"

The kitchen was empty. The big-faced clock ticked. It was six-fifteen.

She emerged from the steps to peer into the adjoining hallway where her sister could have been hiding. Nobody. Everything was still. All the windows were shut. There wasn't a stray breeze in the entire house.

A wide smile broke across Mira's face. She knew. She knew. It was one of those supernatural beings she'd been trying to call up. A poltergeist.

Finally! What took you so long? She went back down to the basement, and waved in her unseen accomplice. *Don't just stand there like an idiot. Come, help me.*

THE THERMOSTAT READ ninety-five. Mrs. Park's head lay on the dining table as the slow blades of the ceiling fan massaged the still air above. Her sweat-soaked hair spilled across the vinyl place mat, a sickly black mop covering her eyes. Her shoulders heaved with REM breathing and her arms hung down at her sides, two meaty plumb lines.

This is what Ma would look like dead, Rosemary thought gloomily. She plucked the cordless out of its cradle and took it back to her room.

"Hello?" Arik picked up, sounding groggy.

"Hi. It's me, Rosemary Park. If this is a bad time, I'll hang up."

"No, no, it's fine. I was just . . . I must have fallen asleep without realizing it, on the couch."

"That's crazy! My mother's asleep at the dining table."

"No way. My mother's sleeping, too, in her chair! And so's my little brother. They're both asleep in the middle of the freakin' afternoon. And the whole place smells like kerosene from her dry-cleaning shit."

"Oh, wow!" Rosemary laughed. "It's like a sleeping virus! Wouldn't it be funny if, like, we walked outside and found that every single person was asleep except for us?"

They both laughed quietly.

"I'm so glad you called," Arik finally said. "You wanna hang out?"

"Yeah. Yeah. Totally."

"Like, now?"

"Sure."

Rosemary walked into the Rite Aid after locking her bike and checking her underarms for BO. She was instantly greeted by Arik, who was standing by the tower of blue shopping baskets and holding two ice cream cones—Rocky Road and strawberry cheesecake—already melting despite the profuse AC.

"Hey!" He handed her the strawberry cheesecake. He just knew. "There was a clerk at the ice-cream counter. It almost never happens, so I went for it."

"Thanks," Rosemary blushed, in spite of herself, and reached for her wallet.

"No, no. It's on me," Arik grinned. She noticed that he'd shaved off his Fu Manchu patches.

They walked through the store, licking their cones. Arik gave her a smile as they passed the eye-level display of Preparation H suppositories. "My mom uses that stuff."

He looked irresistible in his Green Day T-shirt and the cargo shorts that ended high enough to showcase his down-covered calves. She'd touched those legs doing various exercises in Workshop but never socially. The back of his T-shirt was sweat-dappled and stuck to him.

At the freezers in the back of the store, they pressed their backs against the cold glass doors and sighed in unison.

"Aisle seven, by the lozenges," Arik muttered, talking through one side of his mouth. "Toupee alert!"

Rosemary spotted the old guy in a cheap golf shirt wearing a lopsided hairpiece. She giggled.

"World's fattest Ethiopian," Rosemary said, tipping her chin at an anorectic lady squinting at vitamins through bifocals.

"World's skinniest Iowan." Arik arched an eyebrow toward an obese woman, who was panting as she struggled to take two steps in her walking frame.

"*Planet of the Apes.*" Rosemary directed her elbow at the bearded Armenian gent circling the painkillers aisle, graying chest hair popping out of his singlet.

"Watch it, you're talking about my people here!" Arik laughed. He stretched out his fur-lined arm for Rosemary. "I'm getting there myself. It's my genetic destiny to turn into a werewolf."

Rosemary resisted the temptation to stroke his arm like it was some sort of cute hairy pet. "An Ewok, maybe."

They held their gaze for a moment, then Arik turned away, blushing.

"Hey, look, an old dude flirting with the male pharmacist," he said. "Well, I suppose it *does* say pick-up window."

Rosemary craned her neck to see the in-store pharmacy, and gasped. "Oh, my God, that's my neighbor!"

"You're kidding, right? The old dude or the pharmacist?"

"The old dude. He lives next door to me. He's, like, a famous writer. Raymond Van Pelt."

"Never heard of him."

"I've never read his stuff either. He's very early-nineties. Genre, but supposedly ironic."

"I hate irony!"

"I know. Me too!"

They watched Raymond sign for his prescription, take the little paper bag, and bid goodbye to the young pharmacist. Rosemary hadn't seen him in the wild—he actually looked kind of happy, kind of handsome, kind of youthful, a completely different person than the grump-a-lumps she knew, perpetually engaged in a muttering argument with himself. She'd never noticed his feet before either, and saw that he wore green loafers made of swank crocodile leather. He was possibly the only person in the history of Rite Aid who wasn't shopping in footwear assembled by Indonesian child slaves.

"I bet it's Viagra." Arik crunched down on the last of his cake cone. His fuzzy arm brushed against Rosemary's but neither of them budged.

"He's too old to have sex, probably." The little hairs on her arm stood up. Arik was so close. So close.

"I don't think that's necessarily true." Arik grabbed her hand and suddenly lunged forward and kissed her on the lips. His lips were cold and soft from the ice cream. She kissed him back, parting her lips slightly as she had done with Mr. Z. Their tongues clashed and he moved his body over hers, pressing her against the icy door of the freezer. Her hands reached instinctively for his lower back.

He forged ahead with the confidence of someone who'd spent hours practicing on his inner elbow. She felt her lips plump up and every touch from him became a shivery thrill. He moved one of his hands under her T-shirt to grab her waist. The freezing glass against her back and Arik's burning body on her front put her in a contrapuntal dream state—cold, hot, cold, hot. She allowed herself to drown. Arik K., the guy she'd been secretly staring at for a whole year, was kissing her, for real.

Finally, they had to break for air. They looked at each other guiltily, with bedroom eyes and bashful smiles. Their lips were rimmed pink with light abrasions.

Arik put his hands on the small of her back and reeled her in for another kiss. Another wave of desire washed through her and she closed her eyes. "I feel like we're invisible," she said. "And inaudible."

This time, she clasped her hands behind his neck. She was surprised by how smoothly everything came to her, and his reactions were just as natural. She sucked on his tongue; he responded by thrusting it deeper into her mouth. He pushed his lower torso toward her and, meeting with no resistance, rubbed himself against her, following whatever rhythm felt good to him.

A man cleared his throat near them.

"Excuse me, lovebirds," he said. They unglued their faces, dazed. It was a portly African American in a Dodgers jersey. "Could you both just scooch over a little. I need to get to my ice cubes."

"Sorry, sir," Arik said, still hugging Rosemary as they moved aside.

"Don't you apologize, son," the man said. He reached into the freezer and grabbed two large bags of ice. "Lord knows I wish I had your youth. Carry on." He winked at the two of them, then waddled off, a bag balanced in each arm.

Arik released himself from Rosemary and pressed his front against the cold freezer door, throwing her the goofiest, straight-from-the-heart smile.

"Shall we get out of here?"

She kissed him, and they ran.

The heat outside greeted them like an old friend. Arik grabbed Rosemary's hand and led her to the back of the Rite Aid. Wordlessly, in the shade of the loading area, they wrapped themselves in each other. Arik pinned her against the wall and continued to rub his groin against her as they kissed. Heat rose from the concrete, and they were very quickly slick with sweat.

"I hope . . . this isn't bothering you."

He moved her hand to the front of his pants. *There it is*, she thought, *there it is*. It was like Mr. Z's, only more pronounced. She didn't know if she should rub her palm over the bulge, or fondle it, or what.

"I want you to touch me, Rose," he whispered into her ear so it tickled. "And I want to touch you."

His hand moved inside her shorts and she hoped she wasn't too sweaty and gross between her legs. He leaned into her, breathing with his mouth, breaking into a smile whenever their eyes met. She unzipped her shorts and helped his hand slide under her panties. She felt his fingertips move gently, anxiously, down her crotch, startled at first by the prickly forest of pubic hair, then venturing on. It felt so good to have somebody else's fingers in there instead of her own, and she tried to concentrate on being the recipient of this pleasure. But she kept pulling herself out of the moment—she was curious, she wanted to watch.

Arik squeezed his eyes shut, his mouth forming an *o* as he found the valley between her thighs and dipped two fingers into the thick, warm wetness awaiting him.

"Oh my God," he panted. "You feel like the inside of a jack-o'-lantern!"

Rosemary whimpered as he moved his fingers in and out of her. She wanted to come. He thrust his tongue inside her mouth for a deep, long kiss, then quite suddenly withdrew both it and his hand. He looked like he was choking.

"Fuck, Arik, are you okay?"

"Oh my God, oh my God!" he gasped, even more shocked than she was. He pushed her away roughly and opened up his pants. Immediately his cock popped out like a long, pink ax handle. It was bigger than she expected, the tip of it made her think of a Pink Pearl eraser. As soon as he grabbed it, thick white liquid shot out of its head. Rosemary jumped away just in time so the projectile missed her and struck the wall.

Arik propped himself up against the wall with his free hand, and Rosemary watched him twitch uncontrollably with his eyes pressed shut until all the milky streaks drained out of him. She tried to contain her horror.

When he was done, Arik stole sheepish glances at her, still panting. His face was red. There were a couple of white Pollocky splats on the wall and she could tell these would quickly get dry and crusted in the sun. He tucked his cock back into his pants and buttoned up. The bulge was still there, but modest.

"God . . . I hope you're not totally grossed out."

She kissed him tenderly on the lips and put her head on his chest so he couldn't see her face. Listening to his pounding heart, she stole glances at his placid, sated face and then down at his pants. The bulge was gone.

MIRA SAT AT the wheel of the sweltering car, mime-driving. From the handbook, she now knew where every control was, from the hazard lights to the wiper, and in theory could back the car out of the driveway without running anyone over. In theory, she could zoom off, if only Rosie would tell her where she'd hidden the keys. She'd drive to San Francisco, then on to Portland and across the border to be a fugitive in Canada, where she'd trade in the Camry for a hybrid and live amongst the multiethnic street punks of British Columbia.

In the rearview mirror, she glimpsed a man in a hooded sweater standing on the porch of the darkened house across the street, the Ireland house, peering through its windows. He was nobody she recognized and from where she was, it was hard to describe him beyond adult male, darkly Caucasian. The lack of details frustrated her: she made a ritual of memorizing faces in case she was ever invited to point someone out in a lineup. At dusk, everything and everyone looked as hazy as a gas station surveillance tape.

The man looked at his watch, rapped on the door, rang the bell several times, waited for a response and got none. That solitary Kate woman clearly wasn't in. Her car wasn't in the driveway and none of the house lights were even on. The man walked down the front steps and disappeared around the side of the house. He was probably one of those hoodie burglars! Mira kept a close watch through the rearview mirror, expecting him to reappear at any second with a sack of jewelry or a flat-screen TV. Then she'd bust him.

Her foot pumped the accelerator anxiously, and in her mind she plotted out the quickest route to the phone and what she would say to the cops. Where were those stupid police choppers now that she needed them?

RAT-a-tat! Knuckles on the passenger window.

It was him! Her mind went blank, her amazing improv abilities lost to panic. He started walking over to the driver's side, her side. She shut her door and locked it.

"Hi there?" the man said. He sounded muffled on the other side of the glass. "Can I talk to you for a second?"

She said nothing and just stared at his face, which seemed so ordinary that it defied description. Brownish hair. Gray hoodie. The big arms of somebody who owned a gym membership. He knocked on her window again, more softly this time.

"Do you speak English?"

She nodded, keenly insulted.

"Mind rolling down your window? I want to talk to you."

She thought it over. He looked harmless enough, and besides, if he tried anything, she could sound the horn and her mother or Rosie would come running. She lowered the window. He casually reached in, unlocked her door and pulled it open. Now he saw her legs; she saw his.

"What were you doing in there?" The man seemed to find her very amusing.

"I'm a ghost."

"That's right. You really scare me."

He leaned into the car and she steadied her palm on the horn, ready to hit it if he came any closer.

"Listen, I need to ask you a favor. You know that lady across the street?"

She shrugged.

"You know when she'll be home?"

She shrugged.

"Hey, I thought you were a ghost. Shouldn't you know everything?"

She shrugged.

"Well, would you pass her a message from me?"

Again, she shrugged.

"Now come on, Ghost. This is real important. I'm an old, old friend of hers. Would you tell her Bluto was here and that I'll be back soon? Could you do that for me?"

She wavered, then nodded slowly.

"Thanks a million, Ghost. I owe you one."

"Wait." She frowned. "Bluto's the name of her dog though."

"Is that what she told you?" He smirked to himself and started to walk away. Suddenly, he whipped back, and she returned her hand to the horn.

"Is she out a lot?"

"I dunno. For a pregnant lady, maybe."

Her words brought a perplexed expression to his face. Slowly this morphed into the delighted smile of a man who'd just won some bet. He gazed up at the full moon and for a moment Mira thought he was going to bay.

"I'll be seeing ya, my pretty little Ghost."

The man retreated. The term *pretty* gave her goosebumps. What did he mean by that? Was he being sarcastic or what? Mira watched him disappear into a safe distance before she climbed out of the car and dashed into the house.

THE MOMENT KATE pulled into her driveway, she saw in her rearview mirror the figure of a girl running madly toward her out of the dark. She froze and locked her doors. When the girl came closer, she rolled down her window.

It was just one of the Park girls. "Hi there?"

A chill shot down Mira's spine. Kate and the man who was looking for her said those exact words with the exact same questioning lilt.

"A man came for you," Mira said. "He says his name's Bluto, like your dog. He says he'll be back."

"Oh? Thank you." Kate conjured up a pained smile. She was reacting so stiffly that Mira half expected her to reach into her purse for a tip. Then came a look of barely concealed anxiety. "If that man ever tries to approach you again, you should run."

"Run?"

"Yes, the act of departing quickly. He's not someone you want to get mixed up with . . . He's got a history."

"History?"

"Yes, things that happened in the past."

UNLOCKING THE FRONT door, Kate's hands rattled. Bluto had stepped into her flower bed and brought topsoil to her welcome mat. What did he want?

A chopper rumbled its approach overhead. They made her jumpy, these airborne invaders. They were so loud, yet seemed so passive-aggressive. Couldn't they just come out and say what they wanted instead of all this noisy intimation? She slipped into her house and shut the door. A second later, she popped her head out, scanned the street, and with a swift tug, pulled the welcome mat inside.

THE FULL, LATE-AUGUST moon shone on Arik like a spotlight, and he was paranoid someone might see him standing outside Rosemary's house and take him for a burglar. All those choppers were still flying by randomly, looking for Al Qaeda operatives.

"I can't get this thing off," he whispered, tugging at the bug screen in her window. "It's nailed to the freakin' frame. What should we do?" He swiveled around nervously for police cruisers. "I feel really exposed out here."

Abruptly her room light went off. Now Arik couldn't see her

at all. He cupped his hands on the sides of his eyes and pressed them against the screen.

"Rose? You there? What're you doing?"

Then slowly, as his eyes got used to the darkness, he got his answer. She was undressing, methodically and completely. Her shirt came off first, then her shorts. She did a 360-degree spin before she removed her bra and finally her panties. She did this simply and without Mata Hari flair, but it was plenty.

"Oh God, Rose, please don't do that!"

She came to the window and pressed her body against the screen to let him feel her breasts through the mesh.

"Your nipples are hard," he gasped. "God, you're so hot!"

He pressed his face on the screen so his cheek rubbed against her chest, but the mesh in between scratched and scraped at both of them. When he pulled away, Rosemary saw pink crosshatches on his flesh. He lunged back to kiss her breast almost immediately, glistening wet tongue lashing at the screen.

"You taste like metal." He laughed, frustrated. "God, I want to be inside . . ."

"I want you in here, too."

She lowered her hand to her inner thigh and started touching herself. They both heard the moist, sucking sounds this made and Arik sighed with increasing torment. Her flesh looked so grabbable, so bitable.

"Christ, Rose, I need to be inside *you!*"

"I have to get back to my bed, okay? I can't come standing up." She moved onto her bed a few feet away, and switched on her Jesus night-light so he could see her.

"You're driving me crazy, Rose! I am so hard right now. I want to"—he lowered his voice to a whisper—"plunge my cock deep inside you and fuck you so hard."

Rosemary was deep in her own universe, her eyes half-open and looking at him with a dreamy expression. Her fingers were glistening with her own juice, juice produced for him, just for *him*. He *had* to know what she tasted like, God! He rubbed his face on the screen, the smell and taste of rust and dust suddenly sexy.

"Rose," he moaned, unzipping his fly. "I want to hold you down and push my tongue inside you. I want to tongue-fuck you till you come and come . . ."

His incantation worked. She closed her eyes and arched her back. Her legs began to thrash. From the Internet porn he'd seen, he knew this to be a good thing; yet live, right in front of him, it was a different matter. He was terrified by Rosemary's private epileptic trance. He was completely cut out of it.

Rosemary stifled her scream with her free hand. She bit into her fingers and her face scrunched up. Her torso trembled in waves—intense, protracted quakes as she curved her back some more, her fingers still thrusting, then she writhed with shorter, shallower aftershocks. Her eyes popped open and she gasped jaggedly for air, like someone dying. In seconds, her body went limp and she smiled at Arik like a docile doe.

"That's just my first one," she murmured. "I can go on and on and on . . ."

Out of nowhere came the grumbling buzz of a chopper. The ferocity of its approach suggested it had found its target.

In the racket, she thought she heard Arik say "I love you," but couldn't be sure. Whatever he said, Arik was gone. She listened as the chopper whipped over her roof and up the hill toward the mountains.

First thing next morning, she slipped outdoors. The crusty, yellowish streaks she found below her window made her feel warm and fuzzy, and yes, loved.

THE SICK ROSE

Mary-Sue had come a long way since the days she dreamt of outrunning the world on a pogo stick and flipping off her legions of doubters. She knew people still flung adjectives like "kooky," "screwy" and "desperate" behind her back—but she learned to put her fists away. Over the years, this tolerance evolved into indifference, and as she stopped fighting back, she stopped hurting.

She grew to like her own company. It wasn't the kind of loneliness she had experienced among the ascetics in Humboldt long ago, but the solitude of voluntary singlehood. Any non-asshole who entered into her orbit was gravy. After all, you could buy single-serving frozen pizzas these days, with all kinds of toppings. If she wanted to dine out, there was no dread in it; no longer did waiters throw pitiful looks at lone women. She always tipped well. There were also things called DVDs if she didn't feel like going to an R-rated movie by herself.

Florida suited her. She was glad she had the opportunity to discover this for herself. It wasn't only the immigrants and migrants, she realized, who roamed around America looking for a place to call home, it was everybody. And it was this restless wandering, this endless self-creation, that made this country dynamite. The alternative, she supposed, was to calcify into some kind of stupefied Amish tree stump, doomed to have happiness motor right by.

At sixty-six, after the end of what had admittedly been an abnormally long adolescence, Mary-Sue emerged a confident, independent woman. She might have been alone but she was no longer lonely. Her dear Kate still meant the world to her, of course, but as hard as it was at first to accept, it was healthier for them to be apart—Kate was probably happier, too, without her hanging around. Whoever said no man was an island obviously wasn't speaking about women. Women were superb at being by themselves . . .

FORGETTING TO RETURN a phone call wouldn't have been strange for most people, but this was Mary-Sue, who, whenever Kate called, always sounded like she'd leapt for the phone from a hundred yards away.

Scenarios ran through Kate's head, all unpleasant: Mary-Sue, her hip broken on those slippery back porch steps, writhing in pain as raccoons came by and mauled her; rifle-toting Cuban bandits making her compound the base camp for their drug-smuggling empire; migrant-worker thieves who, when caught climbing in the window by Mary-Sue, hacked her head off in cold blood. The world being what it was, even the prosaic worries were wearisome—coyotes, whiplash, twisters, aneurysms. Could she have been planning an expedition, an elopement or a suicide?

It wouldn't have been out of character for Mary-Sue to slip, unannounced, out of this world. Kate was well acquainted with the cussed, childish way her mother insisted on crafting her own fate and woe betide anyone who got in the way of her narrative. She'd never consulted Kate on the move to Florida—she said she was going off on a vacation, then came back announcing she'd bought a house—as if this secrecy proved what a great captain of her own destiny she was. As if Kate was the jailer she'd been patiently plotting to escape for years.

Kate hadn't slept in days—she'd lie like a beached whale watching *Conan*, waiting with clenched jaws for the Lunesta to kick in. Two hours later, still quite alert and surfing the movie channels for anything that wasn't vile or stupid, she'd pop an Ambien. She was lucky if, at five, she'd catch an hour or two of dreamless Zs.

And then there was Bluto's return. Why couldn't he just leave a message on her voicemail, like any other regular person? Had he come back to kiss her or kill her?

She was keeping the baby. Somewhere along the way, she'd made her decision without even fully registering that she'd done it. By not doing anything about it, she supposed. Having the baby would be a turning point in her life. It would reorient her after all those years of feeling out of whack. It would be, in a word, redemption. She'd guard this redemption fiercely—Bluto would have *nothing* to do with it.

But she had yet to break the news to Mary-Sue.

After a full week with no word from her mother, Kate felt it was time to take action. She tried to recall the name of Mary-Sue's Bible-nut neighbor whose backyard was sinking into the Everglades. Larry something. Or was it even Larry? She should have paid closer attention; even a lousy parent would have casually noted the name of her child's playmate. Now there was absolutely nobody she could call to drive by her mother's house to see if things were all right. She tried the local sheriff's department but was put on hold for so long that both times the line went dead.

The next morning, she was on a plane to Miami. In the air, with nothing else she could do, she kicked off her shoes and took a nap against the window—her first unfettered sleep in days. She woke up when the plane touched down at Miami International, a low-key airport that made her think of the shopping malls built in the eighties, when land was infinite. She bought herself a shot of Cuban coffee from a cart strung with plastic bananas, and roused herself. The West Indian coffee lady gave her a genuine smile, full of Caribbean hospitality, a far cry from the resentful scowls of the vendors at LAX who made her feel bad when all she wanted to do was overpay for bottled water.

"Take care, sweetie," the lady said as Kate tottered away.

The rental car clerk gave her a complimentary upgrade and handed her the keys to a Lincoln Town Car for no apparent reason. It was only when she got out to the car and saw her own reflection in its polished black doors that she realized why everybody had been so nice. It wasn't that Florida loved its tourists better, it was that she was a woman with a five-month baby bump who was traveling unassisted and looking completely exhausted, overwhelmed, lost. Those fanny packs under her eyes. She was supposed to be radiant.

Within an hour, Kate found herself effortlessly steering through the flat grids of avocado groves in Mary-Sue's neck of Homestead. The sultry, subtropical air flooded the car's interior as soon as she rolled down her window, and condensation bloomed on every surface. The steering wheel instantly went damp. This was air so loafy it would prop her up if she fell asleep standing. And she did very much feel like sleeping.

She drove up Mary-Sue's long driveway and parked beneath the palm-lined porte cochere. With the right owner, this plantation-style villa could have been the kind of Southern colony where crazy old widows lived with their hundred cats and washed their woes down with moonshine. It was no place for any civilized woman to be living by her lonesome. She got out of the Town Car just as a symphony of insects was starting up.

Mary-Sue's car wasn't there. But there were no stacks of mail or newspapers piled at her door either, and those were the things Kate had been most afraid of finding, ahead of the decomposing body. From the doorstep, she smelled no scent of rot from within; through the windows, the rooms looked undisturbed. A couple of lamps had been left on; perhaps her mother had simply gone to the store and would return anytime.

As she walked back to her car, she saw the outline of someone lumbering up the driveway with a Quasimodo limp. He was short, with a wide barrel-chest and arms that hung low on his sides; this was either an orangutan or a backwoods boogeyman come to gnaw at her flesh.

"Howdy!" he thundered. He carried a flashlight and beamed it up at his own face, ghost-story style. The shadows didn't do his features any favors—with his beaky nose and slab of a forehead, he was a gargoyle prized off the Haunted Mansion at Disney.

"I didn't mean to scare ya," he said, closing in on her. He was a gray-haired guy in a Buccaneers T-shirt so long you couldn't see his shorts. "I'm Larry, your momma's neighbor from next door. You came to visit with my sinkholes the other day, remember?" He reached out to shake her hand. "Katie—that right?"

She nodded, relieved. "Yes, that's right. Hi there?"

"I saw your car drivin' by, and took it for a hearse. Darn near leapt out of my skin!" He chuckled. "So I strolled over to see what the matter was."

"Where's . . . do you happen to know where my mother is?"

His smile weakened. "I'll take you to her." He gestured for her to follow him. "Come. We'll hop into my wagon."

Kate trailed after him—he was a fast walker in spite of his limp. With the butt of his flashlight he struck random bushes, warning off snakes, critters, maybe even alligators. Bugs blew out of there like dust off a beaten rug, but the cicadas squawked unperturbed.

"Is my mother all right?"

"She's doing okay. Your momma's doing okay." He turned back and glanced at her pregnant form. He paused, about to say something paternal, then changed tack. "Hope you have some DEET on you. Or these skeeters here'll have you for supper."

"No. I got on the plane without much planning."

"Ah, don't you worry. I have some in the van."

"What about yourself? You're wearing shorts."

"Oh, no, they don't want my blood. My blood's poison to them. Ever since I started my chemo, but even after I stopped."

She didn't probe. They came finally to Larry's driveway. He had a modest ranch house surrounded by palms and ferns so well pruned they looked artificial. His wagon was a white Ford panel van, the kind pop culture tied to child molesters.

As Larry's vehicle tooled through the rural grids, he told her he'd been picking up Mary-Sue's mail and *Miami Herald*s every day, and making sure that the green things around her house didn't overgrow and "make the place look like Andrew hit it." He was referring, of course, in his parochial way, to the hurricane of '92 that still showed its traces in the area. Kate thought he was fishing for gratitude, and so she thanked him. Then, just as they locked their doors and sped through a less prosperous neighborhood, he told her how impressed he was by the way Mary-Sue had driven into "the colored parts" to take the elderly to the polls during the last election, and even bought them lunch without making a fuss about it. It was the first time that Kate had heard about this, and she was surprised by her mother's sense of civic duty.

"I respected her for doing that though my politics and hers don't mesh. At all. It was like what they say—never the twain?

But we're gettin' there, we're gettin' there." Larry smiled ruefully. "I reckon most folks are good people, no matter who or what they are. They just want what's best for them and their families. And if it makes me a darn liberal for saying that, then so be it. Sticks and stones." He glanced at Kate's belly for a second. "Tell me if you need to throw up. I'll pull over."

Kate watched the broccoli-shaped silhouettes of fruit trees melt into the black velvet nightscape. She hadn't seen a single light in miles. They merged onto placid Dixie highway, flanked on both sides by curved-neck orange street lamps that evoked a fuzzy tropical melancholy. They passed big box stores, pet hospitals, jet ski wholesalers, and key lime pie bakeries with windows long boarded shut—murdered in their sleep perhaps by the Pillsbury Doughboy. So many stores but not one bookshop or library. This was the land of people who couldn't tell you what a dust jacket was. Yet, this was her mother's land now.

"Your momma's a real spatial lady." Larry shook his head. It was the third time he'd said that, in that manner, and Kate had to wonder if he was in love with her. In the past, Mary-Sue would never have had the patience for anyone with a Jesus fish stuck on his bumper; now Kate couldn't be so sure.

"Don't know how you can stand to live so far away from her," Larry said.

Kate scowled. Okay, now this cretin was trying to lay a trip on her. He had no right, he didn't know her at all! And who asked him anyway? Then when she caught the soft look in Larry's eyes, she realized all he'd meant was, *Don't you miss her?*

"God bless her, she's a tough gal," he said. "Never loses hope."

"Just tell me what happened to her."

"With all due respect, I will let her tell it to you herself."

He signaled at the sign for Homestead Hospital, and Kate's

hands gripped the edge of her seat. The angry part of her that raged to tell her mother, "This is what you get for living out in this godforsaken place on your own," melted away. She fought the queasiness that had overcome her.

"Why didn't *you* call me?" her voice was breaking. "I was so . . . worried . . ."

"Because—well, I didn't think it was my place to go against your momma's wishes. You know what she's like."

They pulled into the parking garage. Larry had the three dollars for the attendant ready in advance, obviously a regular visitor. He took one of the hundred empty spots.

"What's your last name, Larry?"

"You're not going to tell the cops on me now, are you?" he smiled. "It's Burk. Without the *e*."

"If this ever happens again, can I call you?"

"Let's better hope this dun happen again. But yes, honey. 'Course you may."

MARY-SUE WAS SLEEPING on her belly like an infant when Larry escorted Kate to her room. Apart from the Band-Aid on her left temple and the outlines of gauze under her hospital clothes, she looked pretty much the same as she'd always looked. Kate was relieved. With her eyes closed and her body rising and falling in a steady rhythm, Mary-Sue even looked restful. But Kate could hardly bear to glance at her mother. Each glimpse of her in that bed was a confirmation of some unstoppable truth— we aged, we got weak, we didn't love our mothers enough.

The room was decorated à la *Golden Girls*—salmon, jade, brass, all thrown together in a budget-conscious stab at island style. It was also shared. The other bed was occupied by a large Jamaican lady named Maggie, and Maggie's way of celebrating the recovery of her collapsed lung was to crunch through a colossal bag of spicy Doritos.

"You her baby girl?" Maggie asked, looking Kate up and down. Kate nodded, bracing herself for the usual comments. "You look just like her."

Kate scanned Maggie's broad, smooth face for traces of sarcasm and was surprised to find none.

"You're right. She does look like her momma." Larry gazed at Kate with avuncular tenderness. "What nature didn't do, nurture made up for. They hold their heads in the same way, talk in that same voice . . ."

"The hands. They have exactly the same hands."

Larry patted Kate's back as if he'd read her anxious mind—*it's all right, we're all family here*. With a Southern gentleman's bearing, he glided over to Mary-Sue and took her hand in his, pressing it gently to rouse her.

"Good morning, milady . . ." he cooed. "Look who we have here?"

Mary-Sue's eyes peeled open slowly. She looked around in a disoriented haze until she spotted the unusual new thing in the room—a pregnant brunette standing with her back pressed up against the wall.

"Katie?" Mary-Sue's voice was hoarse. Larry brought a cup of water to her lips.

"Get closer to her, child, she ain't gonna bite ya." Maggie laughed heartily as she watched Kate keep her distance. "Or is she now?"

"Mom," said Kate. She took tentative steps toward Mary-Sue.

"Baby, what are you doing here?" Mary-Sue said. The control freak in her was waking up. She eyed Larry. "How long has she been here?"

"Only a few minutes." Larry closed the pink divider curtain

between the two beds, and went over to whisper something to Maggie when she objected. Then he tiptoed to the door.

"Larry? Larry!" Mary-Sue croaked. "Where do you think you're going?"

"I'll be right outside."

"Come back and take Kate with you. I don't want her to see me like this!"

"Now, Mary-Sue . . ." He gave her a *be good* look and closed the door.

Kate stepped into Mary-Sue's sightline. "Mom, what happened to you?"

"Wait for me at the house," Mary-Sue said. "I'll be back in a couple of days."

"Will you stop being such a fucking martyr?" Kate pulled a chair close to Mary-Sue so neither of them had to strain their voices. "Why won't you tell me what happened to you?"

When Kate sat, her swollen belly settled before her mother's eyes—and Mary-Sue registered the pregnancy for the first time. Her shocked face crinkled with tears.

"How long were you going to keep this from me?" She reached out to touch the mound. "How long has my grandchild been in there?"

"I left you messages. You never called back."

"Yeah, yeah, yeah." Mary-Sue sighed and looked away. "I fell down in the parking lot and hurt my back, that's all. It's nothing."

"Oh, was that all? And you preferred to have me worried sick, thinking you were attacked or murdered, than return my calls?"

Mary-Sue shuddered at the word *attacked*. Kate softened her approach. She held her mother's hand, moved at how tiny and pale it had become. But Mary-Sue pulled away before Kate could see the happy-face scar on her inner wrist, ☺, her souvenir from the unfortunate encounter with a Prius in the Publix lot. (Mary-Sue hadn't heard the damn car coming; the driver didn't stop because he never realized he'd hit her. It was a prosaic, irritating, humiliating, expensive mishap.)

"I'll pay you back for your airplane ticket," Mary-Sue said, "if you want to go."

"Don't change the subject. Mom, who did this to you? I'm not going to judge you or think you were asking for it."

"Of course I wasn't asking for it! I don't want to discuss it anymore." Mary-Sue's eyes ignited. "I hate being this frail, okay? You think it's fun being old? Catching up with friends, finding new hobbies? That's all a pile of horseshit. Propaganda from drug companies, corporate America and the fucking AARP!"

Mary-Sue calmed herself down by staring at Kate's belly.

"Is there a father in the picture?"

"No."

"Well, who's going to take care of you when the baby comes?"

"I'm the age you were when you got me, and you did it on your own."

"How many more months?"

"Four. I think."

Mary-Sue paused. "Move out here. Let me take care of you, and the little one. At least till you've figured it out." Then realizing the ridiculousness of making this offer while she lay in a hospital bed, Mary-Sue started laughing.

"Don't burst those stitches." Kate placed her head on the bed next to her mother's arm. A wave of exhaustion swept over her and she closed her eyes. She felt like climbing onto the bed and curling up by Mary-Sue, sucking in her Mommy smell. She could sleep right there, she could reclaim every one of the million and forty winks she'd lost.

Neither of them heard Larry open the door.

"Oh, forgive me, ladies. Take your time. I'll be right outside."

"No, Larry, don't you go." Mary-Sue jerked her head up. "Take this woman with you. I've got to go to the bathroom anyhow, and I doubt that either of you want to be here for that." She reached for the nurse's call button and pushed it. "And don't you let her come back till I'm on my feet." She elbowed Kate to get up. "Hospitals are so damned depressing. If I were you, I'd go to the Coconut Grove and get myself some piña coladas—and yes, they make virgin ones for persons in your condition. Or South Beach, where the young people like you congregate. Take an airboat ride through the Everglades. Just don't come back here. Hospitals are such awful, awful places. And Larry?"

"Yes'm?"

"You be her jailer. I'm holding you to it."

"Yes'm."

SCHOOL WAS BACK on, and as usual it felt like a long-running CW show that's sprung back from hiatus. The same, only older and more emotionally promiscuous—more laughter, more tears, often both at once. New haircuts, new clothes and new backpacks to fit the better-defined character arcs everyone had acquired. They strove to open themselves up to new ideas and new friends, and there was always much mingling between the sexes, the cliques, the tribes, this first week.

By the second week, all the old storylines and allegiances would kick back in. Winners and losers would head to their respective turf; those who were neither to their former corners, sick for the long, unconfused days of August. But this was only the fifth day and the laissez-faire spirit hadn't yet dissipated. Arik had on his faded Green Day T-shirt—now his "lucky shirt"—and

Rosemary wore a peasant blouse with baggy blue jeans, and they walked side by side through the piazza around which the school revolved. Where they previously would have each taken elaborate detours to avoid this heartless runway, they now crossed it with nary a qualm. For years, the mock-Grecian balustrades on three sides of the quad had been claimed by the seniors, who text-messaged and people-watched until the last bell rang, sparing no one their withering commentaries, especially not the awkward freshmen in pastel sweaters dispatched by BMWs like unwanted Easter eggs and the pierced punks who drove their moms' mini-vans. The ongoing remodel of the piazza had left these social predators homeless; without their perch, they now struggled to find pillars to lean against in order to look cool.

Rosemary and Arik sauntered to the Shakespeare wall, a garish mural (purportedly of Stratford-upon-Avon) created by talent-free sixth-graders bussed in from some "urban" pocket right after the 1992 riots. The Wall was where the ragtag theater geeks hung out—not that Rosemary and Arik belonged with them either—hunched around stone benches, exchanging sacred texts of Kenneth Lonergan's *This Is Our Youth* and Playbills saved from trips to see Dame Judi Dench on Broadway. All of these kids, with the exception of Arik and Rosemary, dreamed of being on an HBO series. A handful absorbed the annoying tics of various characters from *The Sopranos*, though the person who did the most chillingly precise impression of Tony Soprano was a petite Latina named Ana Baretta. A couple of the kids had headshots made for their birthdays, and chattered about building up their resume of special skills; the boy who took juggling classes in London over the summer showed off with little beanbags ("English juggling's more evolved than American juggling"), the girl who went to mime camp paddled through imaginary rapids, and the South Asian twins, Anil and Ashok, who called their comedy duo the Aryan Brotherhood, shared fresh material about "kikes" and "Chinks."

Three months ago, Rosemary would have found these people vaguely amusing; now, she saw them for what they were. Repellent loveless outcasts. Freaks.

"Fuck me, it's the phantoms!" said the fat boy who asked to be called Betty. "Where have you been? You two just vanished from class like Vin Diesel's career."

"I had to go to my grandma's in Oregon," Arik said, calmly. Rosemary almost believed him—he'd become such a good actor.

"*Et tu*, Lucy Liu?"

"I quit," Rosemary said. "Lost interest."

"Oh." The boy tried to fathom how anyone could have lost faith in something that meant the world to him. "You're still welcome to hang out here though, if you like." He lowered his voice. "We badly need to improve this gene pool."

Rosemary and Arik gave each other a look—*Let's amscray*.

As they fled the Shakespeare Wall, Betty called out after them in his falsetto: "In case you're curious, we've been reading the canon with Mr. De Souza, who's even more pretentious than Mr. Z, if that's even possible. No farces—imagine!" He made a face. "He's issued a *fatwa* against Neil Simon . . ."

BEHIND THE ALUMINUM shed that stored the theater props, Arik and Rosemary stood in a foot of fallen leaves. There were five minutes left to steal and they devoured them greedily. Once their lips locked, it became impossible for them to keep their hands off each other. Rosemary wouldn't let Arik pull away even after the last bell rang.

"Let's cut school today," she gasped.

"If we did that today, I'd never come back."

"Then let's not come back."

"What about Workshop?"

"Fuck that, it's retarded."

"Rose . . . you're crazy. Where would we go?"

She was effortlessly coquettish all of a sudden. Her hand slid down the waist of his jeans until it found his swollen cock. She fondled its tip, and rubbed the silky-soft ridge. Arik trembled.

They kissed deeply again. He put both hands down the back of her jeans and squeezed her ass. "Oh, Rose, I want to fuck you . . . I *need* to fuck you."

A few feet away, there was a rustling in the leaves. They looked up, expecting the groundskeeper, José. But it was Mr. Z, approaching the props shed with a heavy red backpack in his hand. When he saw them, he froze in his tracks, as if he were the one caught in the act.

"Mr. Z," said Arik, his voice all jittery. "We were just practicing. For Workshop this afternoon."

"I see," Mr. Z said. He cast his eyes on Rosemary for her excuse.

Instead of speaking, she reached around Arik's waist. He flinched, self-conscious in Mr. Z's presence. Still, something egged her on—she rested her head on Arik's chest and gazed back defiantly at Mr. Z, her fingers tracing the edge of Arik's fly.

"Well," Mr. Z said, giving her the lifeless stare of a disappointed parent. Dark rings were forming under his eyes. His chore at the shed interrupted, he turned to leave. The red backpack seemed to weigh down his arm even more than before.

"Workshop is canceled," he said, in a neutral voice, "indefinitely."

"What?" Arik turned his wild, bewildered eyes to Rosemary for backup, but got nothing. "Mr. Z! Why are you mad at us? We're just doing what you told us to do!"

"All good things must come to an end." Mr. Z said this calmly, and began walking, the dead leaves crackling under his feet. "Goodnight, sweet prince, and flights of angels sing thee to thy rest."

"Wait! I don't get it!" Arik was about to cry. He pulled away from Rosemary and took three steps after Mr. Z. "Please! What's going on?"

He looked back at Rosemary, who watched Mr. Z's departure with folded arms. She shook her head: "He can be so fucking corny."

SHE WAS FINALLY ready to do it. With a branch cutter she found in the garage, she made a *U*-shaped tear in her window screen that could be lifted up like a dog door.

There was a shuffling of slippers and the rapping of knuckles at her door.

"Baby, why you lock door?"

"Because I'm not seven years old and I want some privacy, that's why!"

"Where you put car key?"

"What do you want it for?"

"Give me car key, Rosie." Mrs. Park continued knocking in her quietly insistent way. Groaning, Rosemary tossed the branch cutter under her bed and closed her curtains.

She opened the door. "Tell me what you're planning to do with it."

"Just give me car key." There was a new hardness in Mrs. Park's tone.

"Okay, okay." Rosemary twitched. "It's in the bathroom cabinet, inside my box of tampons."

WHEN NIGHT FELL, she slipped outside to wait for Arik. She found a hidden spot behind the camellia bush and stood there, fending off ants and bugs by repeatedly stamping her feet in a ridiculous goosestep. She should have worn jeans instead of shorts but it was too late.

Finally, a male silhouette materialized, walking up the center of the street. She ran out to greet him.

"Hey!" She waved at him to hurry up, and he obeyed.

When her guest came into view, under the moonlight, Rosemary froze. It wasn't Arik.

"Well, hello, Ghost," said the man. He approached her like an old acquaintance, a bemused smile across his face. He wasn't particularly threatening—he was much too ordinary-looking for that—but his tone of intimacy made her hair stand. "How's it going tonight, you?"

She didn't know what to say but common courtesy told her she had to say something. "Fine."

"Glad to hear it. Glad to hear it." He glanced at the darkened house across the street. "She's gone AWOL again, hasn't she?"

"Who? The lady who lives there?"

The man looked at Rosemary with a teasing grin. "You're being awfully coy tonight, Ghost."

Slightly insulted, she gave up what she knew: "She's gone out of town, not sure where. She asked my mom to turn on her sprinklers for her. I have no idea when she'll be back."

His response made her blood run cold. He groaned in agony, and he cracked his knuckles. She peered past his shoulder and hoped that Arik would show.

"I've got something here for your trouble," he said. He reached inside his denim jacket and pulled out a necklace with a gold, heart-shaped pendant. "Here, take it."

"I can't." She backed away. "But thanks."

"It's even got your name on it." He moved the pendant into the moonlight, and swung it; she saw how pretty it was—engraved with the block letters *B.A.Y.*

"My name's not Bay."

"Beautiful and young. That's you, my Ghost. That's you."

Swiftly but gently, he grabbed her hand and dropped the necklace into her palm, the metal as cold as ice, then closed her fingers over it. His hands were manly and thick, and his caresses were unambiguously sensual, as opposed to Arik's improvised groping.

"I can't . . ."

He turned, and was gone.

ARIK ARRIVED ON his bike five minutes late, hurrying and clumsy and apologetic. He seemed to her even more of a boy than ever—a sweaty, unreliable schoolboy whose breath smelled of blue Gatorade and marinara sauce.

Rosemary peeled open the window screen from her room and he climbed in with only a few nicks from the wire mesh. Before he could even kick off his shoes, they were entwined on her bed, him on top of her. His mouth covered her neck and shoulder blades with kisses; his hands grabbed her breasts under her bra.

"God, I've been waiting for this for, like, forever." He pulled off her shorts and pressed himself against her.

They both stripped, kissing every time another garment came off. Then they were completely nude except for the new gold necklace around Rosemary's neck.

"You look really hot tonight."

The tip of his cock almost reached up to his belly button and every time it touched Rosemary's bare skin it jerked. They threw the covers off the bed and he moved his face down between her thighs.

"I want to eat your pussy." As those words escaped his lips, he was shocked at how lurid they sounded, and he giggled, high-pitched and girly. He repeated the line in parody Count Dracula fashion, "I vahnt to yeet your poo-see . . . I vahnt to yeet your poo-see, dahlink!"

She wished he would stop. Couldn't he tell he was making her feel gross? When she parted her thighs, she saw that he was immediately intimidated by what he found there. He gave her slit a few light licks, avoiding the slimy areas, then puckered his lips and hastened back up to more familiar territory. Her gold pendant he sucked on like it was candy, metallic candy that would chase away the taste of the ocean on his tongue.

"Arik . . ." She wrapped her legs around him. "Arik, I want you to fuck me."

"Wait," he gasped, "hold that thought." He bounced off the bed like a golden retriever sent to fetch the paper and rummaged through his backpack. Hands shaking, he pulled out a thirty-six-pack of condoms: "I was being optimistic!"

He plucked open the box ceremoniously so she could see it was sealed and untouched, and withdrew a chain of little foil packs. Fingers trembling and breathing heavily, he removed one and tried to peel it open with his teeth.

"Hurry, Arik! You're already dipping."

"I'm trying, I'm trying." The foil wrapper finally tore. He spat out the loose flap, wincing like a baby when the tang of spermicide hit his tongue. Now he had to get the thing on. "I want to . . . ram myself inside you!" Even as he said this, his cock grew soft.

"Hurry . . ." Rosemary went over and kissed him hungrily.

He rose for her again. Everything smelled of rubber gloves and antiseptic, like the hospital where she'd had her tonsils snipped off.

"Let's just do without it," she said.

"Are you crazy?" The condom kept slipping off. Finally she flicked it off his penis and it landed on the rug like a piece of skin.

"Great, now there's going to be dust and hair and bacteria all over it."

"Don't be such a girl about it." She pulled him by the hand, and he followed, all buzzed and confused. "Just come to bed."

"Rose, you're crazy . . ." Then he reached between her legs; she was sopping wet.

She lifted herself up to meet him and gently rubbed her bush against his balls.

Arik smiled, daffy, dazed and full of mixed feeling. "I love you, Rose."

She let that line hang in the dark so her mind could authenticate it before her heart lapped it up.

"I love you, too, Arik." She stuck her tongue into his ear, making him quiver and moan.

He relented. He let her pull him down on top of her. After another lingering kiss, he pushed himself inside. She was so slick that he was halfway in before he realized what had happened. They were no longer virgins. He gasped with joy, almost laughter. What a relief. He looked down at Rosemary and saw her face all scrunched up.

"Are you alright?"

"It feels good," she said. He wasn't convinced. But it didn't matter. As soon as he felt her relax around his cock, he pushed in deeper. She moaned. He closed his eyes so he didn't have to see her agony. He moved, and kept on thrusting, pooling sweat in the twin dimples on his lower spine. He was about to ask her again if she was okay when spasms overtook him. He grunted and twitched with the strongest orgasm he'd ever known. At the last minute, he remembered to pull out and came in violent spurts that struck her face and his face, her neck and his neck, her breasts, his chest. She squealed.

"Oh shit! I should've . . ." he panted, catching his breath as he collapsed on the bed next to her. "Oh God, I hope I didn't . . . I hope you're not . . . Oh, fuck!"

She shushed him and kissed him and held his head as he melted into sleep.

While he slept, she played with herself and came five times, her fingers covered in a glaze of both their juices by the time she was done. She watched it dry and coat her fingers like candle-wax. Then she woke him for round two.

THE NEXT MORNING there was a red envelope wedged in the crack of her locker door. It was addressed to "The Sick Rose" in cursive writing and sealed with red wax, like an old-timey valentine. She took it to the ladies' room and peeled it open in the privacy of her stall, while a trio of AP English girls put on eyeliner and debated the Jewy hotness of actor Adam Brody.

Inside the red envelope was a piece of college-ruled notebook paper, transparent in its cheapness. On it, in familiar chicken scratches, was a hastily copied poem:

> *O Rose thou art sick*
> *The invisible worm*
> *That flies in the night,*
> *In the howling storm,*
>
> *Has found out thy bed*
> *Of crimson joy:*

And his dark secret love
Does thy life destroy.

Wm. Blake

She felt a little heartsick; the poem sounded so old and so bitter. Yet, her heart swelled with pride that she'd provoked such a jealous response from Mr. Z. She resisted the urge to run off and find Arik so they could giggle over the fact that Mr. Z had him pegged as an "invisible worm." It would probably send him galloping to Mr. Z's office, contrite and begging for forgiveness like the approval-hungry boy that he was.

After school, she saw Mr. Z walking to his car, solemnly gripping a thick biography of Stanislavsky and a cup of Yoplait. He backed the Nissan out of his parking spot with a hasty screech, almost running over a teacher talking on her cellphone. Waving an insincere apology, he sped away, his exhaust fumes toxic and black.

When Rosemary got home, the Camry was missing.

She panicked—her mother had driven it off. Then the panic coalesced into cold, hard fear—her mother had abandoned her.

She ran into the house with knees like jelly. "Mira! . . . Mira?" Her legs gave out in the hallway and she found herself crawling on her arms to the bedrooms, panting and breathless, on the verge of tears. "Mee-rah!"

A heart-stopping shuffle of slippered feet, emerging from the kitchen.

"Baby, what is matter?" Mrs. Park was in her housedress beating eggs in a bowl. "Why shouting? Mira still in school. Be back later."

"Oh." Rosemary was relieved *and* disappointed to see her mother. Her legs came back. "What happened to the car?"

"Quellie Soo help me to sell it."

"What?" She pulled herself off the floor. "Why didn't you ask me first? I'm starting Driver's Ed next week!"

"No worry—you can study the driving in Korea."

The blood rushed to her head. She wanted to fling a chair at the alien woman standing in the doorway, the one who claimed to be her mother but was in fact so persistently foreign, so persistently unloving, so persistently strange. Hot tears of rage flushed down her cheeks; she was equally furious that she had failed to hold them back.

"You fucking insensitive *bitch*!"

With those words came the bite of instant regret. She kicked the wall.

Mrs. Park eyed her daughter calmly. "No shouting today. Today is my birthday. Don't tell me you forget." She returned to the kitchen, and checked on the fetid pot bubbling on the stove.

THE DINING TABLE was covered with traditional Korean dishes. Small plates of boiled mung beans, pickled cabbage, tiny fried fish, tofu squares. Larger plates of omelet with pickled root vegetables, dumplings filled with green mush and mystery meat. Bowls of goopy buckwheat noodles in a cold, grey, sour broth. The spread managed the feat of seeming at once grand and hopelessly bleak.

"I don't eat taupe-colored food," said Mira. She prodded the dumplings with her chopsticks.

Mrs. Park chomped away heartily, savoring the flavors of her youth. She was in grandee mode.

"Today, I am forty years old. We eat Korean food."

The girls said nothing. It wasn't their birthday.

"Mira, thank you for birthday present." Mrs. Park held up a plastic wind-up Tweety Bird, the prize in a Happy Meal long gone.

"You're welcome. The pony will have to wait till next year."

Another meaningless minute of silence. Mrs. Park turned to her elder daughter.

"You the quiet type, Rosie." Mrs. Park said it like a vet diagnosing fleas. "In Korea, you study hard, go to college, become doctor." She concluded with her master stroke: "No need worry about husband."

Rosemary gritted her teeth and kept quiet until she could take it no longer. "You don't even *know* me."

"How you say this? I am your mother. I know you since you born, baby."

"That's exactly my point." Rosemary gripped her chopsticks till her knuckles were white. "Fuck this shit."

She picked at a limp mung bean sprout. Their mother chewed on a slice of pickle in silence, no doubt thinking a million negative things. Mira found herself in the unlikely position of family peacemaker. With no choice but to be a good sport, she swallowed one of the dumplings.

"This is pretty tasty." She looked at her mother—who was still expressionless, still locked deep within herself.

"Ma, say something. Say: fo' shizzle my nizzle."

"What? Why?"

"Just say it."

Mrs. Park cast her eyes away but Mira kept at it.

"Ma, say it. Ma, say: fo' shizzle my nizzle. Come on! Fo' shizzle my nizzle, Ma."

Mrs. Park put down her chopsticks. "Fosheezer ma neezer."

"Yaaaay!" Mira hollered enthusiastically and gave her a standing ovation.

Mrs. Park found herself smiling in spite of herself. "What is meaning, Mira?"

"It means," Mira beamed, "I agree with you, my delightful friend."

- 11 -

THE SILVER BULLET

The haunting, if it even was a haunting, continued all summer—doors left open here, ectoplasm there, the dial on his radio tuned to Mexican stations and the volume set at Earth-Shattering. More than twice, mariachi trumpets had him leaping out of his skin. And those yowling disk jockeys—who or what the hell was La Raza? Could his ghost be some Latina who salsa'd around his house to this kind of thing?

As the weeks passed, Raymond started looking forward to the visitations. He liked the radio tampering. He liked the mounds of cookie crumbs neatly piled like anthills on his staircase. He liked especially the sexy puddles of ectoplasm. He started talking to her. This had all the makings of a buddy movie: aging horror writer and his dead Latina confidante, an *I Dream of Jeannie* for the twenty-first century.

"The blue Hugo Boss shirt or the green Thomas Pink shirt?"

When these disturbances stopped in the last week of September, he felt bereft.

He had started a log. The visits only occurred when the security system hadn't been on. When he had it activated, with its beep-beep-beep "On" sound, the ghost seemed to respect his wish not to be disturbed. Some nights, he left the entire system off just so the ghost wouldn't feel unwelcome. But recently, even when he had it off for a week straight, his friend didn't show up.

He knew it was nuts to miss her, much less court her by consciously refusing to put on his alarm. Coming and going was the prerogative of ghosts, after all. Whenever he left the system off, the old paranoia returned—punks invading his house, smashing his precious things and taunting his graying manhood. Just last week a guy in a hooded sweatshirt had held up a woman at gunpoint five houses away. It became a real conundrum—turn the system on, and his ghost wouldn't come; turn the system off, and he might have human monsters to contend with.

As it was, the only hauntings he received now were the incessant phone calls from his father.

"Oh, Ray, just a little longer—"

"I told you. I have a very important meeting I have to get to."

"But today's Sunday!"

"The literary world never sleeps, Dad. You know that."

"I sure as shooting do *not*."

"I gotta say. I do love your way with words."

He hung up the phone, and if a man could kiss himself, he would have. The solution to his dilemma had suddenly revealed itself to him.

THE BUILDINGS GOT shabbier as he drove south and west away from Santa Claus Lane. Sub-divided Victorians became halfway houses, Baptist churches became crack dens. A sign proclaimed: THIS CHURCH IS PRAYER-CONDITIONED. Haha. Young men idled on street corners in baggy blue jeans and white muumuus they seemed to think were T-shirts. He could scoff at them safely in the daytime, but come nightfall, when they pulled on their black hoodies and merged into the night, he knew he'd be quaking again.

Just before the eight lanes of the 210 came into view, a burst of redevelopment: beige shoeboxes overlooking the on-ramp with "New York–style lofts," the trapezoid of a Mormon temple, a block-wide fortress with "All Welcome" sermons in Armenian, Tagalog and Español, offering last-minute salvation before drivers braved the freeway.

So many churches. Not *too* many, just *so* many. Raymond didn't have anything against them personally—they'd been good to him. His last relationship had been with a married man— father of two and husband to a movie publicist shrike—and the only place they could rendezvous without the risk of running into anyone they knew was a church. Like Abelard and Heloise who tiptoed into a musty refectory to rut like minxes, or Matthew Lewis's monk who ventured down to the crypt to ravage his love, Raymond found his neighborhood Presbyterian church, with its neo-Gothic nooks and crannies and cornices and curlicues, sympathetically disposed to urgent romance.

It also looked like a swell place for a funeral.

He thought about this as he drove. He'd always believed that endings should be quiet and full of champagne, assemblies as awkward and giddily meaningless as what had come before. But even on a speculative level he couldn't summon up a list of those who'd come to commemorate his. Lena Ozova would fly in from New York maybe, if she wasn't stuck in a love-in with some hot new memoirist, and perhaps one or two of his former editors, if their fond memories outnumbered their foul ones. He had no siblings, no close living relatives that he could name, and he couldn't imagine any of his former lovers being sentimental. What about his neighbor Kate, that strange, elusive soul? Not likely—they weren't *real* drinking buddies. This left only his face-less fans—with their depressing single-use cameras—and his energy-vampire father.

From the beginning, his father never had the inclination to understand him, and had never made any effort to feign it. It wasn't Raymond's sexuality that was the problem, though it did have its problems. His father had a congenital mistrust of anyone who toiled only with his fingertips. He was the original enemy of fiction.

The on-ramp was fast approaching. He accelerated and merged. Zen driving.

In high school, Raymond had to justify why he'd skip dinner for an Ingmar Bergman marathon at the film society. "Don't get artsy," his father warned him. And Raymond would say: "Swedish movies, Dad. Blondes. Titties." He used to be good at that kind of doubletalk. But what euphemisms were there for limb-tearing, butt-fucking, heart-eating zombies? How did you explain that blood wasn't blood?

He wished he'd had the clarity to write his father into his fiction as the ultimate monster, whose special power was spiritual Chinese water torture. Drip, drip, drip. *To my Dad, without whom I would never have gained such insight into one man's ability to drain the life out of another.*

He glanced at the clock. Seven minutes late. He cut into the carpool lane and a glossy Latina in a Lexus SUV gave him the finger. He knew, he knew—to younger people he registered as a seedy old creep. But he did his best against the merciless wear of gravity; that woman driver would know it too in a few years, when her arms grew thick as *jamon* and her boobs sank like papayas. If she could see through to his true self, the one underneath all the wrinkles and balm, she might feel pity for him instead of spite—she'd be moved, for instance, that he was a man who kept a prescription for Cialis just so he could have sex with himself.

He'd never cruised for tail, oh, no; yet he hadn't banked on being romantically alone this early in life either. He'd even wanted children, at different points. Vital, wholesome boys with trampoline feet, pecs covered in varsity letters. They'd outrun him, outwit him, outlast him.

The best candidate for co-father had slipped through his fingers years earlier. That was Fletcher, the Brit who audited him during his flush New York years in the mid-eighties. The only man Raymond knew who could look sexy in a cardigan. While the going was good, it was great. They were both tall, lean, and often mistaken for brothers. They test-ran fatherhood on dates to Broadway with Fletcher's teenage son. But Fletcher discovered that America was such a conformist country that even its deviants cleaved to convention. And so he, too, fell in line. He never advertised his sexuality and avoided all the souks where AIDS had cast its pall; his preference was to act as if he belonged to a separate caste, if not species, from those he called "the gays."

Several years after Fletcher's departure, Raymond left Manhattan too. As he packed his bags, Lena sent him off with her peculiar form of fare-thee-well: "The bad thing about Cullifornia is that you'll be surrounded by ee-juhts. The *good* thing about Cullifornia is that you'll be surrounded by ee-juhts."

RAYMOND'S JAGUAR SLUICED through Eagle Rock, once a scraggly enclave of flag-waving blue-collars but increasingly home to vegan "creatives" and the offspring they in full sobriety named Axel or Tito. In spite of—many would say, because of—these new migrants, some of the ugliest new architecture in LA

County had sprouted in and around Eagle Rock, clinging to the hillsides like Bauhaus dingleberries.

There, on the main boulevard, Raymond found free street parking. It was less of an LA miracle once he realized where he'd parked—nobody wanted their car jacked in front of an adult video duplicating service; just imagine going in there asking for help. He sprinted the half block down to The Green Man, and was baffled to find that it had the stained glass windows and rustic oak door of an old-school tavern. He checked the address on the printout in his hand.

Inside, the place reeked of old cigarettes, but it was unmistakably a vintage gun store. Old-fashioned firearms of every kind were displayed behind glass on every wall. Minding the cash register was a jowly lady with gray-blond hair. A T-shirt cheetah stretched across her ample chest and tail-eating serpents circumnavigated her arms.

"What can I do for you, sweetheart?" she said.

"This is The Green Man, isn't it?"

"You mean the old Irish pub? That's long gone." She blew a puff of Lucky Strike at him. "I kept the exterior just to fool suckers like you inside so I can sell you an 1889 Winchester."

He humored her with a smile. He knew words like "harridan" were retrograde, but sometimes the right words were necessary. "I'm looking for Duckie."

The woman bellowed to a chunky teenage boy dusting off revolver-shaped candybars at the back of the store.

"Zeke? Would you go and tell Duckie that her boyfriend's here?" The boy nodded and lumbered to an Employees Only door. "My daughter will be with you in a minute."

On the wall behind her were dozens of faded celebrity photos, eight-by-tens like the ones displayed braggingly at dry-cleaning establishments all over Los Angeles. But these were entirely of children. Little girls, in particular.

"Customers?" he asked, while he waited.

"No, no. See here's Tracey—and her big sister Missy. They peaked in the early eighties. Missy made it first, then Tracey won that part on *Growing Pains*. But they were both cursed with what I call ensemble face." She sighed. "Here's Jodie, circa *Taxi Driver*, look at those cute little freckles! . . . And here's Heather, remember her? She was the little one in *Poltergeist*. Passed away when she was twelve . . . Well, she watches over me now." She trailed off on that note. Raymond privately noted the bottle of Jack Daniel's behind the counter. "They're all my children. My little babies."

"How exactly are they your children?" He tried not to sound too judgmental.

She bristled. "What d'you mean *how* are they my children? I watched them grow up before my very eyes. Followed their ups and downs through the years."

A teenage girl with magenta hair ambled over unhurriedly. She wore her stars and stripes tank top with great significance, but Raymond couldn't tell how ironic it was supposed to be, if at all.

"Bryce? I'm Duckie," she said to him. "Follow me."

IN THE DANK stockroom behind the Employees Only door, Duckie pulled out a metal briefcase and opened it out to Raymond. In a dell carved out of gray foam was a pistol engraved with clichés—roses, vines, thorns. He flinched when she took it out and pointed it at him.

"Relax, man!" Harridan-in-training. She clicked open the cylinder for his inspection and spun it. "Just letting you see this beauty from every angle."

Six empty chambers, making it a handsome holder for cigarillos. There was something about this thing that made it too unserious for the business of bullets.

"Pretty, huh?" She pulled out a thick catalog, opening it to a dog-eared page. "It says here that this is modeled after the pistols used by real vampire hunters in Transylvania."

"I highly doubt that."

"I'll give it to you for a thousand bucks, fully loaded."

IN THE KITCHEN, Mrs. Park slid over something slick that sent her tumbling on her ass. The puddle was clear and thick, like mucus, and she gasped in recognition.

She heard the creaking of floorboards directly overhead. She looked up, and as she did, a drop of goopy, clear fluid fell from a crack and landed in her left eye.

"*Ssi-bal!*" Shit. It didn't sting, but its cool, jellylike contact came as a shock.

More creaks from above. Mrs. Park ran to the hallway where, sure enough, her suspicions were confirmed. A ladder perched under the open attic hatch.

"Mira!" she screamed. "Mira, what for you steal my eggs?"

She grabbed a flashlight and started up the ladder, and as soon as she neared the opening, an odor as pungent as fish sauce rushed through her nostrils. She shone her light into the black. There, a frantic shuffling began. Eventually the beam of light found Mira, crouching in the darkness, her arms bent like shields against the glare.

"Mira!"

The girl had eggshells in her hands. When Mrs. Park moved the spotlight around, she saw little maggot-looking pods everywhere. Some were perched in the centers of cobwebs, their tiny feet hanging onto the weave. They were her dried shrimp, which she used—very sparingly—to flavor soup. There was more: Little firecrackers dangling from the rafters? No, wait, they weren't firecrackers at all—they were *tampons*, at least ten of them, stained with use, hanging from their strings like crimson party lights.

"Mira! What are you doing!"

"Stay outta my Kool-Aid, ho."

"Speak English! Why you no going to school?"

"You're making us move to Korea so what does school matter?" Mira showed her the empty bottles of Thai fish sauce. "Every white person's nightmare."

"Why you do this? Why you steal my eggs?" Mrs. Park sounded more hurt than angry. "Why you keep tampons?"

"I'm feeding my termites."

Mrs. Park started down the ladder solemnly. "Quellie Soo is coming today. She helping me sell this house."

Without a further word, Mrs. Park shut the hatch to the attic and bolted it from the outside. Once she got back to ground level, she squeezed the two legs of the ladder closed and carried it out to the garage.

ARIK LED ROSEMARY into his room and engaged the clumsily installed dead bolt, forcibly tilting down the clasp so it would catch. He lunged toward her for a kiss, grinning so wide that her tongue smashed into his wall of teeth.

There was a pungent, sterile odor in the place. She looked around for its source. His room was slightly smaller than hers, even with the bed pushed against the wall to make space. Posters of baseball players she couldn't name lined the walls, limited edition Beanie Babies sat on a shelf above his bed, strangely dust-free; Arnold Schwarzenegger watched over everything from a faded *Terminator 2: Judgment Day* one-sheet.

"Why's it smell like rubber in here?"

Arik reached into the trash bin under his desk and fished out a crushed-up wad of notebook paper which he unpeeled to expose three oily condoms.

"I've been practicing." He pulled off her sweater and her bra and nuzzled her boobs, but earned no reciprocation.

"I think condoms are overrated."

He did an irony-scan of her face. "Unless you're on the pill or whatever, I don't see how I could . . . you know." He pulled off his jeans and his cock poked out of his boxers. "I'm so addicted to you. I need to have you, every day and night . . ." He laughed. "Four, five times a day if I could. I want to tie you to my bed, never let you leave, and come all over your gorgeous face till you beg me to stop."

He lashed his tongue inside her mouth, bracing her face tight in his hands, until she felt a beautiful kind of suffocation, and weakened. They remained new to the game; each kiss still had the power to amaze. They gave each other bedroom eyes— dark-rimmed, shadow eyes that looked relaxed and ravenous at the same time. He locked his hands around her buttocks and rubbed himself against her so her jeans rode down her thighs, releasing soft, taut flesh. He helped himself to her panties, pulling them down her legs, pushing two fingers inside her slickness, planting kisses on her bush.

"Arik, being with you is like the only beautiful thing there is . . . in all of this darkness."

"You know, Rose, you're real different. There's something so mysterious about you that's just so . . . fucking *addicting*."

She wanted to correct him—addic*tive*—but held her tongue. Some of his beauty faded.

He sat up and peeled off his clothes. The hickey she'd left on his collarbone from their last time came level with her eyes. She reached to feel if it was bumpy or smooth—it was smooth. She wished she could be marked like that but every bite he gave her vanished within seconds into her sand-colored flesh. He probably had blunt teeth.

Suddenly he disappeared and returned with a metallic square in his hand. His boner hadn't waned.

"Arik, I don't want us to use them."

"What do you mean?" He ripped open the foil packet and exposed the rubber disc. "I'm not letting all my practice go to waste."

"I don't like the way they smell."

"Well, fuck . . . Maybe you should've said something before I wasted all my money on, like, a box of fifty . . . I mean, how am I going to come inside of you?"

Rosemary said nothing. She massaged the small of his back and licked his neck, culminating at the depression just behind his left earlobe, a spot that always drove him to the edge. He whimpered, and dropped the half-opened rubber.

"Rose . . . you scare me."

She raised her hips so that her crotch met his, then opened her thighs so he could enter her. With one leg hooked over his butt, she reeled him down on top of her.

"Rose . . . wait . . ." He jerked up and reached for the condom.

"No, don't . . ."

"What do you want?" There was frustration in his voice. This was new.

"I want you to come inside me."

"That's really fucking insane . . ."

"I won't mind . . . if we had an accident."

"What exactly do you mean?"

"I mean . . . I'm not going to object if I had your baby."

When she looked up again, Arik was standing at the foot of the bed, cramming on his boxers. His penis dangled like a wet sock.

"What's wrong?" She was nauseated.

He shook his head in bewilderment, as if he was about to say something, then held it back. He slipped his T-shirt over his head roughly.

"Come back." Her words wavered. She reached out nonetheless.

"Don't touch me!" He slapped her hand away. "Are you fucking kidding me?" He stared at her with such contempt.

"I just meant, *if* it happened . . . You wouldn't even have to take care of it . . ."

"God! That is such a *lie*! You're trying to trap me!"

He circled the bed like a wounded lion. All his boyish reserve was gone. His face was wracked in teary spasms and the rage that came from his inability to control them. Rosemary felt naked all of a sudden—and reached for her clothes.

"My dad was right." The tears streamed down Arik's cheeks. "Some girls will try to hook you in and destroy your life. My mom trapped him by getting pregnant and she completely wrecked his life." He yanked the tear-stained Green Day shirt off his chest and flung it across the room. "Fuck you! You've forever cursed this shirt for me!"

He picked up a stool and hurled it hard at the bed, missing Rosemary by inches. Then he grabbed books, CDs, anything he could snatch off his desk and began pelting her. She took cover behind his pillows, holding back her screams in case his brother or mother heard. Item after item flew at her. A Nick Cave CD case, *Jude the Obscure*. When he ran out of things, he crumbled into a shuddering heap on the floor, his joints all gone soft. He tucked his feet under his buttocks and curled into a fetal ball, rocking himself back and forth with his eyes pressed shut. His lips had turned purple and he was shivering. The explosion of rage had sucked all the heat from his body.

Rosemary went to the door and undid the bolt. She let herself out quietly, watching as he swayed to some intimate, primal beat. He never turned to see her go.

"HELLO . . . ?" SHE SAID. "Is this . . . Bryce?"

After a pause, a petulant reply. "It is."

"I'm Rose."

"I can see that. I have caller ID."

"Why did you cancel Workshop?"

"It was obvious to me that your hearts weren't in it."

"That's so not true!" Her voice was still thick from crying. "It's the only thing I have left that's worth living for!"

"That's a little melodramatic. Even for an actor."

"Mr. Z, I'm sorry . . ." She was going to start crying again. Another pause.

"Please," she said, "just say something."

"I don't see how that would change anything."

"I want to go back to before. When we could talk. When you said I could call you to talk about anything."

"And you appreciate that now? In retrospect?"

"I could come to your house."

"Please don't. It's best not to burden my spouse with my extramural obligations."

"Why are you talking like this?" A lump caught in her throat. Not him, too.

"I'm in a meeting right now."

"At school?"

"No, not at school. Look, I really shouldn't be on the phone."

"Can we talk though? Later?"

"I'll send you a text. I have to go now." In the background, she heard murmuring voices and recognized the familiar screech of chair legs on institutional linoleum.

Less than a minute after they hung up, Rosemary's phone beeped. She breathlessly scrolled to its text screen:

"C U @ end of St Cls Ln. 5 PM. Lets hv dinner . . . I MISS U"

Her tears evaporated.

"WHERE'S MIRA?"

Mrs. Park shrugged, her eyes fixed on the TV screen, fingers cracking open chestnuts and popping them into her mouth. Her favorite Korean soap was on—a period weep-a-thon about an insufferable maid who kept the imperial household together with all her cooking.

"I heard you two fighting earlier."

Mrs. Park shrugged again.

As she walked down Santa Claus Lane, Rosemary noted that every house on the street—with the exception of the gay writer's, Kate Ireland's and theirs—had some kind of Halloween adornment. Foam skeletons hanging from rafters, plastic pumpkins doubling as lamps, rag-doll witches sprouting black tinsel hair. She was reminded again of Arik's remark that she felt like the inside of a jack-o'-lantern.

This year, without Mr. Park, their front porch sat bare. Last year, when their father was still alive, the girls had badgered him into buying a couple of pumpkins, and together they'd carved toothy smiles into them. The girls were surprised by his deftness with a hunting knife, even as he complained that Halloween was a pagan festival.

Rosemary heard the Nissan Maxima whirring up the street at five sharp. The recent rain had melted away the smog and the whole neighborhood was given a new, glossy alertness—Mr. Z's car looked especially shiny, like it'd been driven right out of a commercial. Rosemary opened the door and sank into the passenger seat. She sucked in the musky fumes of his car deodorant and was ready to go to sleep right there.

"Hadn't heard from you in weeks. How's the honeymoon going?" She pursed her lips.

"I suppose I'm here to run back to when things go south. You must know how insulting that is. It makes me feel like a parent."

"I'm sorry."

"Don't say that unless you mean it."

"I mean it." She brandished the red Buca di Beppo pen she'd lifted from his car months before. "Here—I'm returning this. I stole it."

"Keep it." He drove on. They passed autumnal foliage and evergreen shrubs, crack houses and kindergartens, liquor stores and libraries, and merged onto the freeway. "You hungry?"

THE WAITER KNEW instinctively where Mr. Z wanted to sit. Though the restaurant was deserted—it wasn't yet six o'clock—they were led to a corner booth in the Grotto, a private room two steps down from the main dining area. There, the walls and ceiling were covered in a tangle of plastic grapevines, empty wine bottles and more reproduction vacation photos than Rosemary had ever seen.

"This is such a cool, cool place." She leaned back and gazed at the decor.

"Glad you like it." He called a waiter over. "A pint of Moretti for me, a strawberry shake for the young lady, and garlic bread for the table, to start."

She liked how confidently he ordered, without consulting her or the menu, and how he said, "for the table, to start." Her father would have taken an eternity to make up his mind, plus he'd never order alcohol at any non-Korean establishment because he was paranoid about being cheated.

"I love it here," Rosemary said, finally. "It's so unique."

"Can you imagine, a bunch of suits sitting in a Minneapolis office park, deciding what goes on the walls of each one of these eighty branches?"

"Wait. This restaurant's part of a chain?" Rosemary's enchantment dipped.

"Oh, my poor, poor bunny." He gazed at her. She detected a little sneer at the edge of his lips, then it vanished. "Look at the prompt service, the organized clutter, the large yet homogenized menu. How could this be anything but a chain for Americans who think they're individuals who eat at special places but don't want the anxiety of the strange menu they'd get at a real Italian restaurant."

Along with their drinks, a large clump of garlic bread arrived, steaming with heat. Mr Z. asked for chicken parmigiana and something called "strangled priest," again without glancing at the menu.

The garlic bread burned the roof of Rosemary's mouth, but she could eat this food forever, with Mr. Z sitting across from her, their feet occasionally bumping, famous arias flowing from the speakers. She sucked on her strawberry milkshake and leaned back. The shake had a comforting synthetic flavor, reminiscent of her early childhood with its store-bought quilts and Barney the purple dinosaur singing, "I love you, you love me."

"Do you take your wife here?"

"Why do you assume that married people are joined at the hip, that we do everything together? We're both busy individuals. There are things we enjoy together and there are things we enjoy apart."

"My parents did everything together," said Rosemary. "But I doubt they loved each other. I never saw them once, like, hold hands." She paused. Hoping to seem innocuous, she looked at her nails and said: "What's your wife look like?"

"Well, you could say she's not hideous. It's not like I keep her in the attic."

"Do you have a photo?"

"I had one in my wallet. But that wallet got stolen."

"Do you love her?"

He looked into her eyes: "We're quite married."

"I know, but . . ."

"What I mean is that we're *quite* married. As opposed to *very* married. Why this sudden interest?"

His shin grazed hers. She moved her legs away, but his legs came back and found them again. She felt his foot rubbing the back of her calf like a needy cat, and all she could think of was whether he'd leave mud tracks on her freshly laundered jeans.

"This is what you were really asking, isn't it?" He reached for her hand now, and kneaded her finger joints. "Rose, you know how fond I am of you. You needn't have been so coy. Not with me."

"Coming through!" warned a voice. Mr. Z released Rosemary's hands abruptly. The waiter lowered two huge platters—one holding fried cutlets and another with wormy strands of pasta mixed with beef ragu.

"I told you not to fill up on that garlic bread," he said, jauntily avuncular.

She counted the seconds until the waiter was gone. "I'm not actually hungry. I just wanted to say . . . I feel so safe with you. I think you're perfect." Her eyes welled up at that word. "I think your house is perfect . . . and I'll bet your wife is perfect, too."

Mr. Z was halfway into his first cutlet. "Nobody's perfect. You know that."

"What I'm trying to say is . . . my mother's kind of a psycho . . ."

"Everybody's mother is kind of a psycho, kid."

She nodded. "I know it's probably too late now, but I was wondering . . ." She stared at her strawberry shake. "Would you and your wife consider adopting me?"

Mr. Z took a big gulp of his beer. She knew she had to ram home the rest of the pitch now, sway him before the word *no* formed in his mouth.

"I'm totally low-maintenance, I'll get after-school jobs so you wouldn't have to, like, give me an allowance and stuff. I'm quiet, good with chores, I'll keep getting scholarships. And I can enter-tain myself—I don't watch much TV, I'll stay out of your way." She felt herself floundering. "It'll be adoption in name only. I promise I won't bother you guys for anything . . . It's just that my mother's threatening to ship me to Korea and I just . . . I just . . . I can't go, I *can't* leave here."

Mr. Z appeared to be thinking. She pressed on:

"I'll pay you back as soon as I can. For the lawyers and paper-work and so on."

"You know," he leaned in toward her, and she mirrored the move with great anticipation, "I wasn't quite expecting that from you, kiddo. You threw me a real curveball, I have to say. That's not fair."

"But you said, you said I could talk to you about anything."

"Furthermore . . ." He lowered his voice. His smile was sugary but his words were not. "Furthermore, here is neither the time nor the place to discuss such a matter. I can ill afford to put myself in a situation that could be of a criminal nature."

"Yes, but I'm not asking you to do anything bad. It's just that I don't want to have to go . . ."

"Rosemary, that's all very well, but I'm your teacher, nothing more." He pulled his legs away from her as he said this. "It's important that you remember there are boundaries. *It's beyond my control.*" A direct quote, from the coldest moment in *Dangerous Liaisons*. He glanced at the plates. "Are you going to eat any more of that?"

She shook her head, and he instantly gestured for the waiter.

A couple of minutes later, they were walking briskly to the exit. By the door was a table with a basket full of red Buca di Beppo pens. Rosemary fished out Mr. Z's pen from her shoulder bag and returned it to the pile.

THE HOUSE WAS dark when she returned. It looked like nobody was home, although she knew that wasn't possible. The stupid choppers were at it again, combing the evening skies, probably looking for the same carjackers or home invaders they'd been tracking for the past six months. Except for the chubby couple walking their whippet and the sullen clanks of dinner cleanup, Santa Claus Lane was shut down for the night.

Rosemary entered her house, feeling the kind of loneliness that in recent weeks she thought she'd banished for good. Once inside, she was struck by a strong bleachy odor—clean, industrial, unkind. Mira's bedroom door opened, and Mrs. Park emerged, her face made strange by a collage of shadows.

"Did something happen?" Rosemary asked.

"Nothing, nothing. She having period, veh tired. Is nothing." Mrs. Park pushed her toward her room. "You go sleep."

"It's only seven-thirty."

"Baby, you go bed. You mind own business." This time, Mrs. Park pushed more insistently, even opening her door for her. "This not you business."

Rosemary went to her room and locked the door. It was just as well. She rushed to her window, half expecting Arik waiting outside, mad with remorse, a ready boner tenting his pants. But there was nobody.

She pulled her curtains shut and took out her cellphone. No new messages. With a few taps on the keypad, she deleted Arik's number from her directory, along with the cartoon icon of Apu from *The Simpsons* she'd assigned to him. Scrolling down to Archived Messages, she played her favorite, received a week before and saved away like the rarest ambrosia. She pressed the phone to her ear till her lobe ached:

"Rose, hey, I know your phone is off and you're probably asleep right now but I wanted to leave you a message that I, uh, don't have the balls to say to your face. I am so deliriously out of my mind with you, man. It's 3 A.M. and I can't go to sleep right now thinking about you, and how, I don't know, like, I want to be inside you all the time . . . [laughs] I hope I'm not freaking you out. I probably sound like I'm high right now, but, well, I guess I am high, on you. You're entirely responsible for this. You make me feel like everything's possible, like we're spiritually bound [giggles]. Yeah, that's it. And I just want to be with you, you know, and fuck you and fuck you and fuck you. Oh my God, I love the way you wriggle and squeal when you're coming. I came like eight times today thinking about that. I hope this

doesn't sound too insane or stalkery or anything, but
I'm so hard again right now and I'm gonna come so
fucking hard for you . . . Um, what else do I have to say?
Oh, right . . . I'll kill for you, I'll die for you. I swear it.
Iloveyou, bye."

With a few icy thumb strokes, Rosemary erased the message and with it, every trace of Arik Kistorian.

Knocking on the door. Some idiot was toggling her doorknob.

"Okay, okay, I'm coming . . ." She hid her phone.

It was her mother, in yet another deplorable, shapeless housecoat.

"Why you lock door?"

"I'm not in the mood to be lectured. What do you want?"

"Next week, terminator is coming. We go somewhere."

"Could you say that again, in English please?"

"Next week, terminator coming here. We having many termites. They putting poison inside the house, killing termites."

"So?"

"Poison, Rosie! Everywhere. They cover up house, every things. We cannot stay here. It's FDA legal poison! We go away for three days, mandatory. I already talk to Quellie Soo. She says we staying at her house."

"No way am I staying in some stranger's house. Have you told Mira any of this?"

"Notchet. She sleeping."

"At this hour?"

"She has period, same like me, very tired. Do not disturb."

"I'm positive both Mira and I won't want to stay at Quellie Soo's. Couldn't we go to a hotel or something?"

"Hotel expensive, Rosie."

"I didn't mean the Ritz. I meant, like, Slumber Inn."

"Okay, I ask Quellie. I ask."

At long last, her mother went away. Rosemary waited till her footsteps subsided and the electronic hum of the TV in the den had developed its steady tinniness. Then she made for Mira's door.

It was unlocked, and she stepped right into the darkness.

"Mira?"

In the moonlight, she made out her sister's silhouette on the bed—flat on her back, hands clasped over her heart like Snow White in her glass coffin. The chiffon drapes were billowing slightly, which was strange because all the windows were shut.

"Mira, are you asleep?"

A small, mournful voice—more escaping air than voice—answered:

"Not really . . ."

On any other day, Rosemary might have guessed Mira was pulling her leg, cackling secretly under her comforter. Not tonight. She wanted to embrace her baby sister but feared encountering chilly, sepulchral flesh.

"What happened? Are you okay?"

"She locked me in the attic . . ." Her voice was hoarse. "She hates me. She always has."

Rosemary was queasy with guilt. She hadn't even included Mira in her adoption request to Mr. Z. In her selfish pursuit to be understood by boys, by men, by everybody else, she'd completely forgotten her true best friend.

"I'm so sorry, Mira. I'm so sorry I wasn't around." She swallowed back her tears. "I won't let it happen again, I swear. No matter what happens, everything will be fine if we stick together."

She reached out for Mira's hand, which turned out to be feverish, and not at all cold. "You're my little Gas Rat."

Mira tried to laugh but instead hacked a chesty dry cough and it sounded as hollow as a forgotten room in an old house. Its severity spooked the both of them.

"Want some water?"

The shadow shook its head.

"What were you doing in the attic anyway?"

"Nothing . . ."

"You mustn't provoke her. I know it's hard but, please, we cannot provoke her."

Mira kept quiet.

"Why are your hands clasped like that?"

"I was praying . . ."

"You don't have to do that. You know it doesn't work."

A gastric yawp from Mira's stomach chirrupped through the silence. It sounded like a cricket in her ribcage. "I'm praying to the Devil," she said. "I think She listens."

GIVE ME SOMETHING GOOD TO EAT

Quellie Soo called them a Bell cab. Rosemary canceled it and called for a People's Taxi. Quellie Soo booked them a room at the Motor Lodge. Rosemary canceled that and reserved a room at the Slumber Inn.

"Who cares what she wants?" Rosemary told Mrs. Park. "That person's not part of our family."

"But, baby," her mother said, "she's our realtor."

As their cab departed, all three Park girls craned their necks back and watched as a team of swarthy men pulled a giant red-and-white striped tarp over their house, lifting it strategically so it wouldn't catch on the chimney, the satellite dish, the falling-apart gable. The men climbed up and down casually. They had a lot of faith in shingles.

One waved to the cab. Then with a heave-ho, his pals pulled the tarp square down the sides of the house and its familiar form disappeared. The big top was in town.

"I lost the war," muttered Mira. Rosemary squeezed her hand.

At the end of Santa Claus Lane, they encountered another cab driven by a younger man coming in the opposite direction. Both drivers rolled down their windows and traded greetings in battle-ax Armenian. Rosemary had assumed that their driver was Iranian or Pakistani from the giant GOD BLESS AMERICA decal on his window.

"That guy," the driver explained as he rolled up his window, "his wife always asking for money. Never enough money."

"He should get a divorce," said Rosemary. Her mother elbowed her.

"He already did. This is third wife."

KATE WONDERED WHERE Mrs. Park was taking her daughters in the taxi that had just crossed paths with hers. She got an answer when her own cab pulled up to her house and she saw the giant tent across the street.

Her driver clucked his tongue. "Now all their rats will run away to your house, and next year it'll be your turn to make your house to wear the dress."

Kate paid the tab gruffly. "Could you wait till I get inside and wave at you?" Her driver struck her as sort of shifty-seeming, but at least he was young and had hairy fists.

"No problem. You go. I wait here." He rolled down his window and lit up his cigarette.

Kate started climbing out of the cab, but was knocked back by her still unfamiliar new center of gravity.

"Could I ask you to do something else for me?"

The driver nodded.

"If you see a man—brown hair, early to mid-thirties—trying to enter the house while I'm in there, could you sound your horn twice, to warn me?"

"No problem, lady. You go." He exhaled a big puff of smoke. "I have only one question."

"What's that?"

He looked at her form, placing her pregnancy at six or seven months, from personal knowledge. "No-good husband, huh? If you want, I have friends who can make him go away." He mimed a gun.

She smiled wanly. "Thank you"—she glanced at the driver's ID on the dash—"Mr. Kistorian."

Five minutes later, Kate gave him the thumbs-up from inside her living room. He waved back and started up the cab.

SHE MADE THE offer and Mary-Sue jumped for it. Kate had feared conflict, and even worse, mixed signals, but her mother had jumped at the chance to move back to Santa Claus Lane, at least until after the baby was born.

"I'll be out of your hair as soon as you can manage on your own," Mary-Sue had said, instantly assuming her old self-sacrificing bossiness even as she hopped along on crutches. Kate found this comical and poignant. Both were new reactions—she'd previously felt only guilt at her mother's frequent gestures of martyrdom.

Her job now was to get the house shipshape ahead of Mary-Sue's arrival in two weeks. The empty Scotch bottles had to go. The floors swept, carpets vacuumed. The ironing board taken out of her mother's old bedroom, along with the piles of clothes she'd been meaning to take to Goodwill for three years.

She began with the bottles—out into the recycling bin. When she reentered the house, she was alight with the euphoria of someone who was finally in control of her life.

"Boo." It was Bluto.

She shrieked and backed violently into the fridge, bumping her elbow.

"I didn't mean to scare you."

He was laughing. His big arms straddled the kitchen doorway and he gazed at her belly with a strident possessiveness. "Your front door was unlocked."

She snatched a bunch of bananas and hurled it at his face, still hyperventilating.

He—great reflexes—caught the bunch. "Aren't you even going to say hello?"

"You creep!" Her eyes darted to the counter—the butcher's block was there, but where were all the knives?

"I put those away." He gave her a wounded smile and stepped in closer. "Kate, for God's sake, it's only me. *Me.* The only person who ever *got* you, ever."

She remembered the delicate high school Bluto, not this corrupted copy, with the crow's feet and the new facial muscles that gave his dimples a hard edge.

He moved toward her, then passed her altogether to shut and lock the back door behind them. "I'm never going to hurt you. Or our baby." He watched for her reaction. "I'm not sure how it could have happened, but nothing's a hundred percent, I guess."

"Nobody said it was yours." She heard the lack of conviction in her own voice.

He stretched out his hand, edging closer. "Can I feel it anyway?"

Hold still, she told herself. She stood her ground. "They still haven't found her, you know. That girl."

"Who, Brittany?" He let his hand dance in the air like a shadow puppet before his fingers made a gentle landing on her belly, and she held her breath. "I'm long over her."

His touch gave her goosebumps. She backed away. "What did you do to her?"

"She ran out on me. I misjudged her. She was bad news. I made a mistake, okay? People make mistakes."

"How can she be 'bad news'? She's fifteen years old."

"Yes, I'm well aware of that. Do you want to go on punishing me or do you want to hear what I've come to say?"

"You've got nothing to say that I want to hear, Paul."

"Paul? So now I'm just Paul again." He took a step back. "Look, I had nothing to do with whatever happened to her."

She opened the fridge and poured herself a glass of milk. She had to keep moving.

"I don't want to debate this," he said. "You've got no one and I've got no one. You know me like no other and I know you like no other. Don't you see the grand sweep of our narrative? Clean slate. Square one. Baby steps." He reached out again for her belly.

"We're not sixteen years old anymore. I've moved on. I really have." She brought out a bag of lollipops from the larder and emptied it into a ceramic dog bowl. "Trick-or-treaters will be here any second now."

He unwrapped one of the candies.

"Think about it, Kate. Clean slate. You and me." The doorbell rang: trick-or-treaters. He stuck the red lollipop into his mouth and gave her one last look. "The knives are under the sink."

THEIR WINDOW ON the third floor had a view of the parking lot with its charming pair of matching potholes. On the ground floor was an alarmed exit by a dumpster where they'd watched the chambermaids eat burritos and bum cigarettes off two separate delivery boys. Other than that, more rooms, and more rooms.

"Couldn't you at least have picked a place with a pool?" Mira said.

"You don't even swim," said Rosemary.

"I was welcoming the prospect of a glamorous drowning death."

Mira exhaled onto the windowpane and scrawled a skull on the condensation before it vanished.

In the facing wing, a geezer with a sunken chest watched TV in his underwear. Above him, an enormous woman holding a bag of chips in one hand closed the drapes with the other. Three windows from her, a good-looking man in a business suit sat on the bedcovers, clutching his head. Each window was a vignette, limited in narrative scope and yet compelling in its immediacy. They never saw any children.

"Hey," Mira said, "do you think people are staying here tonight to avoid trick-or-treaters?"

"Maybe. But there's someone here who's already in costume." Rosemary turned to their mother, who was snoring in one of the two queen-size beds—sleeping mask covering her eyes, shower cap over her hair, sheets pulled up to her chin. They cackled.

"Hot damn!"

"*Hot damn!*"

RAYMOND BOLTED FROM room to room, turning off the lights and checking that every single window and every door was locked. When the house was completely secured and darkened, he activated the alarm system. *Armed to Stay, No Delay.* He sank into his favorite armchair, whisky by his side, loaded gun on his lap. The curtains remained parted so he could see exactly who or what was coming at him. If he'd simply wished to avoid those candy-grubbers, he would have checked into a motel for the night. No, he was keeping watch. Out the picture window loomed the cropped panorama of houses and hills, twilit guardians of secrets that would never be shared. It was up to him to look out for himself. He knew how tempting a target his home was. It was Halloween.

Then, from somewhere close, the scratching sounds began.

He sat up alert as a hound. With the pistol in his hand, he rose slowly, ears as his guide. Little hands, little fingers, little nails were chipping away furiously at hard wood—a door or a wall, it seemed. Someone was either trying to get in or trying to get out. At the base of the stairs, Raymond realized that the ruckus was coming from upstairs.

He went up the steps steadily, wincing when he released a creak. The scratching instantly ceased. Fuck! He held his breath. Then the scratching resumed, more avidly. He cocked his gun at the top of the stairs, and took a deep breath. The sounds were coming from higher still. The attic. There was a swift patter, a movement from one side of the house to the other. Clearly, something was up there, and it sensed that he was coming.

He pulled down the retractable stairway and climbed toward the attic door. *Shine little glow-worm . . . glimmer, glimmer . . .*

He sprang open the door. Three gray rats the size of pumpkin-bread loaves stood in the threshold on their hind legs, their tiny pink hands perched in midair like Hanna-Barbera cartoons of themselves. One lost its balance and was about to keel forward when Raymond slammed the door against it. More pitter-patter as the rodents dispersed. And then, shrill critter chatter.

"Jesus! Fuck!"

Where the hell had they come from? Raymond backed down the steps quickly. Out a small window he glimpsed the red-and-white tarp over the Parks' house and instantly became enraged. He'd seen it, yet he hadn't *seen* it. He hadn't been officially notified. Wasn't that illegal? He would have made preparations against the rodent exodus.

Exactly seven years ago this hour, he was driving back to his hotel from the Wichita funeral home where he'd bidden farewell to his mother's body. Plastic skeletons colonized every housing tract, taunting him with their gap-toothed grins, offering no solace, no dead man's wisdom. He recalled the hotel valets—willfully ignorant numbskulls—hiding their inbred pug faces behind rubber devil masks and mistaking his black cloak for a costume.

"I vant you to believe . . . to believe in things that you cannot." They quoted Bram Stoker at him in Bela Lugosi-ese.

Out Raymond's picture window, the ragtag Halloween parade was just starting up. Pint-sized monsters and fuzzy-wuzzy animals trailed behind taller chaperones. A towering Statue of Liberty waited for a junior hobbit to finish tying his shoelaces. Bevies of grade-school princesses teetered on heels like pygmy whores, their mothers egging them on. This was the twilight crowd, gormless blackmailers who wanted little more than petrified fruit chews and praise for their crayon whiskers. He didn't have to worry about them calling at his door—they never did. He'd tucked his Jaguar in the garage and turned off all his lights. As far as the outside was concerned, nobody was home.

In this "changing neighborhood," as his realtor had termed Santa Claus Lane, the night folk were what people had to worry about. Hooded teenage boys roaming the streets, their faces shadowy, anonymous. He remembered the uproar the previous Halloween when a band of ruffians, all minors, assaulted three women in neighboring Sierra Lucre—the only time he'd ever felt sympathy for soccer moms. These fiends had no respect for boundaries, not on a night like this. These were trickster lords who cared nothing for sweets; they'd scratch obscenities on your windowpane with switchblades and piss on your doormat without so much as a "trick or treat?"

He'd seen these boys prowling in packs on Halloween nights

past, swigging from plastic bottles of rum, clucking, whistling, hollering, strutting down the center of the street in their oversized pants like kings of the netherworld, all cheekbones and demon eyes and not a shred of soul. These kids had no code of honor; they shot babies and slashed old men. With them it was all death, all darkness, all the time, and they spooked him no end. When he was writing his Deathwatch books, his flesh-eating zombies were bourgeois, milquetoast innocents, wronged by the indignity of death. Every time he saw one of these street hoods he was reminded how fey and parochial his imagination had been. How could he return to writing horror when he no longer understood the form?

He took a gulp of whisky and tried to think of jollier things— spending the rest of his life in flannel pajamas, watching *Law & Order* reruns.

The sun was gone now. The little ones had taken their costumed selves home, laden with teeth-rotting loot. A while later came a burst of three separate sirens: one fire, one cop, one EMT. Living in the neighborhood, Raymond had learned to tell them apart. Then they, too, faded.

A hooded figure came up to the porch. He rang the bell with a long, thin, green finger, then stood with a solemn watchfulness. The blade on his scythe glinted.

"Optimist," Raymond hissed and crouched out of view. He gripped his gun.

An old nursery chant slipped off his drink-slicked lips:

> *Hinx, minx, the old witch winks.*
> *The fat begins to fry.*
> *Nobody's home but Jumping Joan,*
> *Father, Mother, and I.*

Stick, stock, stone dead.
Blind men cannot see.
Every knave will have a slave,
You or I . . . must . . . be . . . he.

The hood, the Reaper—whatever he was—slinked away.

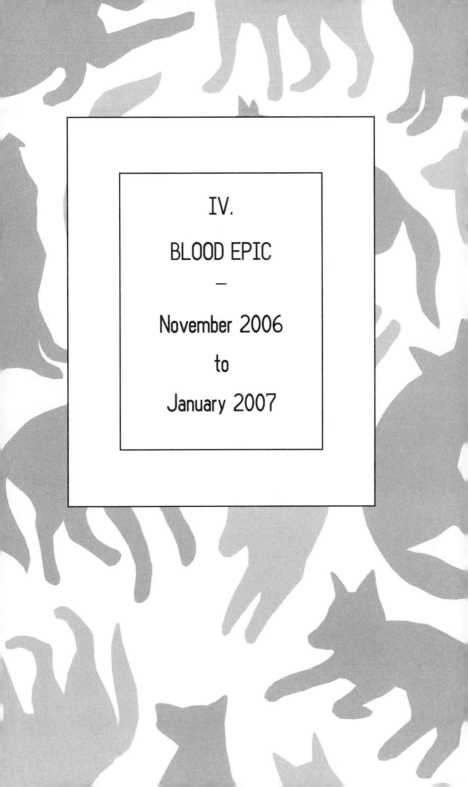

IV.

BLOOD EPIC

–

November 2006

to

January 2007

- 13 -

LIGHTS UP

It had to be done—this was tradition. Every Saturday morning after Halloween, the gnomish retirees and elfin Boy Scouts of Santa Claus Lane peeled themselves out of bed and got to work, undetected and without fanfare, driving trucks, snipping foliage, hiding cables behind thickets.

Mary-Sue arrived just in time to see these Christmas lights go up. Five years away and she'd almost forgotten how much she liked it here as the holidays approached. Santa Claus Lane seemed even more out of place and time—with its shaggy firs, wood cottages, and view of purple mountains. It was the only time of year the deodars were completely appropriate and not just endlessly shedding nuisances. Her lair in Homestead was so set apart from its neighbors that she'd forgotten what a normal street was like. The memories of raising Kate in her house came rushing back, brought on by cooking smells from next door. But of course, Kate was no longer her little girl, generous with hugs and laughter. Now, there wasn't room enough in Rome; Mary-Sue found herself stepping out for air. She had to remind herself why she was back: it wasn't Kate, it wasn't California—it was the baby. The baby was going to reset everything.

Still on crutches, she hobbled along Santa Claus Lane, watching over the volunteers as they pruned the deodars, and shouting alerts to them whenever they missed a branch or something was dangling funny. She'd made herself enough of a nuisance that a smiling delegate from the neighborhood Holiday Committee approached her the next afternoon with a "very important" task: procuring a new Santa for the festivities now that Mr. Shields, the longtime go-to, had died. Mary-Sue was about to volunteer Larry, then remembered he was on the other coast and ached a little.

"I'll find you a Santa," she told the committee. "So long as you promise me his sleigh won't be one of those electric cars. If he runs somebody over, you'll have a public relations catastrophe on your hands."

The final week of November—*voila!*—the deodars of Santa Claus Lane were completely trimmed with colored bulbs and the street itself lined with inflatable snowmen, those cheery apparitions best savored with mulled wine and an SUV. The ordinary became sublime. Everybody dimmed their headlights, and cruised the street like U-boats in the ocean deep.

The Santa deadline loomed.

RAYMOND FELT AS though he'd been on the phone with Dartmoor since the summer ended.

"Your dad has SAD," said the nurse. "Your father has been diagnosed with SAD, seasonal affective disorder. The doctor's put him on paroxetine and we need your approval for the light therapy. We'd like to install full spectrum bulbs and a dawn simulator in his room, which brightens his existing lamps to simulate the sun about an hour before he wakes up."

"Sounds reasonable. Bill me."

Then the doorbell rang. Out his picture window, he spied an aged bird in a lumpy sweater standing stiffly on his porch like one of those Salvation Army grifters outside the supermarket— except for her crutches. Those crutches dignified her. He combed his hair.

"Raymond?"

"Yes?" He saw now that it was Kate Ireland's mother, the one he assumed had died when he stopped seeing her poking around years ago. "Oh, hello, it's you!"

"Listen, would you like to be this year's Santa Claus?" She didn't beat around the bush, this one. "Every year, as you know, we have a Santa on the street. And I'm thinking you'd be a great candidate."

She was met with Raymond's stunned silence.

"I was going to ask Silas Brown at 1041 but that's a huge way to hobble for Tiny Tim here," she lifted up her crutches. "Silas was actually my top choice *because* those nazis on the committee told me it would be upsetting for young children to see a Santa of color. Can you believe it? Those fuckers *actually* said that out loud!"

"And I'm your second choice, why? Because I'm a member of another oppressed minority?"

"Oh, for crying out loud, it ain't brain surgery!" She thumped her right crutch impatiently. "Look, you want to do something good for the goddamn world, don't you?"

The twitch in her lip as she said *goddamn* warmed his heart. "So, just fat suit and ho, ho, ho?"

He was actually entertaining the idea. Mary-Sue smiled. "There's a booth where you'd sit and have those rug rats come up to you. They no longer have them sit on your lap. That's now considered unhygienic, etcetera."

The phone started to ring. He left her at the door to get it. It was the nurse at Dartmoor again.

"Mr. van der Holt, I'm so sorry for calling back. But your father's just said that he wants very much for you to visit at Christmas."

He put the receiver down and ran back to Mary-Sue at the door: "And what do I get out of this?"

"Well, let's see, a momentary sense of goodwill? Free cocoa?"

Raymond was back inside and on the phone. "Look, tell my father I've got a professional engagement at Christmas. I'll see him later."

He hung up the phone hastily and returned to Mary-Sue with a slight shortness of breath. He stretched out his hand to her: "I'm all yours."

RAYMOND CHERISHED THE colorful stacks of toilet reading that showed up at his door near the end of each year. It was marvelous how marketers located his home address and worked out his weaknesses—monogrammed linen stationery, shawl-collar cashmere robes and an endless onslaught of shearling slides and alpaca scarves. The art museum catalogs had modernist scarves from Japan that looked like ghost scarves, the ethereal remains of silk scarves that had died and gone to scarf heaven. And fleece everything—how he loved the smiling sound of "fleece."

He was especially grateful for the catalogs this year because they distracted him from a particular MoMA greeting card that had arrived that afternoon, a minimalist black triangle standing in for a Christmas tree. It was signed: *You Know Who*.

Who the hell was You Know Who?

Dear RvdH,
You know what.
You know why.
You know when.

> *X,*
> *You Know Who*

Raymond stared at the black triangle. He inverted it. Now it was some modernist pubis, like Miro's version of what that naked girl slapped against his window.

He banished the card and photo to the corner of the living room where his grotesque Pop art monographs lived. He had his father's winter blues. As repellent as it was to him to face up to the sly workings of DNA, this fact sealed their connection. He had for years spent December and January indoors, in a flannel robe thrown over silk pajamas. Every man in their family handed his melancholy down like some pauper's heirloom. The blues was his link to his cousin, Gus, who sat in a Sioux City jail for shooting a co-worker in the ass when he misplaced his lunch pail; it linked him also to his paternal grandfather, a lapsed Klansman, who on his deathbed had requested sex with "Hebrew Sally," a girl from his youth. He had the blues in his blood. While researching one of his books, he'd come across a reference to the blues in the *Getica*, the sixth-century text that chronicled the diaspora of the Gothic tribes. The author, Jordanes, wrote that on the isle of Scandza, or what would become modern Scandinavia, people went through a schizoid cycle of joy and sorrow with the continual light of midsummer and the interminable darkness of winter, and were "like no other race in their sufferings and blessings." His winter blues was not a faddish new ailment, like ADD, carpal tunnel or Tourette's. Why fight history?

He drank his Scotch and picked up *The Waning of the Middle Ages*, which was gathering dust on the coffee table. He'd underlined a passage years ago about how everybody in the Middle Ages was perpetually high-strung: *So violent and motley was life, that it bore the mixed smell of blood and roses.*

And where was his houseghost during this time of need? He'd disengaged his alarm system specially for her. But no, she was spurning him. What did he have to do to bring her back? Beg? Cry? Strip? He'd do all three.

"I'm vulnerable right now," he bellowed into the emptiness. "Come get me!" The ice-maker rumbled and plopped out some consolatory frozen phalanxes.

He undressed and lay supine on the sofa. He clicked on the remote and found the show called *Desperate Housewives*, which the critics said used to be funny, or good, or popular—he couldn't remember which—and fell asleep.

QUELLIE SOO HAD been showing up often, and the girls heard her anxiously repeat the word *staging* as a noun, which repulsed them. One morning, a furniture rental truck dropped off two antique side tables, three frilly lamps and a bordello-style chaise lounge with red chenille fabric. Quellie and Mrs. Park spent the day dragging these pieces of alien furniture around the house until every room felt strange.

"Quellie Soo says staging is like making theater," Mrs. Park said to the girls at dinner, whether they were listening or not. "Realtor is producer, owner is director, children is actor. We make our house the dream of buyer. We stage open house on day after Christmas. Sale can be very fast, Quellie say. Very few houses in California, very many buyer. If buyer ask for one-week escrow, we must say yes, believe you me."

Rosemary frowned. "So, we could effectively be thrown out of our own house by New Year's? It's December seventh! Where will we stay?"

"No worry," Mrs. Park stated calmly. "I already book airplane ticket."

Mira backed her chair away from the table noisily and slid off it like a jellyfish.

"Mira, where you go?"

"Leave me alone. I need to pray."

HER ROOM HAD been transformed into some deranged Martian's idea of what a girl's room should look like, but the makeover had been half-assed. Plastic wrap covered two cheesy framed prints of butterflies to be unveiled at some future occasion, and stuffed animals neglected for a decade were given pride of place on her shelf alongside her books about unsolved murders, UFOs and poltergeists. On Quellie Soo's genius advice, her mother had hired an old Korean couple to paint the bedroom walls a peachy pink to match the new Martha Stewart Kmart quilt that would grace her bed during the open house. Her old sheets were still on her bed, faded blue Care Bears marching across the mattress, goodwill shooting off their bellies. There was a brown stain from one of her periods that had never washed off, and the way it blotted Daydream Bear's head made him look like the victim of a maniac's sledgehammer. She'd always liked that about it.

She retrieved a shoebox from under her bed and took out all the little religious icons she'd been collecting. She mounted them on her night table: a rubber Buddha, a wind-up Moses with a bowlegged stride, a family of genderless Peruvian worry dolls, a garish clay Hindu Ganesha, Rosemary's Jesus nightlight, the milk-chocolate dreidel her classmate Ruth gave her back in third grade, and a series of laminated prayer cards featuring Catholic saints in action poses, sometimes leaking blood. These cards she cherished the most, and she blew kisses at each one.

Some mornings, instead of taking the bus to school, she would ride in the opposite direction to downtown LA, hopping off at the Cathedral of Our Lady of the Angels perched atop Bunker Hill. She felt comforted by the cathedral's egalitarian, Southern Californian approach to worship—Catholicism with all its dark cavities filled in and sanded out, designed to welcome the stampeding population of twenty-first-century Los Angeles with its head-spinning diversity of casual footwear. It was light and airy, yet sturdy, a terracotta mesa with such clean lines that it came closer to a modern art museum than a place you went to contemplate your failings. The wooden benches for congregants even came with butt grooves. But Mira's single favorite thing there wasn't the enormous tapestry with its multi-ethnic kids in sneakers marching in solidarity behind Boniface and Mother Teresa, nor the chipper tablet in the mausoleum dedicated to "Beloved Dad" from his "Little Buckaroos." Her favorite thing was the gift shop, which sold a dazzling array of knickknacks and keepsakes, from biblical-themed nail files to statuettes of US Marines with guardian angels looking over their shoulders, sized to sit atop TVs. It was there that she began her collection of sixty-five-cent prayer cards, purchased one at a time like ecumenical trading cards. The twenty she'd amassed were the pride of her shrine, glued to the inner walls of the shoebox like stained-glass panels. There was one of Lazarus, stray pups sniffing at his toes, another of some lady holding up a washcloth embossed with Jesus's placid visage ("the Holy Face"), but her dearest was the one of a New World saint—Kateri Tekakwitha, the Lily of the Mohawks, a blessed virgin who, on the card at least, resembled Rosemary to a tee.

In the dark, Mira lit up a semicircle of tea lights. After placing the shoebox chapel behind the menagerie of deities, she opened her palms:

> *Tyger, Tyger, burning bright*
> *In the forests of the night,*
> *What immortal hand or eye*
> *Could frame thy fearful symmetry?*

ROSEMARY PEDALED HARD. Two weeks with no practice left her winded as she rode up the hill. The body forgot things, got dumb. Every step became an education all over again. Even the seat felt bizarrely foreign, as if molded under someone else's butt. She was a block from Mr. Z's house when she realized it was Mira's lousy old bike that she'd been riding. How could she not have noticed the spastic tassels sprouting from the handlebars? Why was it so freaking dark out tonight?

When she came to the blue cottage at the top of Mount Curve, she dialed Mr. Z on her cell. He took forever to pick up. Three rings, four . . . The curtains were drawn and she couldn't see a thing. Warm lamplight upstairs and downstairs. In one upstairs window, an erratic flicker—somebody was watching TV. Five rings. Two cars were in the drive, neither of them his but he'd probably parked the Nissan inside the garage, given how fastidious he was about his things. The stupid bull fucking terrier swaggered outside the front door, tethered, watching her. Six. Just when she thought his voicemail prompt would trigger, he answered, his voice crushed and slurry, like he'd been asleep.

"What's up?"

"Do you have time to talk?"

"It's really kind of late, you know."

"I'm outside."

"What?"

"I'm standing outside your house. Right now."

She waited for him to look out. Maybe wave. Not even a flutter in the curtains.

"You're on Mount Curve?"

"Yeah. I really need to talk to you."

"You know it's not possible . . ."

Rosemary waited for him to state a reason.

Instead: "Can I call you tomorrow?"

"Tomorrow? But I'm right outside your house now." She waited. "Please, I won't take much of your time."

She heard him sigh. He put his hand over the mouthpiece and said something to somebody, probably his wife. Footsteps, a door opening and closing. When he came back, his voice was even quieter: "Listen. Go home. I'll call you in a while."

"You promise?"

"You know, really, you're being a little . . ." He sighed again. "Yes. I promise."

She stood in the dark for another five minutes after hanging up, waiting to see if Mr. Z would finally peek out of the window. Or if his Indian wife would step into the path of some light and have her silhouette cast against the drapes. Nothing. A patrol car cruised by, its headlights momentarily blinding her. It slowed but didn't stop and she heard the Christmas carol about the Little Drummer Boy drifting out its open window. Pa-rum-pum pum-pum. She got back on the bicycle and noticed for the first time that Mira had attached a reflective sign at the back of the seat: DON'T LIKE MY DRIVING? CALL 1-800-EAT-SHIT.

As soon as she cycled away, the demon dog in the yard started yelping like a crazed lover who missed her and wanted her back in his life right now.

WHEN SHE GOT home, Arik was in her room. He sat on her bed, wearing only underwear.

Not an apparition. The window, he got in through the window.

She kept the lights out. The darkness took from them the terror of eye contact.

"I miss being inside of you, Rose."

She kept quiet.

"I really need you, Rose. You know? And I was wondering, even if you needed time to forgive me . . . if, during this time, we could still, like, fuck anyway?"

She could smell his garlic-bread breath.

"Say something, Rose. I get hard just thinking about you." He grabbed her hand firmly and brought it to his groin. His erection pierced through the opening in his boxers.

She recoiled just as her fingers felt the goop at the tip of his cock. In the dark, she might as well have touched the tongue of a cow or a manatee.

"Rose? Say something."

She snapped. "I actually find you pretty gross right now. Sleeping with you is the last thing on my mind."

"You're lying. You don't have to lie. I know you still love me."

"Are you insane? I *don't* love you!"

"I'll do anything for you. I didn't mean to dump you like that . . ."

"Jesus fucking Christ! You didn't fucking dump me!" She wanted to scream, but kept her voice down. "You're the one who's so fucking needy. Mr. Z was so right about you . . . Do you know what he called you? He called you the Invisible Worm."

A frozen pause.

"Mr. Z said that?" Arik's voice cracked. "Really?"

She heard him wiping his wet nose on his sleeve.

"Stop crying," she said. "You're *such* a girl! And by the way, you're always Mr. Z this, Mr. Z that. You're obviously so in love with him. It's pathetic! I mean, can I ask you something, Arik? Are you gay? 'Cos Mr. Z and I think you might actually be."

He lunged at her, and knocked her back onto the bed. He grabbed her hair with one fist and cupped her mouth with his free hand. When she stopped struggling, he loosened his grip on her hair and reached under her skirt to pull her panties down. "I'm going to rape you. If you scream, I'll kill you."

Doing all this he instantly lost his erection, and he wriggled up against her body, desperately trying to reinstate himself.

"Fag . . ." she said softly. She enjoyed how it hurt him.

"Fuck you!" He persisted, grunting in frustration.

"Yeah, good luck . . ."

He bit her on the neck, hard. It only made her giggle, mockingly, so he slapped her, right across the face. This got him hard. He freed both hands and began to jerk himself off.

She stretched her arm out to the nightstand and groped around. When her fingers took hold of a library book, she swung its thick spine straight into his left eye. The impact it made on his soft flesh unnerved her but not so much she didn't slam it in his face a second time—twice as hard.

The first strike left him too shocked to react; now he wailed: "*Rose!*"

She leapt to a position of safety at the foot of the bed. "Stay the fuck away from me!" She threw her shoes at him.

Arik grabbed his clothes. He climbed out the window into the moonlit night. She heard his ragged breathing and his footsteps in the grass recede.

Insistent knocking now on her door. "Baby, who make a big noise?"

"Nothing! Nobody."

JUST BEFORE MIDNIGHT, Mr. Z called. Rosemary's hands were trembling. A chopper was hovering over the house just then, rattling all the glass panes and her bones. Perhaps the cops had seen Arik clutching his eyeball on the street.

"What's that racket? Want me to call back tomorrow?"

"No, don't. I'm sorry—it's just a chopper. Probably looking for evildoers."

"Make sure you stay hidden then. You're not going to like prison."

She laughed, a little stiffly.

"Well, Rose?" His voice was calm, but she could hear the edge in it. "What did you want to talk about?"

"My mother's bought plane tickets. I may not be here for New Year's."

"I'm really sorry to hear that. You'll be missed." Was that all he could say?

"And I want to talk to you about Arik . . ."

"Spare me, please. I'm not Oprah."

She tried again. "Mr. Z, I know I've been a terrible friend to you. And I want you to know that I'm really sorry. For everything." She took a deep breath. "You know, about that play that you wrote? I still want to do it, if that's possible."

A long pause.

"Go to sleep," he finally said. "We'll talk tomorrow."

"I just . . . I need to see you again."

"You will. Now, go to sleep, little girl. Go to sleep." His voice gained a soothing lilt. "And if you can't sleep, take one of those Ambiens I gave to you the other day. If one doesn't work, two should do the trick."

They hung up. A few seconds later, a text from him appeared on her phone:

@};--

His electric rose was the most romantic, most beautiful gift she'd ever received. The semicolon thorn seemed to be winking at her, telling her it meant no harm and was only there for veri- similitude. Unlike the wavering affection of boys, this rose would never fade and never wilt. It could be saved in her Inbox forever. With this thought, she drifted off to sleep.

MR. Z WAS chanting in an exaggerated brogue:

> *How well I know the fountain, filling, running,*
> *although it is the night.*
> *That eternal fountain hidden away,*
> *I know its haven and its secrecy,*
> *although it is the night . . .*

Rosemary climbed into the Nissan Maxima. Her nose was pink from the sudden warmth of his car. She removed her mittens and rested them demurely on her lap, side by side like angel wings.

"Any of this ring a bell to you?" he asked, of his recitation.

She shook her head.

"'Station Island' by the great Seamus Heaney. Some say it's his best poem. It's about the nature of inspiration." He looked at her. "I'm headed off to Station Island myself. County Donegal, Ireland. I leave tomorrow morning."

This was news. It left her gasping, the victim of a senseless mugging perpetrated in broad daylight.

"It's only for a few weeks. I'm going to visit my dream temple at Lough Derg, better known as St. Patrick's Purgatory." He saw the stricken look on her face. "I need inspiration, Rose."

The San Gabriels loomed purple and heathery above them as they ascended Lake, the avenue that ran straight up and up until it lost conviction at the base of the mountains. Rosemary mused on the word *purgatory* and its implications.

"Know what a dream temple is, Rose?"

She braced herself for another hurt-making answer.

"The ancient Greeks built monuments to sleep, where they sacrificed rams, drank their blood and slept in their fleece. And there they waited for messages from the gods to appear in their dreams. On Lough Derg, there's a cave that pilgrims in the Middle Ages slept in for six days and six nights, to get what they believed was a sneak preview of purgatory. They received visions, premonitions—perhaps due more to poor ventilation and hysteria than anything else." He threw her a grin to see how she was doing. "But generation after generation, pilgrims continued to go in there and they continued to emerge with ideas and visions. Many of them were writers with writer's block. I wouldn't be surprised if Seamus Heaney was one of them."

"I didn't think you were religious."

"Religious inspiration isn't the only kind of inspiration, you know. You should read some Heaney."

She waited a while before she tried to bring it up again. "About Arik . . ."

"I'm warning you. Say that name again and I'll throw you out of the car." He turned to watch her reaction, then to shape it. "I'm not his biggest fan. As you know."

He stopped the car at the top of Lake, outside a gated pathway that led up to the Angeles National Forest, its entryway littered with energy-bar wrappers and empty green tea bottles. It was the highest point a civilian car could go. From there, one could look back and see all the way across the valley—Pasadena, Alhambra, the skyscrapers of downtown LA and even the sliver of silver that was the Pacific Ocean.

"Let's get out of the car for a moment," said Mr. Z. They stepped into the biting chill. He threw on a green Polartec vest and she braced her arms around her cotton sweater, nodding that she was warm enough.

"As long as we're not going for a walk," she said.

"We're not going for a walk."

Downhill looked like a steep drop, although she'd hardly noticed the climb while riding in the car. The church steeples that loomed so oppressively were now small, distant, devoid of authority. A bowling ball released from where they stood would gain so much momentum it might actually smash a hole in the wall of that megachurch four miles down.

Mr. Z opened his arms and with his fingers beckoned to her. "C'mere."

She went to him and let his arms fold across her back. Neither of her parents had ever hugged her like this. His hands massaged her spine and warmed her up.

"I have something for you."

For a split second, she panicked. Was he going to push her down the hill like that bowling ball? She grabbed hold of his vest.

"If you let go of me, I'll be able to get it for you." He prized her fingers off his garment, keeping his eyes on her. It struck her that he might be reaching for a knife or a gun. "I can trust you completely, can't I?"

She was shivering now. The lid went up and in the trunk was a lonely red backpack sitting on a spare tire. She distinctly remembered seeing him carrying the pack around school a few weeks before.

"I want you to keep this for me till I come back from my trip."

She hugged him tight.

"Just promise me you'll keep it safe till I come back."

"Why would you need me to guard it?"

"Because my wife's never approved of my dreams. She thinks I'm childish—'self-indulgent' is the phrase she uses."

Rosemary nodded. She hoped he knew that *she* approved of his dreams. "What's in there?"

"Our play."

"The script?" she asked.

"Everything. Kit and caboodle. Deus ex machina."

She reached for the backpack, but he delicately moved her hand. "Remember *The Sorcerer's Apprentice*? Mickey Mouse setting off spells he couldn't control?"

She nodded again. He lifted the bag out of the trunk and from the muscles that bulged on his lower arms, she could tell it was heavy, like a bowling bag. There was a sturdy padlock that kept the zippers locked, and a series of smaller locks, all conjoined with wires. The contents made clinking sounds as he raised the bag. Glass bottles, was her guess. Wine? Liquor? He looped both carrying straps of the backpack gently around her right arm. When he let go, she was shocked by its heft.

"Careful!" His palms darted back as she let it dip.

"What's in there?"

"If I told you, it wouldn't be a surprise. Before your mother takes you away, I promise we'll put on a show. We'll prove to the non-believers that we're something."

Rosemary beamed at him. She jiggled the backpack a little on purpose. It felt like different items, all jammed together, the taller ones keeping the bag from slouching into itself like an old man.

"Don't agitate it. It does neither of us any good if something breaks and causes a big mess inside. And please don't fiddle with the locks. Remember Pandora?"

He removed the backpack from her shoulder and returned it to the trunk. Had she already failed him? She wanted to hold it to her chest like a newborn and prove to him that she was worthy.

"I've been keeping this in my cellar for some time. It likes being in a cool, dark place. Think you can handle that? Put it under your bed or in the basement. It's just too risky leaving it around my house with my wife poking into everything." He shook his head. "I guess some people will just never understand."

"I know exactly what you mean." She put her hand on his.

He gazed into her eyes. "Guard it with your life. I want to enjoy it with you. We'll celebrate."

They got back into the car. He turned it around slowly and they drove down the hill, not braking, it seemed, all the way down, like a freefall. He turned to look at her instead of watching the road. Four, five blocks he held his eyes on her. The butterflies went berserk in her belly, and she couldn't tell if it was from the plunge or the placid expression on his face. He began braking when they approached a red light about three miles down, well past the rival churches facing off with their moveable type billboards, PAYBACK TIME VS. JESUS WANTED US TO LOSE OUR SINS, NOT OUR MINDS.

Back in her room, Rosemary pushed the red backpack into the deep, dark underneath of her bed. As the mysterious items clinked together, she became convinced that they had to be wine bottles. Based on Mr. Z's early comments to her and Arik on terroir, based on the glass-bottle, liquid-glug sounds, based on his saying that the bag had to be placed in a "cool, dark place," and that he wanted to "enjoy it with her later." She tried to imagine what kind of play it could be that had wine-drinking as the central action. A bacchanal or a communion? With Arik out of the picture, perhaps Mr. Z would play the male lead himself. The only thing now was to hope she wouldn't have to leave before the curtain rose.

THERE WAS A strange car in the driveway, a Ford Focus that looked like a rental. Kate had to park on the street. The front door would not open far. It struck something and then ceased to budge. She squeezed herself and her belly through the foot-and-a-half wide opening. Suitcases were the culprit, two large zippered ones and a smaller hardcase Samsonite from the seventies.

"Mom?"

Mary-Sue poked her head out of the dining room like a delicate brontosaurus, her lower back still sensitive to quick movements.

"Oh, that Larry!" she sighed. "Poor dumb man. I told him to put those in the den."

"Larry?"

"He just got here. I told him he could come for Christmas but I didn't think he'd take me seriously." She looked away. "Anyhow, he's in the shower as we speak."

Kate bristled. "You know, if you wanted to invite your boy-friend, you only had to ask."

"Boyfriend?" Mary-Sue gave a high-pitched laugh, like it was the most ridiculous thing. "Let's not be jumping any guns here, missy. Larry's a decent man, but he's more like my valet. He's never been to California so I thought why not."

Kate told herself to calm down—this was still her mother's house after all. The desire to shriek at her was enormous, how-ever. Here Mary-Sue was, making plans behind her back again. Ever since her return, Mary-Sue had been acting like a restless animal, like she couldn't stand being alone with her.

"Oh, Katie, remember that blue sofa bed? He could sleep on that."

"You gave that away to the Parks, years ago."

"Did I? No wonder. I've been looking everywhere for that old thing. Maybe we can go over there and get it back?"

Kate gave her mother a look. "It's been more than ten years."

"I suppose we'll improvise."

Moving haphazardly but declining Kate's help—she'd ditched her crutches for a cane—Mary-Sue dragged one of the large suit-cases to an armchair and plopped herself into the seat with a loud grunt. Grunting again, she planted her feet far apart, sumo wrestler style. She rolled up her sleeves and unzipped the suitcase a crack, then lowered an entire arm into the hole, rooting around before emerging like a midwife with a pearly pair of silk panties. Her face prickled with embarrassment when she remembered Kate was standing right there.

"I had him get some of my stuff that I forgot to take with me."

Larry walked out of the bathroom as if on cue, a damp towel wrapped around his thick waist. When he saw Kate, he jumped and covered his flabby chest with his arms. It was then that she realized she'd interrupted their lovers' rendezvous.

"Well, howdy, young lady," he said. "Your momma said you wouldn't be home for another couple of hours." He lumbered past the women to fumble with the hardcase Samsonite where his clothes evidently were. "I beg your pardon, madams."

"Larry?" said Mary-Sue.

"Uh-huh?"

"Kate says it's all right for you to bunk with me tonight."

Larry immediately turned beet red. He looked at Kate and nodded. "Well, in that case I promise to be a gentleman."

MARY-SUE LOOKED SO excited when they pulled into the parking lot of the Tropicalia shopping mall that Kate nearly wept. She now understood why her mother had decided to put on a silk scarf and an imitation gold brooch, why she had worn actual shoes, and not her usual Scholl's sandals—Mary-Sue thought this shopping mall was going to be *classy*. "O Tannenbaum" was being funneled out via speakers camouflaged in hibiscus bushes.

After Kate turned off the engine, they sat in the parked car, facing the Pottery Barn for a silent minute. Kate thought her mother was mesmerized by the idyll of the home-and-hearth diorama in the store window, but she was mistaken.

"You have to help me out of the car, kid. My body's still non-compliant."

Kate could have kicked herself. She knew how hard it was for Mary-Sue to ask for help. "Sorry, I completely forgot."

The place was all upscale chain stores built over a man-made lagoon and linked by a wooden plank walkway—apparently developers' shorthand for "resort style." This was what they called a "destination mall," a consumerist magnet dropped in the middle of nowhere to further the LA sprawl. Her mother had read all about it in *Parade* magazine, and had been hinting at a visit for weeks.

Kate feigned interest in the window displays, while wishing Mary-Sue would hurry the hell up. Not that she moved like a sprite herself, with her belly weighing her down. What a pair—a gimp and a blimp.

In her bitterer moments, Mary-Sue allowed herself to think that the accident at the Publix had been a lightning bolt sent to her from some joyless Supreme Being, chastising her for darting around with age-inappropriate speed and impatience—a reminder, in other words, that she was an old woman. This was one of her bitterer moments, and she wanted to wallow in it. But the presence of Kate prevented her from throwing the tantrum she would have with Larry. Larry was *the* ultimate shock absorber; she could say anything to him and he'd still come by with cookies the next day. With Kate, say one wrong thing and she'd go mute for a week.

They stopped by a Häagen-Dazs ice-cream stand. Mary-Sue caught her breath leaning against a post, pretending to casually hum "The Little Drummer Boy."

"We can leave if you like," she said finally. "I know I'm a pain in the butt to have to chaperone."

Kate wondered if she'd done something wrong. "We only just got here. We drove over an hour to get here. I thought you wanted to buy stuff."

"I know. But we won't find any bargains in this place. We'll have to go to the Walmart for that."

"Then why are we even here?" It was amazing how quickly her mother swung from poignant to aggravating. "Let me at least buy you an ice-cream cone before we leave."

"Actually, since you're offering, I'd prefer a strawberry malt from Johnny Rockets—it's better value." Kate let Mary-Sue direct her to the kitschy fifties diner, its pink neon and chrome fixtures beckoning from behind a faux waterfall.

The strawberry malt arrived in a gigantic Styrofoam tumbler. Mary-Sue could barely contain her excitement. She accepted it from the waiter as if it were a holy chalice.

Later as they drove, Mary-Sue pushed the plastic straw to Kate's lips. "Here. It's too much. I can't possibly drink all of this."

"Just leave it, Mom. I'm driving."

"It's going to melt. It won't taste as good once it's melted."

"Just put it in the holder. Please."

Mary-Sue peered at the rearview mirror on her side of the car. The sun was harsh on her papery skin. Some women turned yellow or brown or gray with age like freezer-burnt chicken meat, but she was still the same pale shade from her Iowa days, midway between cherry-blossom pink and cucumber green. Wallflower coloring, her mother had once remarked, "a pallor suited to neither powders nor the palette." Mary-Sue never wore makeup in her youth, and she was now at an age when she could scarcely dream of beginning—any touch of artificial color on her would look obscene, past due, like a dead woman violated by rouge. Her hair was mostly white. The bristly, unruly colony on her scalp was harder to comb down than her original chestnut hair. And it was thinning. She regretted not enjoying her good hair while she had it; she'd always opted for those mousy, low-maintenance bowl cuts, as if she worked in a lab or a lunchroom and needed to have her hair out of the way. But she never worked in a lab. She never had to impersonate Dorothy Hamill. What had she been so afraid of?

The ravines running straight down the ends of her mouth curdled her smiles into grimaces. She also hated the wrinkles radiating from the sides of her eyes like tributaries ready to ferry her tears; they made her weariness so absolutely apparent. If left alone, these unkind fissures would spread across her entire body like albino kudzu and turn her into a gnarled lump of elbow-skin. This drying out even happened in Florida, where the air was moist; California would turn her into an alligator purse in no time. But, she had to be here: Katie was going to give her a second go at motherhood. She'd be ready this time around. Until then, be good, make nice, get along.

"Where did you go, Mom?"

"I'm right here."

LET IT SNOW

It was Christmas Eve and Kate staggered to the kitchen in her robe, sleep-webbed. Mary-Sue was there with Larry.

Kate walked straight toward the coffee pot and poured herself a mugful. She almost spat out her first gulp.

"I know what you're thinking," said Mary-Sue. "Coffee's too weak, am I right? Well, you're not supposed to have *any* caffeine in your condition."

"Your mother knows this coffee's as strong as I can take," Larry said. "Half a can of pop and I'm a Mexican jumping bean."

"It's all right. I'm leaving." Kate tucked the newspaper under her arm and headed to the porch.

"Speaking of which," Mary-Sue said, "I've invited three other people to dinner tonight. I hope you won't mind."

Kate froze. Mrs. Park and the girls? "It's your house, Mother. Invite whomever and however many people you want."

"I figured the three of us couldn't possibly finish the turkey by ourselves. And these are holiday orphans. Good people. They have nowhere else to go."

"Mom, you don't have to explain. Invite those people."

"They're not whoever you think they are."

"I don't care."

"We're all going to behave ourselves and have a fine time."

"If you say so."

WHEN KATE WAS little, Mary-Sue would reserve a table at a local hotel every Christmas and take her there for ham, turkey, and pumpkin pie, not because Mary-Sue enjoyed that type of food—she hated tradition—but just so Kate could partake in the cultural norm. Afterwards, they'd go home to watch figure skating and drink mugs of hot Swiss Miss cocoa. There were a handful of exceptions, as when they got dressed up and joined the family table at the home of one of Mary-Sue's co-workers, but these invitations were always one-offs. Tradition for them consisted of three constants—Kate, Mary-Sue and anonymous strangers. After they began living apart, Kate would accept holiday invitations at the homes of friends where the spreads were vast and the mood convivial, but she'd always feel nostalgia for those bland hotel dinners with Mary-Sue, especially the way Mary-Sue would shrug with clockwork predictability and comic exaggeration as she paid the check: "The good news is—no dishes!"

The doorbell rang at four. They were here, the mysterious dear others that populated her mother's world, yet whom she'd consistently failed to bring up in conversation. Her home now ran on old people time—dinner at five, bed at nine, rise at four to write letters to their councilman. Mary-Sue clopped down the stairs in dress shoes and red Amway lipstick a little caked with age. Kate winced—she'd never seen her wear makeup, ever. And there was perfume. Her mother seemed embalmed.

"My Lord! That's one fine-smelling turkey," one of the two men at the door exclaimed. "And *you*, my pretty, are one fine-smelling gal!" Mary-Sue hugged her guests warmly—more warmly, Kate thought, than she hugged her—and introduced them, snickering, as the "two Bills," B. S. and B. M. The men cackled in naughty glee. They were Bill Spragg and Bill Matthiessen, orchid growers from Homestead, both in their early sixties and evidently good-natured folk. B. S. was the sloppy one with the paunch while B. M. was tall, sinewy and Scandinavian in look, though it was he who was the more garrulous. Were they life partners or just business partners? Kate had no idea and didn't dare ask; Mary-Sue made no effort to clarify.

"Your mother told us she's going traditional this year on account of you. None of her usual cooter and gator stew." B. M. turned to Mary-Sue. "We had quite the Everglades Christmas last year, didn't we, darling? Too bad about Larry's stomach trouble, though. I blame the turtle." He handed a bouquet of purple orchids to Kate, "FYI, these are vandas, the Jackie Collins of the orchid world. Tourists love 'em." He lowered his voice, "Your mother shouldn't, yet she does."

The dining table was set in greens and reds. Facing the breast-heavy bird with its immaculately crisp skin, Kate realized that this was her first holiday dinner with her mother that felt the way she imagined a holiday dinner should feel—social, hearty, conventional and more than a little claustrophobic. Her mother had a *world*—close friends, friends who'd fly across the country to eat with her. Kate had nothing like this. Mary-Sue said for everyone to wait another ten minutes for their final guest. Then those ten minutes passed.

She asked Larry to say grace, and everybody joined hands. She clasped her mother's bony, birdlike talon with one hand and B. M.'s leathery paw with the other. Larry and B. S. reached across the sixth empty seat.

"Let's just pretend he's here, in spirit," said Mary-Sue.

THE MEN HADN'T bought any gifts for Mary-Sue because she'd outlawed it. As Kate knew, this was how she kept her own presents in the spotlight. Like Wendy surrounded by her kow-towing Lost Boys. B. S. caressed the slow cooker Mary-Sue gave him, B. M. called Mary-Sue a mind reader because the hurricane lantern he got was just what he needed "for the airboat out in Shark Valley." Larry planted a kiss on Mary-Sue's lips when he peeled open the wrapper and found the back support pillow he'd been wanting for watching TV in bed. Kate accepted her portable breast-milk pump wordlessly, then she switched on the one news channel Mary-Sue didn't object to. "No terrorism," she'd barked. Luckily, because of the holiday, what came on were "human interest" stories—identity theft, mountain lions, and missing children.

" . . . *Brittany Ann Yamasato turned sixteen during the eight months she spent hiding in the Palo Alto fraternity house where her boyfriend, a junior at Stanford, lived. She had not been kidnapped, she told her parents. She lived there willingly. And to protect the young man from prosecution, she has refused to reveal his identity. As to why she finally decided to come home, she says it's all due to, quote, 'the Christmas propaganda' she saw around her. All in all, it's a bitter-sweet reunion for the Yamasato family tonight . . ."*

As old photographs of Brittany Ann Yamasato flashed on the screen, Mary-Sue felt all choked up: Brittany in a pink sweatshirt, posing by a New York subway sign; Brittany eating lobster with her parents in Maine; Brittany on a class trip to Paris. She was an obliging subject, but she always smiled a frozen sort of smile. Was she happy? Possibly. Was she unhappy? Possibly. Her expression was uncannily, unfathomably Kate-like. She wondered if Kate saw the resemblance also—but people never do.

On TV, the girl's parents looked more shell-shocked than

joyous as they faced the news cameras, as if the truth presented to them had to be a hoax because their daughter had always seemed so unfettered, sprawled on the couch doing her nails and watching MTV. They were glad she was home, Mary-Sue could tell, but she also saw that their innocence was no longer intact; their daughter's happiness had been a lie. She felt an affinity with the mother whose pallid lips were quivering under the glare of the lights.

When the report ended, she turned to Kate, whose tense expression was hard to read. Mary-Sue teared up, in spite of herself. "Come here." She stretched her hand out to her daughter, who reciprocated the move. "If you'd done that to me, dear girl, I would have killed you." She grabbed her hand and rubbed it possessively. "I swear I would have murdered you myself."

KATE'S EARLIER HUNCH had been right. Of course, Bluto was in the area. Pheromones, maybe. He was standing in the driveway when she went out with the trash.

She was almost relieved that he'd come.

"I was invited, but I didn't feel it was my place," he said. "Want to go for a little walk? Up the hill to Mount Curve? Stop in at the am/pm to partake in our traditional Mountain Dew, Sprite and iced tea combo?"

"You can't just waltz back into people's lives and expect everything to be the same as you left it, okay? You can't just lurk, and then show your face when it's convenient to you!"

"You heard about Brittany?" He lurched forward and locked her in an embrace. "I came to say goodbye. I'm going back East. For good."

She stopped breathing.

"I've come to my senses," he said. "When did you become one of those lobotomized sleepwalkers?"

She slapped him. Her hands were small and soft and bare. She punched him in the chest. The tears came. "Fuck you, Paul Corot."

He grabbed her hands and shushed her with a light kiss on the forehead. From inside his jacket he pulled out a small parcel wrapped in Christmas paper.

"Open it."

She did. Inside, a stack of folded papers, grimy with age. In the moonless night, it was hard to see what they were. Each page was a pastiche—newsprint, photos, ransom notes? She moved them into the pool of light spilling from the kitchen window. These were the collages they made together as sulky teenagers . . .

"All these years, I carried them everywhere with me, like religious relics. Bill Cosby's in there somewhere, strangling Idi Amin with his sweater. So's our ad for the Sid Vicious birthday cake company." He laughed quietly. "And that imaginary review of *Macbeth* starring Hervé Villechaize, Zelda Rubinstein and assorted Scottish bagpipes. This is all of it."

All of it? She flipped through the artifacts covered in childish squiggles. This was a collection of no more than thirty pages. Somehow she'd inflated their creations to well over a hundred. Seeing them now—so many gags targeting the ungainly, the elderly and the unconventionally shaped—these were the private craft projects of two unhappy teenagers who shared an affinity for certain pop-culture references and were sheltered enough to think that this made them brilliant. In her hands half a lifetime later, the papers seemed so redundant, so . . . unspecial. They made Mr. Park's short stories seem daringly original.

"Keep them." She pushed the pile back into his hands, her own hands shaking.

"I've long outgrown them," he said. "Anyway, they're not for you or me. She might want a laugh or two someday. To know where she came from. Borne of snark, boredom and nostalgia."

Not knowing what else to say, Kate grabbed his hand. After a while, he gently pulled away. She didn't fight it. They glanced across the street at the darkened van der Holt house. It had once been the Corot house, Paul's house, and they had spent many sleepy afternoons there, giggling at the cleverness of their collages.

"She must know we tried," he said. "Merry Christmas."

THE WHITE BEARD made Raymond's entire face itch. What was this thing made of, the pubic hair of ancient hippies? He looked more Rasputin than Santa Claus. Enthusiastic volunteers had plied him with endless mugs of cocoa which, in his absolute boredom, he'd thoughtlessly sucked down. Now he was trudging home to pee.

As he scrubbed away the gumminess from shaking the drool-slicked hands of toddlers, he saw in the mirror the beard-induced rash on the lower half of his face. It looked like sunburn. Goddammit. He felt like slipping into his pajamas and not leaving his house again until the New Year. Only then would he venture across the street to that Ireland woman and conk her over the head with one of her own crutches. What a sap he was, taken in by her Tiny Tim act!

As he stepped out of his baggy red pants, the hairs at the back of his neck stood up. He turned. There was a smeary gray silhouette in the small, frosted bathroom window. Someone was trying to prize the window open from the outside. From where Raymond stood, he could see that the person was wearing one of those hooded sweaters favored by the local gangs. He backed gingerly out of the room in his underwear, then sprinted madly upstairs for his gun. When he returned, the window was open but the prowler was gone.

"I fucking give up!" He stamped his feet and crumpled to the cold marble floor.

When the chill got to him, he pulled the Santa suit back on. His fingers discovered a deep secret pocket in the pants—for St. Nick's hip flask? Haha. He slipped in his gun. Then, with the resignation of a man who'd made no plans for the rest of the year, he reattached the itchy white beard and stared into the mirror. He was Santa Claus, and he would save the day.

He armed the alarm system before setting foot outside, and circled the pitch-black perimeter of his house—no sign of forced entry. Somebody's orange tabby squawked in terror as he bolted down the driveway.

On the sidewalk, a squat Salvadoran in a gaucho hat was selling battery-operated wands with colorful whiskers. He nodded at Raymond in commercial complicity—it's Christmas, *amigo*, let's milk these suckers for all they're worth.

"Did you see anyone walking onto my property?"

"No, no, Santa."

Across the street, the Ireland gals were emerging from their house, followed by a trio of paunchy, lobster-faced guys. He saw Mary-Sue pointing him out to her friends, tee-heeing with great amusement. He was the unicorn she'd lassoed and tricked into costume. He gave her the finger when none of them were looking.

Raymond moved quickly along, avoiding all eye contact. Next door, on the Parks' front yard, an OPEN HOUSE sign swung forlornly in the breeze, joints squeaking. *Good fucking riddance*, he thought, and walked on. House after house, nativity dioramas competed for God's love: some had two Virgins, one had three. The secularists were also out in force, with their giant inflatable snow globes featuring Snoopy and Woodstock. Bulb-encrusted reindeer bobbed their heads in a simulacra of animal indifference—he had to resist pulling out the gun and popping them like a kid at a shooting gallery. Funny how much jollier he felt having a gun in his pocket. Why hadn't anyone told him about this years ago? Packing heat cools heads. Now there's a bumper sticker.

Cars jammed the street, crawling, headlights off, with rubbery baby faces smooshed against the windows. And on every corner, cabals clustered. They sang an old Bing Crosby song about conspiring and dreaming by the fire, and facing the plans that they've made.

"Mr. Claus?" A Boy Scout ran up breathlessly behind Raymond and tugged at his sleeve. "There are six children . . . waiting to have an audience with you, sir. They've been, they've been waiting . . . fifteen minutes, sir." Raymond nodded but continued to walk on past the Santa booth, scanning the street for the hooded prowler. "Mr. Claus?"

He heard a little girl cry, "*See-anta!*" from across the way but knew better than to turn. "*See-aantaa?*"

Something caught his eye. With a leap and a bound, he cut across some grinch's bare yard and stormed toward an unlit, unloved dead-end street named Des Moines.

ROSEMARY AMBLED UP Mount Curve, greedily filling her lungs with the notes of clove, fresh pine and charred marshmallow. The local newscasters expressed incredulity that it'd be 78 degrees on Christmas Day, yet refused to address the issue of global warming. This was why America was fucked. She savored this feeling of fuckedness, already nostalgic. This, she knew, would be her last winter in America.

The hot, dry Santa Ana winds appeared to have blown

somebody's nylon Santa off their roof, leaving him dangling limply from the eaves like a hanged man. Or maybe that was intentional. Oh, how she would miss this messy mixed-messaging of America.

Over There, they'd be living in a grim little apartment in a crowded high-rise, the airless corridor smelling of pickles and shellfish, each entryway cluttered with the sandals of unseen children, each sidewalk stained by the spatter of old suicides. Over There, unable to speak the language, she'd be considered slow and be ridiculed by classmates. There'd be no coolness factor in being American—the youth of Korea had the chauvinism of K-pop and K-everything. She'd fall in with the wrong crowd, green-haired kids striking for their lack of original thinking, and learn from them how to upload camera-phone videos of herself making peace signs and pouty faces. They'd teach her that selling her used underwear in online auctions would bring her easy cash. Eventually, she'd drop out of school and wind up working bad shifts at a neighborhood 7-Eleven, one that did a brisk trade in condoms and cup noodles at 3 A.M. There would be a microwave oven at the back of the store she'd have to wipe out three times a day from pranksters heating up cans of mackerel. There'd be the awkward Friday night when she'd recognize a couple of the troublemakers as members of the green-haired tribe from school. She'd pray they wouldn't remember her, and they wouldn't. And that lack of recognition would make her feel even worse. Finally, after three or four years at the 7-Eleven, when she'd gained thirty pounds from depression and *jjajang* ramen, a man so ordinary-looking as to defy description would walk into the store, pull out a long, serrated knife and plunge it into her heart.

"*Pssst!*"

Rosemary was jolted from her fantasia.

"Hey, Ghost! Over here."

She turned. The wind slapped her hair back against her face. The man who'd given her the gold pendant was standing on the sidewalk, outside Mr. Z's house. He had on a long coat and black leather gloves, the outfit of one who'd traversed the continent and hadn't expected to encounter warmth.

She looked around. Nobody for miles. There was a theatrical quality about the setting—backstage at midnight, dark, muted, and witness-free.

"I used to live in that house next to yours," he said. "And then I lived in this very house. It looked less fancy back then though, it must be said."

"I know someone living here now."

"You're friendly with the Singhs? Dr. Singh, with that holier-than-thou look of his? My dad had to sell and Dr. Singh bought. I guess that's capitalism."

Rosemary shut her eyes, her doubts confirmed. He walked over to her, and she felt her skin prickle. Somebody nearby was playing Christmas music—pa-rum-pum pum-pum. The snare-drum backbeat to "The Little Drummer Boy" always gave her the chills.

"I came back to say my goodbyes," he said. "It's become obvious a girl and I were not meant to be."

"I'm here to say my goodbyes, too." Quietly, she started walking away.

"Hey!"

Goosebumps coursed up her arms, but she continued to walk. The man quickened his pace after her. She could hear his breathing close behind. Then he grabbed her with his gloved hands—which felt inevitable. And fierce. And a relief.

He spun her around and saw the tears cascading down her cheeks, soaking her hair. She was trembling. He brushed the wet strands from her skin.

"Kill me . . ." The words slipped out of her mouth in a hiss.

The man smiled gravely. "What a thing to say."

"Please . . . I mean it."

"Come here." She was already as close to him as two people could possibly be. He put his arm around her lower back. "I told you I came to say goodbye."

MRS. PARK WAS tired of waiting. Four times she had yelled for the girls to come to dinner. The pizza was cold. Large Domino's loaded with pepperoni and extra cheese. But this was Christmas Eve—she'd even let them have ice cream. By her second slice, Mrs. Park no longer worried about the food.

One last shot. "Rosie! Miraaaa!" She called Rosemary's cell but it had been switched off and wasn't accepting voicemail. She ran to Rosemary's room. The door was locked. She tried Mira's—also locked—and was overcome by a sickly sense of déjà vu. The hollow silence that was ringing in her ears was the same kind of silence, the same kind of deadened air she'd felt in the moment before she opened the door and found Kee Hyun hunched in that sea of red.

She used the master key and freed Mira's door. The lights were all on but the girl was nowhere to be seen. She breathed again—and thanked Jesus—and was about to leave when the clutter on the nightstand caught her eye. All of Mira's little religious icons had been glued together to form one monster amalgam, the chemical sealant still pungent, and this thing stood in the shoebox framed with walls of prayer cards. In its own clear plastic frame overlooking this pantheistic mess was a five-by-seven photo of Mr. Park in his pastor outfit, filched from the family album. It was the same, sacred photo that had sat on his coffin at the funeral.

She snatched it out of the frame. On the back, Mira had written in her wobbly cursive:

> *Dear patron and assistant of the Pure and the Soaked.*
> *With this prayer I request Your assistance,*
> *And with the aid of the Holy Spirit may You always*
> *protect me*
> *During sickness or in health.*
> *St. Bath, Give me the strength to overcome*
>   *All the rage that lives in my heart*
>   *And the horrors that live in my head.*
> *In the name of the Father, the Son and the Holy Spirit,*
> *Protect my Sister and me from you-know-who.*
> *Amen.*

Mrs. Park always had enough English in her to make out insults. For the next minutes, she moved as if in a trance. She carefully put the shoebox shrine back as she had found it and headed to Rosemary's door. Without knocking, she unlocked it and entered. Compared to Mira's, the room was a haven of order. But there was a draught—the window had been left wide open. Drifting in from the street were jubilant carolers: *When it snows, ain't it thrilling./ Though your nose gets a chilling.*

She shut the window and the curtains. On Rosemary's neatly made bed sat a red backpack, not one she'd seen. She lifted it. It was fat and heavy, and placed atop the bed with great significance. Was she running away? With Mira? Her pulse quickened.

Its stainless-steel zippers held an infuriating family of pad-locks. Nothing budged. The bag itself was made of some heavy-duty polymer, almost metallic, and its back was padded with even tougher fabric, making it impossible to rip. She groped its sides and shook it. Things clanged. Bottles? They sounded like bottles. Certainly glass or china. Her antique vases, maybe taken from one of the shipping boxes? Was Rosie planning to sell them? So she could run away . . . with a boy?

She shook the backpack again. New sounds—the glug-glug of moving liquid. But the contents continued to elude her guesses—she hadn't a clue. Hot tears rushed down her cheeks. First Kee Hyun and now her precious Rosie. Mira she'd always felt a stranger to, but Kee Hyun and Rosie she thought she knew completely and absolutely. Yet these two whom she'd loved more than anything in the world had secretly plotted to escape her. And she had read no signs. She wasn't ready to be bereft again, not so soon.

The door creaked. She heard footsteps moving away from the room. She wiped away her tears and darted to the hall. Could the pizza delivery boy have returned to rob her because she hadn't tipped him?

She rushed to the kitchen and went straight for her sharpest cleaver. There was a strong chemical odor in the air that irritated her throat—industrial cleaner? Was this the termite poison seeping back again?

"Mira?"

She walked unsteadily back toward the bedrooms, holding the knife in the "stab" grip. A shadow flitted across Rosemary's door, and it closed.

"Rosie?" she edged up to the doorway, and opened the door.

In Rosemary's room, again nobody. Just the red backpack.

The knife she was holding had beheaded geese and severed pork knuckles. It should have no trouble, she thought, slicing open an American child's satchel.

She stabbed at it, over and over, weakened only slightly by the sobs that had taken hold of her. This was Christmas Eve! She was a widow! Where were her girls? Why weren't they with her?

There were enough cuts in the bag for her to dig the blade in and rip out bigger holes. She reached inside the biggest opening and plucked out the first thing she could. A clear glass bottle, filled with a red liquid too dark to be wine; it was labeled BLOOD. The other two bottles she extracted were filled with pale yellow liquid and labeled SWEAT and TEARS respectively. This had to be some kind of a joke. But what was the joke? And whose joke was it?

"I not understand!" She wept, gripping the bottles to her chest. "I not understand . . ."

OVERSIZED GRAY HOODIE, blue jeans. Slim and spry, probably prepubescent, most likely a fresh inductee or a look-out. Raymond found the hooded figure a few houses down Des Moines. As soon as he realized he'd been spotted, the boy started running. Raymond gave chase. He dissolved into the shade. Still Raymond chased. He needed to scare him, teach him a lesson.

The faceless hood, darting behind trees and bushes thirty yards ahead of Raymond, took him from Atchison to Topeka, Northfield to New York. The irony of these streets, named for the cities of Raymond's past and located within blocks of his present. He never drove on them, fearing taint. But now he was running at full steam along New York, following a junior gangbanger who was rustling against high hedges, causing dogs to whimper as he passed. He thought of Donald Sutherland chasing a hooded kid around Venice, thinking it was his dead daughter—what was the name of that damn movie now?—only to have a dwarf swivel around and stick a knife into his neck.

Suddenly, silence. No more swishing in the bushes, no more canine protestations. The rascal had vanished.

It was just as well. Three blocks into the pursuit, Raymond was panting. He reminded himself of the pathetic zombies in his books—lumbering, lurching lummoxes that could be outrun by any granny in a wheelchair; they frightened people *because* they moved with unnatural slowness.

He decided to go home. The Santa Ana winds had picked up again, rustling all the trees and bushes around him. His beard flew up against his face like a deranged octopus.

Something made him turn back for one last look.

The hoodie was twenty or thirty feet behind him, cheekily baiting him.

"You motherfucker!" Raymond cried, tugging the beard away from his face.

The kid went sprinting. Raymond sighed, and followed, the sweat soaking through his wifebeater and pooling down the cheap polyester fibers of the Santa suit. In his books, Raymond usually described nights like this as "voluptuous," "doom-coated," or "unrepentantly black." But the night was merely inert, uncooperative. It obscured his vision. He paused to wheeze at the base of Mount Curve, grabbing onto a white picket fence for support. His heart was ready to explode.

The kid stopped, too. For a second he almost believed the kid would come over and offer him a sip of water. But the boy started running again.

"Stop, I said!" Raymond picked up his pace, but the fiend continued to elude him. His rapidly diminishing form was at the top of Mount Curve, and Raymond knew he'd soon be out of sight.

He fished the gun out of his pocket—it'd been pounding against his thigh as he ran, a persistent reminder of its availability. "Look at me!" He cocked the gun, his hands shaking from the excitement of holding it. Nobody had told him it'd feel quite so sweetly *sexy*. He put his finger on the trigger. "Look at me, I said!"

Miraculously, his tormentor stopped, in the front yard of a pretty blue cottage. Nobody appeared to be home. He had his back to Raymond. Slowly he turned.

Out of the black, a snarling white mass of dog shot into the air like a marlin. Its jaws snapped, inches from the hoodie, hoping to find a mouth-hold to propel its ascent. It fell, cursing gravity. A split second, and the dog leapt skyward again. Raymond aimed, and pulled the trigger.

The shot kicked the pistol back, striking his nose, hard. His nose registered the pain before his ears registered the piercing bang.

"Holy . . ."

The smell of burnt gunpowder hung treacherously in the air. He ducked and peered around, expecting a roar of sirens. Some neighborhood mutts started barking, agitated, then lost interest. To the world, it was just another casual gunshot.

His hands were shaking. He slipped the gun back into his pocket and jumped when he felt the barrel burning through the cloth. He looked up Mount Curve.

The hoodie was gone. As was the dog. He edged up the hill slowly to see if he could retrieve the bullet casing. Where the kid had stood was an inert gray lump, a mass of dead skin whose owner had taken flight.

He walked closer, but slow.

He yanked a sprinkler spike out of the wet soil near him and wrenched off the snaking hose attached to its side. In medieval times, a stake this firm would have been dipped in poison and rammed into the heart of a witch.

Fifty feet ahead, the lump of gray cotton and blue denim began to morph. As it moved it took on the shape of a girl, with thighs, breasts, dainty ankles. A slip of a girl. The hood slipped off, and long black hair tumbled down. Twenty feet, a crimson roadmap extended from a hole on her sleeve, expanding street by street like veins. She turned toward Raymond, her eyes flashing with outrage and hurt, her breath jagged. Ten feet, he saw the metal braces glinting from her mouth as she formed the words: "You . . . *killed* . . . me . . ."

He knew her somehow, from somewhere. The fire in her eyes was perhaps unfamiliar to him but he'd definitely seen her face—and those braces—before.

"I *know* you!"

At that instant, echoing his eureka moment, the entire night sky flashed white. They both gazed up, expecting thunderclaps. Instead, seconds later, their ears went deaf from an immodest, crackling boom. The ground rumbled, and the vibrations shook their bones. Apparently, some kind of fireworks had gone off close by, fireworks that gave out big noise but forgot to deliver on the goods. A dreadful hollow in its wake. Raymond dropped the sprinkler stake in active surrender, and when he heard it strike the ground with a metallic ping, knew his hearing had returned. In that moment, too, the girl was gone.

Down the hill was the kind of stillness that came only in the wake of a horrible scare. The white dog whimpered squeakily nearby, cowering by the post it was chained to. It wasn't going anywhere! And it was unscathed—he must have missed it and struck the girl instead.

After a while, dogs barked neurotically behind fences. The sirens he'd been waiting for finally faded in. Then came the buzzing of a chopper's blades—which, like a fire truck's siren, could be heard for miles before it entered the frame. A thick cloud of gray smoke crawled up the hill toward him, against the pitch-black sky. Intermittently, the gaudy crackles of a large bonfire. Yet the accompanying scents were not the woodsy, wholesome smells of burning brush. Raymond detected the melting of civilization. Television cinders, crisped box springs, disintegrating linoleum.

From the shadows of the cloud, a man appeared. No, Raymond adjusted his eyes, it was only a skinny young boy in a black T-shirt with a screen-printed Day-Glo skull. THE MISFITS, it said. The boy marched uphill with his hands shoved into his pockets, the only other person on the street. As he neared Raymond, his bruises became visible—there was a violet hemorrhoid under his left eye and the lid was swollen and droopy. The deadened expression on his face did not match the ferocity of his words: "You fucking homo perv!"

The boy took his hands out of his pockets long enough to shove Raymond onto the grass, then he picked up his pace and ran the rest of the way uphill, yelling: "You sick old fuck!"

Seconds passed in shock. He was shaking all over, but he was in no way damaged. The red on his hands, he realized, came not from blood but from sweat leaching the cheap dye off the Santa suit. He staggered to the sidewalk and sat down on the curb to take in the unfolding drama down the hill.

He heard something collapse, like an avalanche, followed by a (euphoric?) wave of bystander exclamation. Over the roofs, he glimpsed embers fluttering like fireflies and the occasional shot of brilliant orange flame. Except for the aberrant, acrid smells, it was really kind of wonderful.

An ambulance slowed down as it approached him, its siren so unnaturally loud that he barely heard it.

"Are you hurt, sir?" a young man yelled out the window. Raymond shook his head and the driver instantly hit the gas.

Too late to request a free ride. He pulled himself off the ground and hobbled down toward Santa Claus Lane, toward home.

The haze thickened into monumental plumes of smoke. Through the gray, he saw churning red lights and shiny patches of wet asphalt. The fire hoses had won. The street was a tangle of emergency vehicles and gawkers, and it was hard to get a view of anything. As he approached the center of Santa Claus Lane, the locus of the excitement seemed to him sickeningly familiar. His spine tingled and his head went numb.

"My house!" He found in himself the energy to sprint.

Two pairs of arms seized him as he ducked below the yellow tape that was stretched across the sidewalk.

"Sir, you need to stay out of there!"

"But that's my house!" he wailed, through the dark fumes. The smoke put tears in his eyes.

"That *was* your house." A consolatory pat on his back.

The clouds lifted, unveiling a crater where the house once stood, now filled in with rubble. When Raymond saw the singed open house sign on the lawn, he gasped.

"That's *not* my house!" The sudden shift in emotions violently unsettled his stomach—he vomited on the grass in relief.

"Merry Christmas, Santa," somebody said, as an army of firefighters wearing headlamps jumped over his puke and descended into the heart of the darkness.

TWO HOURS LATER, a young Latina officer was assigned to escort Raymond home. As they walked, he tried hard not to stare at the smoldering wreck next door.

"What happened, do you know?" he asked.

"Chemical or gas explosion of some kind."

"Big hole for a gas explosion."

"Yeah. Homeland Security's been notified."

"And will they send someone to investigate?"

"Honestly? I doubt it."

"Was anyone home?"

"They found one fatality."

"Good Lord."

"A woman. Did you know her well?"

Raymond shook his head.

"Well . . ." The cop trailed off, not knowing what else to say.

She watched Raymond unlock his front door, and showed no intention of leaving until he was safely inside.

"If you have any animals, sir, please keep them indoors until further notice."

Raymond nodded.

Stepping off the porch, she said, "You may find some of your windows shattered from the blast but I strongly suggest you don't try to pick up the pieces tonight. You can deal with all that stuff tomorrow, once the sun's up."

Locking himself in, Raymond did see shards of window glass on his floor. He didn't activate the alarm system, well aware of the ridiculousness of arming the house when so many of his windows were broken. Then he went to the bathroom to wash the grime off his face.

His nose was swollen from the gun's recoil, but not broken. He took a long, hot piss. He was alive; his neighbor was dead.

He stripped off his clothing and ran the bath. All hot water. He wanted a deep cleansing. He wanted a new wakefulness to sear into his flesh, then his entire being. The room steamed up quickly. Turkish bathhouse. Russian sauna. Japanese hot spring . . . He plunged one foot into the tub.

"Jesus fucking Christ!" The water was boiling hot. He withdrew his foot, pink as shrimp and trailing drip all over the tile. He reached, burned foot in the air, for the tap. And somehow, because his legs were still wobbly from all that running or because he was getting old and imprecise, he lost his balance. The entire world toppled over with a tremendous crash. As he fell, he pulled the shower curtain down with him and the crummy rod, offering no resistance, came off the wall altogether.

Now he lay on the cold marble floor. Naked, shriveled, the dead nylon skin of the shower curtain lying atop him like a shroud. He screamed, "No more! No more! No more!"

In the silence that followed, he heard the bathroom door squeak open. His heart stopped. From the floor, he gazed upward and saw—upside down—feet first, then the legs, bodies and faces of a pair of little girls. Oriental. Twins, it seemed like. One was wearing jeans. She propped up her smaller clone in a shapeless, bloodstained hoodie—*her!*

The Korean daughters. From next door! He'd never been able to recognize them when they weren't together, yet had never taken the time to tell them apart.

Without a word, both girls got down on their haunches dutifully and helped him to sit up. Both had soft, nimble hands—the hands of children who never had to do any housework. All his muscles were in working order. He'd screamed for nothing. Oh, mortification. He held the shower curtain fast over his trembling privates.

"Thank you," he murmured. "Thank you."

It was not the time to shout at anyone for breaking into his house.

"You shot me," said the smaller girl with the tear-stained face. She seemed sad rather than angry. She seemed not to be in any serious pain. "I'm okay though."

"Except we're *not* okay," said her sister. "We're orphans now." Her words were harder, non-negotiable. Once out of the bathroom, she tipped her head toward the squad car parked out on the street, making it clear that it was in everyone's interest not to get the cops involved. "They're going to try and take us away. You have to help us."

– 15 –

SINKHOLES

It was Kate who had called the police.

After the two Bills left the house, Mary-Sue and Larry lingered downstairs washing dishes and swaying to Handel's *Messiah* on the kitchen radio. Kate went up to her room with a glass of milk, hollowed out after her talk with Bluto. She paused at the landing, thinking it might cheer her up to see what Raymond was up to. His house was dark, and she remembered—he was on Santa duty. The street was so crowded with cars and carolers that no one but her saw the figure climbing out of the Parks' window. It was a teenage boy whose appearance made her hair stand up: he was the ghost of Bluto, crystallized and preserved at age sixteen, except Bluto would never have worn such a corny Misfits T-shirt.

She noted the bruises on the left side of the boy's face. She would share these details with 911.

A few minutes after he slipped away, there was that monstrous bang. Kate felt her entire house shake. Glass broke. Before she could get downstairs, her mother was already hurrying up the staircase, asking if she was all right. Together, they stood on the landing watching the Park house being engulfed by a fireball, too transfixed to worry about whether the flames would leap across to them. Miraculously, the blaze stayed hermetic. Neither house next to it received much more than a minor scorching. In a matter of minutes, the Park house caved into itself as if some dark centrifugal force had sucked the fire down a secret drain.

The next day, Kate, her mother and Larry channel-surfed local news for information, even though the drama was unfolding right across the street. The hazmat crew picking its way through the wreckage had refused to answer Mary-Sue's questions. News vans double-parked on the street made it impossible for them to get a good look at anything, even from the upstairs windows, on tiptoes, with binoculars.

"A vintage Craftsman house on historic Santa Claus Lane in Alta Vista was devastated by a fire Christmas Eve. Witnesses reported a loud blast at around 10 P.M. and fire rapidly gutted the house . . ." Shaky cellphone video showed flames shooting out the roof of the house.

"The body of the forty-year-old homeowner, Beverly Joon Park, was found in the wreckage." In an old photo, Mrs. Park smiled demurely outside All-Friends church. *"She is survived by two teenage daughters . . ."* Day-after shots of the neighborhood.

"Investigators believe arson is the cause. An unidentified young male found loitering in the area has been taken into custody. The motive for the crime remains unclear . . ." Repeat of cellphone video footage. Shots of firemen working through the singed, damaged interior.

"The eighty-year-old three-bedroom house had just come on the market. Experts estimate that the house, given its architectural heritage, would have drawn bids above its $545,000 asking price, more than double its value just two years ago. There is no comment at this time from the family's realtor." Shot of fire-damaged open house sign.

"That's repellent," said Mary-Sue. "This is a culture with more sympathy for the real estate than for that poor dead woman. Or her orphan girls. You've got to wonder about terrorism. It *is* Christmas. We *are* Santa Claus Lane."

"Mom, please stop," said Kate. "Not everything is terrorism."

"You said yourself the boy looked Arabic."

"I said he was a dark-haired, Mediterranean type. I was careful not to say words like Arabic because I know how hysterical people can get."

As she said this, she felt a knocking from deep within her body. Someone was kicking the walls of her womb, trying to get her attention. Up to now, the baby had been very good about not moving around unnecessarily. This sensation was new. She pictured her fetus rappelling up the interior of her ribcage, stepping over the spongy honeycombs that were her lungs, getting a toehold on her breastplate so it could advance toward the gauzy ray of light that had appeared above like a chimera, just out of finger reach. Oh wait, wrong end.

"You too, stop." She patted her belly. "I know you're there. I know you're there."

RAYMOND SURVEYED HIS flourishing camellia bushes. Each bloom resembled a snowman's meaty white fist—if snowmen had fists. He chose the three best and snipped them off. It was astounding how their presence softened the angularity of that mahogany dining table. He'd never fully grasped how severe and grim his things were until the girls arrived. The first week, neither of them had dared place their elbows on the table. Then he realized—his furniture scared them.

As Rosemary and Mira grew more comfortable, they flopped around the living room like the girls in a Balthus painting—hems up, guard down, as they perused his novels, getting to know him tale-by-tale. He liked how relaxed the couch looked with its cushions dented by their bodies, the poised dimples in the chenille pillows lost to rumpled disarray. The paint chipping off the upstairs bathroom door, caused by the girls' thoughtless kicks and bumps, might have been described by Pottery Barn as an "artisanal shabby chic." And it was this type of aesthetic reasoning that helped him justify to himself why he was harboring the girls, why he felt so kindly toward them.

What began as a handshake grew into mutual appreciation. He didn't want the girls to leave. With the young refugees in his care, his home took on an improvisational candor—shoes everywhere, socks everywhere, ponytail scrunchies abandoned in surprising crevices. Now that the bullet graze on Mira's arm had almost completely healed—leaving behind a scenic scar that she proudly showed off—there were used Band-Aids everywhere, triumphal souvenirs of her recovery.

Two kind-faced women from Child Services showed up, telling the girls that their father's cousin in Koreatown was the state's "preferred resource" for their "placement" now that they were orphaned, but also that this cousin had not been responsive to discussions, and his home could not be "properly assessed for suitability." Raymond told them that the girls had assured him that their relatives had no interest in taking them, and that he would harbor them until they chose otherwise, and yes, that he understood this arrangement was dependent on paperwork he was only too happy to fill out with the help of his lawyer.

When the girls ambled in for their interview with the social workers, they looked utterly at home. They called Raymond "Uncle Ray" and snacked messily on home-baked muffins, dropping numerous crumbs into the gaps between sofa cushions.

They'd lived their entire lives on Santa Claus Lane and couldn't imagine a future elsewhere. They were star students at their magnet school. They did not want any further disruption.

Through his flame-eaten privet, after the interrogators left, Raymond gazed over at what remained of the Park house. With its top gone and interior eviscerated, what remained resembled medieval fortress ruins. What could have possessed a fifteen-year-old boy to cover the place with gasoline and then torch it, if in fact he did do it? The suspect, Arik Kistorian, a schoolmate of Rosemary's, was evidently the same bruised boy who'd attacked him that night. He'd seen the boy at the police station when he took the girls in for questioning and was struck, even under harsh fluorescent lighting, by his sullen beauty. He reminded Raymond of many boys he'd known and held. But he also sensed something damaged in this one, an aggrieved incomprehension at the work-ings of the world—as if this crime had been done to *him* and not the other way around. The arson investigation proved chal-lenging. Arik's fingerprints could not be found on the site of the blast; further, his mother—a professional laundress—had cleaned his clothes and his room before detectives arrived at their home. But the cops remained interested in him. Each time Raymond brought up Arik, even obliquely, he felt Rosemary grow more distant, more secretive. Finally, he let it drop.

Two days after the blast, on an early Saturday morning, he'd watched an ungainly Korean woman scurry out of her hatchback and pull, with scowling effort, the singed open house sign out of the ground. She broke one of her high heels in doing so, and limped angrily back to her car. Later that day, scavengers arrived, including one in a dusty Chevy Suburban with Arizona plates. People he'd never dreamt he'd see in the neighborhood showed up—sun-drunk Orange County surfers, Hawaiian shirt–wearing fatties straight out of a *Far Side* panel, an Indian family in rubber thongs, Latino fast-food workers still in uniform. They dived into the site like veterans of archaeological digs, emerging ash-nosed and muddy-kneed with TV remotes, shoes, stock pots, even a gold necklace. Each find would elicit a bigger whoop from the lone female who was, invariably, the designated lookout. Afterward, they leapt into their vehicles covered in dirt, the thrill of free stuff outweighing all matters of hygiene, and took off.

And as far as he could tell, the girls had no interest in anything related to their former home. Neither of them brought up the loss in seriousness or in jest; neither peeked through the curtains for ringside views. Not once did they express feeling for their mother, at least not in front of him. Whenever they drove by their old house, the girls pretended to be distracted by their cellphones. Even by his standards, that seemed repressed. When he questioned them about their wishes, the girls said they wanted to stay on with him until they were older and more independent. This frightened him—he worried about his emotional and financial resources. He spent hours on the phone with his lawyer discussing how best to proceed—legal guardianship was complicated, but possible, if he wanted to pursue it. Training to be a county-certified foster parent (with "psycho-social testing" he was sure to fail) sounded far less mouthwatering. The bulldozers would eventually come and raze all traces of plaster and blood next door; such was the history of real estate. He could just as easily be rid of the girls, his lawyer reminded him. He had absolutely no obligation to take them.

The girls started back at school, and Rosemary was pleasantly surprised to learn that Bryce Zehring no longer taught there. When it made the news that he had been located in Ireland, where he'd fled to escape a statutory rape charge, she felt a ghost tug of responsibility for her own silence. After Alicia Hwang started pointing fingers, the *LA Times* uncovered that Mr. Z had been fired from a co-ed boarding school in Boston two years prior for "improper conduct" with a female student. In the same article, a Nandita Singh of Mount Curve was quoted as saying she had complained to the police multiple times about him spying on her from his car. A "deeply unsavory character," she called him. Yet he couldn't be classified a stalker because he never got out of his car, never did anything outwardly worrying. He simply lurked. When the cops did nothing, her husband bought the family a bull terrier to stand guard.

Rosemary was now more curious than ever about what had been in that red backpack. Were they things, like the props and his playscript, say, that would prove the best of him, or things that would prove the worst? Now she'd never know. Arik, in his funny way, had made her darkest wish come true. Maybe that was the price of not knowing. They would forever be bound, even if they never spoke again.

She pulled out her phone and stared at the electric rose Mr. Z had sent her.

@};--

The wonderful thing about electric roses was they didn't fade, and their thorns couldn't scratch you when you put them in the trash. She deleted Mr. Z from her address book, as she had done Arik.

BARELY TWO MONTHS in and the girls had become many things to Raymond—call screener, door answerer, proofreader (he'd begun outlining a new novel), foot rubber, bath runner, remote-control finder, light-bulb changer, bartender, typist, fan club, cook. They'd reeled him in, hook, line and sinker. He let them drink, on weekends—it was the least he could do.

Once, after a jubilant, mimosa-fueled breakfast, he pulled Mira aside and asked her why she'd stalked him so vehemently, masquerading as a naked daemon.

"What are you talking about?"

There was something in the way she said this, the confusion knitting her brow, that told him she wasn't playing. This child could not lie. A shiver passed through him—first terror, then something better.

She saw his secret smile. She read his creases like a book. "What is it?"

"Nothing. A simple case of mistaken identity."

RAYMOND HAD HAD a ghost. It made total literary sense. In the yard, as he watered his camellias, a flutter of dark wings passed over his head. He felt shadows moving swiftly over him like a hundred miniature screeching warplanes. He calmly stood his ground. No longer would he question casual brushes with the supernatural; he would stay and he would watch.

The flying pests convened in a black cluster midair, squawking plans to swarm upon some rendezvous spot. They swooped down to the Parks' backyard, gathering at the only thing that had escaped the blast—that hideous blue couch. When the flurry of wings died down, Raymond saw them for what they were—the feral green parrots he'd heard so much about. The lore had them pegged as wisecracking macaws who blew from perch to snazzy perch. But they were just basic little birds, mere budgerigars if not for the crimson patches on their foreheads. Parvenus of the parrot world! They covered the raggedy couch in a shroud of pea green and immediately pecked and scratched, as if servicing an itchy rhinoceros. Those nicks and tears—they'd been the work of these winged devils! Their little yellow beaks emerged from the cushions white with fluff. Some bit off more than they could chew and the parts they couldn't take with them fell like tired snow onto the ground. Raymond finally understood birdwatching.

"Ray," came Rosemary's voice.

Raymond turned around and read the terror in her eyes. "There's a phone call for you," she said.

In addition to being weaned off "Mr. van der Holt," the girls had been trained to stonewall unimportant calls. Rosemary did not have to say anything else. Raymond stumbled in place, then started back indoors, pointing absently at the birds to divert her eyes from his anxious face.

She watched him vanish inside the house and heard him ram his foot against the base of the stairs, stifle a cry, recompose himself, and pick up the receiver.

"Good evening, nurse."

AT THE FUNERAL in a small church outside New Haven, he chose silence. He had nothing to share with this roomful of strangers. An elderly female relative from Ann Arbor he'd never met before gave a eulogy about his father's early life and the Depression summers they'd spent together on a Kansas farm. That was where his dad had been "truly in his element," as she put it—he'd once saved a brown calf from drowning in the creek. She twice alluded to his "genial, upbeat attitude to life" despite his having been "robbed of a childhood" due to two alcoholic parents and poverty in general. She then quoted a line from St. Augustine's *Confessions* that brought a tear to Raymond's eye: "The reason why that grief had penetrated me so easily and deeply was that I had poured out my soul on to the sand by loving a person sure to die as if he would never die."

This cousin spoke with the authority and regret of a former sweetheart. But well aware that she was addressing a roomful of people who'd never known the man before he was old, she kept her speech to a brief ten minutes. When the whole room realized that no one else had been scheduled to speak, a couple of caregivers from Dartmoor threw in a few kind words just to extend the ceremony. Their contributions were heartfelt, but hazy— "he was a joy to be with," "funny and warm," "we'll all miss him dearly."

Raymond felt as if he'd walked into a memorial honoring somebody else. He was glad that he had the girls with him, even if he had ignored the paperwork from Social Services that would legally let him take them out of state. The girls weren't going to rat him out. In the pew, Mira held on to his arm, massaging it to make sure his blood was still circulating because one might have doubted it from looking at his face.

"You're shaking," she whispered.

The elderly Ann Arbor relative avoided Raymond at the reception that followed—not recognizing him, he hoped. She spoke instead to residents from the retirement home who treated her as if she were the grieving widow. He watched her from across the room. He saw how she made a hasty exit after spilling a cup of coffee down her crocheted vest.

A middle-aged couple dressed like Midwestern academics came up to the table where Raymond and the girls were seated. They had a small Asian girl with them, about six years old. The man possessed an eager but awkward willingness to make friends.

"Are they from China, too?" were his first words to Raymond, his head nodding enthusiastically. "Our Lily's from Sichuan

Province, in the southwest. She's got a natural taste for spicy food."

"No, no." Raymond smiled, tiredly. "Mine are from Southern California. No taste whatsoever."

"Did you know Mr. van der Holt well?"

"Turns out, not really."

That night, Raymond treated himself and the girls to dinner in Manhattan. Hail and sleet meant that even without calling ahead, they landed a table at a jewel box tapas spot in the West Village that he'd read great things about.

"We're all orphans now." He clasped their hands tightly. "We have to be kind to ourselves."

That night, they feasted on tripe salad, steamed cockles, grilled skate and hare. Hard snow pellets blew down outside the windows. The girls stared out, rapt; neither had been in a snowstorm. He savored the moment. New York's still got it. The skyline has been altered but it was still a place you could take out-of-towners and have them wowed.

After dinner, he dropped the girls back at their hotel and went on his own to see Lena Ozova, who'd had a stroke. Her Murray Hill penthouse was everything he recalled from old soirees to celebrate writers she loved more than him—book-lined, silk-carpeted, pockmarked with cheesy little Hogarth engravings. But the old witch, alas, was not the same. Suddenly quite feeble, she moved around in a wheelchair, her musical snarl reduced to a rasp. He had a lousy feeling that the live-in help, a sulky young woman from the Ukraine, wasn't as kind to her as she was paid to be; she sat in the room the whole time, looking aggressively bored. The Ukrainian ran the house how she saw fit, heating it up like a Soviet sauna and filling the air with the acid tang of artificial pine. Raymond gulped down the glass of lukewarm water she handed to him and said goodbye to Lena sooner than he wished, or expected to. He left knowing he'd never see his old friend alive again, shamed that he'd let himself be intimidated by an unpleasant maid.

On the plane back to Los Angeles, Raymond at last cracked a Xanax smile. This didn't go unnoticed by his hawk-eyed favorite.

"What? Tell me," Mira said, looking up from his novel *Black Grave.*

"I never thought I'd be friends with anyone born in the eighties."

"But you're not. We were born in the nineties."

"Ah. So I was right after all."

When they got home—another surprise. A thick envelope arrived from a Koreatown lawyer. Mr. Park's relatives had decided to claim the girls after all, and they would go to court for their property. It was abundantly clear this was more about real estate than blood. Mira ran up to her room in tears. Rosemary went to the den with a stoical stillness and began watching a documentary about meerkats.

"It'll be all right," Raymond assured his older girl. "We've got a Hollywood divorce lawyer."

After another endless phone call with his friend Ron, the retired, half-deaf divorce lawyer, Raymond found Mary-Sue at his door, unsolicited, with a store-bought lemon meringue pie. She told him what a good thing she thought he was doing, taking in those poor girls, and then prattled on, her hand on his arm, about how adoption was going to change his life. Platitudes. Once she was gone, the pie went flying into the trash.

Those Koreatown relatives the girls hardly knew—were they worth his sweat? Whenever he felt like throwing in the towel, he reminded himself: should he ever be found lying in a pool of his own vomit, Rosemary would be efficient about calling 911. She was observant, industrious, polite. Should he ever need cheering up, Mira was there. All those spontaneous cartwheels she spun on the supermarket floor, she was his little dust devil, his nonstop whirligig. No, he couldn't lose *that*. He'd fight, at least for now.

He had embraced neither girl, worried about smothering them with the pressure to reciprocate. Instead, they shook hands, like comrades. He knew he wouldn't have trouble with Mira but he remained afraid of Rosemary—she was a mysterious black box of womanly secrets. One overcast evening, he watched her as she poked around her former backyard, digging into the raggedy blue couch and unearthing a stack of papers under one of the soggy seat cushions; he knew what they were at a glance—her dead father's stories. She ran back to his house clutching them just as the first drops of rain fell.

In front of him, she acted chaste and never discussed any boy, and especially not the tormented Arik Kistorian, who apparently still roamed free—in Florida. Yet he happened upon her more than once on the phone to somebody, her hand inside her pants. He'd heard her sneak people into her room and felt the tremors on the floorboards as her bed shook. He really didn't want to turn into his old man and leap to judgments, but her silence made him wonder if the fire at the house had been *her* idea, winding up a gullible, hormonal boy like a high school Lady Macbeth. Hah, now there's a character for a book.

Raymond had the nagging feeling that he was failing her, even as she persisted in expressing only the politest gratitude. All that girl ever seemed to say was "cool," "thank you," and "I love it." She behaved as if she was biding her time in his house, cleanly, quietly, as if it was some purgatory from which she would flee into her *real* life, far away. He recognized this behavior from his own youth, but it didn't pain him any less.

One Sunday evening, he surprised them by returning home not with his usual clanging liquor shopping but a bag from Best Buy. He'd bought them a PlayStation 2 to replace theirs, which had perished in the fire. Mira whooped, Rosemary nodded.

Raymond felt he had failed the older girl yet again.

Rosemary in fact did sense her own alienation. Acutely so. She was culpable for Arik's act of arson, and her mother's death, too, by default. Indirectly, but still. Yet here she was, being rewarded. She felt imprisoned by Raymond's generosity. She didn't want the fancy restaurant dinners. She didn't need the cashmere sweaters. She'd gone from one cage to the nicer one next door. Only sex provided her with spiritual relief; only in bed, arching her back and coming hard while a horny senior fucked her, did she truly taste the freedom she craved. Raymond was the opposite of sex. Sure he was lovely in a sad, Miss Havisham kind of way, but how he oppressed her with his expectant, puppy-dog looks. He sought her approval in everything. And why did he have to drink so much? Was it really so difficult being rich and famous? She hated it when his words slurred and his reflexes slowed—and especially the way he spilled food down the front of his shirt after a few glasses of wine. This really, really frightened her; she couldn't understand how Mira could just sit there and cackle. At least their parents had behaved like parents—their kind of tyranny she could navigate. Raymond, on the other hand, was home all the time, and all the time scrutinizing her, trying to get a bead on her, trying to impress her. She finally grasped the seemingly unreasonable desire of that girl Brittany Ann Yamasato to Shawshank away from her perfect, affluent, well-educated parents and their perfect, affluent, well-educated love. It made sense, running off to the boyfriend's dorm, where they could fuck until they were sore and forget where they were or what time it was. It'd be like getting her own island. Maybe being forced to live with unloving relatives in Koreatown wouldn't be so bad—at least they'd leave her alone, plus she'd be in the city and not trapped in the boonies. She was supple, she could absorb disappointment from any direction as long as boys wanted to fuck her.

The three of them sat down with the PlayStation and put on "Katamari Damacy." The game was essentially a graphically advanced version of Pac-Man, just as vibrant and cheerily uncomplicated. The player controlled a tiny green elf who pushed around a supremely sticky ball—the katamari—that rolled up objects that would stick to it, starting with small things like ants and mahjong tiles, and as the katamari grew, larger and larger things (cats, bonsai plants, schoolgirls, sumo wrestlers, fishing boats, houses, giant squids). There was a sneaky pathos to the whole thing. As the katamari got bigger, the world around it got smaller and quieter. During the game's final phases, everyday noises gave way to the gnashing of tidal waves, the bellow of foghorns, and the anonymous rumble of large construction equipment. Everything turned epic, including the isolation.

Raymond didn't have the patience to master the fiddly console but he could watch the girls play for hours, drawn into the katamari's single-minded hustle and the controlled chaos of its pixilated Japan. It relaxed him to see the world looking so clean, so logical, so giddily conquerable. Never in a million years would he have imagined finding satori in a video game.

OUTSIDE, IT WAS anti-katamari. The Santa Anas were in full force again, howling as soon as the sun set. By morning, all kinds of detritus that had been stuck up in the deodars for months, even years, found themselves spilled on the street, sidewalks and lawns. Bird's nests, pine cones, shuttlecocks, hair clips, candy wrappers, drinking straws, against a carpet of green and brown pine needles.

Kate spotted the letter quite by chance. She was backing her car out of the driveway, wheels crunching on all the tree crap, when something flat and pink in the center of the street caught her eye. It was a hassle getting out of the car and bending down in her condition—nine months, just about—but her curiosity won out.

It was an envelope, unlabeled but already carefully opened along its upper edge. Notebook paper was folded within. As soon as she freed the letter—handwritten in black ink, entirely in Korean script except for the sign-off, "Beverly"—she knew. It was Mrs. Park. One of the looters must have either dropped it or tossed it behind a bush when they discovered they couldn't read it.

What was it? A secret confession? A suicide note? She stopped herself from instantly running it over to the girls at Raymond's house. What if it was something really disturbing? Until she learned what it said, it was best to protect them. She put it in her purse and brought it with her to the student she saw that afternoon, Cora Ahn, a woman of Korean origin who was fluent in English but wanted to improve her writing skills.

"I have an assignment for you," Kate told her. "Translate this."

The student took the letter in her hands and glanced at its four solid pages of Hangul. "Oh . . ." she murmured as she gave it a cursory read, lips moving silently. "Oh!"

"Why? What does it say?"

"I will write it out for you." Cora Ahn seized the letter possessively, clearly already drawn into its internal drama. "No problem. I can do it. No problem at all."

KATE CAME IN the door and immediately felt woozy with cramps. Her mother bounced up from the chair by the window and began:

"So, Larry called this morning and we had a long heart-to-heart . . ."

"Mom. Not now, please." She stood in the hallway, wondering if she should sit down. "I'm feeling a little strange."

Mary-Sue pulled down her reading glasses and gave her daughter a good hard look—and jumped.

"No wonder. You're standing in a puddle of water!" She grabbed the phone.

SIX OR EIGHT hours later, Kate woke up in a strange bed, with a deep grogginess behind her eyes and a searing rawness between her legs. She recalled the trauma only in discrete flashes—the freezing stirrups, a cluster of shower-capped women urging her to "push!", the odor of rubber gloves, the coppery scent of blood. She wriggled her toes and the pain sharpened. Her insides ached, deep in some pit. When her nose came to, she smelled antiseptic that made her think of embalming fluid, and this made her gag. She reached out and felt a plastic pan by her side, already the recipient of a drying heap of mush. She recognized the peas she'd had at lunch, and produced a fresh mound over the old.

The walls around her were pink vinyl, along a nursery theme— smiling ducklings bursting out of eggshells—but the good cheer seemed generic and insincere. In the far side of the room loomed a couple of bouquets and a heart-shaped foil balloon that was already drooping. Her mouth felt dry. Everything but the plastic pan was out of reach. She whimpered, suddenly overcome with the desire to have Mary-Sue by her side.

"Mom!" she wailed, from the bottom of her lungs. She was

somehow too relaxed—drugs?—to be embarrassed by this. Then an awareness kicked in and she sucked in her crying before it became a full-throttle bawl.

A nurse with a springy blond ponytail opened the door. Her nametag said PEARL.

"Oh, Miss Ireland! You're awake," she said. "Did you want me to call your mother?"

Kate nodded and looked away, mortified. The nurse came over to her bed and checked her vitals, all the while making small talk to distract her.

"She was here almost the whole time, you know. Left just a half hour ago. Did a whole bunch of crossword puzzles." The nurse put a plastic cup of pills on the wheeled table and rolled it toward Kate while gently raising her bed. "I've got some more Vicodin for ya. It's about that time." Wordlessly and seamlessly, she removed Kate's plastic pan without so much as a shudder. "Hey, you were brave. You rose to the challenge. Just let me know if you'll be needin' anything else, alright?"

"Thanks." Kate tried not to cry in front of the kindly, capable girl probably fresh out of nursing school. Her good cheer was unnerving. There were a hundred questions she wanted to ask her about the pain, about whether the fetus survived, whether it'd been a girl or a boy, but all she managed to say was, "Just my mom, please."

Mary-Sue rushed into the room twenty-one minutes later. She was in some kind of floral caftan that looked like a grandiose housecoat—she had intuitively put on Grandma clothes. A positive sign.

"The doc said she put up quite a fight," Mary-Sue said. "Seen her yet?"

Kate shook her head; her hands went clammy.

"Tiny. I saw her through the glass in the nursery."

Kate said nothing—her mother was liable to say any old diplomatic thing just to get through tough times; at least, it seemed that the baby had survived—for now. Tiny could mean not long for this world.

The knocks on the door tensed her up again. Sensing her anxiety, Mary-Sue grabbed her hands and rubbed them. "Goodness. You can't hold a baby with these icicles. You'll make a lousy first impression. She'll remember."

The nurse stepped in and Kate finally saw It, the creature she'd tried to avoid thinking about, the thing she'd hoped against hope she could miraculously pee or poop away. It was nestling at the bosom of the young nurse, wrapped in a pink waffle-weave blanket. Too docile, thought Kate, to even drool.

"She looks just like me, don't you think?" Mary-Sue said, and laughed at her own joke.

When the nurse put the baby in Kate's arms, she was struck by how much it resembled a hairless, anemic orangutan. Mammalian, but just barely. Black liquid pupils stared back at her, yet they registered nothing. There was no primal recognition. Its eyes darted back to the nurse.

"Oh, for Pete's sake, will you at least smile at your daughter?" Mary-Sue barked now. "You're scaring her. I tell you she'll remember this."

"In about a day, she should begin to understand who you are," the nurse told Kate, stroking the creature's wrinkly pink arm.

"Which would make her far smarter than me," said Kate.

"Or me," Mary-Sue added, a little too honestly. The nurse smiled amiably. This wasn't the kind of humor she was used to.

The plastic bracelet on the baby's wrist came with a barcode, tagging her like merchandise. Ireland. Room 315. Though unlike something from the store, an exchange or return was probably out of the question. Not even if she came with design flaws like the floppy neck she had, or the overbite. Kate imagined the girl at ten, still staring at her with those impassive eyes, waiting for her diaper change. She didn't know what to say. Their first meeting hadn't brought her the maternal elation that movies, TV shows and Pampers commercials had suggested it would. That sense of possessiveness just wasn't there. Her arms quickly grew tired and she found a spot on her lower belly to rest the alien beast. Finally it was of some use—self-heating rag doll perched over her sad crotch, infant balm for her grove of maternal ache.

"You're going to snap her spine! Jesus, Katie."

Mary-Sue snatched the bundle from her. She rocked the baby in her arms, leaving lipstick traces on her little simian forehead.

"Oh, I'm so greedy! I'm just *so greedy* to eat you up, my baby!"

The rest of the evening, Kate barely got another chance to try again. Mary-Sue refused to surrender her. She looked only at the baby, smiled only at the baby, spoke only to the baby. "You've come to save the world, haven't you?" "You're going to do great things, aren't you?" "You'll love your nana, won't you?"

THREE DAYS PASSED in lost sleep and strange new baby sounds and smells. Kate's student Cora Ahn dropped by the house with an inelegant flat of Asian pears to congratulate her, but it was really an excuse for her to bring over Mrs. Park's letter and solicit praise for her translation.

At dinner, Mary-Sue insisted on reading it and Kate was too exhausted to object.

My Dearest Kee Hyun,
I am writing to you on our tenth anniversary because

I have neither the eloquence nor the confidence to share these thoughts with you, face to face. I have always felt that you were like some kind of a saint—a man so wise he would instantly recognize the terrible qualities in myself that I had not even known were there.

At this very moment, while I am composing this letter at the kitchen table, you have locked yourself in the bedroom again to write Sunday's sermon. It is the only time of the week when I feel I am not being watched upon or judged by you. Again, this is not a complaint but an expression of how safe and well taken care of I am in your company.

Many times in the past, when asked why you picked me, you told people: "Because I took pity on her." Although we all knew you were only joking, I felt that there was a truth to this. I am grateful to you for your patience and tolerance. Nobody would have guessed that the girl who was thought too bold in manner and too coarse in appearance to snare a mate would find a husband as devoted as you. Remember how my father mocked me when I brought you home to dinner? He could not understand how a respectable man like you could have feelings for me. Even on his deathbed, he never stopped telling me how awkward I looked and that I did not deserve to be married. I always thought it was a cruel irony that you should have taken over his ministry.

I would have given up all hope of marriage if I hadn't met you that fateful day at church. I still do not understand why you had gone there, as you were a nonbeliever. It was your first time in a church, you said.

Were you lonely? Depressed? Suicidal? This remains a mystery.

Over the years, I have seen your hair turn gray and then white, and the white hairs retreating up your scalp. I have watched your skin sag, your wrists grow thin and your chest slowly collapse into itself. Yet, in spite of all this, I want you to know that you mean the world to me, and that if you somehow vanished from my life, I would fade and wilt. Not even our two daughters would be able to fill the empty space of your absence. I would not want to go on.

I know it was a difficult thing for you, allowing me to have the girls. I know it was never your intention to have any children. I am deeply grateful to you for granting me my wishes against your own, and I think we are raising two healthy daughters who will bring us warmth and security in the future. My only wish is that I understood them better. Perhaps you will change your mind and allow me to teach them Korean?

I miss our homeland very much. This may not seem obvious because I do not keep in touch with my relatives. It is difficult for me to contact these aunts and cousins because every time I pick up the phone, it is like reopening an old wound. There is so much envy and resentment, on both sides. They are always waiting for news of misfortune so they can proclaim me a fool for living in America, a place they believe we will always be treated as second-class citizens. Remember how happy my aunts were to hear about the LA riots? They rejoiced at any news of Koreans being attacked by real Americans. I am often convinced that empathy

does not exist in Asia. What we have there is a Confu-
cian culture of sadism, competition and materialism.
It is how dictators and despots keep people subservient.
Consumerism does the rest. America makes me grateful
and hopeful.

Finally, I would like to express to you my growing
sentimental attachment to our life. Although I began
with deep ambivalence, I now love our old house on
Santa Claus Lane. I feel happy and contented here. I
can see us growing old together under this roof.

Yours faithfully, always,
Beverly

Kate's initial reaction was that her student had embellished
the letter in translation, adding eloquent, sentimental touches.
But that seemed unlikely—Cora was one of the most boringly
honest people she'd known.

"Well, we have to take this over to the girls, don't you think?"
said Mary-Sue, putting the baby down on the sofa.

"I'm not so sure. It could really freak them out."

"Freak them out why? To learn that their mother was a human
being with thoughts and feelings?"

Kate held her tongue. "There's no rush. I mean, the mother's
already dead."

"That's a fine thing to say."

"What I meant was, I don't see what good can come of this.
It's none of our business." Kate pocketed the original letter so her
mother couldn't do anything hasty.

"You're exhausted. Go to bed. To be discussed. Shoo."

Kate conceded, and shambled up the stairs, taking one last

look at the domestic tableau—Grandma and the Blob illuminated by some TV cop procedural. Nobody was going anywhere.

Mary-Sue glanced at the dining table. Kate had taken Mrs.
Park's letter but the English translation was still there, pinned
under her water glass. She wedged her sleeping granddaughter
between two pillows and made sure there was no way she'd roll
off the sofa. Then she pulled on a woolen top and her clogs.

RAYMOND SAT IN his armchair sipping a glass of Jurançon
and listening to Schönberg's *Verklärte Nacht* while the girls did
their homework—or so he hoped—upstairs. As the music came
to a sensual crescendo, the crazy mother from across the street
appeared at his picture window. He jumped. Her glasses were
crooked. Her cardigan was puce. She was probably here to ask for
that five-cent pie tin back. Smiling widely, she pressed a couple
of handwritten pages against the glass pane and indicated that
he should meet her at the door. Déjà vu! Oh no, not more short
stories!

"Girls!" he bellowed from his chair. "Help! There's somebody
at the door!"

Mira came bounding down the stairs, happy to abandon her
books. "I'll get it," she cried, "lemme get it!" and lunged to see
who might be there and what news they might bring.

Acknowledgments

For decades, I've thought of writing a coming-of-age novel about different people finding their groove at different ages, whether 15 or 65. You've heard of Method actors; well, lately I've discovered I'm a Method filmmaker, and now, a Method author, too. I have to get in character to get the work done.

I thank everybody who has helped me settle into Southern California, though this settling-in has taken over twenty years. A special shoutout to John, who, though we're no longer married, remains chief recipient of my rants, the price he still has to pay for having dragged me out to this sun-baked state in the first place.

I also need to thank the other recipients of my rants over the last couple of years: Kate Hurwitz, Sue Carls, Linda Lichter, Mollie Glick, and all at Cinetic and CAA who've had to put up with me. And at home, too, my two gray guys: Graham (the human) and Chubblington (the wombat-cat).

Thank you, finally and most of all, to Mark Doten, editor and friend (friend and editor?) at Soho Press, Rachel Kowal, Alexa Wejko and everyone at Soho and Penguin Random House (and cover artist Vi-An Nguyen) who believed in this book and worked so hard through this difficult period of isolating house arrest (thanks, Coronavirus 2020!) to get it out into the world and into your hands.

Having lived in Singapore, London, New York, and, at greatest length, Los Angeles county, I used to say (too glibly) that I feel equally alienated *everywhere*. But with this book, I've finally written my way home. I now like my noir sunlit. Make of that what you will.

Martinis for everyone when we can meet again.

S.T.
Los Angeles
10/20/2020